Rough Canvas

JOEY W. HILL

Ellora's Cave
Romantica Publishing

What the critics are saying...

ꙮ

5 Lips "***Rough Canvas*** is the perfect title for this wonderful love story. Each chapter is like watching a masterpiece being created by the hands of an artist. You will be captivated and in awe as this creation comes to life. But *Rough Canvas* also manages to be a very hot, sweaty "wow can you really do that?" type of book. There is a lot of delightfully sinful D/s sex, though I have to warn that there are some scenes that may be unsuitable for more sensitive readers."

~ *Two Lips Reviews*

5 Angels / Recommended Read! "Joey W. Hill has hit just the right note. The Master/servant relationship is about control and while on the surface the Master appears to be the dominating force it is but a façade. In reality the servant holds the reins of control in a true M/s relationship. *Rough Canvas* is the sixth book in the *Nature of Desire* series but it can stand alone. [...] The sexual scenes were emotionally wrenching and stripped away all the shields and walls that people hide their true feelings behind. Highly erotic and yet soul searchingly deep, the sensual scenes made this novel a 5 Angel Recommend Read for me!" ~ *Fallen Angels Reviews*

An Ellora's Cave Romantica Publication

www.ellorascave.com

Rough Canvas

ISBN 9781419958434

Edited by Briana St. James.
Cover art by Syneca.

This book printed in the U.S.A. by Jasmine-Jade Enterprises, LLC.

Electronic book Publication September 2007
Trade paperback Publication January 2009

ROUGH CANVAS

Trademarks Acknowledgement

ꕥ

The author acknowledges the trademarked status and trademark owners of the following wordmarks mentioned in this work of fiction:

Armani: GA Modefine S.A.

Bud Light: Anheuser-Busch, Incorporated

Cabbage Patch: Original Appalachian Artworks, Inc.

Chopin (vodka): Podlaska Wytwornia Wodek "POLMOS" Spolka Akcyjna

Coke: Coca-Cola Company, The

Coleman: The Coleman Company, Inc.

Cracker Jack: Rueckheim Bros. and Eckstein; Frito-Lay North America, Inc.

Hallmark: Hallmark Licensing, Inc.

Home Depot: Homer TLC, Inc.

Jack Daniel's Gentleman Jack: Jack Daniel's Properties, Inc.

John Deere: Deere & Company

Karo: Corn Products Company

Maserati: Maserati S.P.A.

McDonald's: McDonald's Corporation

Rockettes: Rockefeller Center, Inc.

Tabasco: McIlhenny Company

Sheetrock: United States Gypsum Company

Shoney's: Shoney's, Inc.

Starbuck's: Starbucks U.S. Brands, LLC

Chapter One

ꟾ

When the shop bells over the store entrance rang, Thomas didn't pay much attention. He was in the back tagging a wood chipper for repair and Celeste was out front to handle visitors. But when he heard the customer speak to his sister, he raised his head. Everything in him went tight, alert.

It was a male voice, the words as unintelligible as her response, but something about that voice stirred something in his lower belly. Goddamn it, there was no way it could be... The sprawling wooden farmhouse and barn which his father had turned into a hardware store supplying this part of rural North Carolina area was hell and gone from New York City. There was no way that voice could belong to who he thought it did.

Thomas drew in a steadying breath, taking in the pleasing smell of old wood. The building had been designed to feel like the farm stores of a hundred years ago. He'd always loved that about it, the quiet, powerful aura of permanence, stability. It blended with the landscape and served as a landmark of a time long past. It had become somewhat of a tourist attraction, so they had a petting area fenced off beside the barn as well as a large paddock and grazing field with a pony, goats, chickens and a pack of pigs that roamed and rooted.

There was even one gentle-eyed ancient cow Thomas' father had rescued from a slaughterhouse. An ironic compulsion for a man who regularly sat down to beef stew, but he'd seen the calf bawling for her mother, who'd already gone up the chute. He'd purchased the baby and brought her home to his six-year-old son as a gift. Though in his gruff way, the old man hadn't called the female calf that. "She's your responsibility from here on, Thomas. You have to take care of her."

A responsibility he'd embraced. It hadn't caused a jagged ache in his gut the way the responsibility of being back here some twenty years later did, despite his attachment to the place.

An ache that was being intensified by a voice Thomas knew too well. Damn it. It wasn't him. He hadn't slept well last night and he hadn't finished breakfast. He'd just keep checking out the chipper, because it wasn't who he thought it was. If some Twilight Zone reality existed and it *was* him, it was better for Thomas to stay back here anyway.

But Thomas sat there, his hand in the machine, resting on some broken but entirely forgotten mechanism as that far-too-similar voice coaxed things to life that he'd buried six feet under his heart well over a year ago.

A murmur in the dark, the touch of a hand passing over his hair as he drifted off to sleep. Waking to that same voice whispering to him, bringing him to life with clever fingers as he was filled deep and hard from behind.

Come for your Master.

His "collar" had been a slim gold waist chain he wore beneath his clothes. A relief, since he wasn't comfortable wearing jewelry that didn't fit the masculine stereotype, but then he'd discovered discretion hadn't been the intent. The chain rode low on his hips, keeping him hyperaware of every shift of his ass. The three-inch double tail of excess chain beneath the joining point had a way of working its way around to brush his pubic area, keeping him semi-erect most of the time.

When they lay in bed in the morning and he wasn't quite awake, his Master would slide the strands so they were at the small of his back, in order to tease the crease between his buttocks. He'd move his long-fingered hand from Thomas' hip to fondle his morning erection.

The fastener had been a locked disk with one printed word. *Mine.* Even the press of that metal piece against his skin, reminding him that he willingly belonged to another, kept him hard.

Jesus, what was he doing? He yanked his hand from himself. He'd been pressing the heel of it on the erection rising fast and hard under his jeans, giving himself some relief with the mild abrasion. He wished whoever the customer was would leave. That voice was too much like the voice he had to forget, would forget.

Even as he thought it, he firmly pushed away the knowledge of how often he got himself to sleep by masturbating to that voice in his head, the remembrance of his Master's hands taking him over, taking control, taking everything and giving back mind-shattering pleasure in return.

When Celeste giggled, he froze. An austere, never-flustered and entirely too serious girl for her twenty-one years, Les did not giggle or titter. She might chuckle, perhaps occasionally laugh if he caught her in an unguarded moment, but the obsessive-compulsive premed student helping him out on her semester break did not giggle.

Son of a bitch. As he started to straighten, he hit the switch to the chipper with his knee.

He jerked back as the motor roared to life, experiencing a harrowing blink of resistance as the blades caught the tip of a finger. He yanked free, stumbling away. The machine snarled its fury. Or rather, the broken part was grinding like it was dying. Given the circumstances, the noise just seemed far more sentient and sinister.

"Son of a bitch, son of a bitch..." It stung like hell, but that wasn't what made him shake from head to toe. *My hand...*

"These hands are the real works of art, pet."

When his Master said that, they'd been in Thomas' tiny warehouse room, which also served as his studio. He'd guided his Master's hands into the paint and they'd stood together at the canvas, hands overlaid. They created something that, while not great art, was as much an expression of life as a child's handprint in plaster.

His Master's white silk shirt had been open, the lean muscular slope of the chest down to the sectioned stomach muscles exposed. He'd removed the belt from his slacks so they'd dropped lower, giving Thomas even more of the mouthwatering sculpted abs and diagonal musculature angling toward the groin. The shirt was loose so there was the hint of the points of his broad shoulders, the biceps disappearing into the sleeves.

Thomas had pressed behind his Master, turned him toward the mirror so he could trace his stomach with paint-covered fingers, taking streaks of color up over the pectorals and hard nipples, all the way to the throat. His Master had even allowed Thomas to run his hands over the expensive shirt so he left streaks of color on his clothes as well as his skin. Then his hands had overlapped Thomas', mixing the colors, making a living tapestry that reflected Thomas' passion for all that was his life.

All that was his life then. Not now. Not ever again. Cracking open an eye, he found he still had five fingers, though the tip of his forefinger was welling blood. A slice had been taken out of the meat and part of the nail was torn. It was more blood than damage. Cursing regardless, he picked up a rag and wrapped it around his finger, holding it to staunch the bleeding. He squeezed his eyes shut so he wouldn't scream out his rage.

Earlier this morning his mother had suggested an improvement to the paint color area. "Why don't you paint a display there, Thomas? Something that will make people see how certain colors work together for their bedrooms and trim. You're so good at that. You haven't been painting since you came home, and you used to love to do it so much."

He thought he might get physically ill if he walked down the paint aisle today.

Fuck it. Whoever the hell it was, he had to see. No way Marcus Aurelius Stanton was wandering around a hardware store in the middle of North Carolina. Surely he wasn't the only one in the world with a drop-your-pants-because-I'm-going-to-fuck-you-now voice.

Thomas strode out of the back room, maneuvered around the repair counter and nearly trampled Les, coming around the corner from the other side.

"Oof." She stopped herself with defensive hands against his chest. "Clumsy oaf. What're you doing, charging out of there like a bat out of hell? I was just coming to find—"

He didn't hear her. Not after the first sentence, when his eyes found the customer standing in the aisle behind her about fifteen paces away, who turned from his contemplation of fixtures at the sound of her exclamation.

Lucifer would have looked like that, Thomas was sure. Temptation, a hundred percent Grade A, tightly packaged in a hard-muscled six-foot frame. He knew what that frame looked like without a stitch on it. Marcus had a faint birthmark on the inside left thigh, but no tattoos or piercings. His lip had curled with disdain when Thomas teased him about it.

"Art is fixed on a canvas for a reason. If well preserved, it doesn't distort or fade. I don't believe time will be as kind to this canvas."

He wasn't wrong about much, but Marcus was wrong about that. Thomas knew the man he was looking at would be riveting until the day he died, even with the sculpted lines of old age. But he didn't need tattoos or piercings. It would be like trying to touch up and improve Michelangelo's David.

He wore his black hair loose on his shoulders. It was silk, the different lengths that fell over his brow and swept back from his aristocratic cheekbones only emphasizing his bone structure. He was the prince of every fairy tale that had ever been written. Not the prince who led the king's armies, but the one who handled his negotiations for peace with a rapier intelligence that was twice as deadly a weapon as any general could imagine. A king might gain capitulation through force of arms. Marcus could acquire surrender through nothing more than a look.

Not only had Thomas touched those sensual, firm lips with his own, they had touched every part of his body. He remembered his arms and legs spread and bound as Marcus' mouth moved over his belly, his chest, nuzzling his throat briefly before he straddled Thomas' face and fed his thick, long cock between his eagerly waiting lips.

His jaw had rubbed against the rough texture of Marcus' leg and the smoother skin of his inner thigh as he'd sucked and licked and done everything to drive Marcus mad. When Marcus' grip on his hair fisted and the thighs hardened to drive himself deeper into his slave's throat, Thomas had felt triumph.

How many lips had touched that impressive cock since Thomas'? Probably more than he could count. Thomas hadn't been anything special. Lots of people knew how to give good head.

He told himself cruel things like that and tried to paste them as words in Marcus' mouth to wean himself from the images that haunted him. He'd been successful enough that they plagued him mostly at night now, or when he'd worked a sixteen-hour day at the store and everyone else had gone home. Then it was just him and the silence of the old building, the sky dark outside and winking with stars that certainly couldn't be seen in the night sky over New York City.

That long cock was contained in dark slacks probably custom-tailored by some impressive name like Armani. A blue T-shirt was tucked into it and Marcus wore a dark suit jacket over that. The Swiss timepiece on his wrist probably cost as much as their John Deere tractor inventory. Thomas knew Marcus would be wearing snug cotton boxer briefs in his preferred black. Glancing down, he saw Marcus wore Italian loafers. New York Upper East Side casual, which would be the equivalent of church clothes around here.

"Tommy, this man had some questions I didn't know how to answer." Les held up a small handful of clips. "How much weight can these hold if you're using grade-two nylon line? I told him he might prefer the twine stock, but—"

"Too rough," Marcus said, his green eyes focused on Thomas' face. "I want something that won't scratch."

"Oh, like to protect a boat's gel coat." She nodded. "How much weight did you say it needed to handle?"

Marcus' gaze dropped, passed down Thomas' torso and back up again. It only took a moment, just long enough that Celeste turned to him as he reached Thomas' flushed face again.

"About one sixty-two. Not that much, after all."

Son of a bitch. Thomas had been one-ninety before he'd come back here. How did Marcus do that?

"Oh my God, Thomas. What's happened to your hand?"

He'd been holding the rag over his fingers, but sometime during Marcus' perusal he'd put his palm on the repair check-in counter top and gripped the edge, hard. A fine stream of blood had dripped past the rag and down the side of the paneling.

Celeste was two steps closer than Marcus, but somehow Marcus got there before her, grabbing hold of his wrist and tugging off the rag to see the bloody finger.

He wanted to snatch back, snap at him, but the feel of those long fingers manacling his wrist, the fact he was now close enough he could smell him… Dry-cleaned clothing mixed with the scent of travel, that expensive aftershave and cologne he wore, just a light touch so it became part of the air around him… Thomas could identify him even with his eyes closed.

The first time he'd followed that scent it had been their initial night together. Marcus had taken him home. The sex had been… Thomas could say it was the most amazing sex of his life, but it had been more than a great fuck. He hadn't even known he wanted to do some of the things he'd done that night until he found his cock responding to nothing more than Marcus' commands.

Afterward, Marcus had given him the courtesy of his own room, but Thomas had been stirred up with all the new feelings, aching inside in a way that went beyond the physical. In the early hours of the morning, he'd found himself following the lingering scent of Marcus to his room. The door had been open and he'd gone in like a guilty thief.

He'd hesitated at the foot of the bed, knowing he hadn't been invited. So instead Thomas knelt on the carpet and laid his head on the mattress, his hand slipping ever-so lightly onto Marcus' calf where it extended out of the folds of covers.

About five minutes later, Marcus sat up, propping himself on his elbows. He'd reached out and touched his hair. Thomas knew then he hadn't been asleep. He'd been watching him, waiting to see what he'd do.

Marcus had opened the covers, drawn him in and spooned around him, his hand giving Thomas' ass a proprietary squeeze that was a demand. Thomas had adjusted his leg and Marcus slid his now-hard cock into his still well-greased ass. As Thomas groaned at the feel of it, Marcus had pressed his lips to his ear and whispered that he would sleep that way. Thomas would just have to suffer with no release until the morning.

The hard yearning ache he hadn't wanted to end that first night surged up in him now at Marcus' touch, so alarmingly intense he tried to pull away. Marcus, anticipating him, planted his feet. They eyed one another like gladiators.

"Stop struggling. You splatter my shirt and I'll kick your ass."

"You could try," Thomas retorted. Under normal circumstances, Marcus' eyes would have glinted with humor and lust stirred by the challenge, but as he looked at Thomas' hand there was nothing amused in his expression. And these were definitely not normal circumstances.

"You still have the shop bells," Marcus observed. A casual comment as Celeste came back with the first aid kit, but Thomas knew there was nothing casual about it.

Thomas had given them to his father one Christmas. His dad had looked a little perplexed, but once the customers started appreciating them, his traditionalist of a father found he liked that alert system more than the fancy but banal electronic buzzer most stores used.

The memory of when he got the bells swamped him like another blow to the gut, propelled by Marcus' intent, knowing expression.

* * * * *

Thomas had seen the bells in the window of an antique store in the Cape Cod village they were visiting. He'd ducked in, flipping Marcus off when he made a comment about gay men's obsession with antiques. Thomas got absorbed in the store, picking out some small prints of Cape Cod scenes done in pen and ink. A music box for his sister. He looked over some pieces of old farm equipment, knowing that when he went home for Christmas he'd describe to his dad how they were put together.

He wished he could take Marcus with him. Even if that was a possibility, he knew he wouldn't dare ask Marcus. He'd think Thomas was a lovesick idiot.

Knowing he *was* an idiot, he even found and bought something he thought Marcus would like.

Outside the store there was a sprung occasional chair, a relic from the nineteen twenties obviously beyond salability, too worn to be anything but a place for patiently waiting husbands. That significance wasn't lost on Thomas as he came out and found Marcus sitting in it, his head propped on the headrest as he caught a cat nap in the sun. He had an ankle balanced on his opposite knee, his slacks perfectly adjusted, one hand lying loosely on his knee, the other stretched along the chair arm.

He still wore his sunglasses, emphasizing the relaxed curve of his mouth, the slope of his cheekbones. Thomas suspected the female foot traffic along the sidewalk in front of the store had increased exponentially since Marcus had taken the seat. Thomas managed to scare off a covey of them lingering as he stepped out.

He heard their titters, their murmurs. "Figures. He's too gorgeous not to be gay."

He dropped to a squat by the chair. After a brief hesitation, he linked fingers with Marcus', for once trying not to care that they were on a public street. Marcus was much more relaxed about it, but then he hadn't grown up as Thomas had. Marcus had made his peace with his sexual orientation at fourteen. Even at seventeen, Thomas had been trying to bury any suspicion by being on every sports team he could find and taking girls to the prom, in order to give his mother photographs to share with relatives and linger over fondly.

Marcus opened his eyes behind the sunglasses and lifted his head, his sleepy glance going from their linked hands to Thomas' face in a way that made Thomas think of every illicit thing they'd done in the course of the weekend. It made him glad he'd dared to touch Marcus this way.

Get a grip. "Check these out." He showed Marcus the bells, explained the use for them and their history for shopkeepers as Marcus straightened, touched them and experimented with the sound. "So you think he'll like them?"

"I'm sure he will." Marcus squeezed his hand, conveying with the simple gesture his awareness of Thomas' rocky relationship with his father.

"I got you something too." Thomas said it casually, even now wondering if he should have done it at all. Marcus had suits that cost as much as Thomas' entire wardrobe, starting with his first baby shoe until the present day.

"Yeah? Do I need to search you for it?"

When Marcus made a grab for him, Thomas fended him off with a grin and a forearm.

"Cut it out. Here." The gift had its own container, a pewter incense house that he now pulled carefully from the protective cardboard box. "You can burn tobacco leaves in it to drive off that flowery shit you wear."

That Thomas loved.

"Redneck Neanderthal. I'll just spray your deodorant around the apartment. Eau de 'I-am-not-gay', aka sweaty sock and pig wallow smell." But Marcus tempered the too-close-to-home barb with a hand to Thomas' jaw. As Thomas looked down and opened the pewter box, Marcus' hand drifted to his hair, his nape.

He couldn't help it, he started to tense. Touching hands was one thing. This Cape Cod village was more open, but it wasn't New York City. If Marcus should try to kiss him here, on a busy street…

He'd tried to mask it, but his Master was too intuitive. Marcus dropped his touch, a brief flash of disappointment on his face before it was gone, replaced by polite interest in what Thomas was offering, making him feel like crap.

"Never mind," he mumbled. "I'll just show you at home."

"No." Marcus reached out, closed his hand over the incense container. "You'll show me now." He lifted the hinged triangular top, blinked.

"It's stupid, nothing you have to wear."

"Shut up, pet," Marcus said mildly, and the caress in the words, underlined by the gentle reproof, left Thomas silent with a whorl of confusing emotions in his lower abdomen.

Marcus lifted out the dragon tie pin and matching cufflinks. The craftsmanship was exceptional on the antique pieces. They were no bigger than a fingernail and had chips of jade for the eyes, the tiny scales individually sculpted by the long-dead artisan. But his art had lived on. No artist could hope for more than that, to know that when his bones were dust, two people would sit on a street corner and admire what he'd done.

"You remind me of a dragon. Your eyes." *Your heat. Your intensity.*

"Sitting on a hoard of treasure?"

That made Thomas smile, the tension in his chest easing. "That's why I brave the flame."

"No. No, it's not." Marcus leaned forward then, caught Thomas' lips before he could draw back. He kissed him hard and thoroughly, his hand gripping the back of Thomas' neck so he couldn't move. He was gasping when Marcus at last pulled back. Their faces were still close, Thomas' vision dominated by green eyes. "That's not why at all."

* * * * *

That day had come back to him with one casual comment, just as all of it came back with that one touch as Marcus held his wrist.

Thomas had heard how your life could pass before your eyes when it was threatened. Apparently every memory of that life with someone else could do the same when your heart was threatened.

Of course, it wasn't as if he didn't relive it all every day in his mind anyhow. He was reminded by everything he saw, every object, scent or element of nature he'd experienced with Marcus. Air, sunlight, water.

He'd gotten better at closing memories out at work, which was why he tried to work all the time. It helped make the burning ache a sweet dull longing over which he could more easily shovel the earth of his daily life to keep what should be dead in its grave.

"It's just a nick," he said.

"It looks like you sliced off the top of your finger," Celeste observed, swabbing at it with alcohol. It stung, but he barely noticed. While to all appearances, Marcus was just holding his wrist as a courteous customer helping out, Thomas felt the strength in his grip. In Marcus' eyes he saw he'd welcome the fight if Thomas chose to try to get loose. So he stood still, glad for the counter to press against, which separated at least by a corner Marcus' body from his involuntary reaction to him.

The desire to struggle often had been part of their more intimate moments, Marcus having to prove he could overpower and Dominate Thomas as if he was also overpowering Thomas' worries about embracing this unexpected part of himself. Though Marcus scoffed at "a part of".

It's all of you, pet. You want to be my slave. You get hard every time I order you to get on your knees, to give me your wrists so I can chain you to the bed…

"You two seem to know each other," Celeste commented, taping on a bandage. "Is this one of your friends from New York?"

"I handle Thomas' work," Marcus answered with a professional nonchalance that didn't match the look he kept locked on Thomas' face. He was covering every feature, and when he lingered on Thomas' lips, Thomas felt saliva gather in his mouth. He couldn't help it, he swallowed. Marcus' fingers tightened on his wrist infinitesimally. From the way Thomas' body reacted, it was as if Marcus had in fact slapped a manacle on him right there.

"He's the serpent in the desert," a voice said acidly.

The reaction was instinctive. Just like a high-school kid surprised with his hand up his girlfriend's shirt, Thomas jerked back at the first syllables from his mother's voice. He succeeded in freeing himself, though he also managed to tear loose the bandage Celeste had been molding over his finger. The guilty reaction of course made the situation more apparent to everyone, including Celeste. Her eyes widened, shifting between the two of them even as Marcus gave him an unreadable look.

"What are you doing here?"

Marcus turned, as calm and composed as Thomas was disturbed.

His mother had been gardening, he saw. Wearing her neat jeans and smock printed with wildflowers, she carried her garden gloves in one hand with her dusty spade. While she colored her hair now to keep it ebony, her skin, tanned from her time outdoors, showed attractive lines around her blue eyes.

The deep lines around the corners of her mouth were not as appealing, particularly since she didn't often smile since his father had died and Thomas' brother Rory ended up in a wheelchair from a tractor accident. An accident Thomas knew she felt wouldn't have happened if Thomas had been here. And of course she was right. Right or wrong, it wouldn't have happened.

"The last time I checked," Marcus responded, "you weren't my mother. So I don't see that why I'm here is any business of yours."

"Marcus." His face might be inscrutable, but Thomas knew the reaction simmering under the surface. For all his polish, Marcus became a mean son of a bitch when his temper was provoked. He could wound a person terminally with the clever cruelty of his tongue, and his mother was far too vulnerable a target.

"New York fag," Rory snarled. He'd been just behind Thomas' mother, so he rolled forward now, jutting out his chin and pinning Marcus with a glare.

Marcus swept him with a dismissive glance. "But one who can walk. Would you prefer being a New York fag if you could walk again? Or punch someone in the face who told you to fuck off?"

Celeste drew in a horrified breath. No one talked to Rory like that. In fact, he'd been pretty much coddled like a newborn since the accident. He was drowning in self-pity. As his brother and the de facto head of the family now, Thomas knew it was something he should be doing something about. But with the store and everything else, and his own pain…he just hadn't. Maybe Rory wasn't the only one with a self-pity problem.

"Marcus—" Thomas warned as his mother stepped forward, her expression taut with anger. Her hand automatically landed in reassurance on Rory's stiff shoulder.

"Your mother asked what I was doing here. Fine." Marcus drew a check out of his coat, turned and handed it to Thomas. "I thought I'd personally deliver your earnings from the work you left with me."

"But we pulled my work…months ago."

Before Thomas left New York, Marcus had decided to include him in an upcoming gallery showing with bigger names. While Thomas' credentials from art school and awards had been exceptional enough to make his presence in the show acceptable, he was an unknown. Therefore, he'd worked his ass off on the handful of pieces, knowing Marcus was giving him the type of break most artists didn't get offered twice.

His walking out after finishing only half of the promised work brought an end to that. Not to mention it was a credibility blow to Marcus as a gallery owner. Marcus had been in the business long enough to weather such things with a shrug, especially from a nonestablished artist, but Thomas was fairly sure Marcus had never had a lover do it.

While Thomas had missed his chance at the show when his father had the heart attack, it was when Rory's accident brought him home again less than a month later he knew his career as an artist was over. He'd come close, but it wasn't meant to be. He'd known then he wouldn't be going back.

"Since you said you didn't care what was done with them, I decided to feature the pieces in a recent show I held, for deceased artists." The light trace of sarcasm would go undetected by his family. Not by Thomas. Even as Thomas' jaw tightened, Marcus continued. "I set the prices at what I felt they were worth. I thought you might appreciate the extra income."

Thomas still hadn't looked at the check, but then Celeste's hand was on his, tilting it. "Oh my God, Thomas. Twenty-five… It's twenty-five thousand dollars."

Pandemonium broke out. Rory pushed his chair forward, nearly running over Les' toes while she continued to exclaim. "Thomas, this is…oh my God. Your art…" His mother stood there speechless, though he could tell a hundred thoughts were rocketing through her head like mortar fire, her body stiff as if having to withstand the barrage.

But he couldn't help looking down at it himself, touching the ink. Five figures. Five fucking figures for work he had done.

A gallery check. Marcus' logo. Marcus' signature. Thomas' lips tightened, anger filling his mind with heat.

Give him the damn check in front of his family. Like a gift from God.

Pulling the check away from Celeste and Rory, he strode through the store, hearing the shop bells chime as Marcus exited the building ahead of him. His mother called after Thomas, her voice stammering as she tried to marshal her defenses, but he was already past the defensive line. His own fury could carry him through this. He would handle it.

Chapter Two

ꟸ

Marcus had walked to the end of the parking lot at the edge of the barn and storage area. He now stood looking out at the pasture where the cow raised her head and stared at him. She chewed her cud, as perplexed by him as he seemed mesmerized by her.

"You son of a bitch."

Marcus glanced at him as Thomas stepped over the curb and crossed the grass to the fence. "An accurate statement, based on what I know of my mother."

"What is this?" Thomas waved the check. "What the hell are you doing here?" The ache in his chest was suffocating him. He stopped three paces away because—God help him—he didn't trust himself closer. He might go to his knees and beg, and he didn't know for what. He was the one who'd walked away, and nothing had changed about the situation. If anything, it had gotten worse, confirming that he'd made the right decision.

"This is the cow." When Marcus turned fully to study him, Thomas had to lock his jaw and plant his feet to meet his gaze. "The one you mentioned the day I said you wouldn't be able to sell a picture in my gallery with a cow in it. You told me not only would it sell, I could put it up for auction and people would try to outbid one another for it."

Marcus, always one to take a challenge, had agreed he'd put the painting up at the next auction. Which had never happened because Thomas left. Thomas forced himself to respond. "Yes, that's her. Kate. Her name is Kate. Les named her."

"I should hope so. Else you would have been outed long ago. No straight farm boy names his cow, after all."

The slight edge to Marcus' tone helped Thomas remember the point. He lifted the check. "What is this?"

"I told you. It's your percentage. All of the pieces sold. Even the sculpture, though we both know that's not your best medium. Oils. In your hands, they can become anything."

As Marcus' attention drifted to his mouth, lingered, Thomas couldn't bear it. He crushed the check in his fist.

"Bullshit. Total bullshit. No way an unknown—hell, one who hadn't even gotten his Master of Fine Arts yet—would get this kind of money. It's you. Your signature, your gallery. There were no buyers. You think you can buy me into being something I can't be, like some boy whore you picked up on the street?"

Marcus' green eyes rose, narrowed. "Do you think I'm that desperate, pet?"

No. He didn't think Marcus was desperate at all, whereas Thomas was going to choke on his own misery if he stood here another moment looking at what he wanted so much and couldn't have. *Please God, just let him vanish and be one of those million dreams I've had of him before I do something stupid.*

"You aren't desperate. But you're used to getting what you want. That's all this is about. You don't want me. You just can't stand that I walked away. I should have expected you sooner. Keep your money, and like I told you then, keep those pieces. Burn them, toss them in the trash. It doesn't mean anything here. Nothing. You don't mean anything here."

He slapped the check against Marcus' chest, hard enough to shove him back toward the fence.

He'd overlooked it in his fury, or perhaps he didn't care, craving the fight and the violence, some outlet for everything churning inside of him. While cultured, elegant and beautiful, Marcus was also bloody strong, dangerous as a wolf and knew how to fight in ways far beyond Thomas' skills. He was deadly when crossed, and he was a sexual Dominant.

Not to be confused with an alpha male, though he was that. Thomas had been naïve, unaware of all those terms until he got direct experience in what they meant and what things it unlocked in himself.

Marcus' hand clamped down on his wrist, holding it to his chest. Catching Thomas by the back of the neck, he stepped forward aggressively. Riding on anger, Thomas was unbalanced and so Marcus was able to thrust him against the section of the barn wall that formed a corner with the fence.

Marcus immobilized his legs by thrusting one of his own between them, holding the hard pressure of his thigh against the base of Thomas' testicles, his forward weight making it uncomfortable. The slam against the barn wall also knocked the wind out of him, pissing him off further. He could beat Marcus in a fair fight, but nothing about this was fair, not with his head so fucked up, caught off guard by Marcus' presence in his world, a world Marcus had never been a part of. Could never be a part of.

"Settle down," Marcus said shortly. A short brusque command he emphasized with the pressure of his leg, the squeeze of his hand on his nape. "Settle," he repeated, and Thomas realized his clenched hands were gripping Marcus' shirt just above his waist under the coat. Ostensibly it was to thrust him away, straight-arm him, but Thomas found his hands were squeezed into tight fists, holding onto him as desperately as he was trying to push him away.

When Marcus shifted against that needy ache in his groin, Thomas did something he'd not done since he was thirteen years old. Without warning or plan, not even a frantic moment to try to stop it, he came, his cock spurting hard inside his jeans. His hips jerked, grinding him against the muscular steel of Marcus' thigh beneath the pressed slacks even as he wished for the grip of his hand, those clever fingers.

As if he knew Thomas' mind as well as his cock, Marcus slid his hand in between them, cupped him, took him through it, a desperate, over-too-quickly orgasm cut short by Thomas' own shame and fear of being seen. But they were screened by the barn wall, so for one minute his mind shoved that away and allowed him to savor the feel of Marcus' possessive touch on his cock, his intimate knowledge of it that helped him find the head unerringly and rub the ridge.

Marcus stroked his knuckles up Thomas' turgid length, then down to the balls to hold them in a firm grip, squeezing.

"Oh God." Thomas shut his eyes. One of his hands had now moved to Marcus' shoulder, clutching it, seeking to steady himself because the ground was no longer stable.

"All right, then?" Marcus' voice. The anger remained, but there was something ragged and tender beneath it. He had his hand on Thomas' nape still, only now he was stroking him. "You didn't ask permission to come, but I think under the circumstances I'm flattered enough to overlook it."

"You can't be here. You can't do this to me."

"It appears I did, regardless." Still, Marcus drew back, considered him as Thomas looked away over the field, trying to catch his breath, find a balance. Marcus didn't let him go, though. Nor did Thomas release his grip.

"I did buy one of your pieces. Just one. The one with the cow."

"Nobody else wanted it. Like you said, right?" Because Marcus was always right. It didn't change anything, though. Being right didn't make things right. He wondered if Marcus had ever understood that in his whole life.

"No. I auctioned it as I promised. For ten thousand dollars."

It took Thomas' brain a moment to register it. When he did, his face went rigid with shock.

"I had to bid against seven other serious bidders. It created quite a bit of excitement, as well as the accusation that

I was driving up the price for my gallery. Didn't matter. They fought me all the way for it."

"For ten thousand dollars." Thomas couldn't even get his mind around it. He was weak enough to wonder what it would have been like to be there, see people wanting his work enough to compete against each other for it.

"But…why that one?"

"You know why."

He did know.

* * * * *

They'd been in Marcus' bedroom, which Thomas had started to think of as "theirs", since he'd practically moved in by then. He'd been naked on his stomach in their bed and Marcus had been straddling his ass, working his hands down his shoulders, helping him work out one of the muscle kinks that came with a too-intense studio session.

"So…this cow picture? I might have an idea for you."

"You're just trying to sabotage the bet. Get me to paint something that wouldn't be picked up at a yard sale. Cows playing Mahjong."

"That *would* be picked up at a yard sale." Marcus chuckled, his hands kneading, fingers tracing curves of muscles in ways that had Thomas aware of his every shift against his buttocks, the press of Marcus' thighs on either side of his hips, holding him down.

"I see you standing against a fence, farm boy. Leaning there like you've just finished a day of plowing. You're sweaty, streaked with dirt and you've taken off your shirt."

"Of course." Thomas grinned, but he let out a moan of sheer ecstasy as Marcus hit the kink in his shoulder. "Right there."

Marcus obliged. "You're wearing those working jeans that have no style, but they're riding low on your hips.

Because you're leaning against the fence, they're straining over that fine ass you've got." His fingers trailed there, but he'd told Thomas not to move, so he didn't, though his balls drew up tight and hard from his Master's provocative touch. "Maybe a cowboy hat dangling from your hand."

"Bill cap," Thomas said automatically.

"Excuse me?"

"It's a baseball cap. We don't wear cowboy hats."

"All right, then. The sun's setting behind your precious cow and sunlight is just barely touching you, outlining your body. I can see the hint of sweat on your shoulders." He smoothed his hands over them. When his fingers grazed Thomas' jaw, they paused to caress his lips. Thomas closed his eyes.

"He's just a farm boy taking a break after a hard day, never realizing how breathtaking he is in that one perfect moment. Everything about him is in that picture."

"You're so full of shit." Suddenly uncomfortable, Thomas flipped and attempted to heave Marcus off him. Instead, he found himself pinned full length under his Master's aroused body. He'd struggled, but when Marcus fisted his hands in his hair and kissed him hard, his tongue sweeping inside to claim his mind, that was that.

It had lingered with his muse, though, so he'd created the painting. He'd never done a self portrait and was glad to do it from the back. He did a photo session to get some perspective on points of himself he'd never seen, which included some close-ups he'd had to forcibly wrest from Marcus to destroy.

In the end, he'd found it oddly difficult to paint himself, trying to put together the pieces from photographs. The final effect gave the painting a brilliant starkness, almost as if the artist had painted the figure from inside to out, starting with the skeleton and forming muscle layers over which the skin was painted. The figure of the man was an absorbing contrast to the easy beauty in the green of the meadow, the vibrant colors of the sun.

* * * * *

"I kept that farm scene, because your soul is in it. You're living up to your responsibilities." Marcus nodded toward the hardware store. "But you're looking toward that sunset, all the colors, the miracle of it, yearning for it.

"It was one of your best pieces. It was you. I wanted it." Marcus' tone lightened, but Thomas heard the edge beneath it. "As you said, I get what I want."

Marcus leaned against the fence. There was just the space of one man between him and Thomas now. When Marcus put his foot up on the bottom slat, Thomas couldn't see if he was as turgid and aching as Thomas had been only moments before. And would be again in no time if Marcus didn't remove his chiseled face, sensual lips and lean strong body from Thomas' senses soon.

"I have a proposal for you. One that I hope you'll consider. It would allow you to be here and nurture your talent both. Are you ready to listen, or do you need further attention?" He flicked his glance over Thomas, letting his gaze slide down like the lazy path of hot oil on heated skin.

Oh yeah, in no time at all. "Just tell me."

Marcus inclined his head. "Artists come to New York to make it because that's where you can get hip deep in the industry, make connections. You've done that. My gallery is in the center of things and the reaction at that auction says I can market your work without you. J. Martin is one of my biggest clients and he doesn't make public appearances at all. If you never want to cross the Mason Dixon line again, you don't have to. You provide the art, I'll sell it, get it distributed, build your name."

"What do you want in return?"

Silence was a weighted thing, and Thomas felt it in Marcus' gaze. Suddenly, beneath it, he felt so out of place. Everywhere. He didn't belong here, but it was where he was needed, had to be. He didn't belong in Marcus' New York world anymore either, but when he'd been with Marcus, he'd felt like he belonged anywhere. Wherever Marcus was.

He couldn't be thinking like this. He started to fumble open the work apron and spread it over his damp groin. Marcus spoke.

"One of the buyers was Hans Joyner, a hotel mogul who's salivating to see more. He'd like to put about fifty original pieces in his exclusive male salons across Europe. No restrictions on the subject matter. Fifteen thousand each upon delivery. Take out my sixty percent and you're still bringing in six thousand dollars per completed work, in addition to what else you'll start selling when your name starts growing."

As Thomas hesitated, Marcus sighed. "Thomas, you're working short-staffed at a hardware store that, while admittedly a tribute to a bygone age, only makes enough to break even. Barely. You run in the red half the time. You still have debts from your father's funeral and Rory's astronomical medical bills, not to mention that expensive medical college your sister's scholarship won't cover beyond the first year. If one of the big home improvement stores goes up in a nearer town in the next few years, it will end you and you know it."

"You've no right to dig into my business."

"No right." Abruptly, the civilized veneer was gone. Thomas was blasted with the unexpected heat. Marcus pivoted and shoved him back into the same corner, slamming his palm against the side of the barn so Thomas was caged between Marcus' arm and the fence. Violence and desire always rode the same horse when it came to his feelings about Marcus. Despite a desire to shove back, Thomas abruptly wanted the taste of that mouth again, the feel of those hands gripping him so roughly. Gripping him any way Marcus desired.

The green eyes flickered with the knowledge. With fire.

"Do you want to kiss me, pet?" Marcus asked huskily. "Do you think I don't know just my voice can make you hard? You were hiding that stiff cock of yours behind the counter from your sister, because your body remembers everything about responding to my voice, my touch, the whisper of a command. Did you cream yourself when I grabbed your wrist?"

His hand dropped to cup Thomas' balls again, his thumb rubbing slowly along the ridged head of his cock. Marcus swore softly as Thomas groaned, clenching his teeth. He wouldn't stop him, but Thomas grabbed the edge of the fence in one hand, holding it so his knuckles whitened, so he wouldn't be weak and seize Marcus again.

"What you want is for me to bend you over this fence and fuck you hard, fill you where you've been empty for far too long."

"Haven't…been."

"I'm sure. There's a wealth of eligible playmates for you down here." Marcus' gaze shifted briefly over the open field. He leaned even closer, his lips a hairsbreadth away, his breath caressing Thomas' face. God, Thomas wanted that tongue, needed it pushing into his mouth the way he wanted Marcus' cock pushing into his ass. "But that's not the reason I know that. You're mine, Thomas. You've been mine from the beginning. If you let any other man touch you, I'd kill him."

With that one statement, Marcus put it out there. Thomas had walked away, convinced himself it was over, whereas Marcus had never released the end of the leash. Perhaps that's why Thomas had never felt the chain had been broken. Because it hadn't.

A hard shudder ran through him despite himself. Marcus' eyes grew more intent, more brilliant. Perhaps his mother was right. A serpent in the desert. Marcus' complexity, his gentleness, his urban polish, his humor, all of it was underscored by a generosity that was limitless. He even at times had a loving, nurturing nature.

But all of that was twined like a serpent's coils with this, a ferocious darkness, a Dominant's need to possess and control that Thomas had not realized he would match with an equal submissive hunger. From the beginning he'd wanted to belong to Marcus and only Marcus, in ways a boy from rural North Carolina wouldn't have imagined existed inside himself.

"No!" He shoved Marcus away from him and backed into the open space of the parking area where he could breathe, though the world was teetering dangerously as if it wanted him to slide right back into Marcus' grip. "Don't fuck with my head. You don't need to pull that crap just to get me to make more money for you."

While he said it only to hurt, he needed the defense. Besides which, in his heart he knew it was true. Not the part about Marcus using him for money. Even before he walked away, Thomas had always known Marcus would tire of him in time, no matter how intimate they'd gotten. These were Thomas' roots and he needed those roots. He had to live up to them, because they were permanent and real. Unlike Marcus' attraction to him, which he knew was only permanent and real in his most fantastical dreams.

Marcus' face transformed into a mask of indifferent politeness, which told Thomas he'd hit the mark with enough accuracy to make his heart hurt. "I knew you were gutless when you walked away from me. I didn't think you'd resort to being that stupid redneck kid again as well."

Thomas' spine snapped straight, his chin jutting out like his brother's. "Now you're trying to start a fight."

"If it makes you remember the will to have one, gladly." Marcus nodded once. Coldly.

"This is who I am. Where I'm staying."

"Is it what you want?"

"It doesn't always get to be about what you want," Thomas said between clenched teeth. "Life sometimes is making the best of what you're given."

Marcus considered him. The breeze moved his hair on his shoulders, a strand brushing his firmly held lips. "Fine, then. Ignore your feelings about me, bury them. Try to destroy them by throwing asinine insults at me, but do the work, send it to me. I'll sell them at the contracted price, send you the money and it will supplement your income to keep your family going.

"If nothing else, I'm still the gallery owner who has the connections to get your work noticed, Thomas. Your talent is phenomenal. You've only scratched the surface of it. No matter what you think about me, people don't spend thousands of dollars on a piece of artwork from someone whose name they don't even know, unless the talent is so remarkable they don't care whether it's a brand name or not."

"Stop." Thomas shook his head. "You know I can't handle that kind of shit. I can't…I haven't thought about…"

As Marcus' eyes narrowed, Thomas felt the gnawing teeth start up on his gut, as vicious as the blades of the chipper.

For months, the ideas had been elusive, formless, ruthlessly kicked into a hole in his subconscious like a swamp filled with sucking mud.

Because of that, he couldn't allow himself to accept what Marcus was saying. Couldn't even enjoy the vision for a moment, though a greedy part of him wanted to bask in the idea of achieving success as an artist. Instead, Thomas almost felt sick. When he moved his hand to knead his stomach, he forced himself to stop as Marcus' sharp attention went to it.

It wasn't Marcus' fault. He knew that. He'd always known that. It just wasn't meant to be. Thomas took a deep breath, let it flow out of him, let the anger go. "You know your business, you always have. When you say things like that…it scares the hell out of me. It also…there's a part of me that's just fucking amazed by it."

A light smile crossed Marcus' face, but didn't reach his eyes. "You deserve to let all of you be amazed by it. Not just a part."

"It's not there anymore." Thomas forced the words past stiff lips. "I need the money, but I wouldn't know where to start. Everything's insecticide, feed, and 'what size couplings do you need for your plumbing'?" He gave a half laugh at Marcus' raised brow.

"I'm sure I don't want you to explain what a coupling is to me."

Thomas shook his head, reached out a hand. It felt as if it weighed three times what Kate did. "Thanks for dropping off the check. I'm sorry for how I acted. You…you didn't do anything. It was all me. I took it out on you. You just surprised me, is all. Wasn't ready to see you here."

"I don't exactly fit in this painting, do I?" Marcus looked around, still not taking the hand, though Thomas kept it out stubbornly.

"No, you don't."

When Marcus clasped it at last, Thomas tried not to show how the contact rippled through him, ached in his bones as if he'd been gripped by the flu. Already the sandwich he'd packed to have at noontime was something he knew he wouldn't be eating.

"Give me a week."

"What?"

"You've been here eighteen months, working six or seven days a week with no time off, no breathing room at all. I think they can cover for you a week, particularly if it means they can add a significant source of income to the annual budget. I've got a friend's place up in the Berkshires for a month."

Still holding Thomas' hand, Marcus reached inside his coat with a free hand and drew out an airline ticket. "The date's transferable. I'll be there for the next thirty days, working out of the house and visiting some of my gallery contacts and artists in that area. Come spend the week in the house, bring your sketchbook. I promise you beautiful scenery, wonderful eccentric communities and quiet spots of nature." His eyes gleamed. "A wide variety of things to resurrect your muse."

"You'll be there."

Marcus nodded. "I'll be there."

"Marcus, I can't... I can't promise you anything."

That wasn't what he'd intended to say. *No, I can't start this again. I can't be with you even a week. A day.*

But Thomas didn't say that. Everyone knew an addict couldn't have just one drink, one fix. But no matter how strong Marcus' hold over him, they both knew the building behind Thomas, the people waiting in it and all that meant would always call him back. The question was whether it was worth it to him to give himself a week of Marcus again, now that he knew how intolerably hard it was to walk away from him, be without him. Knowing he'd have to sever that link and do it to himself all over again at the end of the week.

But Marcus and his art together...even if Thomas had to let Marcus go again, if he rediscovered his art, he could have that. Maybe that would help fill the aching void enough that it wouldn't be as difficult this time.

And maybe Thomas wanted Marcus so much he just didn't give a damn how hard it was going to be to walk away again.

"No," he said. "No. I won't."

Marcus nodded. "Hold onto the ticket. It's yours to use or not to use."

Thomas held it out. He couldn't afford the temptation. "No. You take it back. Give it..." The words "to someone else" hung on his tongue as if he were pierced by a fish hook whose barbed tip he couldn't dislodge.

He'd tortured himself with images of other hands on Marcus' body, other men seeing that thick cock, Marcus thrusting into them. He woke from dreams about it, wanting to smash and tear something. He usually settled for going out in the middle of the night in nothing but his pajama bottoms to chop wood, the pain singing through every muscle, his fingers knotting with the agony of clenching the axe too hard.

"I can't, Marcus. I just can't."

Marcus turned for his car. Didn't take the ticket. Thomas clutched it with the check Marcus had picked up, smoothed and handed back to him. He swallowed. Goddamn it.

"Marcus, are you—" He bit it off, knowing it was wrong to show how he felt. As powerful as the physical attraction was between them, it was even more dangerous to give Marcus the edge of knowing how much deeper it went for Thomas still. In fact, if he was forced to look at himself in a mirror and be brutally honest, Thomas knew he hadn't realized how much he loved Marcus Stanton until he left him. He was pathetic.

Marcus turned at the driver's side door. He'd put his sunglasses back on, distancing himself, and Thomas felt exactly like what he was, an awkward, gangling kid dealing with a man who was one step ahead of him on everything. Swiss watch, self confidence and a strong sense of his identity.

"What, pet?"

The endearment was uttered in a neutral tone Thomas knew could hide anything from hurt to scornful amusement.

"Are you...are you being careful? I'm not...fishing. I don't have any right to be, to ask anything. And I'm not," he added quickly. He just knew Marcus. Knew that there was a reckless side to his personality, odd moments of melancholy that had once been known to compel him to go out for an evening's entertainment wherever he could find it, not giving a damn about protection. It was a side of Marcus few knew about, and he'd only picked up on it from bits and pieces of things Marcus had revealed about himself, most of them inadvertently.

Thomas had been able to balance Marcus' dark side, calm it, where friends who'd known him longer couldn't even touch it. When Thomas had asked Marcus about that, to determine if he was imagining it or not, Marcus had been sitting on the balcony staring out in the night, seeing shadows Thomas didn't understand.

"It's because you're an artist, Thomas. I don't mean a person who paints or sculpts, though that's one form your perception takes. You see into the souls of others more easily. It should make me want to close all doors against you, because my soul is the last thing I want anyone to see. But—"

"But..." Thomas had prodded. But Marcus had said nothing else, his green eyes lost in the darkness.

"I just want to know you're taking care of yourself," Thomas said, coming back to the present. "You matter."

Marcus left the driver's side, came back across the gravel in his Italian shoes. Thomas held his ground as Marcus picked up his hand and ran his fingers over the tip of the injured one. "Same goes, pet." Though the shades concealed Marcus' eyes, Thomas felt the intensity of his focus. "Come to the Berkshires. The address is written on the back of the ticket. Don't say no. Just think about it and be willing to give it a try. One week."

"One week when you'll try to get me back in your bed."

"Oh, there won't be any trying on that one, Thomas. We both know that's not what's in question." Marcus' lips curved. Thomas felt his cock respond as if on a chain that Marcus could jerk to attention whenever he wished.

"You'll be in my bed."

Chapter Three

ᏪᏍ

Marcus managed to drive to the end of the dirt road, weaving through the flanking trees that put him out of sight of the hardware store. Then he had to stop. He gripped the steering wheel, fighting the urge to pound on it. He wanted to destroy something inside the car, rip it apart to make it match the way he felt inside.

God, he'd wanted to just eat him alive. Eat him alive and then force him into the car, drive away from the deceptively picturesque rural scene that was tinted with the backlight of hell, because it was a prison for Thomas.

"Jesus Christ. And here comes the warden," he muttered under his breath.

Thomas' mother stopped her late model SUV behind his rental, got out and moved with purpose toward his window, a steely glint in her blue eyes. Marcus toyed with the grimly amusing idea of rolling the car forward just a few feet to see if Elaine Wilder would chase him. Instead, he pushed the window control, met her stare for stare as she squared off with him and crossed her arms.

Her face was hard and strained, unattractive in this light, showing all that had happened to her over the past year. He wasn't feeling particularly sympathetic right now though, even as he acknowledged the wear and tear.

"You can't leave well enough alone, can you?" she said. "He didn't come back into the store. Just walks away from us. Across the field, as if he'd rather be anywhere else."

"Imagine that."

Her lips tightened. "This is his home. Where he belongs. You don't know him the way you think you do. He needs roots, a home. He doesn't belong in a big city like New York."

"That's right. There are no families in New York. We're all just a bunch of wandering nomads addicted to Starbuck's."

"Don't get fresh," she snapped. "I'm not saying people can't be happy in that life. But he can't live that way. If you care for him at all, you know it. Someone like you is not going to be happy with my son forever."

"Please tell me this is not the crap about gay men being unable to commit."

"Your unnatural sin, and the fact you've dragged my son into it, isn't the point. You're far more sophisticated than he is. Older."

"Not by much."

"You and I both know there's a big difference between a man's mind at twenty-seven and a man's mind at forty. And you're the type of person who runs in circles most of us around here only see on TV."

"Are you saying he's not good enough for me?" He delivered it with sarcasm, knowing being a wiseass was not going to help the situation, but he wasn't in a peacemaking mood. Not even close.

"No. I'd never say that." She lifted her chin, stared him down. "I'm saying that's not what will make him happy."

Marcus had to swallow the urge to swing open the door and knock her off her sturdy and hideously ugly garden clogs, but she continued, her voice cold. "My son is special, a pure soul. But I can see your soul, Marcus Stanton. You're the kind of man who won't look past your own selfish interests to see what he really wants and needs."

"Well to borrow one of your quaint country sayings, isn't that the pot calling the kettle black?" he snapped. "Have you looked at him lately?"

At her blank look, his control broke. Marcus unbuckled the seat belt and came out of the car, abruptly enough she started back. He slammed the door behind him, making the vehicle rock from the impact.

"He's dropped thirty pounds since I last saw him. He's got pits under his eyes, so he's not sleeping, and what the fuck is this nervous tic he's got going?" He took his hand, rested the heel of it on his hipbone and pressed his thumb into his abdomen above the navel area, below the rib cage. "He did this four times while I was talking to him. His stomach is bothering him."

"You don't realize what this family has been through, what—"

"We all go through shit," Marcus said bluntly. "None of it gives any of us the right to crush the dreams of the people we love."

"He's lost his father. His brother is crippled. He has a lot of responsibility—"

"All of which you've dropped on him and made him turn his back on what he was meant to be. An artist."

"His art celebrates a lifestyle damned in the eyes of God. If he has to give that up, it's the sacrifice he must make to save his soul. You dragged him into that lifestyle."

"Oh, for Christ's sake. Nothing is going to make your boy straight, Elaine. I didn't drag him into anything. But you're absolutely right. This is a battle for his soul, and while you may think I'm Lucifer, you sure as hell aren't God. This isn't about you or me. It's about the gift that defines his soul more than you or I will ever hope to do. If he doesn't have that for himself, neither of us will have anything."

She opened her mouth to retort and he took another step forward, shamelessly using his height to intimidate her. To her credit, she planted her feet this time and clenched her fists, but he pressed on.

"And while we're on the whole God thing, would you like to know what an ignored ulcer is? It's a suicide."

Being a Catholic, she snapped to attention, as he expected her to. "What are you—"

"When a person who is torn between who he is and who everyone wants him to be gets an ulcer, and then ignores it, it's because some part of him hopes for the day it explodes into something that allows him to escape the frigging Prometheus' rock he's chained on."

"You're talking nonsense. He just needs to get his mind straight here, marry Daralyn…"

"What?" Marcus' eyes narrowed. Apparently his expression became cold enough to make her hesitate. "What the hell are you talking about?"

The profanity snapped her spine straight. "Daralyn. He's been seeing a girl while he's down here. They've talked about being engaged."

"Really?" He lifted a brow. "Poor girl, if you actually screw up Thomas' head enough to get him to go along with that."

"Before he came to New York, he never showed any inclinations—"

"Oh, bullshit," he snarled.

Her hand flashed out, slapped his face. The sting and the shock of it reverberated between the two of him. During a long, frozen moment, something shuddered up from his gut, a primal, violent urge he hadn't unleashed in a long time. Apparently Elaine recognized it, because her voice went up an octave, becoming shrill.

"That's the last time you'll curse at me," she said.

"That's the last time you'll ever raise a hand to me, unless you want to be slapped right back. And I hit harder."

He didn't bother to modulate the menace in his tone, even took some pleasure in the paling of her expression. As if suddenly realizing how isolated she was on this part of the road with him, Thomas' mother took another step back, her eyes widening.

"Don't believe everything Rory tells you about fags," Marcus said, low. "I can assure you that most of us are *not* pansies. You lie to yourself all you want, but you won't lie to me. The mother is almost always the first to know. You noticed it when he was young, maybe even three or four years old. You probably weren't experienced or worldly enough to put your finger on it, but you knew your son was different somehow. Something about his makeup that set him apart from Rory or Celeste.

"It isn't always the stereotypical things," he continued, "but very often it is. You saw it, you knew it as he got older and particularly as the world changed, enough that it touched even your closely sheltered life.

"Thomas is a gifted erotic artist who focuses with absolutely unparalleled passion on the male form. He's got more talent than anyone I've ever seen, with one exception, and I think he'll match that man in time. A man who, by the way, pulls in well over a million a year now from his art."

"Money is Satan's tool."

He nodded. "It's God's tool too. Otherwise, I expect churches wouldn't have collection plates. It can keep this place going as well."

Shaking her head, she backed away, this time he suspected from the threat of his words instead of his fists. Her jaw tightened, visible evidence of the wall she was between him and Thomas. Seeing the tears she was struggling not to shed in front of him, he knew she recognized everything he'd said, and didn't want to hear it. He shouldn't have taken it this far. He'd stepped hip deep into the well of blind, impotent fury goaded by her bigotry and his roused feelings about Thomas' situation.

Thomas would kill him for locking horns with his mother. But damn it, she'd tracked him down, and her timing was lousy. He was beyond rage, seeing the lost weight, the hopeless resignation in Thomas' eyes, the fucking cut on his hand from handling a fucking wood chipper, for God's sake.

Thomas lived in his right brain, where creation took place. He mislaid keys and credit cards regularly. He'd leave his car running on the street outside his pathetically small warehouse lease to go back in and get something. While he was there, he'd get an idea for a painting and start sketching it out, completely forgetting about the car or where he'd been going until Marcus stopped in and found the car had run out of gas. And then he'd just shrug, smile that beautiful smile, his lashes sweeping down as he kept at what he was doing.

Marcus had concluded that Thomas' guardian angel had to be the one who guarded Eden with a hundred flashing swords, because while living in New York City, he'd never even had his wallet picked. His neighbors and total strangers actually took turns finding his keys, cards or other mislaid belongings and returning them.

Had the episode with the wood chipper been the same thing he'd just pointed out to Elaine? A subliminal suicide wish for his hands, so the loss of his art was no longer a choice which could eat at his soul? It made Marcus even more furious.

"Just go away and don't come back," she said, her voice breaking over the syllables.

"That's up to your son to decide. If he needs me, I'm here for him. It's between the two of us, not you."

"You're just manipulating him for your own purposes."

"Manipulating? That's a pretty big word for around here. You must be filling up your lonely evenings with extra courses at the community college."

Okay, that was petty and downright cruel. Thomas *was* going to kill him. It was past time to get out of here.

"You think you have us all figured out, don't you?" Elaine squared her shoulders, not even swiping at the tears that had fought past her restraint and spilled onto her cheeks. "Narrow-minded, ignorant backwoods country people who pound their Bibles. Well, I've raised children long enough to recognize one with a chip on his shoulder I didn't put there. You think twice before you use this family as the whipping post for your past, and sacrifice my son on the altar of your demons."

Marcus stopped, his hand on the car door. He increased his grip, holding himself where he was instead of lashing out at her as he wished to do.

"Why is it so fucking difficult for you to love him as he is?"

"I do love my son. How dare you—"

"No, you don't." He cut across her. "You love what you want him to be, something you want so much you've convinced yourself it *is* him. He senses it, knows it, and so he'll spend his entire life here, trying to be everything he thinks you want him to be and nothing that he is."

"Aren't you doing the same thing?" she shot back. "Don't you love him only for what you want him to be?"

He inclined his head, flashed his teeth. "I want him to have it all, everything his talent deserves, every dream he's ever had. I want to see it happen for him."

All I ever wanted was…him.

To hell with it. He shouldn't be doing and saying things she had no way of comprehending, things that would just feed her revulsion and fear of who and what he was, but he was weary of anger. He stared down at his own reflection in the window, spoke to it instead of her.

"When he was living with me, there was one night… I couldn't sleep. I got some wine, came back and leaned against the bedroom door. There he was, asleep, the moonlight on every inch of him." Every perfect naked inch.

When he turned his head, from the color in her face, he knew he'd made that clear enough, but he had no intention of stopping now.

"Those incredibly talented fingers were on my pillow. He did that whenever I got up at night, to know when I came back. I looked at him and I couldn't speak, couldn't swallow. Couldn't even move."

He made a fist, pressed it against his chest. "I wanted everything for him. I wanted to see him achieve every dream, embrace every desire. I wanted to protect him from anyone who would cause him harm or a moment's pain, tear them apart with my bare hands. Never let him out of my sight, even as I wanted him to stretch out his wings as far as they could go and soar. And at the bottom, top and middle of it all, I just wanted to stand there, just that way forever. Not disturb him. Just look at him and love him. Do nothing but simply love him for everything he is, a creation too perfect to be anything but God's gift to the rest of us."

He straightened. "You may recognize my 'chip', but you don't know what that chip made me. Don't you *ever* assume you fucking know who I am."

Getting into the car, he slammed the door and left her standing on the side of the road. Her face was in her hands, her shoulders shaking. His gut was in a hard aching ball. No wonder Thomas was probably getting an ulcer. But even as he thought it, he couldn't ignore the way it felt, leaving her like that. He was a bastard. A selfish bastard. Just as she said. Just as Thomas had said.

You don't know him the way you think you do…

"Want to bet?" he muttered grimly. *You have no idea.*

Chapter Four

ꙮ

You'll be in my bed.

A hard shiver went through Thomas, as it had every time that arrogant statement stroked through his mind, making his blood run hot and thick through his vitals.

He was insane. Two weeks had passed. He hadn't intended to go, had known he was risking too much. That check, the bills it immediately made disappear, couldn't help but factor into it. But Thomas knew it was the least of his reasons for driving away from the hardware store and swinging onto the interstate.

When Marcus left, Thomas had walked out into the field with Kate, kept on walking. For one weak moment, he'd been overcome with this irresistible warm…glow. Marcus had come for him. He didn't believe it. Couldn't do a damn thing with it, but for just a little while, the horrible ache that had been with him for over a year had settled down.

It would be back in the dead of the night, of course. Probably ten times worse for having seen Marcus. But right then, he'd pushed the consequences away and stood in the field, aching in a good, stupid way, like a kid who'd gotten his first kiss.

Marcus had written his cell number on the ticket, but he hadn't used either the number or the ticket. He knew he might back out if he stopped for anything, even to park at an airport and check his bag.

So he'd just gotten into his ancient Nova and driven. He had to stop twice along the turnpike to coax the car back to life, but his worn-out faithful steed revived each time, as if knowing she had to get him to the end of this quest.

However, nineteen hours later, as he drove through the winding two-lane highway deep in the Berkshires, populated with small towns where houses were likely to be constructed by their owners and locks weren't included as part of the design, he was tired enough to be concocting horror stories about what he might find.

Marcus might have given up on him and invited someone else to come.

His lips twisted grimly. Well, tragic irony would be a good jump start, if that was the type of thing that got his artistic muse going. Unfortunately, it wasn't.

Images had once flowed through his mind as if the muse had set up house there. He could see the possibilities in…well, everything. For months, since the block occurred, he hadn't had the energy or the courage to face what had caused the muse to depart so abruptly, cutting off the power, clearing out and leaving nothing.

He only knew at one time he'd been able to translate all the raw emotion of life to a canvas. Despite how close that emotion cut to his own life, his soul had somehow found a safe haven from which to observe without becoming a paralyzed part of it.

It had been a week since Marcus had visited. When Thomas had made the decision to take him up on his offer, his mother of course had been the most difficult obstacle, Rory a close second. Only Celeste, after all the screaming and tears were done with, had squeezed him in one of her generous hugs, bringing her bony body close, and whispered, "Have a good trip."

His mother had gone to church right before he left. She'd likely stay until he returned, holding a solitary prayer vigil.

He'd told her he'd be back in six days. Made himself say it only once. Left the ledger out where she could see it, see what money like that on a regular basis could do for them.

With each mile between home and Marcus, he was torn between sick apprehension and excitement. Need. Arousal. He'd taken a box of sketchpads, his pencils and charcoals, but he didn't know what he was doing or going to accomplish. He might destroy what was left of his sanity.

He'd left Marcus abruptly, both when his father died and then shortly thereafter when Rory was hurt. Then he hadn't come back at all. If nothing else, they could do the proper goodbyes. Best case scenario, he'd get his muse jump-started from the beauty of the Berkshires, be Marcus' lover for a week, be as generous and grateful as he could be, leave on friendly terms, and that was that. He'd handled it badly before, like an immature child. Marcus deserved better than that.

So it went, a jumble of thoughts he recognized as nervous babbling and rationalizations as his foot pushed down on the pedal even harder. Nineteen hours, and he never even turned on the radio, just letting the cacophony of his mind keep him company. A couple times on the Pennsylvania turnpike he thought of hurtling over the edge of a cliff.

Now at last, he made the turn off the two-lane highway and drove for a few miles into deeper forest until he was on a dirt road. When he saw the red cedar mailbox that was the landmark for the house, he made the turn.

As he went up the hill, he saw the brown wooden cottage, blending into the close surrounding foliage. It had the look of a custom-designed chateau. The house was on pilings with a generous shaded patio below, while the upper level had a glassed-in sunroom that led out to a deck with a lattice-enclosed area for a hot tub. Turning around, he saw the incline gave the house a view of the layered vista of hills.

There was only one car, Marcus' Maserati Spyder. Of course, he could have brought someone. He could be in there with a lover. Thomas put the Nova in park, gripped the steering wheel.

Don't be a complete pussy, Thomas. Get out of the damn car. But his mother's tears, Rory's accusing stare, the ache behind his eyes and in his back from driving like he had demons on his tail…the miles between this place, what it symbolized, and a farmhouse hardware store a handful of states away, loomed in his mind like a crash wall in a driving test. Getting out would be like flooring a car that had no brakes. Nothing would stop him but the crash at the end of the road. The end of this week.

If Marcus had told him to come to New York, he couldn't have done it. Perhaps Marcus knew the quiet setting, the familiarity of trees and nature all around, wouldn't only inspire his muse but reassure him, give him that final gentle push. He knew the Berkshires. Now that he was here, though, it wasn't enough. He couldn't get his hands to let go of the steering wheel, couldn't reach for the door, get out. Who was he kidding? This was a mistake.

Then Marcus stepped out on the deck, glass of wine in hand. He wore slacks and a pale yellow shirt, open and fluttering loose, showing the smooth pectorals, ripple of muscled abs, the hint of his waist, the intimate crease of armpit as the breeze tried to edge the shirt off one broad shoulder. One hand was in his pocket and his feet were bare, his hair loose on his shoulders.

His green eyes were brilliant, even from here, filled with an intensity that washed over Thomas, drawing him into the fantasy of a tranquil, emerald lagoon where everything else was sucked out to sea, to be churned in the surf where it couldn't touch him. Not for one week.

He got out of the car, looked up at the other man. "One week."

Thomas said it out loud first thing, because he knew it was the only restraint that would apply here. The limitation of time. From the look in Marcus' eyes, he knew he understood that quite well.

What was that question, so often posed in movies between lovers in whimsical moments? If you only had one week to have something you always wanted that you could never have again, would you take it?

It was a banal reality show question whose significance he hadn't appreciated before. Yes. He would. Even knowing that walking away from it at the end of the week was more than he could bear.

"Leave your things for now and come up here." Marcus nodded to the outside stairwell that led up to the deck. "I've got a good Shiraz." At Thomas' grimace, he grinned. "But I can probably scrounge up a beer."

"Now you're talking."

A nice, even conversation. Like everything was fine, like the air wasn't so charged with energy that a single spark could ignite the forest around them.

Thomas came up the stairs, found Marcus already returning from inside, sliding the glass door back with a knee, beer in one hand. His favorite label, Bud Light. Marcus rarely drank beer, and when he did, it was an import.

"You knew I'd come."

"Yes. For your art, I knew you'd come, even if you wouldn't just for me." There was no censure in his tone. Calm, civilized.

When Thomas reached out to take the beer from Marcus' hand, Marcus set it down on the rail before they made contact, absurdly disappointing Thomas. He needed to play it cool, easy and Marcus was helping him.

He didn't want Marcus to help him.

His stomach was taut with all the things Thomas did want, such that his hand shook as he took the bottle to his lips. He covered it by turning away, looking at the view, when all he wanted to do was look at Marcus. "Spectacular. This place is a new one. When'd you discover it?" *With someone else?*

"Friends of mine own it. They're in the Bahamas, at my place there. We swap."

Thomas nodded. Swallowed. He felt Marcus' eyes on him and made himself turn his head to look at him. Leaning his hips on the rail two feet away, Marcus drank his wine. The wind made the tail of his open shirt feather against Thomas' forearm, drawing his attention to the fact there was only a foot between their hands on the railing.

Marcus' long fingers, manicured, his knuckles perfectly proportioned. Thomas' hands, calloused from farm work, several knuckles enlarged from a lifetime of drawing, brushwork. The tip of the one finger gone.

As if following his thoughts, Marcus reached out and brushed the scarred tip with his forefinger, held it there, head cocked. "Does it hurt?"

Thomas shook his head, tried to relax his beer hand. It allowed him to press the point of his wrist into his stomach. He rested his forearm on his hip bone as he shifted to lean his side against the rail.

"You should have used the plane ticket." Marcus' gaze took in the amount of bug matter on the hood and windshield of Thomas' vehicle. "You probably only stopped for a vat of those boiled peanuts you think are food."

"They stopped making them at the state line."

"Thank God for the limits of the Mason Dixon. I have some Chinese takeout, plenty for two, and you're going to eat all of it." Marcus straightened abruptly, moved toward the glass doors.

"I want..." Thomas stopped. His hand gripped the beer bottle in a tight fist, as if squeezing could call back the words.

Marcus stopped and looked back at him. Thomas wished he knew what Marcus was thinking, feeling. He knew what he needed, didn't know if it was fair, was afraid to ask.

"What, pet? What do you want?" It was the gentle tone that did him in, made him blurt it out.

"I'd like...while I'm here. I'd like permission to call you Master... For one week." He had to add that, had to be honest, even as he flinched at the flash of derision that crossed Marcus' expression.

But then it was gone, and there were just the shades of green in Marcus' eyes. All the mysteries of life were there, all the answers. Marcus inclined his head.

"Then you will."

Thomas let out his breath. He couldn't explain why that gave him a sudden sense of grounding, much of the awkwardness melting away, though it did nothing to alleviate the sexual tension. That was still hot enough to make him think he was feeling the heat of a southern sunset, instead of a New England one.

"Come here."

Putting down the beer, Thomas walked across the deck, not conscious of any sounds his shoes were making. All he could see was the outstretched hand against the fluttering pale yellow of Marcus' shirt, the silhouette of Marcus' body revealed fully and then cloaked by it, like an unconscious strip tease.

Marcus slid the door open, tugged Thomas so he stepped into the room in front of him, into a quiet and cool living area that was a warm, masculine comparison of wood tones, highlights of deep reds, the scent of wood reaching his nostrils. Dim light. A lantern and some candles. A fireplace.

Marcus had been reading, for there was a newspaper open on the sofa, Neal Boortz's fair tax book facedown on the arm. Cell phone and organizer next to a scattering of notes. His watchband was stretched out next to them. All familiar things, set out in a familiar way. Marcus had a method of arranging his personal belongings like carefully monitored chess pieces, whether he was at work or leisure.

It gave Thomas what he knew was a false illusion. The sense that he was home.

The door slid closed behind them and Marcus pressed against his back, sliding his arm under Thomas'. His hand moved to the front of the jeans Thomas was wearing and palmed him through them. Already semi-erect just from Marcus' proximity, Thomas hardened immediately, his cock pressing against the restraint of denim to get to that touch.

He was fueled by the energy of having thought about Marcus from the moment he'd gotten behind the wheel. Or since he'd come into the store, or after Thomas had walked out of his life. Oh hell, even before that, from the moment they'd met.

It seemed everything inside him had been about Marcus always. Since Thomas knew that kind of thinking made sense only to people ridiculously, passionately in love, it made it all the worse to be unable to deny it.

Marcus' lips whispered along the back of his neck, his jaw brushing Thomas'. "I want you naked. All the way. Now."

He helped, his fingers slipping the button of Thomas' jeans with strong, sure fingers, tugging at the zipper and taking it to half-mast before he withdrew his hand and stepped back. Waiting.

Thomas took off the shirt first, pulling it free and tossing it to the arm of a nearby chair. He had to bend to untie the shoes, bring one up off the floor to tug at the heel. When he did, Marcus' hands gripped his hips, steadying him even as the touch seared through him, sending his emotions rocketing off balance.

After he got the shoes off, Marcus withdrew again. Thomas removed his jeans, still feeling Marcus' watchful presence behind him like fire coursing over every inch of skin he was revealing. His cock was leaking, no surprise there, so erect it brushed his belly.

"Turn around."

He did, feeling inexplicably nervous. Marcus was physically perfect, and Thomas knew he'd dropped a lot of weight, even though he'd kept his leaner muscles hard from all the manual labor at the store. He hadn't even gotten a haircut before he came up, had decided to go without a shave for the last twenty-four hours in finalizing things at the store, dealing with his mother's final last-ditch effort to stop him, Rory's biting insults.

Hell, he'd basically fled like a fugitive with a small duffel of balled-up clothing he'd barely looked at. All that had mattered were the sketchpads and pencils. And Marcus.

As Thomas completed the turn, Marcus' voice was a quiet command. "Keep your eyes down."

His hands clenched, then opened as Thomas nodded, let out a breath. It had been like this the first time Marcus had taken control, dominated him as his Master.

He hadn't wanted to call it that then. Marcus hadn't been his first sex with a man. Thomas had a couple of tangles with men in New York who'd validated with pleasant skill what he'd always known about himself, that it was a man's touch he craved.

Marcus had revealed a whole other level to him that took him by surprise. The click of the cuffs locking had been an answer to a question in his soul he'd never been brave enough to hear, let alone ask. It was as if the need had always been there, just waiting for him to look toward it.

Thomas didn't even know if it was a level he would crave with anyone else. He didn't look at men and think of being restrained by them, marked by them. He might be attracted to them, but it became clear that was about sex. Apparently, there was only one man he wanted as a Master. Whether that was something about Marcus or something about himself, or about their chemistry together, he didn't know. Any other sex was just sex. He didn't know if that was a blessing or a curse.

What he did know was that Marcus' way of taking him over fed his soul the same way his painting did. It fulfilled a yearning inside him that had no names. No form, only a dense substance that could choke him with feeling, like now. Which was yet another reason why it was fucking crazy to be here.

But that was the type of thing Marcus was so good at. Showing up after just the right amount of time had passed, when he'd had a shitty enough week to be tempted. Tempted beyond refusal. So he told himself.

Marcus closed his hand around Thomas' cock. Thomas shut his eyes, his balls drawing up dangerously.

"Don't you dare close your eyes."

"I'm afraid I'll come. Master."

"Turn back around and get on your knees. Elbows on the floor. Spread your thighs out so I can see you."

Thomas swallowed, that universal sign of nervousness, but complied. He heard Marcus walk away. Though he kept his head down, Thomas managed to sneak a look at him moving across the room and down the hallway, leaving him there waiting in a position to be fucked at his Master's pleasure.

Marcus looked so good it hurt to see him. The curve of his bare heels, the way the slacks fit his ass and thighs. Not tight. Marcus was *GQ* all the way. To get a good view of his ass, Thomas had to wait for him to wear jeans or be naked, and holy Christ, even if it took until Judgment Day, it was worth the wait.

The view coming back was as good or better, because it was easier to see the line of his cock, the weight of testicles. Particularly when the former was aroused as Marcus' cock was at this point, straining the fabric, making Thomas swallow the excess saliva pooled in his mouth.

Marcus had chest hair, the finest layer of down over the pecs and a narrow point arrowing down to his navel. Thomas wanted to reach out and touch, rub his face against it. Lick Marcus' nipples to hard points, close his palm strong and sure over the prominent arousal, feel the steel of it, grip the length and be awed at the privilege of touching it.

Marcus would snort at that, of course. Call him a fucking idiot even as he'd let Thomas do it, the green eyes disappearing as his head dropped back to his shoulders and he let Thomas work him.

Marcus straddled his back now, his calves and feet on either side of Thomas' thighs. Reaching under him, he took hold of his cock without fumbling. Thomas bit down on the inside of his cheek, trying to hold onto his control at the touch of bare hand to bare skin. He felt straps and the metal of a chain a moment before they bit into his flesh, the cock harness cinching tight at the base of his cock and the second loop binding his balls.

Marcus had never used a cock harness on him. It gave a different edge to this moment than they'd shared before. It made Thomas remember that he'd left Marcus and had stated practically from the moment he got out of the car he intended to do it again.

So Marcus was going to make him suffer, and God help him, all Thomas felt was an overwhelming flood of response in his loins, his chest, in the tightening of every muscle of his body in reaction, in the desire to be with him. His arousal ratcheted up exponentially.

Marcus ran his hand over his ass. Taking hold of the left buttock, he squeezed hard, his fingers deep between the cleft, brushing the rim. Thomas shuddered and was thankful for the cruel pinch of the harness on him. *God, please fuck me.* It would hurt, because it had been awhile, and Marcus was well endowed. Not to mention Thomas knew he was a tight fit, but he welcomed the pain. Wanted it with a savagery he couldn't explain. *Punish me. Hurt me.*

It made him think of places Marcus had taken him, just to watch. Club dungeons they had visited where Marcus fondled him under the table or in plain sight while others performed. Slaves stripped and flogged, muscles tightening against pain even as the slave groaned with the pleasure of it, begged for more. For the release that pain brought, to be just who they wanted to be. The slave of their Master, the beginning and end of who they were, because everything they wanted was within that boundary, and the pain reminded them of it.

"You want me to beat you. Stripe your ass raw. I can feel you trembling for it." Marcus' voice, husky, capable of pulling Thomas over the edge with just the intonation, a simple uttered command. "But I won't let it be that easy, Thomas."

Thomas heard the unfastening of the belt, the tongue coming loose. The unzipping of the slacks was a sound that skittered down his spine, the soft rush of clothes falling to the ground, being kicked to the side. The yellow shirt was abruptly before him and Marcus folded it over his eyes, tying it behind Thomas' head, as if immersing him in a sun-drenched room. A room that smelled like Marcus' heat.

Thomas wanted to weep. He wanted to roar. He wanted to turn and take hold of Marcus with both hands, tear at his flesh with teeth and sheer ferocity until he could get inside of him.

Marcus would have made a good horseman. He anticipated everything. Like the knotting of Thomas' shoulders as he tried to thrust himself up from the floor and turn on him. Before he could do it, Marcus had a hand firmly on the back of his neck, gripping as he knelt, pushed his weight against Thomas' ass so he hissed through his teeth, trying to push up, but Marcus had all the leverage.

Before he could think to roll, Marcus parted his buttocks and thrust home. Rough, non-lubricated, raw and painful possession that burned like the fire in Thomas' chest and stomach.

"Stay still and take it, or I'll make it much rougher, farm boy."

Jesus, Marcus was big. And Thomas wanted more. Despite the command, Thomas pushed back, tilting up, telling Marcus he wanted it, telling the bastard he could take anything he could dish out. Even with his dick tied in a knot in that harness, unable to release. Thomas already felt like he was in the throes of an orgasm, he was quivering so intensely.

"There you are. Rock that ass, fuck my cock. Tell me how much you missed me and I might let you come."

Thomas sobbed in his throat, snarled and shoved back against him, hurting. Marcus' hand curled in his short hair, held him with brutal efficiency as he slapped himself against Thomas' ass, hard. Again. And again. Fast, then slowing it down, making Thomas feel every inch of that cock deep inside of him, burning down his shields, leaving raw exposed flesh inside and out.

"Marcus...Master." He said them both, breathed them both, and he had Marcus' answer in an unintelligible noise that meant nothing in words, but spoke directly to something inside him. A harsh breath, and Marcus kicked his knees out wider, dropping Thomas down almost on his face as Marcus held his hips with both hands now.

Thomas cried out at the pain, a pain matched only by the agony in his balls, drawn up so tight and wanting to spew come everywhere, mark all of Marcus' scattered things. The book his hands had touched, the wineglass where his lips had been, the pillow he'd put his head on. He wanted to give it all to him. But Marcus wasn't going to allow it. Not yet.

His Master came in a sudden explosion of brutal force, jetting into Thomas. The heat flooded him, stroked that gland inside so sensitive to such stimulation. He wondered if Marcus had intentionally not used a condom, and why he didn't care, even though he knew they were both being stupid bastards.

But this moment had nothing to do with any of that. It was raw, primitive, and would have been as appropriate in the forest outside, perhaps more. Which made him imagine Marcus as a lion, hunting Thomas down, fighting with him, taking him down.

Marcus withdrew, drawing a quiet moan from Thomas. He was so close to orgasm he knew he would have come without the restraint.

"Up on your knees. Ass on your heels."

As he obeyed, Marcus inserted a lubricated dildo into him Thomas hadn't even seen him bring out. It was a good size, filling him tight. "Jesus..." It whistled out between his clenched teeth, and Marcus' sexy low laugh made Thomas want to do all sorts of dark, deadly things.

"Now sit back on your heels, holding that in."

Thomas wondered if a person could die from withheld release, for if it was possible he was going to have a meltdown. Only Marcus could do this to him, take him beyond thought or reason, desiring only to release, to please his Master. In the nastier, more insecure moments, he'd wondered if it was just the advantage a slick New Yorker had over a country boy with little experience, but he'd held his own.

From the first time Thomas had seen him, he hadn't known who or what Marcus was, just that he wanted him. Wanted to be his. And the fact Thomas had thought of it that way should have given him a clue to the hidden craving in his own makeup. An unexpected sexual preference. Preference. There was a grimly amusing word. As if any need this elemental was a choice. Just as Marcus had always said.

As Marcus trailed his fingers along Thomas' shoulder, the blindfold loosened and fell away. "Hands behind your back now, pet. Lace your fingers and let me see you pull your shoulders back."

Oh God. The position squeezed his buttocks together more tightly, stretched his cock up in the restraint as if he were some sort of overly endowed fertility god. He couldn't see him yet, but Thomas could feel Marcus looking.

He imagined it, Marcus' eyes lingering on his cock, his lashes fanning his cheeks, his eyes just hints of emerald in the dim light. He was in the cave of a dragon, a wild animal in truth, waiting to be devoured. Wanting to be consumed and not caring. Just wanting to feel the hot breath wash over his skin, the hunger pressing him down.

The dragon moved around him, bringing dangerous grace into his vision as he crossed the floor, circled the couch to go into the kitchen. Marcus went behind the counter island and Thomas heard running water, then Marcus returned with a basin of water, washcloth and soap. He set them down on the coffee table, three feet in front of Thomas.

Standing there, tall and naked, he wet the cloth and began to clean his own genitals. Slowly, working the soap up and down his shaft, under the broad ridge of the head, cleaning the slit, then putting the cloth back into the basin to rinse it, wring it out again and wipe away the soap with more water.

Now Thomas knew for sure he was just going to die of need, right here. The ache in his gut was as excruciating as the chronic pains he'd been feeling for the past six months, only he wanted this ache. It was like a knot drawing tighter and tighter, but when it released, oh God, it was going to feel so fucking good.

Marcus' hand touched Thomas' jaw, his thumb at the corner of his lips. Somehow he'd been so overwhelmed he'd closed his eyes. But when he opened them, Marcus was putting the blindfold back on. His expression was focused, intent, his mouth a firm line. No give. No mercy.

"Take my cock and suck it back to life. Then I'm going to fuck you again. When you've made me come three times in your ass and three times in your mouth, when your jaw is aching and your ass feels like I've given you an enema with Tabasco sauce, then I'll let you come. But not a minute before. And when you do come, it's going to be the best and worst orgasm you've ever had."

Beneath the blindfold, Thomas squeezed his eyes shut again, a shudder running through him. Okay, Marcus was pissed. Seriously pissed with him. But he'd do it. He could torture him three times that number of times, and he'd still do what he had to do, though his cock throbbed so hard now he made sounds of growling need in his throat as Marcus fisted a handful of his hair and began to roughly fuck his mouth. Thomas still reveled in it, in serving his Master, clutching at that sense of completeness he hadn't had in over a year.

He'd forgotten that Marcus never lost control. Even if he was pissed, he never lost sight of the ultimate goal. As he worked his cock back up to a full erection, night closed in. After spilling his seed down Thomas' throat, he switched positions, removing the dildo and taking Thomas' ass, pushing him to the floor again, until he snarled his release and Thomas' body shuddered in an agony of need.

Time ceased, details blurred. There was only flesh meeting flesh, penetration, burning. The blindfold removed again, Thomas watching with glazed, watering eyes as Marcus washed himself, that sensual torment of seeing the soap-and-water slicked fingers moving over the cock that had been deep in both orifices of his body. Then his lips being stretched again. Rocking against that rubber phallus, holding it in with his heels. When Thomas couldn't see, it was all intensified, the slide of Marcus' body against his, every rough thrust, every light caress.

There was one blissful point when Marcus stopped deep inside of his ass and pressed a kiss to the back of Thomas' neck. It was possibly the most unbearable moment of all as Marcus slid an arm around his waist and held him, his palm over Thomas' thundering heart, just before he came again.

He should have been keeping count, but he wasn't. It all became about serving Marcus until his Master was ready to have him do otherwise. It was all he was, all his mind wanted to be.

Once when Thomas was eight, he'd been dared to swim a hundred laps in the community pool. He kept going and going and going. Someone stopped him by reaching in and grabbing his arm, pulling him up. He'd been dazed, disoriented, because it had been all about proving he could keep going. The number was no longer important.

The blindfold was untied again. Marcus brought back the room, the features now sharp-edged in their clarity. The book. The wineglass. The edges of the coffee table and frame of the picture over the fireplace. It was twilight outside. The room smelled of sweat and sex, old wood and lubricant which Marcus thankfully had started to use on the second penetration.

"Back on your heels, pet." But this time Marcus didn't put the dildo back in and Thomas was glad, because his ass was so sore. "Hands clasped together at your lower back again."

The now constant quiver in Thomas' muscles increased when he felt the pressure of velour cuffs being wrapped around his wrists and then ankles. Marcus hooked the two sets together, so he was completely helpless.

Then his Master went back to the sofa and sat. Thomas fastened hungry eyes on him. Marcus' chest was slick with sweat, hair damp. He'd been kind enough not to pull on his slacks and so he sat there completely naked. For the moment, his cock rested on his thigh and the nest of his testicles as he considered his slave. His green eyes were still that of a dragon's, laced with fire and power, the simmering fierceness of his climaxes still in his face, the sensuous, taut set of his mouth.

Thomas' attention lingered on the slope of his chest, the tapering to the stomach. God, but it was mouthwatering terrain. No one could look at Marcus' smoothly muscled upper body and not want to take a hard, deep bite. Suck and lick him like an ice cream, like the curves of a creamy vanilla double scoop. The long thighs and narrow calves, all roped with the clean lines of a cyclist's muscles, were equally tempting.

Even the graceful arches of his feet. Every inch of Marcus stirred Thomas, kept him hard, and he suspected the harness was going to leave a permanent collar imprint on the base of his cock. He didn't like to think just how appropriate that was.

Marcus reached for his wine, took a swallow. His hand rested on the chair arm, his palm on the upside down book. Thomas could imagine him picking it up, choosing to pass the next half hour in reading another chapter or two while his slave suffered watching, the hard-on making him dizzy as he contemplated the perfect beauty of his naked Master, hungered for his hands, his mouth. Any kind of attention at all.

Marcus was not in a mood to be that cruel anymore, however. Thank God. He rose, picked up a folded hand towel from the kitchen and came around the table. As he dropped to one knee before Thomas, Thomas' shaking increased. Cupping his jaw, Marcus framed his face, ran his thumbs over Thomas' lips so that he parted them. Thomas tried to catch a finger in his teeth.

"Sshh. Be still. Keep your eyes open."

Did Marcus know how hard this part was for him? Had always been? Staring into his Master's face, seeing the way Marcus looked at him as he gently caressed his jaw, his forehead, touched the corners of his eyes, traced the line of his nose.

"So straight, pet. You've got such a patrician nose."

It was a far different torment than all the rest, because it was the one Thomas hungered for most. Despite all the sweat-covered images that haunted him, these were the memories that plagued him most of all.

Marcus leaned in, fitted his mouth over Thomas', his hand holding his jaw and throat, controlling the moment, controlling everything even as Thomas shook as though he had an infectious fever. Marcus made an approving growl deep in his chest. With his hand he restrained the sudden fierce need Thomas felt to crush, tangle tongues like combatants. His Master kept it slow, steady, wet.

Marcus' aroma was in his nose, the damp hair on Marcus' forehead brushing his, then his cheek and jaw.

When Marcus reached down and gripped him, Thomas groaned in his mouth and Marcus answered with a quiet murmur of pleasure. The straps loosened, fell away. It was all Marcus' fingers running over the cruelly chafed area, stroking up the length of Thomas, the sensitive underside, closing around him firmly, a sure knowledge of what would jack him off in no time. Damn if the bastard was able to set just the right rhythm while still keeping his mouth moving on Thomas' in that erotic, slow swim of a kiss, tongues tangling, lips sliding and teeth gently nipping.

Thomas' hips jerked and he yanked against the bonds on his wrists and ankles. Oh God…this was… He didn't know how long it had taken to bring Marcus to climax six times, but all the images and remembered sensations slammed back into him, assaulting him to mesh with the movement of Marcus' hand.

"Master, I—"

"Another ten seconds. One…" Marcus' tongue invaded, swept in, fucked his mouth relentlessly now as Thomas made noises of wordless protest, begging. Marcus' hand increased in strength on Thomas' jaw as his grip down below did the same. "Two…"

He wasn't going to make it.

"You better make it, pet." Menace, threat of more torture infused in the words like hot flame. Marcus' thumb rubbed the tip, pressed against the underside of his cock. Thomas arched up, his thigh muscles straining. "Oh God… Shit…"

"Wait." Marcus snapped it once, reining him in like a stallion who'd had the bit ripped against his mouth. He couldn't let go. Not until his Master said. Oh, but fucking hell, he was going to die. The world had slowed to a crawl, moving toward that countdown.

Marcus' hand left his jaw, found the towel. "Seven…eight…"

"Ten."

He couldn't help it. The climax exploded from him, so violently that he tried to buck, yank upward. With his hands bound to his ankles he lost his balance, falling forward, nothing to stop him except Marcus' ready hand, sliding around his shoulders, holding him, his face pressed into the side of Marcus' neck and bare shoulder.

Their knees became interlocking puzzle pieces, one of Marcus' in between his legs, one on the outside, Marcus' cock and balls brushing Thomas' kneecap as he jerked and spewed against Marcus' hand under the soft abrasion of the terry cloth he had cupped firmly over him with one deft hand.

It was a cleansing, a scalding of the nerves of his body from his brain to his cock and through all the limbs, leaving Thomas quivering like an oak after the furious passage of a violent tornado. He felt every point of contact between their bodies, not just the clasp of Marcus' hand commanding his cock, but his cheek against his temple.

The still damp, amazingly semi-erect dick against his knee, the fingers around his neck, caressing the side of his throat, his pulse pounding beneath the pads of Marcus' fingers. As Thomas tried to straighten, the world tilted as if he were a bug in a jar being tumbled by a cruelly curious child.

"Easy." Marcus steadied him.

Acting on desire and instinct, Thomas shifted, inching backward a slight movement at a time, hobbling on his shins to the short range of the ankle cuffs. Then he pressed against Marcus' touch, trusting him to balance him as he began to lean forward, down, down. He didn't know if Marcus would permit it, but he did, his face a soft blur, then Thomas' cheek was on Marcus' knee and he was bent forward all the way, his back curved, legs folded under himself.

His belly pressed on his spent cock as he brought his lips to Marcus' cock, brushed his cheek against his leg. Opened his mouth and drew him in, slow, savoring him, sucking him into the back of his throat.

"Jesus." Marcus' soft utterance was like a prayer. His hand splayed out on Thomas' bare back, his other hand curling loosely over Thomas' bound hands, holding the joining point of the cuffs. His fingers betrayed a slight quiver Thomas savored as much as the taste in his mouth. He began to suck slowly in an almost trancelike state, licking, working the organ he knew as well as his own, trying not to think if there were others that could share that distinction.

This was now. He had no right to demand any more, certainly knew it would have been fair to expect far less than what Marcus had given him already. For now there was just the velvet steel of Marcus' cock in his mouth, elongated enough to press into the back of his throat and stretch his mouth again as Marcus splayed his knees and took over, pushing down on him harder.

It took a lot longer this time, because they'd both flat-out exhausted each other. But Thomas didn't mind taking it slow and easy. Marcus' groan as he released at last was a lullaby to Thomas. He swallowed the thick salty taste of him, thinking of how much of Marcus he had inside him now, both orifices.

He kept his head down, eyes closed, forehead pressed against Marcus' sticky cock, inhaling the scent of him as Marcus' palm rested between his shoulder blades, holding him there as Marcus breathed deep, shuddering breaths. Then the thighs shifted beneath Thomas' face as Marcus leaned forward to unlock the cuffs.

As Marcus raised him, they faced each other naked, knee to quivering knee. When Marcus brushed hair off his own brow with his forearm, Thomas watched, wishing. Marcus seemed to understand, because he tilted his head, his attention moving to Thomas' now free hand. Thomas didn't pause, afraid Marcus would change his mind. Reaching out, he threaded his fingers into that dark, thick silk. A lion's mantle added to the creature's virile beauty, and so too did Marcus' dark mane.

Thomas dared to let the heel of his hand caress Marcus' damp brow, the side of his cheek. When Marcus' hand closed over his wrist, he could feel Marcus' desire to remove it, take control of the intimacy. Thomas curled his fingers into his hair more deeply in response, tangling.

"When you were counting, before I came…you skipped a couple numbers, didn't you?" He noticed his voice was hoarse from the abrasion of taking Marcus four times down his throat. From the flicker in his Master's gaze, Thomas suspected Marcus liked hearing it. "You forget how to count?"

"You weren't going to make it. You were ready to spurt like a twelve-year-old with his first copped Hustler."

"Asshole." Thomas made the comment without rancor, for Marcus had let him go, was running his knuckles lightly along his forearm as he let Thomas keep his fingers in his hair.

"Let's get some food in you." Marcus at last pulled Thomas' hand free, kissed his palm and then set it away from him, rising. While Marcus smiled, Thomas noticed it didn't quite reach his eyes. So much could be said with the violent power of sex, but it could leave emotions lingering in the air like the sharp, poignant residue of gunpowder.

When Thomas rose, he was forced to catch hold of Marcus' arm abruptly, causing them both to sway. As the two men regarded each other, Marcus' jaw at last relaxed into a rueful grin, easing some of Thomas' sudden tension.

"Look at us," Thomas managed. "Like a couple of drunk sailors."

Marcus snorted. "You start singing *In the Navy,* you're sleeping in that junk car of yours."

Chapter Five

Marcus woke early, for him. Most of his work involved lunch meetings and nighttime gallery showings, networking parties that might not start until close to midnight. But as if his subconscious knew that every moment with Thomas was precious and not to be wasted, he stirred when the sun was still in the process of rising.

Not only that, he'd surfaced several times during the night. Once, he'd found Thomas' head on his chest. Marcus had his arm resting across his back while Thomas had his arm securely wrapped around Marcus' side and waist, his leg twined over one of Marcus'. Holding him in sleep as if Thomas was afraid he'd lose him.

"I missed you too, pet." Marcus had stroked his head, pressing down to increase the weight of that precious skull against his heart. Thinking of how Thomas pressed on the burning spot in his belly so often, he wondered if this gesture was the same thing. A way to assuage the pain.

Fuck, saying he'd missed Thomas didn't cover it. He thought he'd understood the full extent of it, but when Thomas had pulled into the driveway, it had landed on Marcus like an asteroid.

It pleased him how deeply his farm boy slept. He'd made sure to wear him out physically. Just thinking of it made him want him again, but for now, Marcus wanted Thomas to sleep like this, shed some of his emotional and physical exhaustion.

But holy God, he was a beautiful kid. Broken down, the individual features didn't seem like much. At a glance, his nose appeared small, precise. But when the light hit his profile, it was a sharp blade sharing the same angle with the jaw and cheekbone, perfectly aligned.

Dark eyes, large to balance that small nose. Thomas' ears were larger, but again, somehow it worked. He had heavy brows that Marcus at first thought should be trimmed, plucked down, but very quickly he'd realized they were the perfect accent for the dark eyes and all the emotions that moved behind them, like silken streaks of clouds over a stormy sky. One dropped lower over the eye than the other, giving Thomas' face further intensity.

Though it was starting to curl, Thomas' hair was soft and short under Marcus' stroking fingertips, a conservative cut appropriate for a man raised in a rural county all his life. Shaved short sideburns, the hairline sculpted up and over the ears and trimmed properly above the collar. Marcus could almost imagine Thomas sitting in his mother's kitchen getting the cut, his eyes closed, nearly asleep after a hard day as her hands, those working woman's hands, touched his man's neck, the nape.

As she did it, Marcus was sure Elaine would be remembering the vulnerable shape of it as a boy. Isolated, that part of the body never lost the ability to project innocence.

He knew she loved Thomas. He'd never doubted that. The love was in Thomas' eyes as well when he spoke of her, protected her. It didn't make any of it easier. If anything, it made it harder.

His mother wasn't completely wrong. Marcus was well aware Thomas would never be an urbanite. He was at heart what he'd been raised. Modest, quiet. Not flamboyant in the least. Shy even, at times. He had a bashful tendency to look away when he smiled, but the smile was sexy, black Irish. Except when painting or at ease with Marcus, he typically had nervous gestures while he was talking with strangers.

Thomas was the type of person to hold a door for a woman, no matter what. He'd avert his eyes, uncomfortable and yet a gentleman if a woman's breast was exposed when she leaned over in the grocery line, or if he saw one nursing a baby in public.

Then, just as Marcus would decide Thomas was *too* gentle and boyish, something would raise his ire. That brow would lower, the eyes sharpening, all those straight lines of his face hardening, such that you were looking at the face of a man who wouldn't back down, wouldn't think of it, no matter the odds.

A man as irresistible as a hearth fire in winter. His proximity was heat and comfort at once.

Marcus had drifted off to sleep again reluctantly, only because he knew he'd need rest to enjoy Thomas fully. Now he found himself alone with the rising sun. He made himself lie there, pushing down panic. Glancing toward the half-open door of the bathroom, he located Thomas' shaving kit, along with a hairbrush with bristles so thinned out it looked as if Thomas had possessed it since puberty. Marcus suppressed a smile.

Rising, he slid on a pair of sweatpants and followed intuition out to the main room. Coffee was brewing. Thomas didn't drink it often, but he knew Marcus did. Getting a cup, rubbing sleep out of his eyes, he padded out to the back deck.

And there Thomas was, as welcome as the sunrise Marcus was rarely up to see. Marcus leaned on the rail, looked down at the lower patio. Thomas had set up three easels with pads and there were two more sketchbooks on the ground, held open to the desired place with rocks he'd found from the surrounding natural area. He was doing a combination of pencil and charcoal renderings.

Thomas had always been fascinating to watch work, and Marcus knew he was one of the few who'd gotten the privilege. He compared it to the chance glimpse by a hiker of a rarely seen wild creature. Some part of his subconscious realized what a gift it was to be trusted to stand this close.

Knowing the creature might disappear any second made every moment it lingered that much more precious. Impossible to compare this to seeing its facsimile inside the manufactured environment of a zoo. Because of that, this was what Marcus wished Thomas' mother could see.

Had he given Thomas any room to think last night, Marcus was sure he would have started to worry. What if the muse didn't come? If she was truly dead? A worry Marcus had known to his marrow was completely without merit.

She'd obviously dragged Thomas out of bed sometime in the early hours before dawn. Marcus would have liked to have seen it, but he would enjoy this and not regret the missed moment.

Thomas would take the three or four concepts he was developing and bring them together into one layered image before he was done. Marcus knew he should be studying what Thomas was doing from a marketing standpoint. Start planning how he'd present it, reach the target buyer. But all he wanted to do was look at the artist. As incredible as Thomas' work was, it was nothing next to the work of art the artist himself was.

Marcus watched Thomas balance himself on his heels as he studied the work he'd done thus far. He had the unconscious grace of a dancer when he moved. It wasn't obvious, but with the dropped weight, it was even more enhanced.

His skin was brown from the Southern sun, the muscles on the rawboned physique nevertheless rolling beneath it like the powerful curve of a waterfall at the break point. He ran a hand through his hair, back and forth, a gesture he made when he was thinking. It amazed Marcus, how he remembered every detail about him. It was as if he'd reviewed every gesture and feature in a photo album daily since he'd left, but he had no pictures of Thomas, except the painting he'd bought.

Now Marcus wondered why he hadn't gone after him sooner. But he'd always told Thomas when he wanted out, he wouldn't hold him, wouldn't make it uncomfortable. That was the way it had always worked in his relationships. But he'd discovered he didn't want it to be that way with Thomas.

Maybe Thomas was thinking this week was all they had. To hell with that.

Quietly Marcus took the side stairs off the deck and leaned against one of the support posts. He wanted to be close enough to smell Thomas, to see the faint gleam of the sun on his shoulders, the slightly paler strip where the jeans he'd pulled on were a little loose.

God, he felt like a teenager. Even his heart pounded a little faster as he got closer. Marcus couldn't help it. He didn't want to disturb Thomas' concentration, but he reached out anyway, caressed his nape. Thomas didn't start at all, telling him either he'd been aware of his presence all along or Marcus' touch was so integrated into what he was doing it didn't disrupt him.

It had been like that once between them. Marcus could let himself into Thomas' dingy warehouse space he rented as a combination studio and apartment and ten minutes later, Thomas would start talking to him as if they'd been conversing all along.

Sliding his arm around Thomas' waist from behind, Marcus let his hand drift up to a nipple and pinch. Putting his hips firmly against his denim-covered ass, he let Thomas feel how his cock was already semirigid.

"Insatiable bastard," Thomas murmured. Marcus smiled.

"Did I abuse you, pet? Leave you too sore?" Though he was darkly thrilled to know his lover's muscles might be sore, his ass tender from being taken so brutally and often.

In answer, Thomas turned and sought his mouth, urgent. His arousal pressed against Marcus' thigh. Marcus muttered a curse at his own lack of control and cupped the back of Thomas' neck, delving deep, tongue and teeth clashing in wet invitation.

God, Thomas had the most delectable tongue. He couldn't have it in his mouth without wanting it other places. As if Thomas was reading his mind, he moved to Marcus' throat, biting him sharply. He caught hold of the sides of Marcus' open shirt and yanked it down his arms, pushing forward so Marcus found himself shoved back against one of the deck pillars, his upper body under the provocative suggestion of restraint.

Thomas ducked his head and nipped at his chest, tasted his flesh while he licked, suckling his skin, kissing him as fire roared through Marcus' blood.

"So fucking hungry for you," Thomas muttered, and the words seared through Marcus' mind down to the root of his cock. "Want to eat you alive. So fucking perfect. Too perfect."

Marcus shattered, overwhelmed by Thomas' sudden surge of passion, the desperation of it so at odds with his almost shy submission last night. There was pain and longing under this urgency. The elephant was still in the room, the specters of anger and regret circling. Forgiveness couldn't be asked, because Thomas still held the knife that would likely stab Marcus again at the end of the week.

Family. Duty.

Marcus tightened his grip on Thomas and swept his legs, taking them both to the patio tile, managing to cushion somewhat the fall of both their weights. He pulled at Thomas' jeans with a grunt. He'd left the top button unfastened, the fricking tease, and there was no underwear beneath. Even with Thomas' struggles it wasn't so hard to get them off and end up back on top, Thomas flat on his back.

"No." Thomas tried to shove him off, but Marcus was solidly between his thighs, his stomach pressed against Thomas' hard cock. At the friction, Thomas groaned, his resistance turning into a slow rub of movement. Marcus lifted up enough to seize both of Thomas' thighs, raise them and make Thomas clasp his hips with his muscular limbs.

He found his anus with a finger. At the brief stimulation, Thomas writhed and threw a clumsy punch at Marcus' face. He ducked it as he slid the finger ruthlessly into a well-greased ass. An ass Thomas likely would continue to grease, knowing how demanding and spontaneous his Master could and would be.

At the next punch, Marcus seized both Thomas' hands and used his weight to pin him, holding his thighs up with the weight of his upper body and abdomen pressed hard against him. If Thomas put his whole heart into it, he could likely slip the connection, but the minute Marcus was at the right angle and slid his cock in deep, he knew the fight was over.

Thomas squeezed his eyes shut.

"No you don't." Marcus growled. "Look at me." He worked himself in, let go of Thomas' arms to pull his thighs up to a higher angle, forcing him to lock his legs around Marcus' back as he rocked, made Thomas feel the penetration as they lay nearly chest to chest, eye to eye. He had a mere two or three inches on Thomas in height, but it came in handy.

Thomas had dropped his hands out to the sides, his hands fisted, but when Marcus feathered a hand over the side of his face, he exploded, wrapping his arms and legs more tightly around Marcus. His fingers grasped Marcus' shoulders, face buried into his neck as Thomas raised his hips higher for deeper penetration. Marcus responded in kind, pistoning in and out, feeling Thomas' hunger and knowing as insatiable as he himself was, he might not be able to match the storm of need he felt quivering in Thomas' every muscle.

"I've missed you too, pet. So much." He whispered it hoarsely, repeating what he'd said to the darkness over Thomas' sleeping head. "That's it, love. It all belongs to me. Not just that fine ass I'm fucking."

His stomach muscles rubbed hard against Thomas' turgid cock. With a sudden groan and convulsive buck that pressed it painfully like a rod of steel into Marcus' flesh, Thomas released, flooding the narrow area between their bodies with hot fluid. It jetted against Marcus' belly, his chest, the warmth of it as welcome as mother's milk. Thomas' muscles squeezed on him and Marcus let himself go over, reaming Thomas hard, knowing he was abusing the privilege, but wanting Thomas to understand his need was just as desperate.

Only when they both shuddered to a halt did Marcus let his lover ease his legs back down, put his feet flat on the patio tile. Marcus kept his full weight resting on Thomas, enjoying the feel of Thomas' wet cock pressed between their bodies against Marcus' lower abdomen, the sac of testicles against his upper thigh.

Thomas' hands were still on his shoulders, but his fingers eased into more of a rhythmic stroke than a clutch. He started to look away, to avoid the intimacy of the close eye contact, but Marcus anticipated him. Cupping his jaw, he bent and kissed him. Slow and thorough, teasing his mouth with lazy strokes of his tongue until he felt a faint quiver in his slave's muscles.

Always leave them wanting more. The only problem was that was a double-edged sword with Thomas.

When Marcus finally drew back, Thomas gave him a shaky half smile, one hand dropping back to the ground over his head, his other fingers still caressing Marcus' bare shoulder. "Well, that was a hell of a good morning."

"It was good coffee." Marcus kept his voice light, even as he passed his thumb over Thomas' lips once just to feel the moistness of his mouth, to see those dark eyes go darker. He wanted to roll off Thomas, but only to turn him in his arms, hold him close here on the unyielding patio tile, feel Thomas' head on his shoulder, his muscular body sprawled tangled with his, his thigh over Marcus' leg as his spent genitals pressed against his leg. Marcus wanted to lie here, knowing it was all his.

But it wasn't. He was determined to get Thomas to change his mind, come back to his life here, but he couldn't cut himself open fatally to do it. He flat out wouldn't survive if he failed.

However, before he could move, Thomas drew him down, circled his back with his strong arms and held, his face pressed into Marcus' neck, temple against his jaw.

"I've missed you, Master," he said against Marcus' throat, increasing the size of the jagged lump there. "I know it's fucking unfair of me to say that, but for what it's worth..."

Marcus nodded, his eyes closed. He pushed away, rose to his knees and surveyed the beauty of what lay before him. Thomas went up on his elbows, possibly to roll to his feet, but Marcus shook his head. "Stay just like that."

Marcus sank back on his haunches, the same position Thomas had when surveying his paintings, only he studied Thomas. The splayed thighs, the cock lying in an inviting curve on his balls. Marcus moved his attention leisurely up the six-foot frame, over Thomas' pubic area, his flat stomach, then to his chest and shoulders, back to his face.

There was a yearning need there, and the Master in him couldn't help but respond to it. Reaching for the coffee mug he'd put down on a patio table, he took a sip. Still hot, but not scalding. He dropped back to one knee, pushed Thomas flat on his back again and tipped the mug over his chest, enough to splash a generous flow of the hot liquid over a sensitive nipple.

Thomas quivered, jerked, but otherwise stayed still, his eyes fastened on Marcus' face. His lips parted to handle the explosion of breath, his reaction to the stimulation of the pain. His cock started to harden again. With a curve of his lips, Marcus bent and sampled the good coffee, only now with a bite of that taut nub, a lick of the uneven texture of areola, and out to the muscular flesh.

"Arms to the ground, pet," he murmured, a second before Thomas' palm would have touched his hair.

The proximity hovered, a sense of air movement between two objects, but then Thomas' chest heaved under Marcus' mouth as he shifted, both arms falling back above his head, which arched his chest closer to Marcus' lips.

At length, Marcus sat back on his heels and resumed his enjoyment of the coffee from his cup. He lifted his gaze to survey the artwork arranged in a semicircle around them, acutely aware of the man who obeyed his Master's Will by lying open and accessible to his desires.

There was some roughness in what he suspected were Thomas' first two attempts of the morning, when Marcus assumed he'd still been struggling to reach his muse behind an army of doubts, insecurities. But as the dawn burgeoned, the pencil had moved more freely, because Thomas had a hands-down kick-ass muse. One that couldn't be denied except under the most extreme circumstances.

Which was perhaps why, of all the things he'd seen in North Carolina that concerned him, what had concerned Marcus most was Thomas' admission that he couldn't reach his muse.

Folds of bed covers. When Thomas painted it, he would turn the linens into the suggestion of water on canvas, sensual, undulating, like the movement of the bodies on the bed that had created the impressions in the fabric. The curve of buttock, tangle of leg.

He was doing it as a series. Another canvas showed a hand gripping the covers as if in the throes of some passion, stimulated by an unseen lover, seeking an anchor amid a storm. Then the third rendering. After the storm was over, that hand again, lying flat on the coverlet seeking the lingering body warmth of the lover who'd left.

Scribblings for free forms, expert pencil pressure and contour lines for shading. Even with it in draft form, Marcus could visualize it finished, the way Thomas would create it, that oddly disjointed layered style of his that always hinted at meanings beneath meanings.

Because of his family's needs and a resulting shortage of cash, Thomas hadn't been able to complete his MFA. But Marcus had spent nearly his whole life ferreting out talent, not only from graduating classes and shows but places other gallery owners wouldn't look, and he knew Thomas would stand toe-to-toe with the best, with or without the degree.

Never overt or overly sentimental, but something that teased the senses as well as the emotions. Thomas' work could compel people visiting Marcus' gallery to walk back and study it five, six, even ten times in the same visit. They felt the pull of it even when they couldn't put their finger on the why.

It was much what Marcus had done in his mind countless times over the past eighteen months. Coming back again and again to what it was about a North Carolina farm boy that wouldn't let him go. The promise of something he wanted so deeply it was impossible to give a name to it, but it could be sensed like the instinctual need to survive. It didn't need to be nurtured—it simply was, a primitive fact of life.

In some ways, he carried a gallery in his mind, all paintings of Thomas that Marcus had created, looking at him in a hundred different ways. This moment was a new addition to that priceless gallery of mental images he would be no more willing to part with than any masterpiece in the Smithsonian.

His lover, now on his elbows again but still at his command. Naked, legs spread, upper body slightly red around the nipple area with the heat of the coffee, some dark drops caught in the crease of his stomach muscles. His nape damp with perspiration, beautiful eyes watching Marcus' face. His paintings waited in a half crescent behind him, a testament to the layers of meaning behind the man.

Marcus laid his hand on Thomas' inner thigh, his thumb passing over the damp ball sac. "A series of five?"

"I think so. That's what it feels like right now."

"Just remember it only counts as one, since it has to be sold as one. Joyner will want the whole group. I'll suggest he hang them together along a wall, but spotlight them individually."

"Mercenary." A slow grin eased its way over Thomas' face, even as his eyes lit with quiet pleasure at the implied praise.

"You forgot the bastard part." Marcus rose and tugged him to his feet. "It's still there, Thomas. Just waiting for you to tap into it. It never went anywhere. It's you who shut the door on it."

Before Thomas could react to that, Marcus let him go, turned away. "Let's get some breakfast. I'll let you get back to it after that."

"I don't really need—"

"You're eating," Marcus said bluntly. He picked up Thomas' jeans, tossed them at him. "You look like a scarecrow. I don't care for bony lovers."

He saw with satisfaction the flash of temper, the abused ego. Gay men didn't like to have their appearance criticized. If it got food into Thomas' stomach, he didn't mind taking advantage of that fact. His lover was going to need a lot of energy.

* * * * *

Thomas helped him cut the tomatoes. They both liked to cook, but Marcus decided to keep it simple today, scrambled eggs and wheat toast, some chopped up fruit from the fridge he'd already prepared for himself.

As they ate at a bistro set on the deck, Marcus also tried to keep the conversation light. He knew he'd taken a low shot with his barbed remark about Thomas shutting the door on his muse. He also knew the emotional intensity of what they'd done before that still had Thomas' mind reeling. He felt a little raw from it himself.

"I have a friend with a pet elephant."

Thomas forked up a small piece of egg, chewed carefully and paused before he swallowed. "In New York? That must be some house."

"No, he lives on a private island. But it makes it easy to make old jokes. You know the one about the elephant in the room?"

"If I recall, that's not really a joke." Thomas glanced toward him.

"I want this to be a good week for you," Marcus said casually, gauging Thomas' wary look. "So let's just deal with it. You left me and your art because you felt your family needed you more, and you've been raised that your first duty is to your family. You're the first son, and now considered the head of the family. I accept that they needed you. All right?" When Thomas nodded, Marcus reached out briefly, squeezed his hand.

Okay. That seemed to go passably well. Thomas appeared to be more relaxed. Enough that he fell into an old habit, which pulled at Marcus' gut even as it provoked a familiar amused frustration.

When Marcus sat back, picked up his fork and reached for the salt, Thomas slid it out of reach with barely a pause in his own eating. "What was your last blood pressure reading?"

"So low they thought I was dead."

"You already salted the eggs when you cooked them. That's plenty. And you're such a liar." Thomas nudged it further behind his elbow, where Marcus would have to stand up to grab it. He took a swallow of his juice. "I can always tell when you're lying."

"Oh, yeah?" Marcus made a feint for the salt and Thomas sent it over his shoulder in one economical move that took it off the deck. The fortunately plastic shaker bounced off the patio, rolling under one of the easels. Thomas didn't even glance back, as if hurling condiments fifty feet through the air was a routine breakfast practice for him. Marcus sat back, lips twitching. "I'm pretty sure you're supposed to throw a pinch of salt over your shoulder for good luck, not the whole fucking thing. How can you tell I'm lying?"

"If I tell you that, you'll stop doing it."

"A little salt isn't going to kill me. Asshole." Marcus picked up his coffee as Thomas made a noncommittal grunt. Marcus shifted his attention to studying the strands of Thomas' hair in front, which were just long enough to be ruffling over his forehead with the morning breeze. Reaching out, Marcus threaded his fingers over Thomas' ear. "I bet your Mom thinks you need a haircut."

"Yeah, I do. Anyone around here?"

"I'm sure we can find a barber to hack it off with a buzz saw in the best rural South fashion." When Thomas had stayed in the city, Marcus had talked him into growing it out long enough that soft dark curls tangled along the top and over his forehead, the natural curl making itself known with the length, giving Marcus a lot more to tug on. "How is Rory? Is he in that chair for good?"

Thomas put down the juice. Swallowed again. "Why are you asking?"

"Why do you think I'm asking?"

Thomas tried to quell the surge of annoyance. Damn it, Marcus had just fucked his brains out, made him lie beneath him spread like a woman and stare up into his face, feel his lips on his mouth, those eyes so close and overpowering...he'd made him vulnerable, and then fired off a question like that. It couldn't *not* be strategy. Thomas wasn't going to be dicked around.

As he searched for a response, Marcus' jaw tightened. "You may be able to tell I'm lying, but for some reason you don't seem to know when I'm asking a simple question," he said in a deceptively mild tone. "Which suggests a problem with trust. So I repeat, why do you think I'm asking?"

"You want to know what leverage you have," Thomas said bluntly. "When you want something to happen a certain way, you break down defenses. Then you gather pieces of information, assemble them into a plan and execute it when someone is off balance. Like 'Item One, his brother might get better, so I can use that to—'"

Marcus rose so abruptly his knee hit the table, jarring the glassware. Fortunately, nothing toppled, but the clink of glass and silver was enough to stop Thomas mid-sentence.

Marcus had fixed a hard, cold gaze upon him. When he said nothing for several moments, Thomas felt like squirming. If Marcus was silent now, it was because his temper had been simmering and suddenly had gone to open boil. The passive-aggressive energy that had been moving between them—the elephant in the room—was about to stampede. But goddammit, he wasn't wrong. He knew Marcus. He'd seen him do it before. Not in personal shit so much, but somehow Thomas figured there was a line they'd crossed where all was fair in love and war. Or had he imagined it?

"You walked out on a gallery showing we spent months planning and promoting," Marcus said at last, in a flat, deadly tone. "You called me from an airport hundreds of miles away to tell me that your father'd had a heart attack and died before you could even make the connecting flight. You told me you didn't need me—"

"I didn't—"

"Shut. Up."

Thomas clenched his teeth, but he shut up.

"You didn't want me to come, even though I could hear your voice breaking over the phone. I told you I would do whatever you needed, be whatever, wherever you needed me to be, when all I wanted to do was go to you, stand by you, while you faced one of the hardest moments of your life. You came back, thinking you could pick up some of the pieces, but I should have known then it hadn't been resolved. Your brother got hurt and you left again. In the middle of the night, because you couldn't handle saying goodbye."

Marcus leaned down, bracing his knuckles on the table and stared hard into Thomas' eyes. "I wanted to know how your brother was because he's your brother. Because I haven't been able to find out from you how you're doing or how your family is doing. It matters to me, because *they* matter to *you*.

"How many times have you told me stories about you and Rory as kids? How he tagged along after you, wore overalls without a shirt? How you fished him out of a creek when he was eight so he wouldn't drown? The way you watched over him when your dad and mom had to keep a farm and a business running while you all were growing up?

"I asked," he continued in that low tone that was striping Thomas' insides, "Because I love you so fucking much, and I wish I could change everything that's happened to you. But because I can't, I can at least ask how things are going, so maybe I can figure out a way you'll let me help you."

Thomas started shaking his head. Marcus had never said he loved him. He was using it now like a weapon of mass destruction, trying to wipe away all his defenses, use it to…

"Fuck you," Marcus snarled abruptly, upending the table, sending it crashing against the railing. Crockery spun and shattered, juice and eggs splattering them both. "For your information, you selfish prick, I can read everything in your face. I've never lied to you about anything. Ever. The only one lying to himself here is you. You tell me 'one week'. That's it, that's all you'll give us. Well, since I'm on a roll, let me continue to be perfectly honest with you."

Marcus leaned forward again, his face hard. "That has nothing to do with your family. You've accepted a man can want to fuck another man, but you can't accept they can love each other. That's what's eating a hole in your gut. Your dad dying when he did was just an excuse. You were getting too scared of where we were going. And it wasn't just the way you feel about me. You're not only gay, you're a fucking sexual submissive. Wouldn't that just send your mother over the deep end?"

"My mom's been through a lot. You don't understand."

"No, I don't," Marcus shouted. "I don't understand what it's like to lose someone when I'm not expecting it. Have my heart torn from me and be told it's something I just have to accept."

He straightened abruptly, stepped back, his eyes like emerald fire, heat blasting off him. "At least she knows what she wants is dead. What I want just refuses to be with me. Maybe I should compare notes with her on what's worse, for I swear to God sometimes I think if you were dead this would hurt less."

"Fuck you." Thomas leaped up and backed away from the upended table, moving toward the stairs. "I won't listen to this bullshit. You're just trying to confuse me."

"You do that well enough on your goddamned own," Marcus shot back. "Run. Run from it all you want. Go home to your little farm and pretend there are all these noble reasons to be there rather than the truth, which is you're a coward. Afraid to face who you are and what you want."

Thomas spun on his heel, an angry retort on his lips, but Marcus was already turning away with a disgusted look. He went back into the house, slamming the sliding door with enough force to make the entire rear wall of the house quake, shuddering through the pilings below, matching the quiver of rage that went through Thomas' own limbs.

Son of a bitch. Bastard. Asshole. Fucking shithead. Thomas stomped down the deck stairs. But even as he thought it, something was shaken deep inside of him. He'd never seen Marcus have an outburst like that, the sarcasm and intellectual scorn abandoned for raw, pure feeling.

Halfway down, Thomas became aware of a sharp pain in his foot. His pulse was racing so hard in reaction to Marcus' words he hadn't noticed it at first. He hobbled to the bottom of the stairs, sat down and looked at the three bloody spots where shards of broken glass had lodged in his bare heel.

I love you. Marcus had never said the words, but Thomas had felt something from him sometimes in a quiet moment, an urgent need, a sudden powerful stillness as if there were such words there, just waiting to be said. Thomas had never said them himself, believing it was just his own desire to hear Marcus say them resonating, reflecting the desire of one heart, not two.

Marcus didn't love him. He couldn't.

I've never lied to you.

Thomas looked across the patio at his mounted sketchpads. Always a comfort, but now they mocked him, particularly the one in the middle. Just that splayed hand, the fingers inviting touch even as they gave the impression of looking for something that wasn't within reach. Was it Marcus' hand, or his soul? Thomas rose, went to it. Putting his hand over it, he saw there was a splatter of egg at the top corner, fallen from the upper deck.

It hit then. Sometimes the pain in his lower abdomen grew to such proportions it compressed his chest, and then he couldn't breathe through the pain of it. Couldn't breathe…

I love you… Coward… Father was just an excuse…

Thomas dropped to one knee as if shoved. Holding onto his chest, he tried to suck in air that wasn't there. Perspiration, cold along his skin. *God,* don't *do this here.*

There was broken glass on the tile, one of the saucers that had been propelled off by Marcus' violent reaction. Despite the pain in his foot, it wasn't enough. Thomas grabbed one of the shards, gripped it hard enough it pierced his palm, competing with the pain in his gut, but it was too far gone. The cut of the glass was just a feather brush compared to the sick green fire there.

He managed to get to the edge of the patio before he threw up the breakfast he'd eaten. The labored wheezing was his own, mixed with a peculiar sobbing noise in his throat. He was choking on his own failure, his inability to get any of it right. *Can't breathe…*

"Hey. Hey!" The snapped command made him realize Marcus was there, kneeling with him, hand on the side of his jaw and throat, dragging his attention up to meet his stern gaze. "Thomas. Breathe. Slow, pet. Breathe. It's all right. I'm here."

That strong hand on the back of his neck, the other over his abdomen, steadying him, giving him back the rhythm of his heartbeat, slowing it down. "Ssshh, sshh…"

"I'm…sorry. Should just go. Not…fair to you—"

"Thomas." Marcus' voice sharpened, silencing him. "Stop thinking about it. It's okay." His grip tightened and Thomas brought his face back up again. Marcus' green eyes. So green. Peaceful, turbulent, beautiful. Everything was in that green. "It's going to be all right, okay? No matter what, it's going to be all right. We're just fighting, pet. Couples do it all the time. Come here."

Down to the cool tile of the patio, his shoulders hauled across Marcus' thighs as Marcus held him, legs stretched out while he stroked Thomas' hair, his other hand still on his belly. Marcus rocked him, murmured to him. Helped him breathe, breaking the clasp of the panic attack. Everything would be all right. He could hear Marcus' heartbeat beneath his ear, pressed against his firm abdomen. Steady, thudding through Thomas' body. He gripped Marcus' calf under one hand, an anchor.

"Oh, Jesus." He closed his eyes. Mortified, as reason returned. He would have tried to sit up, reclaim a little dignity, but he wasn't sure he wouldn't pass out just yet. "Guess I won that argument, didn't I?"

"Just as every swooning Victorian heroine does." But despite the smartass comment, Marcus didn't smile or look remotely amused. He shifted his grip, tilting Thomas' head up, his thumb on his jugular so Thomas could feel his own pulse, as if Marcus had the right to decide if he lived or died, as if he were his slave in truth. Perhaps he was. Perhaps he'd rather die at Marcus' hand, if it would save him from hurting Marcus or his family in any way anymore.

"How long has this been happening? And don't you even think of lying to me."

Thomas wasn't a good liar on his best day. Under the undeniably intimidating stare, he wasn't going to try today. Much. "I get them every once in a while. I usually know the signs, so you're the first person who's ever been treated to the pathetic sight of one." The joke fell flat. He closed his eyes. "Marcus, I should go home. This was a mistake, you know it as well as I do. I'll paint what I can there. You're right, I want to get back to it, and there's no reason I can't—"

"I don't give a damn if you don't paint anything this week other than a paint-by-numbers rendition of a Cape Cod lighthouse. Hell, you can give me a crayon drawing of the Shoney's kids' menu. I don't give a fuck about the painting. Can you pull your head out of your ass long enough to get that one thing through your stubborn head?"

Thomas swallowed. He was one of the few people who knew what Marcus was like when he was genuinely pissed off. Normally, he'd prefer to have some distance physically from it, because it came off him like an explosion from a volcano, but the anger in Marcus' eyes was only matched by the tenacity of his grip on Thomas' upper body, sprawled ignominiously over his knees.

"This is serious, pet." Marcus increased the pressure of his hand on Thomas' stomach and Thomas couldn't help the wincing. "You're twenty-seven years old and you're having weekly panic attacks, and you have an ulcer."

"Weekly? How did you—"

"Because I'm a lot smarter than you, and despite your inability to lie to me, you have a tendency to try to fudge the truth." Marcus cupped his jaw. "Are you listening to me? You promised your Master a week, and that's what you're giving him. We've both said what we needed to say to get it off our chests for the time being. Let's leave that right there, okay?"

"I didn't mean it." Thomas had to say it, make Marcus understand that one thing. "I just—"

"I'm the only person you can strike out at that you trust to handle it." Marcus adjusted his grip, the hand on Thomas' throat now firm enough to be a collar, silencing him and riveting his attention. He kneaded against Thomas' vulnerable windpipe. Despite the moment, it drew Thomas' attention to Marcus' mouth, which made some of his energy drain to his lap. From the flick of Marcus' eyes, Thomas knew he registered the reaction. He struggled to focus.

"Even so, I shouldn't have—"

"It's over now." Marcus squeezed, silencing him. "Go get your swimsuit and a towel. I'm going to pack up a few things. Today, we're going to drive to Cape Cod and go to the beach. It's warm enough. Then, this evening, I intend to take you to a new place I've heard some good things about."

At the sudden shift in Marcus' gaze, something else tightened in his raw lower belly, just as searing but a lot more pleasurable. "What kind of place?"

Moving his hand off Thomas' stomach, Marcus captured his wrist, raising it to study the cut hand. Ignored the question. "If you want pain, Thomas, you'll ask your Master for it. Not cause it to yourself. You understand me?" He brought the palm to his lip, sucked the blood off, licked Thomas like an animal.

Thomas curled his fingers, touching Marcus' face, suddenly needing more of him. But he stayed still, a hard quiver going through him at the stimulation of Marcus' mouth.

Shrewd green eyes shifted to Thomas, demanding an answer.

Thomas managed to nod.

"Good. We're going someplace tonight where I can remind you what trust between a slave and his Master truly means. You're overdue for the lesson, and I think I've let you have a little too much slack. My mistake, and I'm going to fix it."

The sensual intent in his eyes and the emotional impact of it made Thomas unable to respond. They'd visited some clubs, but their play there had been soft, easy, with few exceptions. But the look in Marcus' expression suggested tonight would be anything but. Despite the apprehension that flitted through Thomas' mind, the warning of the emotional cost, his body reacted to the idea eagerly.

There was a smear of his blood on Marcus' lips. Thomas found himself reaching up to it. His arm was trembling, and Marcus put his hand against it, steadying him as he ran the pads of his fingers there. Marcus bit one finger and held it, sending a current of fire through Thomas' veins. Jesus, weak as a baby and still he had a hard-on.

"But until tonight," Marcus continued, "we're going to give your body a rest and have some fun. Something else I think you've forgotten about. Got it?"

Thomas pulled off another nod, his mind too scrambled to come up with anything more coherent.

Marcus saw Thomas mulling it over. He knew he'd planted the seeds, and it would rapidly grow into a multibranched tree of possibilities in Thomas' mind the closer they drew to the evening. But it was the kind of stirred-up he wanted Thomas to be experiencing. It would help crowd out the rest.

He helped Thomas to his feet, sent him on his way up the stairs, not giving him an opportunity to protest. They needed to get out of here, get some breathing space from the intensity of that argument, let it air out so it didn't soak in and poison them.

Once Thomas went in, Marcus got the hose and washed the breakfast Thomas had thrown up off into the more distant grasses. His hand tightened on the rubber tubing. Thomas had only eaten eggs, no tomatoes, but there were insidious red veins running through the yellow, undigested mess.

There were places in the world that trafficked in human slavery, for despicable reasons. If he could have teleported them to such a place, where Thomas could have no freedom save what his Master permitted him, Marcus would have happily transplanted them there right now.

While he knew the thought was based on his frustration, Marcus did know that willing submission in a D/s relationship could bring the submissive a freedom he often lacked in his real life. Where slavery became the chance to stretch one's wings without being afraid of whom they would let down, what expectations would be failed.

The place he planned to take Thomas tonight might help them exorcise some of Thomas' demons…and provide a safe environment where Marcus could beat the living shit out of him to exorcise his own.

His lips twisted, but the wry amusement died as he remembered how he'd sensed it in Thomas the first time he'd met him. Strong, creative souls often had a submissive nature. It helped them balance the chaotic impulses barraging their minds at all times. They felt things more deeply, saw nuances of things many didn't. Most people had mental insulation against the stark, painful realities of human nature. The best artists didn't, which was why most of the ones he'd encountered seemed beset with all sorts of neuroses and addictions.

A Master could take control, give them an oasis of quiet amid all that. The first time he'd told Thomas to get on his knees, making it a command, a deliberate requirement that his lover obey him consciously rather than a request or a physical shove that could be passed off as mere passion, Thomas' cock had leaped against Marcus' hand. Those dark eyes had flashed with a response, something Thomas didn't even know he wanted until the plate was offered.

A true submissive wasn't forced to submit. He was simply shown the right room in his soul. Sometimes when he stepped into it, he wrapped his way around his Master's heart and tugged him in right after him.

That not-so-long-ago night, Thomas had barely breathed, almost seeming in a trance as Marcus pressed on his shoulder, took him down to his knees. Fire had roared in Marcus' own blood, a contrast to the gentle touch. Marcus had plenty of experience in being a Dom, enjoyed it, was fond of the men he'd exercised it upon. But it was the first time in his life he couldn't look away or think beyond the moment as Thomas bent his head and brushed his lips over Marcus' knuckles, a non-choreographed compulsion, pure obeisance.

Marcus put away the hose and stood staring at the side of the house, struggling to find his own center for balance. Thomas' mother thought she was fighting for her son's soul. Thinking of the eggs, Marcus wondered if the real battle was for her son's life.

Chapter Six

ꟹ

The Cape Cod beach Marcus chose was one known by the locals to be primarily populated by men who preferred men. For once, Marcus appeared to be indulging his lover's self-consciousness about his sexual preference. Thomas wryly suspected his Master's intention was for him to be anxious only about the things Marcus *wanted* Thomas to be worked up about.

When they got there, it was easy enough to find a spot for their beach chairs, towels and umbrella, rented from a beach vendor.

As Thomas set up his chair, he watched Marcus shuck off jeans and shrug out of his buttoned shirt to reveal his swimwear. He was one of the only men Thomas had seen that could pull off the brief style bathing suit. Black and sleek, it molded his ass and groin area in a way sure to have every tongue on the beach unrolled and gathering sand. Including his.

Only what he was looking at, he was allowed to touch. Impulsively, he bent and rooted in their duffel, retrieving sunscreen. For some inexplicable reason, he wanted to make a proprietary move, make it clear who Marcus was with.

Marcus was obviously familiar with the area, this beach. There could even be men here he'd been with in the past. It was an ugly thought, coming from an ugly part inside of him. Thomas tried to push it away, close that door. They'd already fought once this morning. He didn't care to repeat it. Catching Marcus' attention, he gestured awkwardly with the sunscreen. "You haven't been in the sun for awhile."

"I know you did not just imply I look like the underbelly of a fish."

He didn't, but Thomas tucked his tongue in his cheek and raised a brow. "If the shoe fits…"

Marcus gave him a narrow look, but turned his back, staying on his feet, weight shifted to one hip. His attitude was one of practiced indifference, whereas the view sent a hard shot of longing arrowing through Thomas' stomach and groin.

Marcus had queued back his shoulder-length hair, so it was easy for Thomas to grease up his hands and run them over the broad shoulders, down the smooth back. For all his urban polish, under his clothes Marcus had the body of a lean, hard-eyed street fighter. From the time when they were practically living together, Thomas knew he didn't go to a fitness club. He went to boxing clubs and martial arts centers, where he worked out with a fierceness that suggested he knew what it was to fight for his life.

Yet Marcus had no scars. Nothing, not even the lingering mark of a childhood stove burn, a cut from mishandling a cooking knife. It was as if there was no map on Marcus to show the direction to his past. Whenever Thomas asked Marcus about his family, or where he'd come from before he became a gallery owner in New York, Marcus kept his answers to brief, professional steps on the career ladder. He simply refused to answer questions about any time before then.

Why should he? Thomas was nothing special compared to anyone else, just the same as any other man. Right? But he'd said *I love you.* Thomas wasn't sure of anything anymore.

"A nuclear blast isn't going to get through that cover on my shoulders," Marcus commented. Thomas started out of his thoughts, moved down. When he reached the thin elastic waistband of the suit, Thomas couldn't help sliding the tips of his fingers beneath it to tease the bare rise of Marcus' ass, the indentation between the taut muscular cheeks.

Here on this beach, with its reputation for being a hangout for gay men, things could get pretty blatant. Maybe it was that environment making him so bold, knowing there'd be no disparaging looks as he did what he wanted to do. If Marcus commanded him, he might take him down his throat now. The pain of their words this morning, the difference between wishing and reality, made him reckless. Time was short.

And maybe he wanted it clear. *Yeah, you might've gotten to grab his ass in the past, but today I'm the only one who gets to do it.*

Jesus, what an ass. His thumb still hooked in the elastic, Thomas' other fingers moved over the outside, the stretched fabric of the suit, digging into the taut buttock beneath, even as he kept the other hand moving, spreading the lotion.

"Do the legs." Marcus' voice was low. "I want to feel your hands between my legs." He was aroused, Thomas could tell just from the tone, even if he couldn't see him from the front.

Swallowing, he took his hand from the waistband, put more lotion in his hand. Then deliberately he dropped to one knee and ran both hands up either side of Marcus' left thigh as if he were a personal slave attending the needs of an Egyptian prince.

Though Thomas stopped just short of his tightly compressed scrotum in the snug, way-too-brief black swimsuit, he could feel the firm round testicles graze his fingertips. With his fingers coated with lotion, he ran the sunscreen over the other thigh and then between again, Marcus obligingly spreading his legs to his touch, flexing that magnificent ass within inches of his face. Thomas wanted to sink his teeth into the meat of it and growl. No man should be so goddamned sexy.

Finished with both legs, he withdrew his hands reluctantly and moved to Marcus' front. He stifled a groan. Marcus was huge, straining against the suit so that the broad head was in danger of coming out of the top. Marcus gave him an amused glance as Thomas positioned his body in front of him before he began rubbing down his shoulders.

"You caused it, pet. Now you're going to try to hide it?"

"Shut up," Thomas muttered. He grabbed up a towel, ostensibly to wipe his hands but he slid it around Marcus' hips, tucked it in. "You've got no modesty at all."

"You've got enough for both of us." Marcus closed one hand on both of Thomas' over the tucked and rolled knot of towel and cupped his face for a light brush of lips, just a taste that left him hungering for more. "Farm boy."

"Hey!"

Thomas turned to see a couple men calling out to them from the volleyball net. "We need two more. You up for it?"

"A scene from *Top Gun* comes to mind," Marcus noted, appraising the two men who appeared to be bodybuilders in their spare time. "What do you think?"

"All brawn, no brains or quickness," Thomas said, with a forced careless grin.

But as Marcus dropped the towel and Thomas squatted to tuck the sunblock back in their pack, something compelled him to ask the question. "Master…" He hesitated, startled he'd used the address in such a public place, though no one was close enough to hear. He turned, looked up at Marcus. Marcus reached out and brushed his temple with his thumb, his expression unsmiling, waiting.

"You always brush it off when I ask. Are you ever going to tell me anything about your past?"

Something shifted in Marcus' expression. It was a beautiful day, with a clear blue sky and sun sparkling on the water and sand. The promise of volleyball added to the relaxing, pleasurable feel of the day. But as Thomas was caught in that expression, it got suddenly cold and dark. He felt the brief, shuddering grip of a quiet, terrible place where Marcus wasn't the Marcus he knew. Someone far different. But strangely, perhaps more real.

"Who I am now is all that matters, pet. Let it go." Marcus turned away, bent and picked up the towel.

"But… Ouch!" Marcus snapped the towel at him again, landing another stinging blow on Thomas' ass. "You son of a—"

Marcus took off with a grin, catching the ball midair as they got closer to the net. He tossed it to Thomas, occupying his hands before he could retaliate.

But Thomas wouldn't forget. He wondered. His family and upbringing were so much of what he was it was hard for him to imagine who he'd be without it. But from Marcus' reaction, he wondered if he was ready to know more. And Marcus of course had made it easy to put off the decision, shifting it back on his footing again.

Ben and Andrew were fitness club trainers. They liked the beach as a way to soft-recruit new customers as well as to enjoy some healthy competition, when they could scare it up.

Soon Ben and Andrew had them and some other men joining in, getting a full game going. Marcus was on the other side of the net and several times he and Thomas had to come up against each other to fight for the ball's placement, with mixed results.

When Marcus' cell phone rang, the noise reaching them from where the phone sat on his beach chair, it distracted him enough that Thomas spiked the ball under his arm, winning the point to the cheers of his teammates.

"Lucky."

"Yeah, right." Thomas grinned as Marcus backpedaled to his towel, picked up the phone and answered.

When Ben raised a questioning hand, Marcus waved him off. "More important name on the other line. Deal me out of the game." At Ben's deprecating comment, he flashed a grin. "Bite me."

"Love to," Andrew responded. Marcus flipped him off to laughter from the other players. Ben looked over at Thomas. "You staying in?"

"Yeah, let's go another round." Thomas tried not to pay attention to the affectionate smile that crossed Marcus' face as he took the call, indicating it was more personal than business.

Though he couldn't help watching Marcus' body language as he settled into the beach chair. Was he imagining the infinitesimal tightening of his grip on the phone, the way someone did when talking to someone they cared about? The rock of his heel in the sand, the way Marcus laid his fingers over his knee, stroking his own skin absently. Thomas couldn't hear the words at this distance, but he could definitely hear the tone.

Carl, the newest member on the team, passed Thomas the ball. Or rather, pressed it to his stomach, his other hand brushing the small of Thomas' back. His fingertips swiped just below the waistband of the cut off jeans serving as Thomas' swimwear. "Your serve, sweetmeat."

* * * * *

"Why the hell are you calling me when we're two weeks away from the Prague show and you owe me one more piece?"

"Well, hello and how the fuck are you?"

Marcus grinned. "If I'm nice to you, you'll think that you're hot shit and lose your focus. How are you, Josh?"

"You know how I am. I'm calling to see how *you* are. Lauren said you called her this morning to scope out some pretty scary symptoms. I know I'm not running late enough to cause you an ulcer, so what's going on?"

"It wasn't for me, you idiot. It's for a friend I'm worried about. To get an ulcer, you have to have a conscience. You know I was born without one."

"Horseshit." Josh sounded distracted, telling Marcus he probably was up to his elbows in sculpting medium, but it would be a mistake to assume his second favorite artist and closest friend was not paying attention to every word he was saying. With his next words, he proved it.

"Lauren mentioned you made a trip to North Carolina a couple weeks ago."

"I had a craving for barbecue and pickled pigs' feet."

"Is he with you? Did you bring him back?"

"If I hang up, you'd just call back, wouldn't you?"

"Worse. I'll pee in a jar, put an anatomically correct naked orange Gumby in it and call it a statement about the decay of a materialistic society. *That* will be the last Prague piece."

"You're a vicious bastard. I talked him into spending a week with me in the Berkshires, getting his work off the ground again. Out of his ass where it had crawled."

"Nice visual. And you and him?"

"A work in progress."

"Keep me posted."

"Why? Are you starting a betting pool on the Internet?"

"Absolutely. My money's on you. You said you're in the Berkshires? The Zone just bought out a fetish club up near Boston. It's been renamed Detonation, catering mainly to men. Tyler has a part interest in it. You could take your work in progress there."

"I was planning to. But now that I know Tyler Winterman owns a part interest, I may spend my money elsewhere."

"You're just mad because he outbid you on that Takahura sculpture."

"There was a real samurai blade in it. I keep hoping he'll trip on it one night on the way to the bathroom and lop off his balls."

"Ouch. Sore loser. You just can't stand the fact he's more arrogant and just as obnoxious a son of a bitch as you are. You should have come and crashed his wedding with us. He wouldn't have minded."

Marcus snorted. "One arrogant and obnoxious S.O.B. at a function is enough. I can't believe he found a woman willing to put up with him."

"She's a Mistress. I did a private on her that would have had you salivating."

"Tyler married a Domme?" Marcus chuckled at the thought. "Oh, there's karma for you. Two Dominants paired for life. Sounds like they have a competition problem they decided to turn into a lifetime psychosis."

"No, it was a good thing. I don't know why it works, but when you see them, you know it's right. Tyler is one lucky bastard."

"Does Lauren know she has competition?"

"Stop it," Josh said mildly. "You know that's crap. You're sure it's not you that you called about?"

"Everything is not about me, you know. And before you can say it, fuck off." Over Josh's chuckle, Marcus continued, "I should set up a show with you and Thomas. If he survived the heart attack at the mere idea of it, you two would make me a tremendous amount of money."

"Shut up, Marcus." Josh's voice lowered. "You know Lauren and I love you. So we're here, all right? If he hurts you again, I don't want to be anywhere near him."

The line went dead. Marcus knew Josh had done it on purpose, denying him the ability to come back with something flippant, a rapid parry before the weight of those words could strike his shields and land a harsh blow on his defenses.

"Asshole," Marcus muttered.

When Marcus flipped the phone closed, he saw they'd brought in another guy to balance the teams. He could enjoy watching Thomas at his leisure. He stretched out in a reclining position in the low beach chair and set the phone aside, laying his head back on the headrest to take advantage of the sun and keep an eye on his lover at the same time.

It amazed him, how unaware Thomas was of his own appeal. The way the other men checked him out, the passing of the ball that allowed them to brush hands, make those subtle overtures that when men were involved were not so subtle. The occasional slap on the back or somewhat lower, for a point well played. The beach environment removed inhibitions, and of course there was always the chance of some quick action in the dunes if you could get a prospective partner stirred up enough.

Marcus watched the newest man, whose name he caught as "Carl", maneuver closer to Thomas, his hand lingering on his shoulder as they spoke strategy. It dropped briefly to Thomas' waist as he told Thomas something that caused a quick smile. Thomas moved out of range. Not as far or as deliberately as Marcus would have liked, but then it was a close contact sport. Ben, evidently a peacemaker, murmured something to the man, shooting a discreet glance toward Marcus' location.

Carl laughed, pushed him away. Since Marcus was downwind, it was easy to catch the gist of the response. "—shouldn't leave his ass alone then—"

As Marcus studied the man behind the screen of his sunglasses, he wondered how Carl would look with his foot stuffed up to the ankle into his own rectum.

On the next rotation, the man made another move, far more blatant. This time his hand closed in a flirtatious squeeze on Thomas' ass before he took the ball. Thomas pushed away, but not with anger. He elbowed the man away with a grin. A fucking *grin.*

Marcus' eyes narrowed, taking a harder look at that replay. Thomas didn't grin that often. Usually it qualified as just a smile. This grin had been high wattage, a little forced. And yes, that was definitely an eye cut in his direction.

The bastard was trying to make him jealous. Seeing if he was paying attention.

Marcus set aside the sunglasses and rose. He inclined his head at Andrew when he was noticed, but he moved toward the water, indicating his intention to take a swim. He held Thomas' gaze a fraction of a second before he continued past the play area.

As Thomas watched Marcus move down to the water, he was sure of two things. Marcus had noticed his pathetic adolescent act. And in his sophisticated way, he'd given it the attention it warranted. Thomas had walked out on him and only committed to one week with him. Who the hell was Thomas to make demands?

He was the guy who was here in front of Marcus, damn it. The one who'd come at Marcus' encouragement, despite his mother's tears and his brother's crude accusations. Despite the fact his gut was going to eat him alive when he had to walk away at the end of the week, while Marcus would go on with his urbane, privileged life.

Carl made a muffled protest as Ben elbowed him aside with little fanfare and took the ball from Thomas' hands. "Thanks for joining us."

"What—"

Ben corralled Thomas with a friendly but firm arm around his shoulders and shepherded him to the edge of the court. He dropped his tone. "If you don't go after that after the look he just gave you, you're an idiot. Stop being stupid and dicking around with this snaker." He raised his voice. "Later today, why don't you and Marcus plan on joining us for a coffee? There's a great place not far from here."

Practically every man on the beach, as well as the few girls, had simply stopped what they were doing, even if they pretended not to, to watch Marcus walk down to the water in nothing but that brief scrap of swimsuit. He'd always been completely aware of how attractive he was, but Marcus didn't flaunt or minimize it. It was just an asset. An asset Thomas knew carried the potency of a lethal weapon.

Ben gave him a friendly, firm push. "Thanks again."

"Our pleasure," Thomas managed, saving face with the response before he turned on his heel and walked away with forced casualness toward the surf. Marcus was already in to his waist, showing remarkable fortitude for the New England temperatures. Even in late summer, Thomas' blood was more accustomed to the southeast coastline. But he could use cooling off anyway.

He splashed in, gritting his teeth at the surge of cold water, and followed Marcus as he moved further out. He resented that he didn't look back. Resented that he was the one following him like a puppy, resented that fucking phone call and whoever'd been on the end of it. It would have been better if he'd stayed in North Carolina. At least there his tortured imaginings of Marcus sleeping around were exactly that, not actual, in-his-face realities.

Marcus went under and came back up, water running off his shoulders down his back, his now-wet ass in the briefs visible for a glimpse as a wave passed. He dove under it as Thomas closed in, moving past the surf line into the quieter waters. Marcus didn't resurface.

Thomas turned to see if the current had pulled Marcus further down the beach. The water swirled around his legs, the brush of something his only warning as Marcus surfaced behind him, close enough to shoot an arm around his neck and sweep Thomas' legs out from under him, taking them both under the next wave.

Thomas struggled, throwing elbows. Marcus hung on even as they surfaced on the other side, now deep enough the water lapped at their chests. He had his arm wrapped around Thomas' chest, holding him back against him. His lips were close to his ear. And his cock was a bar of iron pressing against Thomas' all-too-eager ass.

"You wanted my attention, pet. You got it."

"Let go. You're not going to fuck me as a surrogate for whoever just got your dick hard on the phone." Thomas normally wasn't crude, but he was angry and helpless as Marcus' hand grazed over his nipple, made it draw up in response.

"You were the one who got my dick hard, farm boy. Trying to tease me with that piece of shit." He had his grip clamped on Thomas' opposite side under the biceps, a highly effective and uncomfortable restraint, and Marcus was using their several-inch height difference to his advantage, making it difficult for Thomas to plant his feet and shrug him off.

"You need a reminder of who your Master is, so you won't be so quick to doubt?" Marcus dropped his other hand neatly into Thomas' shorts, their loose fit and lack of underwear making it easy to grasp a buttock, pull it aside and slide two fingertips just inside the tight pucker of his anus, teasing him.

Thomas struggled, his cheeks flushing, biting his lips. "You son of a bitch, when I get free, I'm going to—"

"You're going to what?" Thomas bucked as Marcus' fingers started pressing in.

"Stop..." Thomas caught hold of the arm Marcus had across his chest, anchoring himself as Marcus pressed in, squeezed. His bare feet stepped on Marcus' as Thomas clumsily tried to find a purchase.

"Hold onto my neck," Marcus murmured.

Thomas reached back, latched on, his head dropping on Marcus' shoulder as Marcus released his chest, opened the cut-offs and clasped his hand over his cock, working him fast and hard while Thomas pistoned back and forth like a hooked fish between the two stimuli, squeezing back on Marcus' fingers, thrusting forward into the powerful grip of his hand.

"You...ever..." Marcus punctuated each word with another thrust and stroke as Thomas' breath clogged in his throat. "Let…another man touch you like that…and I will beat your ass until you can't walk. You hear me? You got it?" As if he had the devil's own sense of timing, he stopped, holding Thomas just on that frantic edge.

"Who was on the phone?" Thomas snarled, his breath rasping.

"Stubborn bastard." Marcus started stroking again. Thomas sucked in his breath, came so close and then cursed as Marcus withdrew and settled one arm like a bar back across his upper body, still manacling the hard pulsing cock in his other hand, tight at the base. He didn't move now, squeezing in warning when Thomas tried to, and simply let them drift with Thomas in his arms, vibrating with the near climax.

"Is he competition?"

Marcus chuckled. Thomas' teeth ground together. "Hardly. He's married, and his Mistress is very protective of him."

"But you've fucked him."

Marcus' tone turned cool. "I wouldn't characterize it that way, no."

"Is there another way to characterize putting your dick in someone's ass?"

Marcus' teeth latched onto his throat, bit and Thomas shuddered. "You're spoiling for a fight. Fine. How do you go about it with your little fiancée your mother wants to chain you to?"

"You leave her out of it."

"Your mother I will gladly leave out of any discussion involving sex. However, with respect to this girl…have you made out? How did you get it up? Who would you fantasize about to make her think it was all about her?"

"You arrogant son of a—

"That's what I thought."

Marcus caressed Thomas' balls as Thomas strained, moved backward to try to rub his ass against Marcus' erection. Marcus inserted his thigh between Thomas' knees and sat him down hard on it, latching his arm around his waist, the other around his chest again.

"You're not getting it now. You're going to walk around wanting it all day, your dick hard as a rock. Until tonight, when I get you off however I choose."

A Master's right, to deny, to punish, to reward. Thomas shuddered in his arms, struggling between desire and frustrated pride. "Please..." Thomas muttered it, but Marcus was far from a merciful mood.

"Hush. Be still. Just be still. I'm still trying to decide if I want to fuck you or drown you."

"Could you fuck me first?"

Marcus chuckled. "Christ, you're priceless, pet. Just priceless." His voice got throaty, and he pressed closer.

Thomas took a deep breath. He let himself float, held in Marcus' arms, feeling the long fingers idly caressing his body as they moved together with the flow of the surf. The sky was so blue it almost hurt the eyes, so Thomas closed his, laying his head back on Marcus' shoulder again, turning his face so he could smell the saltwater on his chin, graze his lips on the beating pulse. *Christ, you're so beautiful. What are you doing with me?*

It wasn't until Marcus stilled Thomas realized he'd spoken his thoughts aloud.

"You know," Marcus said casually after a moment. "You used to do that. Wander around your studio, talking half to yourself, half to me or to some imaginary something. You'd look amazed when I spoke to you, because you thought half of the words you'd said had been in your head." He tightened his arm around Thomas.

"Artists are a lot like pilots, sailors, those who depend on powers they don't entirely understand for their intuition, their gifts. Their ability to get from Point A to Point B. You're a superstitious bunch. You think if your gift came to fruition when you were at a certain place in your psyche, you can't ever change, or you'll lose it."

Thomas loved it and hated it when Marcus talked like this. His oracle voice, Thomas had always called it teasingly. Hearing the message might be difficult, but the delivery was like feeling the hand of God strike the earth. It soothed, the solid tone of the words, the way Marcus' arms were wrapped around him now.

"Thomas." Marcus whispered, his breath teasing him. "I promise if you grow up, become a man sure of his own worth, it won't destroy your gift. If anything, it will expand to levels you never thought possible."

Thomas hooked his hands on Marcus' arm. His grip curled in, his thumb sliding back and forth. A caress, but he knew Marcus also would recognize it for what it was, a nervous gesture.

"Do you trust me, Thomas?"

"I—"

"No, don't answer that. I know you don't. We're going to work on that. In the meantime, let this rattle around your mind." Marcus ran his palm down Thomas' thigh, caressing his sac, his thumb passing over his cock before he changed direction to explore Thomas' stomach, following the dent of his navel, brushing his knuckles over the stomach muscles.

"What I have is surface. Grooming, good genetics, whatever. Whether you've rolled out of bed an hour ago without having had a shower for three days, or you're wearing a designer suit, there is a deep, perfect beauty to you that takes my breath away. You miss it because you're looking at some twisted image you've created in your head, full of faults and shortcomings."

"Marcus—"

"Ssshh… See yourself the way I see you. Feel the way my hands touch you, think about the way I look at you. I see all of you, Thomas. You think I don't, but I do. Hide it, don't hide it, I know all of it, feel all of it. You're mine. Just let go. Let go and see it. I always have."

There was a quiet between them then. A floating of the minds, like their bodies in the water. Thomas tried not to be overwhelmed by the emotions the words evoked, but Marcus wasn't done torturing him yet.

"I'm going to ask you the question I asked you earlier. How is Rory?"

Thomas tensed. He felt Marcus' hold compensating, knew he wouldn't get away without a fight. Damn if the unshakable restraint on his arms and chest just aroused him more, even as his heart twisted at the question. The rock of the water and Marcus' mesmerizing words wrenched the honest words out of him.

"Broken inside, worse than the outside. And I'm to blame for it."

"Maybe you are." Marcus said after a silence. "If you'd been there, it might not have happened. If your mother had called him in to lunch an hour earlier, it might not have happened. If it had rained that day, it wouldn't have happened.

"So everyone's to blame, even God, for Rory turning over a tractor he didn't have a lot of experience handling. So how's all that guilt going to help him get on with his life, make something of it? Far as I can tell he's got his upper body. Does his cock still work?"

"Jesus, Marcus." Thomas jabbed him with his elbow. "Yeah. Why?"

"I was figuring on hitting on him if his brother turned into too much of a pain in the ass."

Thomas pushed off the bottom and shoved backward, twisting free and going after Marcus, doing his best to shove him under. Marcus, laughing, backpedaled, then they were both doused by the surf line. Thomas managed to duck back under and got lucky. He caught the edge of Marcus' suit, the elastic at his leg, bringing his other hand into play to close it on his cock, which was still attractively turgid.

As they surfaced, he had a firm grip on Marcus. His nemesis moved into him, bringing them chest to chest. Thomas squeezed, stroked, enjoying the feel of the water mixed with the heat. Marcus kept his hands floating out to his sides, his green eyes fixed on Thomas' face.

Without encouragement, Thomas touched his face, threaded his fingers in the slick wet hair, his thumb following the bridge of Marcus' perfect nose as he rested a forearm on Marcus' shoulder. They were back in deep again, the water at mid-chest where a strong current could take them out. They were both good swimmers, so Thomas wasn't worried about that. He was more concerned about the depth of the feeling in himself, wondering if Marcus was barely treading water there as well.

"I don't want to let go."

"I didn't tell you to."

Thomas slid his grip up the velvet shaft and back down, his thumb playing with the throbbing vein on the underside. Marcus' eyes lost focus, lips parting, his chest expanding. He shifted, planting his feet, and Thomas moved with him.

"Come rub yourself against me, pet. I want to feel your cock."

Not daring to look toward the beach, Thomas took the extra step. Marcus' arm went around his neck and back. Thomas kept his hand pumping on Marcus' organ, but he put his leg up next to Marcus', foot aligned on the inside of his, hip bones brushing as he rubbed his cock alongside the grip of his hand, so the aching curve of his balls could brush Marcus'.

As he did, Marcus guided Thomas' face to him, took his lips in a mind-numbing, wet saline kiss. He growled into

Thomas' mouth as Thomas squeezed harder in reaction, his own cock hardening, pushing more insistently against Marcus, rubbing, seeking friction. Marcus' thumb flicked his nipple. Thomas gasped into his mouth and Marcus' strong hands were on the small of his back, sliding into his waistband, taking a firm hold of his ass as Thomas tried to keep his rhythm consistent.

Marcus was a strong son of a bitch, and his grip now proved it as he rocked Thomas against him, his tongue tangling with his. Thomas was sure it was obvious what they must be doing from the beach, but God, who cared? It was safe here. Marcus had brought him somewhere safe, so he could drink his fill of him.

"Oh—" He choked on the reaction as Marcus' fingers eased into him, working him now as cleverly as Thomas was doing that long, fine cock which was hot and hard in his hand. He fondled Marcus' balls, felt them draw up. He was close. And he was going to explode.

Despite Marcus' threat to refuse him release, they came almost together. So often when they'd been together they'd had the timing down perfectly. Marcus had taught him the searing Tantric pleasure of holding out, so when they both finally came it was that much more intense. Even now, goaded by the urgency of absence, both past and anticipated, they still managed to pull it off.

The liquid heat of Marcus' seed shot past his wrist, against his belly. Thomas fought back his own release for a second to watch his lover's face, the tense jaw, the slight bow to the head as he was trapped by the orgasm. Unguarded, unpracticed, just raw animal reaction straining Marcus' features.

Marcus clung to Thomas' nape, fingers burrowing. Thomas felt the trembling of his muscular thighs as Marcus thrust against his hold savagely, letting Thomas take him all the way over and beyond. Thomas groaned out his own climax then, his hand losing its finesse, jerking hard on Marcus as he catapulted with him into the same realm, those fingers in his ass knowing too well how to take him higher than he expected to go.

It made him forget for a time the phone call and who was on the other end of the line. It also almost erased his apprehension about what Marcus planned for them tonight.

Almost.

Chapter Seven

When they came out of the water at last, it was an effort not to stagger. Thomas' knees were quivering, whereas Marcus looked as if he could run a marathon. In the interest of trying to appear as if he wasn't shaken to the core, Thomas mentioned Ben's offer as he slogged out of the surf.

"Sounds like a plan." Marcus picked up a towel when they reached their spot, pressed it against Thomas' back. "Stand still."

There was a different tone when it was a Master's order, a tone that snapped at Thomas' attention like the end of a whip, tightening up everything inside. Despite being drained literally moments before, his cock stirred weakly. Marcus put his hand on his shoulder, his fingers casually resting on the base of Thomas' throat.

Thomas swallowed against his touch as the towel rubbed between his shoulder blades, down over his ass, Marcus squeezing firmly, briskly, coming around the front to do the same to Thomas' chest and belly. Then his hair, letting the terry cloth momentarily blind him before Marcus pulled it away, dropped a kiss on his shoulder. "You'll do, pet. Lie down on the towel and take a short nap. I'll massage those kinks out of your shoulders."

Thomas didn't need a second invitation. Marcus' touch was often demanding. But when all that strength was channeled into being gentle and firm, stroking over Thomas' shoulders, digging into the muscles, down across the wide plane of his back, sweeping circles, kneading, then going to the dip of his lower back, eliciting a grunt…

"Like that, do you?"

"You always gave one hell of a massage."

"Mmmm. You've always had one hell of a body. You've had an injury here. Like you've tied the muscle into a knot."

"Yeah. Fell off a ladder. Damn step moved."

Marcus didn't laugh. Just kept kneading that area. Thomas wasn't going to tell Marcus he'd been working on something at two in the morning because he couldn't bear to lie on a mattress and imagine Marcus right next to him, hearing his even breath. They'd only lived together officially for a handful of months, and he'd felt like a grieving widower.

A grieving widower who couldn't share his grief with anyone, not even the person whom he had to treat as if he were dead, no longer part of his life. Thomas squeezed his eyes shut, not wanting to go there. He needed to turn off a little while, wanted to just focus on Marcus' hands on him.

Instead, he sat up, latched onto Marcus' wrist. "How many?" he asked, his jaw set.

Marcus' eyes narrowed. "I know you're not asking what I think you're asking."

"I have the right to know." Not because Thomas had a claim on him, but because of the way he felt about him. Not that he could or would say that.

Marcus studied him, his expression moving between anger and something else. "Two. I've gone to the clubs, but there've only been two men I've fucked in the time you've been gone. One of them wasn't exactly…mine. He's a friend and belongs to a Mistress, who is another friend of mine. It was a one-shot deal, unusual circumstances, because he's straight. We shared him. The man I was talking with on the phone. They're married."

Thomas nodded, though he felt like he'd swallowed one of the spiny balls from a sweet gum tree. Marcus had gone to the clubs. Often? Occasionally? A hell of a lot could go on in fetish clubs. He could have been blown every other night.

"It's eating you, isn't it?" Those green eyes saw far too much. "You're thinking of all the things you saw when I took you to those types of places, how turned on you got. When I took you home and fucked you, you couldn't get enough."

"Stop it." Thomas shook his head, reached over to the cooler to withdraw a beer, but Marcus laid a hand on his thigh, arresting him in mid motion. Thomas stared at the long fingers lying on the tense line of muscle, close to his groin.

"You were irresistible," Marcus said in a low voice. "Too shy to ask me to do any of it to you. But it mesmerized you to see others treated that way. Restrained, on public display before total strangers. A Master taking up a whip and leaving red marks on fine skin." He ran his knuckles down the center of Thomas' chest and Thomas swallowed, forced himself to remain still, though he wanted to scramble away from the truth of it.

"Who was the other guy you…you know."

"Some poor, unfortunate—or perhaps he considered himself lucky—complete stranger. It was a month after I was certain you weren't coming back." There was a faint hardening in Marcus' gaze. "I took him to a private dungeon room and fucked him within an inch of his life. Slapped him over a bench, rammed my cock in him six or seven times, flogged him until he had to use his safe word. Then I kissed every welt so he was begging for more."

Thomas closed his eyes, his jaw flexing. His hands clenched into fists on the towel. "You son of a bitch." When he began to jerk away, Marcus caught his arm, held him there with a fierce grip and an even fiercer look.

"Tonight is your turn. I'm going to use you, pet. Drive you crazy. Give you pain and pleasure so you don't know which is which. Don't deny that's what you want, because your hard-on is saying something different." His gaze shifted down, then back up, pinning Thomas in place. "I'm going to do what I've always wanted to do, what you've always wanted me to do. Make you surrender to me utterly."

"But I'm here for a week..."

"It doesn't have anything to do with time, pet. It has to do with accepting what is, no matter what happens. Lie back down on your stomach. Now."

When Marcus had Dominated him before, often in the harsh light of day Thomas had rationalized it as a game, role-playing he'd "allowed". But since their separation, he'd recognized that for the lie it was. Thomas found himself lying down again, despite the resentment burning in his gut. That inexplicable emotional compulsion to obey Marcus' commands didn't care about his wounded feelings. His cock sure as hell didn't care.

All those different times, watching the things Marcus had described, Thomas had sensed something in Marcus, waiting. Something in him had wanted to beg for his Master to take command, do more, though he had no idea what "more" was. Whatever it was, he knew he was afraid of wanting it. But that didn't stop him from wanting it so much.

Marcus' hands smoothed over the muscles that had re-knotted in his back. As Marcus leaned forward so the ends of his hair grazed the back of Thomas' shoulders, Thomas felt his breath there. "After I give you all that pain tonight," his lips brushed Thomas' skin, making his fingers convulse on the sand, "I'm going to kiss every one of *your* welts, soothe everything I've torn apart and put it all back together again."

His last scrap of sanity warned Thomas he should back out of this. They had so much shit tearing up the ground between them, and there seemed no way to make it smooth. Thomas wondered if his passive acquiescence was just a way of stumbling blindly down a road they'd never taken this far to see if a solution would present itself.

Marcus massaged his body in silence for about ten more minutes, until Thomas was both more relaxed and more aroused again. Then his lover stretched out on the towel next to him, apparently prepared to take his own nap.

As Marcus lay on his back in the sun, his sunglasses shaded his eyes, one lean strong arm relaxed over his head. His other palm rested on his abdomen, just above the waistband of that sinfully low-riding suit, drawing Thomas' eyes to the impressive mound triangulated between his thighs. Even at rest it was able to make saliva clog his throat.

"We've always played on the edges, you and me," Marcus said, his eyes hidden, his voice neutral. "It's time for you to understand what me being your Master means. My Will becoming the air moving in and out of your lungs, the blood pumping through your body. You've submitted to me, your heart yearning to be my slave, but you haven't taken that final step. When you do, the chains you've wrapped around your internal organs to squeeze the life out of them might just fall away."

A few minutes later the merciless bastard succumbed to a doze, leaving Thomas like a tightly strung wire next to him.

Eventually Thomas sat, knees drawn up, one arm linked over them. He got a beer and opened it, took a swig. Watching the volleyball players, he listened to the wind and surf.

He also watched over the man next to him. Jesus, even Marcus' inhumanly, perfectly styled jet-black hair was drying in an attractive windblown look, despite the saltwater content that should have made it like bedraggled seaweed.

As Thomas rocked the half-empty beer between his fingers, he thought of Marcus touching that faceless slave, kissing away his hurts. Ramming his cock in his ass.

On second thought, Marcus really could use a rinse.

* * * * *

Fortunately the coffeehouse Andrew and Ben recommended was on the ground level of a yacht club with showers. Andrew was a member.

"You had to douse me with Bud Light? There was bottled water in the cooler, for Chrissakes. Or a good quality wine, at least. I smelled like a college frat punk. Or a mill worker on Friday night."

Thomas grinned without repentance as Marcus returned to their table with damp, newly washed hair and the acid comment. Glancing down as the waitress set a cup in front of him, he thought he was probably the first person who'd ordered plain black coffee since the place opened.

It was delivered in a mug the size of a soup bowl. If he drank all of it, he was sure he'd be bouncing off the walls, and his nerves didn't need any more jangling. Though the dumping of his beer had helped relieve some of the tension, and this relaxed atmosphere was a simple pleasure, he still saw the anticipation of the impending evening simmering behind Marcus' eyes.

Marcus' hands settled on his shoulders, a double-edged reassurance. "Ben, Andrew? I have to go down the street and pick up some things. Would you mind looking after Thomas for about thirty minutes?" He ruffled Thomas' hair, rested his hand on his nape as he straightened. "How's the coffee?"

"Fine." Thomas lifted a shoulder. "I don't need a sitter. You know, I have been out in public before. Where are you going?" *And why aren't you taking me with you?* Gods, was he getting that possessive?

"Hmm." When Marcus signaled, the waitress practically leaped to his side, his obvious sexual preference notwithstanding. "Please take this toxic waste away and bring my friend a chamomile tea." He bent again before Thomas could snarl at him, met him eye for eye. "Your stomach's already upset. You're not going to get out of this by poisoning yourself."

"I can walk away anytime. I don't *have* to do anything."

"You're exactly right. But you're not walking, are you?" Marcus brushed his lips over his, just a passing caress that had

Thomas torn between a self-conscious hunching of his shoulders and a wrenching in his gut for more of that mouth. "You keep your ass in this chair and I'll be back soon. It'll be worth the wait."

He straightened again, nodded to Ben and Andrew and headed for the door. Thomas reached for coffee that wasn't there anymore, scowled as he glanced over his shoulder to watch Marcus walk out the door. Along with every other person with a pulse in the café.

"Someday he *is* going to get old and ugly."

"Let's hope so," Andrew observed. "Too many of us who look like that, don't. Get old, that is."

Thomas turned his attention back to his two companions. Ben had his arm casually hooked on the back of Andrew's chair as he leaned back. Demonstrating the ease of lovers who'd been with each other long enough that the close proximity was as simple as breathing. Thomas took a swallow of the tea the waitress brought him to cover the burning ache that thought created. Jesus, he couldn't do this. He was having enough problems just being around Marcus, and he hadn't completed a full twenty-four hours yet.

"How long have you two been together?"

Thomas poked the tea bag deeper into the cup with Ben's unused straw and swirled it around, hoping to get a flavor closer to the strength of coffee. "We're… not really. I mean, we used to be, but it's not that way anymore." Trying to assume a nonchalant attitude, he shrugged. "I'm up for the week to do some work at Marcus' place. That's all."

Thomas took another swallow of his tea. Damn if it wasn't settling his stomach down. Sure as hell he couldn't drink it around Rory, though. It would kick off a whole new set of homo jokes.

He was usually the nurturing one. Marcus knew how to dress him up, handle certain things, but Thomas had added warm, more personal accents to his penthouse. Made Marcus get off the phone at least by one in the morning and get a decent night's sleep. He'd liked cooking Marcus breakfast before he went to the gallery. For some odd reason, Marcus always seemed disproportionately gratified and fascinated by the domestic touches, as if they moved something inside him.

It came so easily to Thomas, the desire to take care of Marcus, even though Marcus seemed the last person in the world who needed someone to do so. Maybe that was why it felt so…good, the way Marcus reacted to it. Now Thomas sourly wondered if he'd mistaken gratitude for suppressed amusement, a sophisticated lover's fascination with the provincial quirks of his bedmate.

Jesus, was there anything he wasn't going to question about every moment they'd had?

He looked up to find Andrew studying him with narrowed eyes and Ben grinning from ear to ear. "What?"

"I'm willing to bet everything you just said was technically, factually correct, and all of it was total bullshit. We've been together fifteen years." Ben glanced over at Andrew with obvious fondness in his gaze. "And it's been tough. Particularly the first years, when you're still dealing with issues of individual identity, just like most couples. Pride. Then there's family, God help us all."

"Where are you from? There's mint julep in your voice." Andrew handed him the slice of lemon from the sweet tea he'd ordered and Thomas accepted it with relief, squeezing it liberally into the tea.

"North Carolina. My family runs a hardware store down there."

"It's good to know the giants haven't driven them all out of business," Ben put in.

"He says that, but try to get him out of Home Depot in under three hours. He'd live there if they let him," Andrew teased.

"We live in a pretty rural area. That's where the small stores can still make it. And if we don't have it, there's a bigger chain store about an hour or so away."

"You grew up there? In the sticks? That couldn't have been easy. How did you get here?"

"He means how in the hell did you and Marcus ever run into each other?"

"I'm an artist." It had been a while since Thomas had said that, and it was like taking a clean breath of fresh air. He paused a moment, feeling it. "I had a teacher in high school that sent some of my work to friends in New York. When I graduated, they encouraged me to come up and enter an art school there. I started showing my work in a small co-op. That's where I ran into Marcus. He runs a gallery."

"But…it sounds like you're back in the sticks, based on what you said." Andrew frowned. "Did it not work out?"

Thomas lifted a shoulder. "My family needed me. Health issues, death in the family."

No, it didn't work out… I'm an artist… The words mocked him, as did the memory of the store's paint display. Why don't you do a nice mural, show them what you can do with color? You're so good with color… I remember when he painted a princess on a unicorn on the wall of Celeste's bedroom when he was eleven. Everyone thought it came from one of those stencil packets…

What was his mother doing now? Sitting in church, praying, lighting candles for his endangered soul while he sat here enjoying a day at the beach? Was Celeste trying to put on a brave face and counting the minutes until she could go back to school as Rory rolled around in his perpetual cloud of bitterness? Watching his friends hoot and holler their way down the road on Friday nights in their souped-up cars, while their mother went to bed holding their father's picture?

The forested surroundings of the Berkshires and the dotting of farmhouses he'd seen as they headed to the beach and the city had reminded him somewhat of home. But North Carolina was more open, the country area more…country.

When Thomas kept the woodstove going in the winter in the shop, the men would congregate in the morning, drinking the complimentary black coffee, analyzing weather, hunting, fishing… It was a life he'd never fit with, but it didn't mean he wasn't a part of it, the blood of that world running through his veins, giving him his foundation.

"No," he said at last. "It didn't work out."

Fortunately, Ben was intuitive enough to change the subject. They spent the next half hour talking about their respective businesses. Before starting their fitness operation, Ben had been a lawyer and Andrew ran a restaurant. Being with them was calming as well as painful, watching the casual touches, the intimacy of two men who knew they had a present and a future as well as a past.

"It's not easy, Thomas." Andrew broke the thread of the conversation mid-sentence. He either had his own dose of intuition or, as Marcus had pointed out before, Thomas' expression was just too transparent. "It isn't easy for any couple to figure it out, gay or straight. Everything can sometimes work against you. Particularly family. Forget that 'let no man put asunder' bullshit. Even hetero couples know that's wedding day crap when it comes to family and friends."

He leaned forward. "They may call it well-meaning meddling, concern, whatever, but lots of time people in your life, the people you really love, will work to tear you apart. You'll even help sometimes, being your own worst enemy. But the two of us decided a long time ago love *isn't* given frivolously." He glanced at Ben. "If you're given the gift of it, you fight to keep it, on all fronts. Don't think it was a mistake or not meant to be. That kind of thing isn't a mistake, and it's too rare to fuck up. Okay?"

Thomas considered his half-empty cup of tea. "Sometimes I just don't know why he's with me."

"Maybe he needs a compass."

Thomas looked up, surprised. Andrew shrugged. "A man looks at the person he loves, he sees his compass. A man can command all the physical aspects of his world, but if his soul is lost, well…it doesn't mean much. Maybe when you look at him, you see beyond the fantastic looks to what's real, his soul. And maybe that's what he needs from you."

Ben nodded. "You aren't like that sleaze who was trying to snake in today. You can tell you're a family guy."

"And what does Marcus seem like?"

Andrew grinned, discarding the serious tone. "You tell us, kid. You're the one who looks at him like he's the entire universe." Then his gaze shifted, and Thomas knew the subject of their conversation was back.

Even so, his nerves rippled in excitement when a pair of hands slid over his shoulders, cupped. He inhaled Marcus' rich scent, which was an answer all in itself. "Miss me?"

"Were you gone?" Thomas glanced up at him indifferently as Ben chuckled. "You know, I could have pulled weeds out of the parking lot and boiled them. It would have been a hell of a lot cheaper than this crap."

Marcus shifted his attention to the other two. "I should have mentioned if he gets cranky, you can take him to the McDonald's down the street to buy him some cookies and let him roll around in that vat of colored plastic balls."

Thomas bared his teeth at him. Marcus slid into the vacant chair and handed him a shopping bag. "Here, go put this on. You'll need to be dressed a little differently for the plans we have tonight."

The way Marcus' eyes lingered on Thomas gave him the terrifying vision of some leather and chains combination and Marcus requiring him to step out of the coffeehouse adorned in it. Well, he didn't have to do it. Didn't have to do anything.

"Go on, pet." Marcus nudged his foot under the table, his lips held firmly together as if suppressing a smile. Thomas reflected that he really did need to cultivate a better poker face. "We need to get going soon. It's dark already."

Thomas rose and left them for the privacy of the yacht club locker rooms. The white opaque bag at least felt like it held something resembling clothing, but there was a smaller paper bag inside of it that made a crumpling noise. When he closed the door of a private bathing room with sink and mirror, he opened the main bag to find a pair of black jeans in his correct size and a short sleeved heavy cotton tee in a royal blue.

In the brown paper bag was a full harness that would collar the cock and balls, and then run up the back of the ass with adjustable strap and ring for positioning a plug. So of course there was a plug and lubricant. He fished in the bag, found a note.

Put this on. Tighten it so the plug will stay deep in your ass and you'll feel the harness on your cock and balls with every step. No underwear. Put a condom on with the harness. You'll be hard enough, I'm sure.

Under the tee was a pair of loafers and socks. All of the clothes were top quality men's wear that Thomas would never have bought for himself, but they were simple, clean styles he liked. He fingered the soft fabric, saw another note.

Still thinking? Am I your Master or not? Put the harness and clothes on and don't make me wait. And tuck the shirt in. I want to see your ass.

This week. Marcus was his Master for this week. It gave Thomas the courage to strip off his cut off jean shorts and T-shirt that had been suitable for the yacht club coffee shop. The bag also held a razor, aftershave and other toiletries to clean up. Marcus had left no message on them, because the message was clear. It made Thomas flush despite the fact he was alone.

Marcus preferred him to keep his genital area shaved, which made him think of the first time Marcus' fine hand had cupped his smoothly shaven balls. The nerves had felt so exposed, sensitive to every stimulation. Jesus, he was getting harder by the minute, just looking at the things Marcus had bought for him. He was being prepared, and rising along with the anxiety was a hungry ache.

Thomas couldn't deny his Master. Wouldn't. And Marcus knew it.

* * * * *

He'd been worried about the plug. He didn't want to walk funny and give it away, mortifying himself. But the thinness made it more of a probe, and the snug fit of the jeans kept the harness firmly in place, keeping the stimulation right where he was sure Marcus wanted it. When tightened properly, the harness cut a bit, but it was supple and lined, so an adjustment on his now cleanly shaved groin took care of that.

He'd shaved his face too, washed his hair, put on the aftershave cologne. All in all, he admitted he cleaned up well. He typically didn't think about whether or not he was handsome, except when he was with Marcus. Marcus had ways of making him feel…well, like he looked pretty damn good. Good enough to make Marcus want to take a bite.

Nodding at himself in the mirror, Thomas collected the bag of toiletries and beach clothes, and reached for the door. He had to stifle a groan at the tightening and stimulating restraint of the cock ring, the probe, the feel of the straps running along his hips. Bound, restrained. A slave to his Master's desire. A slave to his own. Marcus brought forth in him what no other man could. This unquenchable desire to belong, to submit.

When they'd argued earlier, Marcus had cruelly but accurately pointed out that Thomas was uncomfortable facing the truth of that. But when Marcus was his mirror, it was as if the only two things Thomas had ever wanted were to create his art and serve Marcus' pleasure.

He kept telling himself he couldn't lose himself in this, but hell, damn it all, sure he could. Because after a week it was likely all over. No, not "likely". It fucking was. Who wouldn't take a week offered in heaven before they had to descend back to a life sentence in Purgatory?

Stepping out of the bathroom, Thomas returned to the coffee shop, self-conscious enough to almost blush when Andrew let out a low wolf whistle, turning heads. Ben elbowed him, gave him an affectionate smack on the back of his head as Marcus turned in his chair and let his eyes settle on Thomas.

Thomas was hyperaware of the leisurely track his gaze took, strolling up his body, his green eyes going from warm to slow burn as he crossed his groin, slid up to his face. Thomas forced himself to maintain an easy pace. He didn't want to think about how obvious his erection probably was, compressed as it was in the snug jeans and straightened behind the folds of the tucked in shirt.

"Have a seat, pet." Marcus pushed out the chair next to him with a foot.

Of course he was going to make him sit there and suffer, when all he wanted to do was taste Marcus' mouth, his skin, feel the smooth layers of muscle under his palms. Thomas sat, feeling the plug settle itself more deeply, keeping his cock in ramrod stiff mode.

There was a tablecloth, and Marcus and Thomas had the corner. When Thomas sat, Marcus slid a hand onto his knee, exerting some pressure so Thomas knew he wanted his knees splayed, increasing the tension and the angle of the—

Holy Christ. Thomas' teeth snapped together as the probe started to vibrate silently, as well as the base ring on the harness. Jesus… He clenched his teeth, trying to hear what Ben and Andrew were saying. It wasn't the type of stimulation that would make him come, not for an excruciatingly long time. But it made it impossible to think coherently about anything.

He dropped his hand below the table. It landed on top of Marcus', gripped hard. Marcus' thumb stroked the side of his smallest finger, just a teasing caress.

Ten minutes. Marcus put him through ten minutes of conversation that Thomas was barely able to follow, let alone contribute to intelligently, and the bastard made him actually participate. Not huge long syllables, but having to say yes or no had the complexity of a physics equation. Finally, as Marcus began to make their goodbyes, the vibration stopped. Thomas noticed Marcus withdraw his hand from the pocket of his pants where he obviously held the remote.

Thomas managed a courteous farewell and followed Marcus' lead to the door. When he held the door for Thomas to precede him, Marcus' hand grazed the dip in his back, his fingers brushing the top of his buttocks. As sensitized as Thomas was at this point, it was like receiving a hard electric jolt.

"You let me know if anything starts to hurt." Marcus unlocked the passenger side door of the Maserati for him at their street parking place. "I want you stirred up, not in pain. You understand?"

Thomas nodded, his eyes on Marcus' mouth as he took the passenger seat. He wished they were home, at the cottage in the woods, in that soft darkness like the first night, just the two of them.

But another part of him wanted to be right here, particularly when Marcus leaned in and brushed his lips. Just a taste, even as Thomas strained for more, a stroke of his tongue. Marcus' hand rested on his shoulder, a brief hold to keep it short.

When Marcus pulled away, it was like he was magnetized, for Thomas followed him, trying to reestablish the connection, too hungry to exercise control. Slamming his hand down to pin Marcus' wrist on the frame of the door, Thomas caught his Master's other hand and pressed it to his groin in the shadows of the car. He nearly groaned in gratitude as

Marcus flexed his hand under his grip, pressed the heel of his hand against Thomas' engorged cock.

"Let go of me, pet."

Marcus wasn't trying to pull away, but was ordering Thomas to remove his touch, drawing the line. Making himself let go wasn't easy, not when his thighs were trembling with the need to thrust into that touch, insist.

"Are you going to be bad for me tonight? Make me really punish you, teach you what being a slave is all about?"

Marcus' voice was a husky growl. With the coffee shop left behind, the heat was now turned up. He'd shed the cloak of the courteous lover who'd always let his less experienced leman take cautious steps. His Dominant side was far more out front and less restrained. But tonight Thomas didn't want caution. Maybe not ever again, not when it came to Marcus taking him over.

Raising his gaze, Thomas locked it with Marcus'. "If that's what it takes to get my Master to fuck me. Any part of me. Whatever pleases him. That's what I want."

When he reached up, he wasn't at all surprised that Marcus intercepted him, gripping his wrist. He pulled back but Marcus held firm, strength pitted against strength until Thomas subsided, his gaze still on his Master's, burning with a need to fight…and submit both.

"Take off the shirt and put your hands behind you, on the outside of the seat on either side."

No gentleness, just hard command.

Thomas obeyed, pulling off the T-shirt, watching Marcus' gaze course over his bare chest, down to the substantial bulge of his cock. When he put his hands behind him as directed, Marcus closed the door, went around to the driver's side and slid in, one leg stretching out under the wheel before he turned, reaching into the back.

The rattling of paper told Thomas Marcus hadn't brought in all his purchases. He wondered if there was a limit to the amount of blood his cock could contain as Marcus wrapped one of his wrists firmly in a Velour cuff then the other, snapping them together with a strong hasp behind the seat. It was enough of a reach that it put a strain on Thomas' shoulders, thrust out his upper body so when Marcus straightened it was easy to reach over, run his hand down Thomas' chest, play with his sensitive nipples.

"God." Thomas swallowed as sensation shot straight down to his lap, an arrow of testosterone-charged adrenaline.

It was incredible. He couldn't get loose, an anxious feeling, and Marcus was taking his full pleasure with it, not asking his opinion or anything else, just fondling him like he was his, with a stern set to his mouth and a hard lust in his eyes that made Thomas' body into a tight rubber band of reaction about to snap. Marcus touched his navel, traced the indentation. The heel of his hand was so close, but his Master paid no attention to his suffering cock.

Marcus had closed his door and the Maserati's windows were dark tinted. People were walking along the sidewalk within feet of the car, and Thomas could clearly see them, a disconcerting effect, but he couldn't deny the powerful arousal of it as well.

Marcus reached behind the seat again and this time came back with a dark black strap with a buckle. He placed it against Thomas' throat, nudging up his chin impatiently then buckling it in the back, around the metal bar beneath the headrest, so Thomas couldn't lift his head away from it.

It couldn't help but make him remember the waist chain that had been his "collar" before their relationship went to hell. This was a generic collar, no personalized lock that said "Mine", no adornment. An unspoken barb whose pain was somewhat eased by the new surge of response as Marcus put it in place. Thomas tried to strain, feeling suddenly restive.

"I don't… I think…"

"You don't think. You respond. Fight all you want. It will just make me harder." Then Marcus bent his head and pressed his lips to Thomas' bare sternum, coursing over to his left nipple to lick. Nip.

At the stimulus, Thomas arched even further into the uncomfortable angle, his fingers fisting against the bonds, pulling against a metal clasp that would not give. Marcus' temple brushed him, just the hint of the silk of his hair.

"Please…your hair."

"What, dearest?" Marcus murmured it, tilting his head so his green eyes, that sinful mouth, were so close, just beyond his reach. "Beg your Master."

"I want to feel your hair…on my skin. Take it down." He swallowed as Marcus waited, uncompromising. Damn it. "Please take it down, Master."

Marcus had it queued back. After a long, harrowing pause, he reached up and pulled the band loose so that when he turned his attention back to Thomas' nipple, the shoulder-length strands brushed his bare skin. Thomas closed his eyes. There was a physical component—Lord God was there ever—when Marcus made love to him, but then there were times like this, when it was beyond the intensity of an orgasm, where every muscle was rigid, tuned to Marcus' every touch or kiss.

It was like Thomas was in the rapture of Heaven and torture of Hell at once, too stretched between the two to do anything other than stay in this fixed point in space. In the moment.

That said, if Marcus touched his dick Thomas was going to go off like a geyser. Now he knew why Marcus had required he put on a condom with the harness. Or at least one of the reasons, the other reasons still part of the murky possibilities planned for the evening.

Marcus' tongue was damp and firm, and Thomas' legs were jerking, his hips fucking air. Leisurely, Marcus moved to the other nipple, and Thomas cried out at the very first contact.

"Jesus!" He bucked off the seat. Then the vibration started up in his ass and around his cock again. It shot a current of reaction through him and then stopped in a blink, a hair before he would have come if it hadn't been for the secure fit of the harness.

"I have your attention?" Marcus' breath was hellfire hot on his skin.

"Yes. Shit, yes."

"Good." He lifted his head, lips moist from what he'd been doing. Thomas licked his own lips in reaction. "What do you want, Thomas?"

"To serve you." The words came out of that void he couldn't face on his own, that Marcus had opened in him. He was falling deeper into it than he'd known he could go. The words were the first thing that came to his mind before he could analyze or be spooked by them.

Marcus sat back in his seat, put the key in the ignition and turned the engine over. Laying his hand on Thomas' thigh, he let one long finger stroke to a hairsbreadth below his genitals. "I plan to do a lot of things to you tonight. If you can't handle something, you say 'stop'." Not 'please don't'. Stop is the only word that will change things."

"What? No safe word like 'shoe' or 'New Jersey'?" Thomas tried to sound offhanded, even as he remained hyper-cognizant of the fact Marcus had all the control, while Thomas' arms and throat were restrained, his chest bare.

"No. If you're going to stop me, you're going to have to say it directly."

When he was with Marcus before, Thomas didn't know whether to be afraid or ashamed of his desire to be topped. He hadn't had the courage to embrace it except with tentative, easily backtracked steps. Tonight he'd stepped all the way in, and Marcus had shut the door behind him.

To get back out he'd have to go through his Master. Looking at the way Marcus was eyeing his body, Thomas knew there was no way in hell Marcus was going to step out of the way.

Unless Thomas said stop. The hardest word for Thomas to say to Marcus, and he was sure Marcus damn well knew it.

Chapter Eight

The Zone was one of Florida's most high-class BDSM clubs. The fact they'd bought and renovated the fetish club Detonation meant it likely would soon have the same reputation in this area. Particularly if Tyler Winterman's name was involved in it. Marcus grudgingly gave the arrogant ass that much. The Detonation already was known as one of the area's finest underground fetish clubs catering to the BDSM lifestyle. It also catered primarily to men, and so had many different play options catering to their fantasies and tastes. Marcus had been here before, but not since the renovations.

As Marcus stepped into the foyer area, which was designed to look like the open terrace of a Roman plaza, he showed his card and paid the cover charge. Artfully arranged among the various columns and tall urns of plants were chairs and low tables for the men sitting and ordering drinks, eyeing each newcomer. Except for another couple who had entered just ahead of them, he and Thomas were the only recent arrivals to this front area. Since Marcus knew Detonation's entrance ritual, he decided it was a perfect way to start the evening.

He glanced at Thomas at his side, his arms now free, but still shirtless and wearing the collar.

"Take off all your clothes."

"What?" Thomas' gaze snapped to him.

"Do you need help with your slave, sir?" The maître d' said coolly, looking as if he did bouncer work.

"No. But thank you." Marcus inclined his head.

Thomas saw that the obvious submissive member of the pair who'd come in ahead of them was already stripping for his waiting Master, who was casually talking to another Dom he apparently recognized. Because of the many men lingering here with avid eyes and an anticipatory air, Thomas quickly realized that most of the Masters had their slaves strip off all their street clothes here, preparing for the environment in a very public manner, underscoring the way it was going to be up front.

"Thomas. I said strip."

Thomas nodded, suppressing an unmanly tremor in his hands as he opened his jeans, pushed them down over his haunches, careful not to snag the harness. His ears burned at the whistles from their audience, the explicit comments made about what he was revealing. He tried not to be reminded of movie scenes where a new prisoner was brought into the cell block.

Removing his shoes, he took it all off, folded it up into a bundle. Marcus handed the maître d' the bundle and a tip in exchange for a token on a chain, which he put over Thomas' head. It dangled below the collar. The pewter disk had number sixty-eight on it.

"When we come back for your clothes, that's how we'll get them. However, if anyone other than me speaks to you here, you are Slave Sixty-Eight. Do you understand?"

Thomas managed another nod, though he could barely follow Marcus' words. There must be fifty men lingering in this area. Two more slaves had come in and were being made to strip. One was rebellious. His Master quickly yanked the chain attached to a manacle locked just below his slave's knee, above the swell of muscular calf, dropping him to a kneeling position. The maître d' and another bouncer were brought in to forcibly strip him, his struggles obviously arousing them all.

Marcus pressed against Thomas' side, holding his arm when he instinctively started forward.

"Easy. It's the way he and his Master like it, pet. Things are a bit more high-powered here than at the other clubs you've been to, but it's all still consensual. All right?" His fingers tightened on Thomas' quivering shoulder.

Thomas wondered if he was the only one close to a panic attack. It was too warm in here. Too many staring faces.

"Eyes down, pet. On my feet at all times unless I say otherwise. Hands at side, palms open."

"Leash, sir?" This from the maître d' again. "Cock or collar?"

Holy shit, no.

"Yes. Cock, please." Marcus' hand came into view, snapped it onto the ring on the cuff at the base of Thomas' very erect, sheathed cock. Thomas could see some fluid inside the condom where he leaked.

"Is he up for auction tonight? Jesus, I'd like a bid on his ass."

A male voice, right behind him. Thomas stiffened, almost turned before he remembered Marcus had him tethered. Marcus' hand slid around his biceps, stilled him.

"You'll let the Master look at you, pet. He's complimenting my taste."

I don't like this. I don't. Please, let's go home where you'll touch me and murmur to me in that fuck-me voice I can't resist. But he didn't say it. And his cock got harder at Marcus' touch, the protective authority in his voice.

"He's not up for auction tonight, but he will be on public view. This is his first time here. First time participating, ever."

"Enjoy, then." The man moved away, but Thomas' body remained rigid. Too many people…too close…

"Thomas." Thomas had to fight the urge to look up as Marcus pressed his forehead to his. "Sshh. You're ready for this. No one will touch you without my permission. You understand? They might say things, but no one can touch you unless I say so. It's the rules. This is a safe place. I'm not going to let anything happen to you that you can't handle. Okay? Just enjoy the scenery."

Marcus watched Thomas digest that. He'd never taken it to this level with his shy, tough farm boy, and now he was wondering if that was because of Thomas' underlying innocence, his gentle nature, or something else Marcus didn't want to face in himself.

There were a large group of unattached Doms trolling for partners. They would participate in the auction that would occur periodically, allowing a sub the thrill of a new handler, or his Master the opportunity to share him. Before Thomas, Marcus had shared subs when it would be a kick for both of them, something to increase the intensity. It usually involved laying out the slave over a bench to be fucked by him while his sub went down on another Master.

But he wouldn't share Thomas. Couldn't imagine or even countenance it. Marcus told himself it was too much; Thomas looked overwhelmed as it was. But that wasn't why.

I'd kill anyone who'd touched you…you're mine.

He hadn't intended to say those words that day next to the field, but in the dark shadows of his heart, the place he knew a pure spirit like Thomas should never come near, Marcus considered Thomas exclusively his.

He pushed down a sense of uneasiness. Thomas *was* ready for this. But was he?

He changed his mind about the leash and took it off, set it aside. Thomas obediently kept his gaze on Marcus' shoes…or thereabouts. Marcus suppressed a smile, even as it built the hunger in his gut to see the flicker of lashes checking out his cock.

Thomas was nervous, hell yes. But he was aroused and there was that sexy little tremor to his limbs that tightened all those pleasing muscles. Nerves, but more than nerves. Thomas still didn't consciously understand this type of intimacy enough to know his reaction was normal, but Marcus had been deep in this world a long time, and recognized every sign. As most submissives did, eventually Thomas would take the bit in his mouth and ironically pull his Master where they both wanted to go.

I want to call you Master again…for a week.

"Do you want my cock in your mouth?" Marcus demanded, cognizant they were still standing center stage.

Thomas nodded. Marcus reached out, toyed with the numbered disk on his chest. "When I ask you a question, Slave Sixty-Eight, you will respond, 'Yes, Master'."

Thomas' nostrils flared. "Yes, Master."

Marcus let his fingers trail upward now, hook under the buckled collar, tugging so Thomas moved a step forward. "You want it enough to take it here, in front of all of them?"

Thomas inhaled sharply, but Marcus saw his eyes close, his cock jump another inch. He didn't like it confined in the Latex, but he knew his slave would need it, though there were few things he liked as much as feeling Thomas' semen warming and wetting his skin, smelling the musk of it. "Yes, Master. Whatever pleases you."

There was a wave of appreciative response from those sitting nearby, a reaction to the chance to witness an unexpected floor show. The Dom who'd spoken to Marcus took a seat on a divan behind Thomas, not more than several feet away, where he'd get a good view of every flex and shift of Thomas' tight ass, still penetrated by the probe, the strap running between his buttocks.

Marcus exerted downward pressure on the collar. "On your knees, then."

As he stripped off his belt, he thought what it would be like to leave his marks on Thomas' flesh, hear the pleasurable grunts of pain. He could let the other Master do it while Thomas sucked him off, a suitable punishment for his flirtation earlier in the day, but Marcus wanted the pleasure of marking his skin. He wanted to hoard all the pleasure involving Thomas.

Marcus also thought about having Thomas clasp his hands behind his head, his only anchor Marcus' hand in his hair, pushing him into a bobbing rhythm on the cock he knew was long, thick and hard enough to gag most slaves. But Thomas knew how to take all of him, so good at relaxing his throat. He wanted to feel Thomas' hands.

Thomas' first touch caused a shudder to run through him. Marcus was usually good at masking such reactions, but apparently breaking Thomas into his first high-level BDSM arena was affecting him strangely. Though scared as hell, Thomas was trusting him. And the power of a submissive's trust could blow away anything a Master had to offer.

Thomas unfastened Marcus' slacks, took down the zipper and eased underwear and outer garment down just enough in front to release Marcus' cock to the gaze of the crowd a scant moment before he covered most of it with his mouth, not an easy feat. He took it deep into the back of his throat, just as Marcus liked it. It made him pulse and leak the first drops onto Thomas' tongue. When he felt Thomas swallow, he suppressed a growl of response.

Thomas' strong, firm fingers circled him, his thumb stroking the taut vein beneath as he slid down, up. Slow, letting the crowd see the glistening moisture his mouth left all along Marcus' shaft, polishing it up for them.

Like many submissives when being Dominated, Thomas' focus narrowed only to his Master, so Marcus knew it was likely his slave was no longer even aware he was performing in front of a group. Essentially given no choice, his only task was to please his Master. His tongue caressed Marcus, tasted, mouth pulling, increasing suction. Marcus was overwhelmed by the picture of it, both before his eyes and in his mind.

Thomas on his knees before him, naked. Long, muscular lean body bare in all ways except for the cock harness straps, the probe up his ass, the collar on his throat telling everyone he belonged to someone. At least in here, Marcus didn't have to pretend it was true—or wonder how true it was.

Another couple had come in, another slave stripping, and the energy in the proportionally small area was hot, pounding, pulsing. All of them were sucked into this tableau in the center however, and many of the men had moved closer. There was a circle of aroused, tense males within five feet of them on all sides. Marcus knew it was Thomas who held them riveted.

A new, relatively inexperienced sub on his knees and working his Master's cock in his mouth, his own organ stiff and straight above his thighs like a sun dial, needing release, restrained by the collar cinched around it.

Trying to retain his sanity, Marcus slid a hand into his loose pocket, amazed that he didn't fumble. He removed the remote, held it up so others could see, and pressed it to highest setting, where he knew the probe would do a staccato dance against Thomas' prostate.

The reaction was instant, and gratifying. Thomas jerked, his buttocks squeezing together in a way that caused several groans from their audience. Even Marcus had to suppress a reaction as muscles rippled along Thomas' curved back, his broad shoulders bunching.

"You keep working me, pet. Don't you let go."

Thomas made an inarticulate sound against his cock, part plea, part growl. His hand tightened on the base of Marcus' cock, the other dropping to grip his thigh through the trousers, fingers pushing into hard muscle. Marcus' hips were jerking, cock so stiff it barely moved, but Marcus knew it was ready to explode. Thomas' breath was a harsh rasp, hot friction against him, working him the way only a man knew to do. Ruthless, relentless, fucking fantastic.

"Keep going," Marcus said sharply. Thomas clumsily obliged, trying to keep his mouth moving in a rhythm over him as the probe turned him mindless. Responding to his

Master on instinct alone and filling Marcus with an even more ravenous desire to push him, to make him give it all.

Just when Thomas was sure he was going to come, cock harness or not, Marcus eased the vibration to a slow hum and forcibly pulled his head back, taking Thomas' mouth from his cock, leaving him staring at the broad head, licking his lips from the salty taste of what had come into his mouth, collected on the tip.

He was forced to sit back, despite wanting to feel it deep in his ass, even if it meant turning around and putting his hind end in the air like an eager hound. But Marcus rearranged his clothes over his enormous erection and brought him to his feet with his hand on his elbow. "Come with me."

"That's where I thought we were headed," Thomas rasped. Marcus' fingers bit into his arm and he subsided, though he was pretty certain he saw his Master's lips curve before Thomas lowered his gaze back to his feet as he'd been ordered to do.

Marcus took him down a dimly lit hall strung with lights to show murals on the wall depicting explosions, red and orange streaks of fire. Long strips of cloth hung from the ceiling in a staggered pattern, some translucent, some solid, so the different textures brushed the skin and occluded vision. It was easy to brush against the bodies of those passing in the opposite direction, smell the scents of different men. Thomas kept his gaze glued on Marcus' feet with effort, his Master's grip on his arm firm.

They emerged into the dizzying lights and noise of the main club area. Though he'd been able to mostly forget about the watching crowd from the intensity of going down on Marcus, Thomas was relieved he was no longer the center of attention. Here the music was loud, throbbing. There was a crowded dance floor, darkness and strobe lights giving brief images of all the things going on.

Men in cages suspended over the dance floor. A couple of them dancing while a handler stood on the platform outside, ready with a hot stick or cattle prod if they didn't obey their Master's mandate to perform for the crowd. One of the men had tears on his cheeks, perhaps as new to this as Thomas, but like Thomas his cock was hard. He was dancing with a riveting fury, his hands in clenched fists against the struggle going on within him.

On another two raised platforms, men were bound spread eagle to spinning wheels. People could come by and spin their naked bodies, or… Thomas watched as a man, obviously a total stranger to the bound slave, pulled the wheel around so its occupant was upside down. Then he jammed his cock into the slave's mouth, which was wrested open with a gag ring. The Dom leisurely fucked his mouth while sipping a cocktail and talking to another Dom.

It was hedonistic, like one of the fascinating upper layers of Hell. Dark and shadows. Thomas felt sick and excited at once.

"Your eyes aren't on my feet." Marcus' voice brought him back and he obeyed, but he noticed Marcus had given him time to study his surroundings before he'd reminded him. "I'm letting go, pet. You stay two steps behind me at all times. You forget and look up again, I'll make you do it on your hands and knees like a dog so you can't see anything *but* my feet."

There was something hard in Marcus' voice that hadn't been there in the foyer. The tone suggested he might do the humiliating thing he described. Thomas followed, wondering at the feelings swirling in his stomach. It was like being offered candy, but the wrong kind. He couldn't put a name to it, but some shadowy apprehension was moving low in his belly, the deeper they moved into the club. He wasn't sure…

Before he could complete the thought, they moved out of the dance area into a new space. This was one large room divided by a wall of clear glass. The glass was partitioned into rectangular sections by Ionic columns. Between each set of columns was a carved wooden chair that looked as though it might have graced the judgment hall of a Roman governor.

Metal pieces formed artistic diamond-shaped divided lights in the glass, but they were functional, for there were protrusions bolted onto those metal frame pieces. Because Thomas only dared a quick glimpse, he couldn't tell what they were. He wasn't going to risk Marcus doing exactly what he'd said he'd do, and dealing with how that might turn him on. But not knowing the whole picture, having to rely on Marcus' guidance, was creating all sorts of tangled reactions within him, apprehensive and lustful at once.

Marcus stopped by one of the chairs. He effectively banished Thomas' thought process by opening his slacks again and taking a seat. Almost absently, he fondled Thomas' bare thigh. "Come here, pet. Keep your eyes down."

Because of that, he had to let Marcus guide him. Marcus nudged him so Thomas stood in front of his Master, facing away from him. "There are two handles in front of you. Bend over and take hold of them."

They were at mid-body level, anchored into the metal frame pieces of the glass wall. Now he could see there were people on the other side. A man bent toward him, a mirror image of how Marcus wanted him. His long cock was hanging down between spread, trembling thighs as someone took him from behind. He had his mouth pressed on the glass, stretched open by the rubber phallus mounted there. A duplicate of the one in front of Thomas' face now, sheathed in an unlubricated new condom.

Thomas' own body started trembling as he realized what Marcus intended to do.

"You're making me wait."

As Thomas grasped the handles, Marcus continued in an implacable voice. "Take the dildo in your mouth, all the way, until your lips are against the glass. It's sterile. The attendants clean the glass and replace the condom between every use.

Once you get it all the way in, you'll lift your eyes. You keep them open and staring straight ahead."

Thomas obeyed slowly, reluctant and self-conscious. When he took his lips down the length of the hard rubber cock, he and the man being fucked on the other side were essentially in a kiss, separated by thick double-plated glass. The way the handles were anchored in the steel framework their knuckles would have touched.

The wild drumbeat of the music on the dance floor could be felt through his bare heels. Where the glass was hinged to the Ionic column, there was a slender line of space, so he could hear the grunts of the other slave, as rhythmic and primal as those drums. His eyes were a pale green, his hair red and long. He had a pale, muscular body, with a tattoo of a dragon over the left pec that undulated as he reacted to the thrusts of whoever was fucking him.

Thomas didn't want to keep his eyes open, feeling far too exposed to this man and his submission, but his Master had ordered it, so he did.

I am Slave Sixty-Eight. I obey my Master and that's all. I'm not responsible for anything but giving him pleasure. I don't think about who I am beyond this moment, or what others would think. It's all about this moment…

To hold onto the handles and lean forward the way Marcus wished, Thomas had to bend his knees. The significance of that uncomfortable pose struck when Marcus slid his chair up behind Thomas, removed the lubricated probe, put his hands on Thomas' hips and brought him down on his cock.

Holy fuck. Truer words never spoken. After all the stimulation from the coffee house to this moment, Marcus' cock sinking into him had the searing pleasure of fire racing through his blood. Thomas bit down on the rubber cock savagely. The panic in the other man's eyes reflected his realization that Thomas had just been penetrated, and it propelled him closer to a release Thomas was sure his Master had forbidden him.

Both of them were sucking frantically on the phalluses, a way of goading or controlling themselves, Thomas didn't know. He just had to do it.

Perhaps Thomas was just imagining it, torqued as he was, but he thought he could feel the pressure of the other man's lips, their texture, even as he imagined it was Marcus' cock he was deep-throating, almost choking on it as Marcus thrust deep, withdrew and thrust deep again, full penetration and withdrawal each time. It left a trail of clawing need all up and down the passageway, to the root of him. He heard Marcus' grunt of approval like a gift. God, he'd gone beyond *wanting* to come. He *had* to come or he'd just die.

Thomas couldn't beg with his mouth so occupied, so he begged with his body, his arm muscles banded steel as he held onto the handles with tight fists, hips lifting up and slamming down. Marcus' hands slid down either thigh where Thomas sat on his lap, caressed muscles, then one hand reached between his legs, released the harness a notch.

"Come, pet."

Despite his overwhelming desire to do so, Thomas managed to hold back. Not until he'd brought his Master pleasure. He gripped him with his strong inner muscles, sliding up and down Marcus' delectable length. He longed to feel that hot jetting pulse of his climax, the spasmodic clutch of his hands. Marcus' hands were powerful enough to bruise and they often did. Thomas loved it.

It was submission and yet an exercise of power at once. The desire to serve his Master's pleasure but prove he could make *him* do something, no matter how many times he'd had slaves within walls like these do *his* bidding.

"Stubborn," Marcus said, but his voice was hoarse. Thomas renewed his efforts, so on each slow withdrawal

Marcus was pulling against resistance from muscles oiled with lubricant, that knew just how to stroke and hold him…

Thomas grunted as Marcus abruptly slammed into him, slick and slow gone hot and fast. He hung onto the handles, providing the counterpoint even as need burst into undeniable release. "Oh God…" his voice was garbled against the gag of the phallus.

"Let it go," Marcus growled.

You first, damn it. Thomas' nerve endings had never felt so sensitive. If Marcus touched him anywhere—his elbow, an earlobe—he would go off like a rocket. Though the fire of it was all consuming, Thomas hung on, thinking he could hold on just another second…

Marcus groaned, his hands clutching his hips, shoving up into him so Thomas' body rocked forward, chest to the glass. "Fuck…"

That guttural curse and the spasmodic vibrations of Marcus' body gave Thomas what he needed. He let go, crying out against the phallus deep in his mouth. The man before him ejaculated, no doubt spurred by his reaction. It was like a video screen though, for everything living and real to Thomas was all Marcus. His semen filling him, the press of his thighs and open slacks against the back of his legs and ass. That hard, undeniable cock impaling him.

He was pumped relentlessly. He kept up, his hands slick on the handles, his body rocking even past the point when his release was done, like a dog humping air because it felt too damn good to stop. Only Marcus' hands sliding down to grip his ass and bring him to a stop returned Thomas somewhat to himself.

He rested his forehead against the glass, mouth still full of the dildo even though his chest was expanding fast to get air around the gag. Marcus' hands moved over his back. Reaching forward, he removed the now full condom, a cosseting that moved something in Thomas, creating a lump in his throat.

Marcus had been demanding, even a little mean, but at the end, there was this reminder of tenderness, of care.

If his intention was to keep Thomas off balance, it was succeeding.

Marcus took several of the wipes that were provided in a discreet and decorative wooden box mounted on the column and cleaned Thomas, keeping pressure with one hand on his back to tell him he wanted him to stay in that position. Thomas watched, amazed as the man who'd been fucking the redhead got up and turned over his chair to another.

The redhead gave him a weary wink and winced as he was immediately rutted upon by a new occupant of the chair who'd donned a condom before plunging into his ass with an enthusiasm bordering on violence. Apparently their show had stirred things up.

"He was auctioned to submit to whoever his Master deemed appropriate," Marcus observed. "Either because it pleasures and excites his Master and his slave to be shared, or because he's being punished and he consents to allow his Master to punish him this way." His hands wiped at Thomas' genitals and Thomas noticed the man was watching the tenderness. No, devouring it with his gaze. Was it watching a man's hands on another man's cock? Or like Thomas was he enthralled with the contrast of punishing demand with gentle care?

"Straighten up and turn toward me. Keep hands and eyes down."

Thomas obeyed, turning to find Marcus had apparently cleaned himself and rearranged his trousers so everything was in place. Marcus' long-fingered, beautiful hands rose with another wet paper cloth to clean Thomas' face where saliva had escaped his mouth.

"What are you thinking?" His voice was low, velvet.

That I can't tell if you hate or love me in this place, or if it even matters. Thomas couldn't say that, though. Despite the fact they seemed to have reached a higher plane of intensity, a bond that seemed to make other words unnecessary, some essential component of the intimacy that could exist between them so easily was missing. He just couldn't put his finger on what was off.

"What's going to happen next?" he asked instead.

"Whatever I want to happen," Marcus said mildly, tossing the wad of tissues in another discreetly placed steel can.

"How..." Thomas swept his downward glance toward the other slave, whose eyes were now closed. "How do they stay safe?"

"His Master is standing about ten feet away, watching it all. Making sure every man he's given the privilege of fucking his slave is appropriately protected."

"Will you..."

"Share you? Let another man fuck you, for pleasure or punishment?"

Marcus touched his face. Whereas before he'd wanted to raise his gaze, now Thomas resisted. But Marcus slid his fingers in the strap of the collar, knuckles pressing on Thomas' windpipe to force his head back to meet his cold green eyes.

"Is that what would turn you on, pet? To have your Master whore you out? There's some women here. I could let one barter for some cunt-eating time with my slave. You could practice for that doe-eyed fiancée of yours."

The reassurance that Marcus' tenderness had evoked vanished. "Don't." One word, spoken through stiff lips, was all Thomas could manage. *Don't do this.*

"Why? Is she that precious to you?"

"She's a friend. And you're just doing this to get me to take a swing at you. Which I will if you don't shut up about her. It's not about her. It's about you and me."

"Really? That's news to me. My understanding is it's never been about you and me, to the point I often wonder if there *is* a you and me in your mind."

* * * * *

Marcus told himself he didn't know where the anger had come from. But that was bullshit. He'd been overwhelmed by Thomas' response to him, not just here, but since they'd stepped into the club. He'd expected Thomas' resistance. Instead, his shy lover had surrendered to things that far exceeded what he'd been asked to give Marcus before. Going down on him in this setting, letting himself be spread out and fucked the way he just had. He submitted to Marcus, belonged to him fully, in so many ways. And at the end of the week it wouldn't mean a damn thing.

Coming to a club like this, where emotions could be brought rocketing to the surface so easily, was a mistake. As he'd just demonstrated with the below-the-belt shot that roused the side of Thomas he so rarely saw. When the dark eyes became sharp and direct, the body shifting into a Southern boy kick-your-ass forwardness posture, nothing would back him down.

A muscle flexed in Thomas' jaw. "Would whoring me out turn *you* on? It's not okay for me to let someone else fuck me, but it's okay if it's you doing the letting? Is that what my Master wants?"

Marcus couldn't bring himself to be dishonest about what he wanted from Thomas. Never. He'd made that oath to himself when he went to North Carolina to find him.

"No," Marcus said it fiercely. Then, more softly, his hand gentling on Thomas' neck, thumb stroking over the pulse, a quick pass over the flushed jaw. When Thomas tried to push him away, Marcus turned his hand, gripped his wrist, kept it pinned to his shoulder. "I don't want any other man to fuck you. Ever. The idea of it makes me physically sick, and so furious I can't…" He stopped, shook his head. "No."

"It's not what I want, either." Thomas swallowed and suddenly there wasn't a club, pounding noise and flashing lights. There was just his face, close, his eyes meeting Marcus'. His sensual mouth was held in a line taut with the power of his emotions, spun up and to the surface, so Marcus knew his words were brutally honest. "No matter what happens, Marcus. With Daralyn, with any of it, you're the only man I want. Now or forever. The only man I'll ever let inside me again."

Words of devotion could cut like rusty saw blades. Marcus wanted to quip, wanted to make some dig at how young Thomas was to be making such a rash statement. He was only twenty-seven, for Chrissakes, but Marcus knew Thomas had the soul-deep understanding of himself to make the utterance with the certainty of an oath.

Indeed, it was Thomas' very spiritual sense of himself, his responsibility to those he loved, the wisdom to perceive who needed him the most, that drove Marcus to insanity. Even as it made him want to be with him with a hunger that made him worry he might blurt out the same foolish promise.

The only man I'll ever let inside me again…

When Thomas reached out to touch his face, Marcus stepped back, shook his head. Thomas stopped midair, waited a pregnant second, then slowly lowered his arm. Marcus lifted the Velcro cuffs and gestured to Thomas to turn. When he did, he wrapped the cuffs around Thomas' wrists, trying to keep his mind on what he was doing and not the back of Thomas' neck, so tender and exposed with his head bowed, his eyes cut down again.

Marcus wanted to bury his face there, his nose in the soft line of hair and skin, smell deodorant and aftershave, warmth.

Instead, he latched the cuffs together. Thomas' knuckles rested on the curves of his bare ass, so that Marcus couldn't resist caressing him there. Thomas' fingers twitched but didn't seek to entwine, his shoulders rising and falling, the elevated breathing pattern showing he was fighting a frisson of panic at experiencing the restraints in such an environment.

"Come on." Marcus took his arm. He was crazy to be here, but he couldn't leave. There was too much he wanted to do to his slave. Needed to do to him.

Chapter Nine

ꟹ

As Marcus led him down to a second level of the Club, Thomas couldn't get a sense of his Master's thoughts. Arousal, for certain. The flash of anger, almost vicious resentment, had unsettled him. In these surroundings, Thomas was already unsettled. He needed to be sure of his Master, and he wasn't at all sure of Marcus' mind at the moment.

This area of the club was a circular lounge, where those taking a break could relax with a drink, talk. In the center of the room was...well, he wasn't sure what to call it. He was starting to know what Alice in Wonderland must have felt. Or any character who found himself in a world fantastically, temptingly different from his own.

It appeared to be a large oval-shaped fountain with water pouring over stepped layers of flat slate from a top round disk into the pool. On top of the disk was an excellent reproduction of Michelangelo's David.

There were men kneeling, manacled in a circle around the wall of the pool. The line of the wall was scalloped, so each convex or concave curve formed a separate space for the man placed there. The men's positions were also arranged to form an aesthetic design. Where one man was bent over the wall in the concave space, the ivory rough stucco side pressing against his pelvis as he stared down into the water, the man next to him sat on the convex top of the scallop, facing outward and sitting upright.

Their arms were chained, one man's arm under or over the man's next to him. The ankles were likewise done, legs spread, so the sitting man's jutting cock and balls were exposed from the front as the bent-over man's was from the back, hanging free between his legs.

The floor beneath the fountain and the men was a rotating disk, and they were moving slowly, being displayed from all angles. As Thomas studied the carousel, the rigid faces of the men on their knees or the jerking hips of the men facing forward, he understood.

The cocks of the men bent forward were threaded through holes in the fountain wall, their hips and thighs anchored with straps so they couldn't move back to free themselves. Something in that hole was stimulating them like a man's mouth. Whereas the sitting men were obviously sitting on automated phalluses to fuck their asses. All for the watching pleasure of the wine drinkers in the room.

"Chocolate sauce, sir?" A waiter stepped up to Marcus. Thomas managed to tear his gaze away to see Marcus hand over the required tip before dipping his fingers into the metal chalice offered. Thomas noted all the men on the carousel were marked in some way on chest or back, depending on which direction they were situated, with letters or symbols he didn't understand.

Marcus brought the sauce-covered fingers to Thomas' back. As he stayed still and felt the slow glide over his spine, the caress as Marcus made a symbol of his own, Thomas digested the fact that Marcus was going to put him here. Restrain him, let others watch him get fucked or jerked off by inanimate electronic devices.

This imprisonment of his body, displaying it for the pleasure of others, was unthinkable, and yet he was fascinated by it. He was unable to resist the pressure of Marcus' hand as he was guided to the fountain and Marcus removed the cock harness.

"On your knees, pet," Marcus ordered. "Put this new condom on and then guide your cock into the hole."

Thomas sank down on a knee cushion apparently provided to help the sub hold his position. As he leaned forward, obeying, he felt as if everyone's eyes were on him, but particularly Marcus'. He guided himself into a warm, moist canal and jumped as it automatically closed on him, adjusting for his girth. Then it cinched in a little tighter to hold him.

"Holy Christ." He swallowed. It felt too snug to remove himself without tearing off something he might need.

Marcus fitted the straps over the backs of his thighs and his waist, spreading out his arms to either side, under the braced arms of the two sitting men on either side of him so their forearms touched. There was another vulnerability to this position, for his cheek now pressed on the upper curve of the well wall, mist from the fountain bathing his face as Marcus bound his neck against it with a strap, holding him completely in place.

His knees were nudged further apart and the ankles of the men on either side were briefly released so Thomas' legs could be guided to the inside of their feet. When they were all rebound, he was firmly manacled, their heels pressing against the inside of his calves, almost as if they were holding him spread open. They did not speak, at least one of them gagged, but he could feel the warmth of their unfamiliar flesh, the flex of their muscles.

"This will keep you occupied for a time. I'm going to go set up a room I want to use." Marcus fiddled with a dial and Thomas clenched his jaw as the simulation of a wet mouth began to work him, making his body tense with the artificial stimulation.

"Master..." Don't go, he wanted to say. Don't leave. But there was an element of punishment here he had to endure for the pleasure of his Master. One part of him wanted to tear free, be back home with Marcus where play was between them. Another part of him wanted to be here, showing the world he belonged to Marcus. Which made no sense at all. But what had ever made sense with Marcus?

Marcus was standing where he could partially see him, and he was aroused. Looking at Thomas and nowhere else, and Thomas knew him so well, he knew Marcus was so turned on he could barely speak. It made his own reaction leap, not a wise idea with the stimulation he was already experiencing. He groaned.

Marcus passed his hand over his hair, clenching and tugging to the point of pain. "You're going to make every dick in the place rock hard. I changed my mind on one thing, because you seem to be having trouble remembering to keep your eyes down. You *can* be touched, pet, but the symbol I left on your back says you're mine, that you're not to be fucked."

Thomas bit his lips as Marcus called a staff member to attend him. The oiled-down muscular man in painted-on Latex black pants and black tie carried a shallow crate supported with a strap around his neck like one of the vintage cigarette girls, only he was providing a selection of plugs in sealed packaging. Marcus chose one very thick dildo, paid and tipped him well, then lubricated it for insertion.

Thomas watched him, his mouth dry, unable to speak. When Marcus eased it into him, his fingers gripping his buttock, Thomas' testicles drew up, his cock flexing inside the tight cavern of that automated mouth.

"If you should sweat it off, that's to protect your virtue until I return. Don't let it slide out, pet. Keep that ass tight."

Marcus' fingers whispered down his back and then he was gone where Thomas couldn't see him. With his neck locked down, he could only look at the man next to him or gaze down into the wading pool.

The man next to him was getting ready to explode, bouncing spasmodically, as much as he could with his tight restraints, breath rasping. "Please…Master…"

His Master must be at one of the tables watching him. The wet mouth sucked on Thomas' cock, rippled. Holding his ass tight wasn't a problem. He wanted to slam himself against the wall in response, but he couldn't.

He tore his gaze from the man and looked down into the fountain, only to find that provided no relief. It had a glass bottom, and through the wake of the fountain water he could see the floor of a third level below. There appeared to be a full scale Roman orgy ensuing.

Desire and lust crowding in on all sides, but where the hell was Marcus? Surely Marcus wouldn't go where he couldn't see Thomas? As Thomas rotated with the others, he couldn't see anything, for the carousel was almost full, too many bodies in the way. Marcus had surely only been gone a minute, but without being able to see him, it seemed much longer. He felt helpless.

He heard voices, registered words as Doms walked by, appreciatively fondling those with the right symbols. One gripped the cock of the man about to explode, testing the weight and girth while his companion leisurely took down his pants and drove a sheathed cock glistening with lubrication into the slave on the other side of that man, eliciting a guttural cry which seemed to inspire him to a rougher thrust, a reverent curse. His friend rubbing the cock next to Thomas chuckled and made a comment Thomas couldn't hear.

The man ejaculated, crying out, and Thomas closed his eyes. He didn't want to come like this. Oh God, but he was going to…

Then he stiffened as a strange hand touched his ass, his lower back. A thigh pressed against his, making his thighs widen further. When fingers rocked the dildo in his ass, the explosion of sensation went right to the root of his cock. An electric knot of tension fired through his belly and tributary lines in his chest as if he wore nipple clamps.

That hand was now on his back stroking. *Get off. That's not yours.* Two men. There were two men behind him. He was hemmed in by them, and by the slaves on either side.

He didn't like this. Didn't want this. He wanted out of here. The lobby and the glass wall, that had been just Marcus and him, even surrounded by other people. Where the fuck was Marcus?

Stop it. He squeezed his eyes shut, the rushing of the water filling his senses, but it didn't calm him. If anything, it was like the roar of a crowd watching gladiators, men forced to perform, to bleed, to suffer for cruel eyes and faces.

He wanted to focus on soft green fields, the way the North Carolina mist would lie low on the cut fields on an early morning. The velvet press of Kate's nose in his hand. The feel of Marcus' body curled protectively around him, only this wasn't protective, so the image didn't hold, dissolving away like the empty fantasy it was. Fingers pinched his ass hard, closed around his testicles.

This was Marcus' punishment. His anger, which had been simmering below the surface since Thomas had gone down on him in front of a mass of strangers and they'd left the foyer. That was what was wrong. This was wrong.

"Let go." He tried to twist around, tried to see his tormentors and couldn't as they stayed just out of his vision, playfully laughing at his efforts. "Stop it." He said it again, stronger, and one slapped his ass.

"It says you can't be fucked, Slave Sixty-Eight. It doesn't say you can't be touched." It was a game to them. They didn't know. He should just ride it out. He should just…

"I'm saying it. I'm…" As the man's touch drifted to his front, teasing his nipples, his other hand clamping on the back of Thomas' neck to increase the sense of being pinned, Thomas tried to kick out, forgetting his leg was bound to the floor. He yanked against the hold of the manacles, managing to send a tremor through the fountain wall. It drew startled looks from the bound slaves he could see.

"Stop it. Go away. Damn it, stop. *STOP*."

"Sshh…sshhh."

Marcus. Marcus' touch on his back, Marcus' thighs straddling his hips, the other men moving away at Marcus' murmured word. The electronic stimulation stopped.

"Let me go."

"In a minute. I promise, in just a minute. You need to calm down first. Deep breaths."

"Why did you do this? This wasn't about…like the rest. I'm not…"

I'm not theirs. I'm yours. Thomas wanted to say it, but he didn't. Not right now. He was angry, hurt. He wanted to be let go.

The other man had been removed by his Master after his climax, so Marcus came into his field of vision then, sitting down on the now empty convex scallop of the carousel, sans dildo. Propping his hand just behind Thomas' head, he leaned down over him, so Thomas could see his Master's face. Only his Master's face. Marcus laid his hand on Thomas' cheek, thumb caressing the side of his nose.

"It's different now with us, isn't it?" Thomas managed. He was able to stretch out his fingers enough to grasp the cuff of Marcus' sleeve, capture it between two fingers in a tenuous hold, just a physical connection. "It was easier before, but it's like…we're deeper somehow now."

His intuitive artist. Marcus didn't know how to answer him, how to say that yes, it was more intense. That bringing Thomas here had opened up scars much older than those Thomas had inflicted. That the cut of his leaving had severed stitches over ancient wounds Marcus thought he'd left behind.

Don't sacrifice my son on the altar of your demons…

"Come on." Marcus reached over and removed the restraints on Thomas' neck and arms, the legs and hips. He wanted to touch him, but he didn't. He felt unclean. "You don't belong here."

It was startling to realize that neither did he. Not anymore. Not while he was with Thomas.

Thomas rose. Swayed a little as blood rushed to his head, but still Marcus couldn't bring himself to reach out. It was Thomas who did, catching Marcus' shoulder before he could draw away. He curled a hand in Marcus' shirt lapel to steady himself.

"Is this what you want? What you like?" When Thomas said the words in an odd, soft voice, Marcus could see the weight he'd placed on his farm boy's heart. Thomas was obviously torn between what he subconsciously knew to be true about the two of them and his doubt of that truth. Doubt, because Marcus had betrayed Thomas' trust. Betrayed what Marcus himself knew to be true about the two of them.

"No," Marcus said at last, making himself say that truth. "Not with you."

When he started to turn away, his slave tightened his grip, met his gaze. "Master. It's okay."

"No. No, it's not." Marcus attempted a light tone, failed. "You mess me up, Thomas. In a lot of ways."

A slow smile crossed Thomas' face, a surprising expression considering the gravity of the moment. "And you think my compass isn't spinning around like I'm in the Bermuda Triangle when I'm with you?" He took a breath. "If this is the kind of thing you want, I'll…figure it out. I'll do it. We'll do it."

"No." Marcus pried his touch off his shirtfront and held it upright between them, curled hand over curled hand, like two men taking a warriors' oath. "It's never going to be that way with us. Anything you say "stop" about, I respect. No apologies, no guilt on your part, no feeling like you've disappointed me. I want you to feel comfortable saying it. You want to get out of here now?"

When Thomas looked at him, something shifted in his eyes, something that made everything in Marcus go still. His grip increased around Marcus' hand.

"You said…"

"What, pet?"

"*'Then I kissed every welt so he was begging for more.'*" Thomas moved in, his hair brushing Marcus' temple. They were eye to eye, his lips so close, his body completely naked, pressing close to Marcus' fully clothed one. But it was his gaze where all his energy was concentrated, bringing fire into Marcus' chest at that searing look. "That's the room you set up, wasn't it?"

Marcus nodded, one slow movement.

"Then give me your pain, Master. I can bear it as long as I know your lips will touch every mark when you're done, signing it as your work."

They both knew there was more going on here, but Jesus. As usual it was Thomas who called it forth, gave it a name, restored the balance. And Marcus knew Thomas had no clue he had that gift. He wondered if any Master could deserve him, let alone one as despicable as himself.

* * * * *

The room he'd booked wasn't private. Three other couples were in there. Marcus was fine with that, though initially he would have preferred a room with just him and his slave. He ignored the sly voice that suggested his change of heart was to keep Thomas from making any more soul baring confessions that might drive *him* to his knees.

However, it was silent except for the short commands of Masters to their bound subs, the slap of weapons against flesh. One slave was bent double, wrists bound so he hugged his knees as his Master caned him. Another was over a spanking bench being paddled, his buttocks already a bright red. His grunts came through the ball gag strapped around his head.

Some Masters were like used car salesmen, loud, admonishing their subs as if for a performance. These three couples were quiet, simply giving Marcus a cursory look and a nod as he came into the door. They were into their own scenes, personal between their sub and them. Their presence was stimulating, but not intrusive.

Walking Thomas to the side of the room, Marcus straightened his arms above his head and locked him into a pair of manacles dropped from the ceiling. Marcus did the same to his ankles with a set bolted into the floor, using his knee instead of his voice to command Thomas to spread wide. The chains made a clanking sound.

There was a delicious shiver running through his slave's body now, Thomas responding as Marcus knew he would, making him want to snap and salivate like a wolf. Something was drawing tight, low in Marcus' belly, a feeling he hadn't ever experienced as a Dom before. He'd gotten hints of it before with Thomas, a vision of the places the feelings between them could take them both.

"Master…" Thomas' voice, almost a murmur, sending a ripple of response through Marcus' body. He leaned up against his now immobilized lover, pressing his hips against Thomas' bare backside. He stroked his arms, all the way up, and gripped his wrists just below the cuffs with his own hot palms, as if they were bound together. Two slaves to Fate, awaiting its lash.

Then he got hold of himself. Marcus dropped one hand to Thomas' jaw, holding him steady. "Don't move your lips," he commanded.

He brushed his lips over the firm mouth, the corners, tracing him with his tongue. Thomas clenched his fists in the cuffs. His cock brushed against Marcus' as it rose high again, bumping his groin.

When Marcus glanced down and raised an ironic gaze, there was a tight smile on Thomas' lips, even as his eyes burned with need. "You said my lips. You didn't say anything else."

Marcus pressed his temple to him. "So I did. I'm going to blindfold you now, dearest. I want your focus to be only on what's going on inside of you and what I'm doing. Let everything but that energy go and see where it takes you."

Thomas didn't reply, just stood still as Marcus fitted the blindfold over his eyes, unable to resist brushing his fingers over Thomas' fair lips one more time before he turned him, the heavy ankle chains having enough slack that he could make Thomas face away from him. Then he moved back, went to the weapon choices on the wall.

Let everything but the energy go, and see where it takes you…

That was what Thomas did when he painted. Thomas wondered if Marcus had knowingly provided him the right words to help him focus, give him something to hang onto. So much of the past hour had been instinct, no thought. There was no explaining why. As he strained to hear Marcus' movements, his footsteps, the portentous sound of something being retrieved from inside a cabinet, his body trembled with anxiety and arousal both. His cock was as stiff as it had been when Marcus was inside him, as if Marcus were still inside him.

Like a cruel poltergeist, the thought flitted through his mind of what his family would think. Jesus, would they be glad to accept he was "just gay" if they knew about this? No, he didn't want his thoughts to go there. But there it was. Rory or his mother, or even Celeste, seeing this. Was something wrong with him? Was he sick to crave this so much from Marcus' hand? He was about to be beaten, hard, and all he could think was *yes, please. Give me the release.*

His fists became knots, reflecting what was happening in his lower abdomen. Was this who he was? He couldn't even explain why he desired and wanted this to himself. Was he just fucked up? What if—

The whistle of air announced the lick of flame which sliced down his back in a diagonal line from shoulder blade to mid-back. He arched on a gasp.

"*Let everything go.* You're disobeying your Master. Let me see if I can't help bring you in line." Marcus' voice, stern, implacable, with a rough thread that told Thomas his instant response had aroused him.

Give me your pain…

The lash fell again. Holy God, what was Marcus using? The stinging provided a jolt, the weight of the tail like a knife cut that became a rope burn. But the pain released a wealth of inexplicable emotional and physical responses in him. It simply was and there was no defense against the reaction.

The tableau of broad shoulders, muscles bunching and rippling across Thomas' back, down to the tight flex of his buttocks and thighs, the curling of his toes, made Marcus harder, hotter. He was mindful of his strength, knowing the difference between administering pain for pleasure and pain for pain's sake. He was straddling the line with it, choosing different areas for each stroke, then going back, increasing the agony and the burn, but increasing something else too.

The wall beyond them was mirrored, so he could tell Thomas was getting closer to climax with every blow. His expulsion of breaths, the quiet grunts and trembling, the gleam of perspiration spreading on his smooth, firm skin, told Marcus what he'd always suspected, that Thomas was a sub to the hardcore, even if it was only with him. That exclusivity suited him just fine. If anything, it drove his lust to levels that could easily make him insane.

He closed the distance between them. Before Thomas could anticipate, Marcus laid the hand still holding the whip on his back, letting Thomas feel the texture of the braided weapon along with the fingers holding it.

When Marcus wet three fingers from his own mouth and thrust them deep between his slave's buttocks, he nearly growled with possessive satisfaction at Thomas' groan of response. His thighs strained against the manacles. "Jesus…"

He had raised red welts on his skin, so now Marcus made good on his promise. Touching his lips to those marks, he felt Thomas shudder at each touch of his mouth.

"I'm going to move back in a minute and do it some more," Marcus said gruffly. "Because of the pause, the initial blows will be more sensitive, so the first strikes will hurt. But instead of tensing, I want you to relax. Completely surrender to the pain, and to me. Can you do that?"

Thomas nodded, his head pressed hard against his arm. When he spoke, nerves made his voice shake. "Yes, Master."

"Good."

When Marcus moved his fingers in the tight channel of his ass, slow, steady, Thomas rocked against his touch. God, his cock was so hard Marcus ached. "You're so hot you'd go off like a volcano if I commanded it, wouldn't you?"

Thomas jerked his head in another nod. "Yes, Master."

"I love it when you call me that. When you know it's absolutely true, so I hear it in your voice." Marcus bent his head, soothed another welt and noticed Thomas biting down on the inside of his mouth as if to keep from crying out.

He'd changed his mind. He wanted to hear Thomas cry out. In fact, he wanted to hear him scream.

* * * * *

Marcus was moving around to his front. The heat of his body brushed Thomas, the whip circling his waist, the loop of it dropping low on his ass. When Marcus released his ankles,

Thomas heard some type of mechanism humming. His arms drew taut, his body stretching, his heels leaving the ground…

"Marcus—"

"Be still, pet."

His feet left the floor completely, his shoulders straining with his own weight. He was moving, a conveyor taking him…backward? It was hard to tell blindfolded, but his body came up against an uneven vertical metal surface, like the bars of some type of cage. His shoulder blades, buttocks and heels were against them.

Marcus took him back to the ground again, though he kept him stretched out pretty well, his toes barely brushing the floor. What contraption was he up against? Thomas couldn't remember what all was in the room, so distracted by what Marcus was going to do to him here.

"All points—head, shoulders, heels—stay right against these bars, pet. Or I stop."

Stop what? Then Thomas felt the whip tighten on his hips so he had to pull against him to stay in position. His mind as well as his body froze as Marcus' mouth closed over his bare cock.

Marcus had mouthed him there before, usually after he'd wrestled Thomas to the ground to tease him with the passing caress of his warm breath, the playful sandpaper stroke of his jaw in the late afternoon. But never like this, where Thomas felt the full blissful suction of his mouth taking him deep while Marcus held the whip in a tight grip compressing his ass cheeks.

He used the whip to move Thomas as he wished, making him have to focus on obeying Marcus' order against Marcus' own strength, which had the effect of stretching the rubber band reaction in his lower body even tauter.

When Marcus' tongue flicked on Thomas' head, he gasped. Though he gripped the chain with both hands to try to stay still, he couldn't. Oh God, there was no way… He tried to hold his heels and shoulders in a fixed position as Marcus had demanded, but his body swayed and moved.

"Master, I can't… Oh God…"

Marcus removed his mouth. With swift and ruthless functionality, he closed something over Thomas' chest, shoulders, throat and face and snapped it closed, then did the same across his legs at mid-thigh, leaving just his groin and head area free. It was a tight, constricting fit, making Thomas grunt with need. Marcus ignored him, went back to work on him with his mouth.

He'd put him in some sort of modified iron maiden. Under the blindfold, Thomas was locked in darkness, in the hell-born pleasure of that mouth, its slow friction up and down his length, the lash of the tongue, the addition of strong fingers, moving between his legs to find his rim again, teasing his hips into a jerky rhythm as Marcus slid several fingers back in. It was the knife edge of pleasure, cutting him deep, but he hung onto the blade with both hands, needing it too much to fall off, even if it cut him to the core and split him in half.

Marcus was performing long, slow glides along his length with his mouth. Rocking back and forth on his Master's fingertips, Thomas couldn't contain his response. He made a strangled sound of pain, an attempted warning, but rather than pulling back, Marcus took him deeper, hand curling on Thomas' hip, the cylindrical shape of the whip pressed against his skin, between hot palms and his damp flesh.

As Thomas jerked forward, jetting, Marcus took his release into the back of his throat with expert precision, growling his approval as Thomas cried out with the power of the sensation.

He rocked and bucked, hearing the rhythmic clank of the chains, their clatter against the iron maiden as he jerked. Somewhere else in the room, another slave released among the sounds of punishment and flogging.

Then as he was still shuddering, Marcus pulled his mouth away, removed his fingers. Rising, he moved behind Thomas.

Taking a firm, possessive hold of Thomas' throat with the whip hand, Marcus reached down, put those three fingers back in, thrusting, thrusting. Then a fourth finger. Then a fifth.

All five, stretching the way as Marcus slowly, inexorably worked his hand in until he was fully there, deep in the rectum, negotiating the curves, seeming to know Thomas' body inside and out. His fingers curled and he was fisting Thomas, his forearm between his ass cheeks, his wrist stretching him open.

Marcus had never fisted him before, but Thomas was so open to him in every way now that he trusted, didn't tense, let Marcus all the way in and suddenly found himself fuller than he'd ever been, an indescribable feeling. He thought he'd finished climaxing, but he found he was wrong. His cock jetted anew, as if Marcus was milking a reservoir Thomas hadn't known he'd had, taking the orgasm to a cataclysmic level.

Thomas' shout became a scream, all the thoughts in his mind exploding so there was nothing but this second in time, the universe stopping as everything else vanished. And even then Marcus was not done with him, still ruthlessly working him, keeping Thomas screaming, convulsing in the restraint of the iron maiden as if in a seizure.

He might have blacked out at last. He wasn't sure. All he knew was when he finally came down, he was hanging limply against the cuffs, his shoulder joints aching like hell. His mouth was open, lips stretched back to draw shuddering gasps.

He could hear at least two of the Masters murmuring to one another in appreciation of the stimulation to their own scene, could sense the eyes of the other subs on him. Perhaps envious. Perhaps counting themselves lucky their Masters didn't strip them so raw. But it didn't matter. He was Marcus'. There was no thinking about that, no choice.

His back stung like holy hell and his cock felt wrung out but all he wanted, desperately needed, was Marcus. Enough to beg.

"Please touch me."

He needed intimacy, the emotion behind the physical punch of what Marcus had just done to him.

Marcus moved around him, so close to Thomas' body Thomas felt the brush of his slacks against his knees. The whip slithered over his buttocks and fell to the outside of his legs as Marcus dropped it. Grasping Thomas' waist, a proprietary touch, he leaned in, pressed his lips to Thomas' throat just below his ear, then across his cheekbone. The forehead, the slope of his nose. The eyes beneath the blindfold.

Thomas stood in the manacles, vibrating, overwhelmed with words he couldn't say. Didn't know if he knew how to say them, because they contained all the heartbreak of the world mixed with its ephemeral joy. Waking to the aroma of breakfast when he was eight. Feeling the heat of the setting sun on his skin while falling asleep on Kate's back at ten.

Turning and seeing Marcus for the very first time. Moments too powerful to be contained by the human heart and therefore having a peculiar way of making the soul hurt, as if there was something to mourn in the midst of the happiness. As if happiness itself couldn't exist without shadows to define it.

Thomas parted his lips. He understood his Master would kiss his mouth when he desired to do so, and he was embracing his pleasure by staying still. But when Marcus at last cupped his jaw and pressed his mouth to Thomas' lips, he made a soft noise, a breath of sound into that welcome place, teasing Marcus' tongue, everything in him straining, needing. He never wanted Marcus to remove the blindfold, for truth and desire were easier to hold onto in this cleansing darkness.

"Yours," he said abruptly, a hoarse whisper into that heated cavern. "Always."

He'd said it earlier, in a different way. But he wanted Marcus to know it, to realize it was the one thing he *could* give him without reservation, no matter if everything else in his life took him away from the one thing he wanted above all others, even his painting. Actually, the two were intertwined, expressions of the soul without which he was just a shell. He supposed it was no wonder Marcus was a gallery owner.

"All mine," Marcus agreed, the voice of his soul.

ChapterTen

ﷻ

"Tomorrow's your day," Marcus had said on the way home. "Wherever, however you want to paint. Wherever you lead, I'll follow."

"Maybe hell will freeze over too," Thomas had responded with a snort.

They'd had pie and coffee at a late-night restaurant after they left the club, talked about other things. Art, New York... Hell, what they'd each been catching on television lately, but they'd stayed away from everything that happened at Detonation, both understanding that needed time to settle. When they got back to the cottage and Marcus finally went on to bed, with a mere reserved brush of lips and a steady, long look, Thomas had stayed in the living room, ostensibly to sketch.

In reality he was too wired.

He'd sat up a long time, thinking about everything that had happened. As he put together bits and pieces he'd barely been able to register while at the club, he'd come upon an unexpected revelation that turned him on his axis. Ironically, the twinge of hurt he'd felt at Marcus' reserve when they got home had been the key that opened the door. And what he'd seen in that new room had transformed the hurt into an altogether different reaction.

There at the end, Marcus hadn't been sure of himself. Of what was happening, where they were going. If he'd crossed the line, and he had, several times. It had taken Thomas back to the words of the first night, the ones he hadn't believed.

I love you. At one time he'd have given anything to hear those words from Marcus' mouth, when he'd been naïve enough to believe them. When Marcus had said it that first day, he hadn't wanted to hear it, had really brushed it off with no consideration at all, because the idea was ludicrous. However, sitting on the couch into the early hours of morning, he had to accept that it was entirely possible the words might be true.

The conflict and apprehension that came with that idea made him reckless, restive. He stayed awake, watching the sky start to light, and felt the desire build in him to sketch, create. Images crowded into his brain like rabid fans at a rock concert, vying for the lead singer's attention in a variety of provocative ways. He wanted to shout and rage and spin in circles, the way his mind was doing. He wanted to *go*. Needed to go and wanted to pull Marcus into flight right along with him. Have him beside him to tease and talk to, to share it all.

That was when he got up and made the coffee.

* * * * *

Someone was trying to wake him up, and it was barely light outside, a time no normal person would think of getting out of bed. Marcus cracked open an eye and saw the clock confirm the horrifying truth. "It's not even daytime yet."

"It's seven a.m." Thomas waved the coffee under his nose again, retracted it when Marcus narrowed his eyes to slits. "What, all that beauty will fall apart if you get less than twelve hours?"

"It might. My hair won't style right and my butt will drag the ground all day long."

"Your ass couldn't sag if you tied weights to it."

Marcus closed his eyes again.

A gentle stroking started in his hair, a thumb passing along his temple. It was a soothing caress that perversely made him want to keep drifting, even as it brought him to a waking state. It was almost like the faraway memory of a mother's touch, where all was well and forgiven, even before the sin was committed. Safety and peace.

Since Thomas never came to bed, Marcus suspected he'd fallen asleep on the couch. It wasn't what Marcus wanted, but he hadn't wanted to push. He knew he'd done way too much of that for one night. He still wasn't sure what had gotten into him.

Marcus opened his eyes once more to find ten minutes had passed during his half-doze, half-thought. Squatting by the edge of the bed, Thomas still held the coffee cup in one hand, keeping the aroma temptingly close while stroking Marcus' hair. When he saw Marcus' eyes open, Thomas gave it a tug. A smile grew on his face like lazy morning sunshine. "I almost wanted you to keep sleeping so I could keep looking at you."

"So what's the plan today?" Marcus asked, forcing himself to shift and sit up, take the coffee. Closing his eyes, he let the steam curl up toward his face to wake him in that gentle narcotic fashion that only coffee beans could accomplish.

"I'd like to drive around the hills some. Just wander, see what looks inspiring, set up somewhere. I've made up a lunch, some snacks, a cooler of beer and wine. Packed some of your books. Hid your briefcase and cell phone where it will take you much too long to find them."

"You know I run a very lucrative side career as a phone operator for Talk Dirty To Me. Someone might have an emergency."

"I can tip that cup and take your voice up a couple octaves. Permanently. Your career as a sex operator would be over."

Marcus smiled. "You sound in a different mood today."

"I am." When he opened his eyes, Thomas was regarding him with an odd expression. For some reason, Marcus didn't want to pursue what was going on behind the dark eyes studying him.

"I'll get dressed," he said.

* * * * *

They put the top down on the Maserati. It handled well on the small winding roads that took them deeper into the Berkshires, where leaves danced as they passed and wildflowers on the road side nodded. Marcus found there was a soothing greenness to it all, like the clasp of something familiar, important in its vitality in a way that couldn't be described, that he found vaguely disturbing.

Thomas finally had him stop on a rise, where a sloped expanse of field provided a rolling panoramic glimpse of the forest backdrop, followed by a layering of blue-green hills. Marcus followed him over a fence with the basket, blanket and book. In short order he had the blanket spread out, the basket serving as a side table for his glass of wine. Putting a book in his lap and tree at his back, Marcus set his music player at his side to softly play the programmed selections he'd downloaded for this trip.

While Thomas had packed all those things for his comfort, he paid little attention to Marcus' use of them now, moving about fifty feet away into the field, dropping several sketch pads around him. There he stood now. Staring into space. Shifting.

It was like watching a bloodhound, Marcus reflected. Thomas turning, making slight, erratic shifts that couldn't necessarily be predicted, seeking something no one else could detect. Abruptly he settled, dropping to a cross-legged position in the long grass, opening the sketch pad and letting his pencil take him to whatever place he tangled with his muse.

Marcus had heard of family members of artists who felt excluded, isolated during these times. Maybe he felt differently because of his reverence for what happened in these moments. When the end result captivated someone on a gallery wall, he knew he'd been present for creation, a fly on the wall.

That applied to Josh and some of his other artists. But with Thomas, it was as if his lover's creative awareness expanded and cloaked Marcus the same way the greenness of the trees did. The cool comfort of it was a buffer against the world, as if it guarded something sacred, untouchable in this field. He was a part of this, not just an observer.

Pushing away that thought and the other unsettling thoughts it raised, Marcus focused on his book and wine, letting the breeze and the quiet of the place close in on his mind, fill the troubled spots for awhile. That quietness had substance, for while it was present it seemed to have no room for uneasy ruminations.

Three glasses of wine later, he stretched out on his back, ankles crossed, one arm behind his head as a pillow, holding the paperback up to read. Until it slowly descended and he dozed.

Wheat-colored grass, flowing, rippling like a lover's muscles. Green flowing into the gold like interlocking fingers. Every part different, but all part of the whole. Birds spiraling and speaking in musical tongues, warbling, chirping, trebling, the piercing shriek of a hawk. The occasional rasping calls of the crows, or the surprise of an owl's hoot as the sun rose, giving warmth, a dying god's gift, the promise of renewal as it moved inexorably toward the autumn cycle.

Marcus opened sleepy eyes to find his lover's face very, very close. Thomas was leaning over him, one hand braced on the other side of Marcus' hip, his dark chocolate brown eyes studying Marcus' face intently. Leaning in further, he kissed him.

Marcus raised his hand, intending to cup his head, feel the short hair layered over his knuckles, but Thomas' hand closed over his wrist, held it in the air, his fingers straightening to meet him palm to palm. Then, slowly, Thomas eased both their hands back to the blanket as he shifted and laid his body fully on Marcus'.

Marcus felt a stirring in his lower belly, a need to change their positions, but he was too drugged by sun and the tranquility of their surroundings. He could lie here, for just another moment. One more. And one more.

"Christ, you're going to kill me," he muttered.

As Thomas' lips coaxed his open, his tongue was seduced into erotic play that had his vitals coiling. When Thomas increased the pressure behind the kisses, the passion behind them, his hand dropped to Marcus' throat, squeezing. Marcus responded somewhere between a groan and a feral growl of warning. Even as he did his body was lifting up, back arching to bump Thomas' chest. When he would have freed his hand, Thomas' grip slid to his other wrist, just caressing the pulse.

"Let me," Thomas murmured. "Just let me."

Marcus wondered if it was only incidental that John Mayer's languorous *Gravity* was playing, the words and tone so appropriate.

Thomas' hand cupped the side of Marcus' head, fingers sliding into his thick hair, caressing his scalp, capturing strands and stroking, his body rubbing Marcus' in the slow blues rhythm of the song, chest to chest. Groin to groin, hard, urgent need grinding against the same.

"Wait..." Thomas' whisper held Marcus where he was. When Thomas moved his hand, thumb tracing his ribs, then shifting between them to open Marcus' shirt, Marcus left his hand lying on the grass. Fingers half curled, but palm up, suggesting surrender. He'd never let a lover make love to him like this, but this was Thomas, his pet. His slave. Thomas could do anything he wanted to him, because Thomas was his. And yet, Thomas had never been as bold, as confident as he was at this moment, taking the lead.

Thomas moved his mouth to go for the throat, the sweet pocket of Marcus' collarbone, loosening his hold on Marcus' other hand as he cupped his jaw to trace vulnerable arteries with his tongue. He caressed the smooth muscle of Marcus' chest. The flat hard nipples, the silken hair that formed a thin line down the distinct aisle between the washboard abs.

He kissed, not down, but along Marcus' shoulder, teasing the line of bone and muscle there, rubbed his cheek along it. Raised his head enough to study it, trace it before he turned to stare into Marcus' eyes, peer there intently as he caressed that part of his anatomy. He moved his hips, a slow, dragging stroke, rubbing his turgid cock against Marcus'.

That was all Marcus could handle. His control broke. Seizing the back of Thomas' head, he rolled them, crushing his mouth to Thomas' as he reversed their positions. Thomas' hands clamped down on his ass and squeezed with bruising force, fingers teasing the crease. Marcus pulled at Thomas' waistband, wanting to tear his clothes from him, right now, now, *now*. Goading him to a sexual frenzy with those sexy touches and slumberous eyes, touching him as if he owned him, as if…

When Marcus rose to his knees, Thomas reached for his pants, opening them and reaching in, his eyes now dark and dangerous. It was the unexpected version of Thomas, the one who knew what he wanted and could have it, who closed his hand on the heated steel of Marcus' cock. Marcus let his head fall back on his shoulders at that touch and then he caught the hand that was threatening to make him spew at any moment.

"Take off your jeans, pet," he managed hoarsely. "Down on your side on the blankets." He caressed Thomas' throat, squeezing it deliberately, making it clear who belonged to whom. "I want to see the marks I left on you."

"You could see them long before last night," Thomas responded.

"Off," Marcus growled. "Now."

Thomas stood up on his knees, unbuckled his belt, slid it free and opened the jeans, shoving them down his thighs. Keeping his gaze on Marcus' face, he went down on his side.

Marcus wondered if the extent of his own need, the dangerous power of it, was in his expression.

"The shirt."

Thomas slid it from his shoulders, rising a bit. Reaching forward, Marcus caught the collar, damp with sweat from Thomas' nape, and pulled it all the way free. As he let it fall to the ground, the breeze folding it over, he traced the marks on Thomas' back and ass left from the flogger.

A still, heavy moment. As he touched him, Marcus wasn't sure of Thomas' thoughts about last night. But Thomas was looking up at the clouds shifting, his hand opening and closing on the grass next to him. "My back is sore this morning," he said, low. "I liked it. Liked knowing it was you who made it that way. It turned me on to remember it. And though you've been trying to keep your distance, you couldn't keep yourself from running your hands over them this morning, pressing down so I'd feel it. You liked it."

"I needed to mark you. Fuck you. Always feel like you're mine."

"I am. I've already told you that." Thomas curled his fingers around the belt he'd pulled loose, held it up to him, extending an arm whose the muscles were bunched with tension. "Mark me again."

God, Marcus didn't think he could get harder, but he did, just from those three words.

Thomas saw his reaction. He shrugged out of his clothes fully and then rolled to his stomach naked. Rising on all fours, he deliberately and provocatively adjusted his thighs open, raising his ass for whatever Marcus wanted to do to him.

Pure lean muscles, a farmer's tan, his head bent down, waiting for Marcus' bidding.

Lust could burn, Marcus knew that, but he'd never felt it threaten to incinerate every rational part of him, all the careful, civilized shields he had that made him a functioning member of society, leaving this savage, rutting Neanderthal. Whatever propelled his next actions, thought had been pushed away in favor of sheer response, reaction. He needed, wanted, couldn't hardly breathe with the power of it.

Doubling the belt over in his hand, he brought it down on Thomas' tight muscular ass, the left buttock. It clenched further. He put his hand on the heat of the mark, the heat of the man beneath, and his own hand trembled. He strapped him again, both cheeks, several strikes on the upper back, layering the marks still sensitive from the flogging.

When Thomas drew in a breath through his teeth, it pierced straight to Marcus' heart. Bending down, he laid his lips on one of the marks as Thomas' shoulders flexed under the caress, his head turning to see him, to brush his forehead with his jaw. Marcus threaded the belt under him and wound both ends over his knuckles. Bringing the strap in tight across the flat expanse of Thomas' lower abdomen, he trapped his cock against his belly and made Thomas groan from the punishing friction.

Then he wrenched a deeper groan from him when Marcus thrust in, using the hold on the belt to hold Thomas rigid as he rammed in hard and fast, pistoning, taking them both up.

Marcus needed it, needed it like air, needed some outlet for the emotion that clogged in his throat and made his heart want to explode every time he touched Thomas, kissed him, saw his smile and knew he would go. Leaving a growing emptiness that might dull in time but would kill Marcus in the end nonetheless, because one simply couldn't exist without the other half of one's own body.

Marcus let go of the belt and dropped, covering him and taking hold of Thomas' cock, gripping the pulsing weight of it. A second later Thomas was coming, falling to one elbow. Marcus followed him down, face pressed to his neck as he worked him, felt his seed make his own hand slick, his knuckles wet. Thomas' ass muscles clenched him like a fist as well, making Marcus wish he could stay hard forever, make Thomas come like this forever.

"Don't you hold back on me," Thomas rasped. "Let go."

Marcus tightened his fist, his other hand on Thomas' hip, clutching as his hips slammed against his ass, making Thomas feel the full size of him, pushing against his thighs, driving him to both elbows now. Marcus rolled them to their sides on the blanket so he could keep pumping him, moving Thomas with the force of it, his hand dipping to grip his buttock and open him up further.

"God..." As Thomas gasped it, Marcus set his teeth into his shoulder, letting go, jetting into him.

Sometimes when it was like this, Marcus felt every sensation as if his senses were completely open. A space of total spiritual clarity, no shields against the detailed sensations of earth, air, fire and water moving around him. Of flesh, Thomas' thighs against his own, the quiver of his buttocks, the beautiful way his shoulders and chest lifted and expanded from his breath, reminding Marcus of a butterfly slowly opening and closing his wings. He could almost imagine the patterns and markings on Thomas' shoulders, the network of veins.

A man's soul was a fragile thing when this close to the surface, very much like a butterfly. Maybe that was why time seemed to stop in these moments, as if it was a protection. Once the winds of time resumed, that butterfly would be blown away, as if blasted by the backdraft of a semi. It had to have time to sink back behind the protective wall of flesh and mental shields.

Some of those walls were built thicker and tougher than others, which perhaps explained why it came so easily to the surface for Thomas, whose shields seemed almost dangerously transparent at times.

Marcus molded Thomas protectively into the curve of his body at the thought, holding him securely about the waist, still inside of him as they both got their breath back. Since he had his arm under Thomas' head, Thomas brushed his lips on the smooth inside skin of his forearm.

"Wow," he murmured. "That was something else."

Marcus rose on one elbow then, sliding from him and tugging him to his back to look into his face, needing to see his eyes. "Yeah."

Thomas grinned. "Poets. Both of us." He cast a glance to the right. "What do you think?"

Marcus moved his attention to the series of sketch pads propped up in tented fashion so Thomas could show them to him, the pages anchored with clips against the breeze.

The one he'd been working on was this meadow, a bird's eye view. In the ripples of meadow grass there were the hints of sinuous bodies and limbs. The grasses followed the contours of muscles, as if the meadow held the memory and impression of past lovers.

As remarkable as that coincidence was, the next sketch cinched it. It was the curved back of a man as his male lover knelt in intimate posture behind him, the suggestion of a butterfly's markings upon his back even as one of the creatures fluttered into the picture with them. Just one…

Had he internalized Thomas' work in his dreams, during his doze? Logic told him he had, but something deeper, the thing that tumbled inside of his heart with such strength whenever he looked at Thomas, suggested something different. It was a feeling so strong it could be the essence of joy and fury. Perhaps the two together created passion because it was the struggle to give and take all at once. It told him he would never know if the idea had come from Thomas' mind or his own.

Maybe what Thomas painted was the melding of both of their desires, fears, dreams and fantasies. Maybe that was the real reason he'd never felt excluded when Thomas painted.

"What do you think?" Thomas' tone was studiedly neutral, almost making Marcus smile.

"I think the more free rein you give your talent, the more you're going to amaze the world." Marcus glanced down at him. "But if you want me to go on record, my official comment is I should be able to get a decent commission off them."

"Asshole." Thomas shoved at his chest and Marcus laughed, let himself be pushed away. He lay on his back quietly then, watching Thomas draw his jeans back on, zip them up. His farm boy negligently left the top button open as something in the sketch pads caught his attention. He hopped one-legged toward them, putting on his shoe, grabbing up his pencil. Marcus swiftly moved to retrieve his wineglass from the sure punt it would have experienced, since Thomas paid no attention to what was between him and his goal.

"Use me for sex and then you're done with me." He murmured it, though, not wanting to distract Thomas' concentration. He dressed, found Thomas' shirt, folded it and added it to the pack of their belongings.

When he turned to survey the scenery of the lower level of the field they were in, he found himself eye to eye with another occupant of the same meadow.

"Thomas."

Thomas glanced back, half irritably, and then did a double take. "Where did they come from?"

"I haven't the faintest idea. I think we were a bit distracted when they arrived."

The large black and gray male goat, complete with curved horns and a shaggy long coat, considered Marcus with an interested eye, or rather his books. He began to nibble at the edge of one.

"Hey, quit that." When Marcus raised a hand to shove him away, Thomas made a quick warning noise.

"Not a good idea to push around a male goat. Just take it away, don't push at his face. He'll take that as an invitation to butt heads with you." Marcus heard the laughter in his lover's voice. "And as hard as your head is, I still suspect you'll lose."

"Oh, geez. What is that stench?"

"Him. Male goats piss on their own faces to make themselves more attractive to females."

"You made that up."

"Did not." Thomas came to his side and gazed down the slope past their tree where the rest of the herd, about twenty-five females and a few kids, late summer arrivals, were alternately grazing or studying the two men. Marcus was easing away from the male goat, giving him a baleful look as the goat continued to root at him. His lips captured a piece of shirt and Marcus pulled back.

"This shirt costs way more than they get for goat meat, you pushy bastard," he pointed out. The goat stepped forward, making a guttural noise followed by a snort. "Thomas—"

"Is that panic I hear in the great Marcus Stanton's voice?" Thomas touched his back and burst out laughing when Marcus jumped as if jolted by electricity. "You didn't seem at all intimidated by Kate."

"She was a cow. I know cows. Pigs. Chickens. Goats are…not supposed to be this bloody big. His fricking head reaches my chest."

"It's all right. I'll protect you." With a droll look, Thomas dipped his hand and squeezed his buttock.

"I am so going to kick your ass in about ten seconds."

"If the goat doesn't scare you into scampering back to the car."

"What the hell are you doing in this field?"

When they both turned, Marcus noted that Thomas automatically took a step in front of him. Though to Marcus' way of thinking the goat posed more of a threat than the man, it still gave him an odd feeling to see Thomas do it so instinctively. Enough that he quelled the urge to shoulder him aside for the same reason.

They were quite obviously facing the farmer and caretaker of the goats, for a group of the herd began to move up the hill at the sound of his voice, their steps quickening as if expecting he would be bringing them something interesting to eat. The male goat pushed past Marcus as if he weren't there, making him jump again and leaving a malodorous wake that had his eyes watering.

The man was heavy set, in his fifties, wearing jeans stained with straw and dirt. There was a once white undershirt under his open unbuttoned shirt. His eyes were suspicious.

"We're sorry, sir." Thomas turned and scooped up his sketch pads, drawing them under his arm and extending a hand. "I'm Thomas Wilder, and this is Marcus Stanton. I'm an artist. We're visiting the area and I'd picked this spot out for sketch work because of the view. It's beautiful land."

The man studied the extended hand, didn't take it. "Well, you're trespassing. Get off my land the way you came. If I come back here in ten minutes and find you, I'll call the police." His gaze moved deliberately to the mussed blanket, the picnic basket. "What you do in Boston or whatever big city you came from is your business, but I don't want it happening on my property."

"Well, you didn't have a rest area available for us to molest teenage boys," Marcus said, his jaw tightening.

"Marcus," Thomas hissed, taking his arm. Thomas knew that fired-up look, knew this was entirely the wrong place. "I'm sorry sir," he said quickly. 'We should have asked permission before coming onto your land."

The farmer nodded, a muscle in his jaw twitching in an ironic mirror of Marcus' expression as he turned around and strode away, his herd ambling after him. Some of them returned to their grazing, savvy enough to know it wasn't dinnertime.

"Why didn't you just apologize for breathing his fucking air while you were at it?" Marcus snapped, turning to the blanket and picking it up. He shoved the basket away before the male goat could start investigating the contents or nibble on the wicker on the outside.

"We're on his land. We weren't invited. It was my fault. I'm used to home where I know all the farmers and they know me."

"It's your fault for being gay?"

Thomas set his teeth. "This isn't about that. Not everything is about that. He's just tired of tourists trespassing."

"It isn't, hmm?" Marcus rolled the blanket into a ball, stuffed it into the duffel, shouldering it and gathering the picnic basket. "What do you think he would have done if we were Joe and Suzie Q sitting here, doing exactly what we were doing?"

"He still would have asked us to leave the property," Thomas said stubbornly.

"Maybe. But I'll lay you odds if he did, he'd have chatted them up a bit. Or as he headed back up that hill, he'd get a nostalgic feeling, thinking about him and the missus and their younger days. Sowing wild oats and all that."

"Getting in his face doesn't work. You don't change people by living up to what they think you are."

Marcus lifted a brow. "Have you tried that line on yourself?"

"What do you want, Marcus?" Thomas snatched the basket from him, slammed it to the ground. "Not everyone accepts people who… like…"

Marcus rounded on him. "You searching for a word, pet? Maybe you should be listening more closely to your brother. Homosexuals, gay, fags, rump riders, fudge packers, whatever makes it into something nasty and obscene."

The male goat had retreated to his herd. Despite the fact he applauded the goat's wisdom, Thomas held firm, his brows drawing down over dark eyes that he wasn't even aware were snapping with their own fire. "This isn't about some farmer's veiled insult. The way you're acting—that's about you and me."

"Really? You fucking think so? Artists are such brain surgeons, aren't they? Two seconds ago, I was inside you and you were inside me. Two seconds later you're bowing and scraping and asking for forgiveness for being here, for fucking being who you are. Just like you are with your family. As if it's something to be ashamed of."

"It's not that. You know my mother, her faith—"

"Don't." Marcus' voice was low and vicious, and it brought Thomas up short. "When I've come inside you, lain on you, felt you tremble, felt that silence between us that has everything…you don't think God is there? If there is a God, I've felt It then, and I know you have too."

"Marcus—"

Marcus snarled at him, hefted the blanket and turned on his heel, striding across the field, his back stiff and straight. He went right through the herd. If Thomas hadn't been so angry himself, he would have been amused by how the goats parted before him like Moses.

"Son of a bitch," he muttered, following. But Thomas kept his distance as Marcus went up the opposite slope, letting him work off his mad. And maybe because he couldn't bear for the conversation to continue. They had been…everything had been perfect, just as Marcus said. Was he right? When he'd heard the farmer, all Thomas could think about during his stumbling apology was that the farmer had seen him fondling another man, and how that would color his perception.

But Marcus didn't understand. He lived in New York City, where prejudice was simply swallowed in the sheer volume of multinationalism and multicultures, where it could squeak and irritate but rarely roar and destroy. Where ridicule might come from one person, but not become a wall of reaction from the whole community that could impact his family.

Maybe coming out into the country hadn't been a good idea. He'd sought the familiar, but it was the familiar when he was playing the role of the hardware owner's son, in a community where he'd grown up and they knew him. Where his sexual preference might be suspected because of his looks and absence of a steady girlfriend, but never openly stated.

It wasn't familiar territory when he was with Marcus. He looked at the stiff lines of Marcus' shoulders and knew, as he'd known from the beginning, that this was a mistake. It would always be this way. But he had three more days before he had to walk away and God help him, Marcus was right about his lack of pride. When it came to Marcus, Thomas would take the remaining days because he couldn't have any more after that. This was borrowed time as it was.

He'd accepted that, would let it tear him apart. But for the first time, after his revelation of last night, he thought about it from Marcus' viewpoint. If Marcus was right, if Marcus did…love him, should Thomas be so selfish to take these three days? Could Marcus be as vulnerable as he seemed to be at times, ways Thomas had never perceived him to be before? If he took the full week, what would that do to Marcus when he walked away?

Geez, he was losing his mind. Marcus had a life that normal, average people who stood in grocery store lines, staring at the glitzy covers of magazines, would envy.

A bleat distracted him. A straggler. Then Thomas heard another note to it, a note of distress, and came to a stop.

"Marcus."

Marcus thought about ignoring the call. Actually contemplated driving away, leaving Thomas here, or at least making him think so. He'd drive just over the hill, around the curve. But knowing Thomas, the Southern redneck streak would kick in and he'd probably pick up a rock and destroy the Maserati's paint job.

No, that was more his style, not his gentle Thomas. Thomas would stand there and look like an abandoned puppy, making Marcus feel like shit.

He stopped, expelling a frustrated blast of air and turned to find Thomas waving to him from a copse of trees, an urgency to his gesture that obviously had nothing to do with their argument.

Marcus jogged back down the slope and was halfway back over the field when he figured out Thomas had gone to one knee by an animal lying on his or her side on the ground. It was a goat. A goat whose stomach was distended far above her head, obviously in labor. She paid no attention to Marcus, bleating piteously.

Thomas' hands moved over her belly and between her back legs, his brow furrowed. "Something's wrong. She's dry as a bone and worn out, but she's dilated. We have some of that lubricant in the basket?"

Marcus pulled it out and Thomas poured jelly over his hand and up to the elbow, greasing his fingers up. "Easy girl. I know, Mama. I'm trying to help. Easy there."

Before Marcus could blink, Thomas had eased his hand into her.

She heaved, cried out and tried to get up, but Thomas held her down with one arm. Marcus dropped to one knee and put a tentatively calming hand on her head.

"Just one baby, feels like…and alive, which is good," Thomas said, his eyes distant, intent on what he was feeling. "Go get the farmer. Tell him we've got a kid trying to come out feet first with the head thrown back. She's been in labor awhile. If he doesn't have a vet who can get here on the double, tell him to bring his gun and something sharp enough to cut her open."

Marcus was on his feet at the first command, but at the second instruction, he turned, his brow raised.

"If we can't get the baby around, the mother's suffering," Thomas explained impatiently. "She's really tired. She's been at this awhile. We'll have to take the baby out and end the mother's pain. Hurry. Fast as you can get to him."

"Where?" Marcus had no idea which direction the farmer had taken.

"Over the side of the hill we were on. There was a gate. Should lead to his barn and a driveway. Follow the goats. Oh...did you bring any nylon cord?"

Marcus blinked, then wordlessly reached into the basket and pulled out several pieces from the bottom. Thomas gave him an absent wry smile, pulled out a pocket knife and began to cut a length he apparently needed. "Hurry."

Marcus complied and took off.

It was one of the most difficult abnormal presentations for a kid, Thomas knew. He reached back in, grunting to hold the mother down with the other arm again as he relocated the baby's body, followed the neck until he reached the head. He was in up to the elbow, and the mother was making guttural, heartbreaking noises.

"Okay, Mama, I know. Hang in there." Thomas made himself tune out everything, just like he did when he found the flow of what he wanted to create on canvas.

He'd brought a lot of calves and kids into the world when he was younger, when the farm had raised both in greater numbers. His father had him helping with difficult birthings when he was as young as ten because his dad had quickly learned Thomas had an intuitive sense in his fingers, coupled with his lack of fear about going in. It had led his parents to the mistaken belief Thomas might consider vet college.

Even then, Thomas had been amazed by that canal, meant to bring forth life. He was awed to reach into the chamber where the baby had grown and now wanted to burst free, sucking his or her first gasp of air, taking the first breath as an individual. The miracle of birth was the miracle of destiny, of divinity, of change and continued growth. As an artist, Thomas was drawn to it as much as to his blank canvas.

He could draw the baby's head forward to the legs, but as he feared the little creature was too weak to keep it there. Its head flopped back before he could get a good grasp on the legs to help pull it free.

He pulled out, relubricated both of his arms and made a noose out of one of the nylon pieces. "I know, sweet girl, I know," he crooned. "No, we won't be cutting you open today. But he's a big city boy and he was panicking. Had to give him something to do. Yeah, I'm lying a little bit, but you're going to be okay."

He went back in. The trick was to get the head lying forward on the legs, the way the baby was meant to come out. Thomas took the noose in with him this time and felt around to try to get it over the kid's head. He closed his eyes, using only his sense of what was going on at the tips of his fingers, vaguely registering the mother's sounds of exhaustion, the snug fit of the birth canal, the smells of birthing and struggle.

"Come on, you little bastard. Get over there." There. He had it. He brought the head forward again and positioned it on the front legs. He tightened up the loop and kept tension on the pull, then caught the feet with his other hand, pulling on both the rope and the feet at once.

"There you are. It's okay, Mama. Here he comes." The mother heaved again, as if sensing the shift in the tide. The mother's contraction squeezed his forearm painfully against the wall, and then he was out, helping pull the little body free, giving the exhausted mother additional strength. One more heave and the baby landed in his lap.

"Ah, look at you..." Stripping the shirt he'd put back on during his argument with Marcus, he cleaned out the nostrils, wiped the doe-like face. Mama was already struggling up, trying to reach him. "Easy girl. Easy."

It seemed to have gone quickly, but Thomas saw he was soaking wet from his own sweat. The waistband of his jeans and the front placket were stained with fluid from him and the mother.

And thank God, Marcus and the farmer were there, the farmer with a kit of supplies and a bucket of water to which he was adding a dollop of Karo syrup for the mother. "There, Phyllis, good girl. A hard one this time, but you did all right."

They'd been coming up the hill when the baby had landed in Thomas' lap. As Marcus saw Thomas phase back in, the clouds clearing from his gaze, Marcus recognized it as the same expression he had when he emerged from painting.

He was covered in goop and even now didn't seem cognizant of it as he worked in tandem with the farmer to do all the postoperative things that were apparently needed for a new kid and the mother. Thomas was using newspaper to clean off the kid's body while the farmer tended to Phyllis. And within ten minutes, miraculously, the weak kid was trying to get to his feet. Thomas steadied the little one, though he didn't let go. Apparently the birth had been too difficult. It was going to take this one a little longer to get his land legs.

Marcus looked at those slimy hands, the long fingers against the body of the new baby, new life. He'd never really given thought to what the essence of a farmer was. As he looked at Thomas, he saw a man close to the earth, who in his ironic simplicity understood the complexity of life and all its cycles. Who needed to be close to those cycles in order to be the artist he was. It was reflected in his work, as well as in the way he did everything, even loving Marcus, or protecting and supporting his family.

Thomas and the farmer were exchanging stories of past birthings, all the farmer's earlier hostility just evaporated as if it had never been.

When he touched Marcus, Thomas made him feel things he'd never thought he'd trust anyone enough to feel. This just made him more blown away by the truth of that, and more afraid than he'd ever been that Thomas' mother was right. That the worst possible thing for someone like Thomas in the long run would be someone like Marcus.

"We'll help you get them back to the barn," Thomas was saying. He was turning the kid, now wrapped in a towel, over to the farmer. Bending despite the farmer's protests, he used his younger back and muscles to lift the mother goat in his arms. As he straightened, he shot Marcus a tired grin, twisting something inside of him.

Feeling at loose ends, Marcus gathered up the farmer's kit and their own belongings.

The farmer nodded. "Once we make sure this one's had his first meal, my wife was just about ready to have me sit down with her for lunch," he said. "I'd like for you to join us, you and your friend. You'd be welcome." He gave Marcus a glance that told him the invitation wasn't necessarily so steady as far as he was concerned, but manners were manners.

"We'd love to," Thomas accepted.

Oh hell, Marcus thought.

Chapter Eleven

ꟃ

Cathy and Walter Briggs sold their goat cheese to a select but highbrow clientele, including Zabar's in New York City and several of the gourmet shops in Stockbridge, where the Boston symphony spent its summers.

Thomas had mixed feelings about accepting the lunch invitation. He'd done so automatically, for that was simple courtesy, giving the farmer the chance to repay a kindness himself. Thomas just wasn't sure what Marcus thought of it, or if he'd have preferred to get away as fast as he could.

Given the state of Marcus' temper before they were interrupted by Phyllis the Goat's labor crisis, he was a little concerned that Marcus would make the farmer regret his offer.

Instead, Marcus helped Cathy fill glasses with ice from the basement freezer while Walter showed Thomas where he could wash up, loaning him a shirt and baggy pair of work pants. Cathy took his clothes to wash out and put on the line to dry. They'd apparently recently built the house to replace an older one which had been infested with rot and termites. Walter was still working on wiring for things like the washer and dryer.

Marcus was sincerely complimentary of the carpentry work, most of which had been done by Walter with the help of neighbors and other family members. He particularly remarked on the arched moldings over the windows and the architecture of the vaulted ceiling, making Thomas relax somewhat.

The house had a nice feel to it, a good space, and Thomas could almost imagine it as an artist's Berkshire hideaway, particularly when Walter took him upstairs and showed him the rolling hill view from the windows and described the layers of fall color that would become a vibrant mural as the seasons cycled.

"Your friend looks more comfortable than I'd imagine him to be." The farmer chuckled. He gestured down below, where Marcus had joined Cathy in a trip to the hen house, apparently to collect some eggs.

Thomas watched Marcus take the basket from her, kneel and reach into the first opening in the henhouse, a smile flashing across his face as she apparently instructed him on the proper way to do it. Like most women faced with that smile, Cathy blushed, even though Thomas was sure they were talking about something entirely innocuous. Whatever Marcus said next made her laugh. She put a hand on his shoulder, motherly.

He was sure Marcus would have noticed her stiff knees from her gait, and, being Marcus, he'd volunteered to get down and learn how to pull eggs out.

Walter cleared his throat. "I stomped on you boys a little hard. You should have asked, but even so... We get a lot of them through here, city folk who think like your friend. Like they're better than us and want to change everything they think we should be and feel, without ever knowing who we really are."

"Marcus is a good man, with a generous heart," Thomas responded quietly, glad for the reminder of it right before his eyes, and a little ashamed at the necessity for the reminder. "On some things he just refuses to consider any option other than a confrontation. Like he thinks he always has to make it a fight, or always be ready for one, I guess."

"Sounds like a man who's been in enough of them to make him that way," Walter observed matter-of-factly. "Let's go get something to eat. My backbone's gnawing into my stomach."

Lunch included goat cheese spread on thick slices of homemade wheat bread, a bowl of blackberries and lemonade made just that morning, a fresh and simple meal that made Thomas think of home and his mother's table with a pang.

Cathy was a comfortable conversationalist, asking about Marcus' gallery, Thomas' art, his family in North Carolina. She'd positioned Marcus at Walter's right, her at his left, and Thomas next to Marcus. Thomas wondered if she'd had a momentary lapse of good sense, putting Walter and Marcus catty corner.

"Does your family live in the area, Mr…?"

"Just Marcus will do, ma'am." Marcus took the bread plate from her, passed it to Walter at her nod. "My family's in this room."

He didn't look up from his plate where he was applying goat cheese to the thick slab of wheat bread, but Thomas felt like he'd speared him through the gut with the butter knife. So matter-of-fact and easy.

Was he saying it just to deflect Cathy's questions about his background? He'd surely deflected them often enough when Thomas asked.

Cathy darted a glance at Walter, but he was just as studiously focused on his own meal. "Walter, those eggs should be ready in about five more minutes."

He shrugged. "We're in no hurry. Thanks to Thomas, I shouldn't have to worry about any more birthings today. I just hate I didn't find her earlier. We haven't had a morning birthing all summer. They almost always happen late afternoon."

Conversation turned to their interests in Stockbridge, the Boston symphony. Marcus spoke primarily to Cathy, though he shifted his glance politely to Walter now and again, to all appearances relaxed in his surroundings. Marcus could handle almost any awkward social situation. But just like at the club,

Thomas could feel there was something off, thrumming hard under the surface.

When he glanced down, he noticed Marcus' hand was resting on his knee in a tense half curl, his forefinger rubbing a half-inch track on the fabric. Back and forth. Back and forth. It was obvious, if only to him, that Marcus was finding this a very difficult situation.

But they weren't at the beach or sitting in a coffee shop where most of the people were of the same sexual preference, or expected them to be. Thomas couldn't reach out to offer the brief touch of comfort he was almost certain Marcus needed at the moment, some sense Thomas was in his corner.

Good Christ, he wasn't going to grope Marcus. What was the matter with him? Lifting the glass of iced lemonade to his lips, Thomas reached over and laid his free hand on Marcus' beneath the table. If Walter glanced over at just the right angle, he'd see it, but if he saw it, he saw it. Closing his hand over the top of Marcus', Thomas let his thumb rub Marcus' palm. Gave him a slight squeeze.

At one time, he'd known Marcus' moods better than his own, but how Marcus reacted to certain things could be unpredictable, which was why Thomas tended to be cautious about public displays. In this case, however, Marcus' fingers shifted, coming up between Thomas' to overlap his fingertips, pressing down more tightly than he'd expected, as if drawing some elemental reassurance.

Then, just as quickly, Marcus released him and leaned back, stretching his arm over the back of Thomas' chair as he spoke to Cathy about the symphony. When he hooked his fingers in the slats, his thumb stroked a small spot in between Thomas' shoulder blades.

"How long you boys been together?"

This from Walter, a question that seemed to take even Cathy by surprise. A flash of alarm crossed her face before she apparently processed that he'd asked it in a neutral, not argumentative, tone.

"I met Thomas about four years ago," Marcus said, glancing over at him. "We were together for two and a half years after that. He's just visiting right now, working on some new projects. He wanted to go out today and paint in a natural setting."

"How did you meet?" Cathy asked, a tentative smile in her eyes.

"Thomas was sharing some of his work in a little co-op hole-in-the-wall I periodically checked out. The owner had an eye for good talent, but little money. There was terrible lighting in the place. It was a wonder anything ever sold. Of course, it probably helped some of the work get bought."

Thomas' unexpected touch had steadied Marcus more than he wanted to admit. He didn't want to feel this absurd squeezing sense of panic sitting at the table of a pleasant, average enough farmer and his wife. So now, to keep the boat of his emotions rocking on an even keel, he glanced at Thomas—scooping up blackberries with his spoon, his face in profile, his quick smile at Marcus' joke—and remembered that first meeting.

* * * * *

Thomas had brought in his own lighting. He'd run a drop cord and just finished duct taping it to the wall so it would be out of the way. He wore secondhand jeans and a T-shirt for some BBQ place Marcus had never heard of. As he straightened, he hitched up the jeans, giving Marcus a brief impression of a very nicely shaped ass, then he flicked on the mounted light and angled it over the painting.

Based on the way the man was dressed, Marcus would have assumed he was a maintenance guy, except for several things. One, Richard couldn't afford a maintenance guy. Two, there were flecks of paint on his fingers, as well as the ones he'd missed on the nape of his neck where the hair was shorn away with all the finesse of a sheep shearing. Finally, the dead giveaway—the careful way he arranged the light as if it mattered as much to him as the arrangement of a blanket did to a mother pulling the edge of it up around her baby's shoulder.

The painting had some rough elements. But Marcus knew he was looking at phenomenal talent that wouldn't be raw for long. Or whose rawness might even be a key element to how captivating it was. As he took a closer look, stepping forward, his sharp eye caught it. It was deliberate, that layering effect, and doing it deliberately took more control and ability than doing it by accident.

The subject matter was a man sleeping. There was a poignant loneliness to it, his hand hooked on the iron rail of the headboard, holding it as if holding onto someone, the other hand out of view, somehow managing to convey without crudity that perhaps in half sleep he was touching himself, wishing or dreaming it was the hand of a lover. The tautness of the arm gripping the headboard was intriguing, the build toward release it conveyed.

Often Marcus didn't know what it was about a piece of art that told him it would sell, that it had something special that would make it irresistible to the specific buyers he would contact about it. But he had a gift for it that made him take risks on work his peers wouldn't touch. When his gaze shifted back to the artist, he lingered, studying him with the same intent scrutiny.

Thomas hadn't had any polish, no style whatsoever. Just a straightforward man with a shy smile and not an ounce of artifice to him. Surrounded by all the highbrow urbanity of New York City, he didn't try to fit in, nor did he try to be James Dean and pretend he didn't care or go out of his way to appear different. He was simply himself.

In time, Marcus would learn the city hadn't chewed Thomas up and spit him out, because he staked out his piece of ground and held it. He listened, he learned, he adapted, but he didn't lose who he was. And the restless demon in Marcus' soul was attracted to that. As much as Thomas thought otherwise, Marcus knew it wasn't Thomas who'd been the moth drawn to the flame, but him.

When his "maintenance man" at last noticed him, he'd done a double take. Marcus was so used to it he usually didn't even acknowledge the reaction, but suddenly he was glad he had something to capture his attention. He made a point of never getting involved with the artists he represented, but he wanted the man *and* his art fiercely, immediately. They wouldn't come as a separate package anyway. With true talent, it never did. He knew it because his own soul had been crafted out of the art created by others, after all.

"It's rough," Thomas had said self-consciously, an amateur's mistake, downplaying his own work. Marcus shook his head, stepped forward, close enough to smell soap and aftershave, and to hunger to taste. He cocked his head, appearing to study the painting, and part of him was.

"You can tell the artist became enthralled with the beauty of the model. He stopped, left his palette and touched him in his sleep, which would explain that smudge of paint on his shoulder there, and on his hip. Wouldn't it?" He gestured.

He could feel the young man's attention on him, and it was as if he could already feel the touch of his hands. "Yes," Thomas said at last. "Most people don't get that at first. But I think they sense it."

Marcus turned to face him fully then, only a few inches between them. Thomas' dark eyes coursed over his mouth, then he looked away, the lashes sweeping his cheeks.

* * * * *

"He begged me to take on his work. Embarrassing really, but I had a weak moment."

Thomas choked on his piece of toast, shot him a glance. "Not how I remember it."

"And how do *you* remember it?" Marcus gave him a curious, open expression, all innocence, while the hand on the back of his chair caressed, stroked the small spot between Thomas' shoulder blades, a gesture that spoke as clearly as words. *Do you remember how I had you in my bed that very night, fucking your brains out?*

A dull flush started creeping up Thomas' neck, but he covered it with a cough and glanced at Walter and Cathy. "Cathy, could you pass the lemonade, please?"

Walter was studying them, and now his gaze touched on Marcus' hand, which had shifted to rest on the juncture between Thomas' shoulder and neck. For once, Thomas tried not to worry about what was going through the man's mind and focused instead on the way it felt to have Marcus treating him with such easy affection and intimacy. Like Andrew and Ben.

Walter had touched Cathy as they moved around the kitchen together, a hand to her waist, a brush of thigh, almost unconsciously. Squeezing his arm, she'd gestured to him to show Thomas the upstairs. When he'd grunted, given her a surreptitious pat on her generous bottom before he complied, she'd swatted at him with a spoon.

"Well, if you've got more to do, you're welcome to use my property for it." Humor crinkled Walter's eyes. "And if another of my girls goes into labor and you can handle that between sketches, that would be appreciated."

"Can I see what you were doing?" Cathy asked, stealing a glance at the sketchbooks Thomas had stacked neatly on the side chair.

Thomas cleared his throat. "I'm an erotic artist, Mrs. Briggs."

"Really?" A mischievous grin crossed her face, dropping twenty years from it. "Well then, I definitely want to see it. If something in these fields can inspire those kinds of thoughts, then maybe I'll join Walter on his morning walk more often."

"Cathy." Walter chuckled, waved at Thomas. "Bring them to the table, let's see them. I'm sure it's the closest we'll ever to get to them, what with the prices they charge at those New York galleries."

Thomas hesitated. Marcus squeezed his neck. "You've nothing to be concerned about, pet. They're brilliant, even in pencil."

"Cathy did some painting in college. She even turned her hand to it again these past couple years, since we've hired summer help."

"Walter, I'm sure he doesn't want to hear about that. It's nothing like what he's doing."

Walter snorted at her, rose and disappeared into their bedroom. He brought back a small framed picture, a detail of a purple wildflower Thomas was sure proliferated here in the spring.

"Walter, put that away. That's like a crayon drawing next to what this boy does, if his work is shown in New York."

"Pfft." He arched a brow at Marcus. "She painted it for me when I was sick with pneumonia in the hospital and couldn't be here to see 'em. So it's not available to your fancy gallery at any price."

Thomas laid his sketchbooks facedown on the table to reach across Marcus and carefully balance the small piece in his palms. "This is silk painting," he said, impressed. "You used batik wax on the resist lines. Vibrant color. Cathy, this is really good."

As she flushed with pleasure, Thomas added, "And you created it out of love. That's all that matters." He handed it back to Walter. "I don't blame you for not wanting to sell it. You can't set a price on that. My mother got magnolia blooms and floated them in a bowl of water for my brother when he was recovering from his accident. Not sure he cared much about it, but just knowing she did it for him when he was scared was enough."

Marcus rose. "I'm going out for a cigarette."

Thomas gave him a quizzical look. When his head was turned, Cathy reached for the sketch pad and drew it over to her place before he could stop her, though Thomas reached out in automatic reaction. She gave his knuckles a light smack and winked.

Marcus stopped at the door and turned, eyes narrowing as she and her husband bent over the sketchbook silently. Thomas waited, tension in his shoulders. It was the one of the embracing bodies, etched into the waving pattern of the grasses. He'd done it in graphite, since the charcoal was a more difficult medium to do on-the-go renderings without smudging, but Thomas had tremendous talent with the pencil and Marcus knew where he was going with the ultimate work would be clear.

Cathy tilted it up to the light from the window. "I bet you do these as easy as I breathe. I never could do people. But look at them, Walter. It's like you can feel the wind on your skin, and this is just a sketch. You'll have to drop us a postcard when you have a showing, Thomas. I'd love to see what it all looks like finished. Walter can take me to see the Rockettes like he's been promising."

It was a homey picture. The three of them together, sunlight making Cathy's tidy brown hair gleam. Thomas was watching her, and Marcus could tell he was just dumbfounded. He'd told Marcus he'd never shown his work to his own mother or father. Never been invited to do so. Not since they'd found out his preferred subject material.

Marcus stepped out, closing the door.

Thomas looked over his shoulder at the soft click, watched Marcus move past the windows and disappear around the corner of the house.

"He doesn't smoke, does he?" The question came from Walter.

Thomas shook his head, took the sketchbook back from Cathy when it was offered. "No. I think..."

He wasn't sure what made him say it to the two sitting before him, but the words seemed to tumble free without thought. "I think this reminds him too much of what I'll be going back to at the end of the week. My family. North Carolina. A fiancée, of sorts."

"A fiancée?" Cathy's brow furrowed. "But..."

"My family needs me. She needs someone...undemanding, to take care of her." He said it quietly, zipping the sketches into the portfolio. "We're friends, she and I. If I can't be with Marcus, it doesn't really matter. And I can't be. My mother's Catholic and where we live..."

He put the portfolio down on the floor carefully as if it were glass, because suddenly he had to control the overwhelming urge to pick it up and throw it. The raging frustration rose like bile in his throat, fast and dizzying. "Daralyn. She needs someone. She doesn't know...but she knows I don't love her like that. She's delicate, just needs someone to..." He shook his head. "I shouldn't be telling you this."

"You probably haven't been able to tell anyone else, have you?" Cathy said softly. "It's in your face. You've got enough misery in those brown eyes to break a mother's heart. Sometimes it's easier to tell a caring stranger than the people who are too close."

"What kind of girl wants a man who doesn't love her?" Walter asked, brows drawing down.

"A girl that's been abused by the people she should have trusted most," Thomas said flatly. "Her dad and her uncle. They shared her, since she was six."

"Oh my God." Cathy put her hand to her mouth.

"The father's dead, the uncle took off a few years back, so she's got no one but my family. My mother took her under her wing at fifteen. She thinks it's divine destiny. Daralyn worked in the store one summer and I'm the only man she trusts. She doesn't want…a normal relationship. Ever. She wants a friend to keep her company, protect her. And I do love her, like that. I can do that.

"My brother's in a wheelchair. I know he could do more, he's milking it, but if I'd been there… And my father, his heart attack. My mother feels… And I'd…"

He couldn't go on, was appalled he'd just blurted this all out. The sensation of being unable to breathe was closing in, but he had to say the last words because they were the ones erupting into flame in a line from his gut to esophagus, the ones he'd also been unable to say to anyone.

"And I'd rather cut out my own heart than hurt Marcus, but he's the only one I think will be okay. I mean, look at him. He'll never lack for someone to love him. He's got money, power, everything he does turns to gold. How can I give myself that when my mother is still crying herself to sleep, and the bills are coming in?"

"So is the issue your family needing you, or you not being able to believe someone like Marcus can need you as much?" Cathy asked quietly.

"Maybe he needs you more."

Thomas turned, surprised at both comments. Sometime during his diatribe, Walter had risen, gone to the sink. Now he leaned on it, chewing on a toothpick, studying Thomas. He'd given the sketches a cursory look, obviously uncomfortable with the male/male subject material, turning them quickly over to Cathy, but now there was nothing evasive in his expression. Wryly, Thomas was starting to get the feeling that still waters ran deep in Walter, that his slow talking and watchful demeanor masked a man who did a lot of thinking.

"Your family trusts you enough to show they need you. That tells me they know they can count on you, that they're pretty solid about your love for them. Yeah, that one outside is pretty and put together like one of those fancy ads, but did you notice how my Cathy has a spot of juice on her dress? Her hair's a little messed up today too."

"Walter Briggs." She began to push at her hair, but he straightened and caught one of her hands, stilling her. All the while keeping his gaze pinned on Thomas. "When you know you're worth loving, you can be a little imperfect. Hell, look at me—a lot imperfect. It makes all the difference in the world when you believe someone loves you enough that they *don't* overlook the spot and the messed up hair. They just add it to the things about you that make them love you all the more.

"He's too damn perfect. You were thinking he left this room because it reminds him you're going home and what you're going home to. Maybe." Walter shrugged. "But maybe it's also that he's looking at something he thinks he's never going to have. He said his family is in this room. That's you and only you. And you're not staying. So he's got nothing but those perfect looks that can't in a million years make him believe he deserves a good-hearted man like you."

"But I can't abandon—"

"Young people don't listen. They think it's all about the grandiose gesture." Walter made an impatient gesture of his hand even as Cathy made a soothing noise in her throat to calm him down. "That's all about ego. You don't have to abandon anything. It's about doing what's really hard, day to day. Someone willing to put up with tantrums on both sides and say, 'you're both my family, and we're going to make this work'.

"You don't think he'll stick with you if it gets that messy. From where I'm sitting, it appears you have your heads up your butts. You're as afraid to bring him into your world because it means he might really decide you are some hick, as he is to ask to be invited, for fear of being rejected."

He settled back against the sink, pointed at Thomas with his toothpick as if it were the finger of God.

"Get over it, the both of you. If you do, maybe you'll be sitting at a breakfast table together like me and Cathy forty years from now, thinking you're the luckiest people ever been born."

Chapter Twelve

ꕤ

Marcus knew Thomas had been surprised to see him actually smoking the cigarette he'd bummed out of a pack Walter left on a barrel outside the side door. It was something he hadn't done in awhile, but the acrid burn had suited his mood. Marcus also knew that his foul mood was spawned more by watching Thomas with Cathy than watching him with Walter.

It mattered to Thomas. His mother's love, her approval. The sense she was behind him. *Do my parents love me?* The Achilles heel that every child was infected with at birth like a virus, and spent adulthood trying to overcome in order to be who they were meant to be.

They stayed at the rental house for the next couple days, with no plans for excursions. Marcus encouraged Thomas to spend the time roaming the property acreage for inspiration. Apparently today Thomas had enough crowding into his head, for he'd never got further than the outside deck. He'd sketched most of the morning and part of the afternoon, sometimes standing at the rail, sometimes sprawled over the lounger.

Now he was sitting on the deck, letting his feet hang down off the side of the deck, using the middle railing to prop his sketchbook. As he tore off sheets, he used several empty coffee mugs he'd taken out there to guard against them being blown away by the breeze.

Marcus stayed inside, working in the living room on phone calls and paperwork, but positioning himself where he could watch Thomas through the glass doors.

Thomas was listening to a track by Staind. While the insulated glass blocked out all but the reverberation, Marcus felt the poignant, hopeless, visceral anger to it. Totally fucked up except when you got to be with the person who made it all unfucked up. But you could spend a life functioning while being fucked up. Until it killed you.

Thomas would be going home in a day or two, and maybe that was good. The shadows kept rising. Marcus didn't have time to get trapped in a morbid fog. He had gallery showings…things to do. Plenty of opportunities for…something. He sat there, staring out the glass at Thomas until the cell rang, breaking his concentration.

"Julie, how are you?"

"I'm stalking your fine ass, of course. Heard you're in the Berkshires, and guess what? Girlfriend crisis, so I am too. What do you think of…"

* * * * *

Julie Ramirez ran a theater near Marcus' gallery. He'd been her first patron, now one of many. He'd come to his gallery on a Saturday, dressed casually to pull some receipts, and seen the short, voluptuous brunette hauling out a load of dusty boxes too heavy for her to lift and too bulky for a hand truck. With the same powers of persuasion she'd apparently used to get the landlord to sign a five year, dollar-a-year tax write-off lease on the building she intended to turn into a community theater for the arts, she got Marcus to volunteer his whole afternoon to her.

It wasn't until a week later she learned he was the affluent gallery owner up the street. By then, he was impressed enough with her commitment, her background in a theater family and her willingness to stick her neck out that he was more than willing to hand over a check. Which she cheerfully and unabashedly hit him up for as soon as she learned that "he was mega-loaded".

At the end of that first day, however, he'd sat on the edge of her truck, covered in dirt and cobwebs, his hair yanked back and held by a rubber band they'd found in the debris. She'd leaned back on her elbows and given him a thorough look. "Jesus. Someone who can be that filthy and look that pretty needs to be beaten with a stick. Can I buy you dinner for helping me? Offer you sex? Dinner *and* sex?"

Marcus grinned, leaned back on his elbows next to her, his shoulder brushing hers companionably. He tried not to be a tease with women, but they were so easily, physically affectionate, sometimes it was hard to stay out of range. Just because he preferred a man for sex didn't mean he didn't like the touch of a woman's hand, their different texture and pressure, the rich emotional language they conveyed so easily.

And because they'd been bantering all day, he put a little stretch into the leaning back, drawing her attention to his upper torso, the strength of his arms, biting back a chuckle as she snuck a quick glance at his groin area.

"All right." She punched his shoulder. "You're doing that on purpose. Don't be such a tramp."

"I'll take you up on dinner, but I'm afraid I'm going to pass on the sex. I'd be a disappointment."

"Oh." She digested that. He was prepared to add more clarification if needed, something to salve the ego, but then she brightened. "Oh, for Christ's sake, you're a *man*. It's *sex*. Can't you close your eyes and pretend I'm a guy? We can turn off the lights and I'll talk deep, like this." She mimicked what he thought sounded like a frog with a bad cold. "You can even do me from behind, but I'd kind of like you to get my preferred orifice, if you don't mind."

It startled a laugh out of him, and he'd been delighted with her a hundred ways since. When he met Thomas soon after and introduced them, Thomas had been equally enamored of her in no time.

Marcus considered her a true friend, not only because she was honest and forthright in a brutal, New York way, but carried a heart of gold that came straight from her home state of Oregon.

Unfortunately, Marcus knew while she had a limitless heart for friends and her theater, she'd always fallen for the type of guy who would take advantage of her nature. As a result, at thirty-five, she'd never been married. She still dated, but not too seriously, telling Marcus she'd decided she preferred to be a pathetic hanger-on to the platonic physical affections of gay men and their enjoyable company than fucked over emotionally by a straight male.

"Besides," she'd told him later, after he'd met Thomas. "I keep hoping you'll come up to my place and just stand next to my bed naked and hold the vibrator. Now if you *and* Thomas did it…hmmm…like Thomas would hold me on his lap…he'd be naked too, of course, and you'd do the vibrator thing, and it would be like a real fantasy. I wouldn't have to worry about the stilted 'I'll call you' bullshit conversation. You guys would even fix me breakfast. Those pancakes you make are *so* good."

When Marcus mentioned Julie's birthday was coming up, it was Thomas who said, "Let's go give her that fantasy she wants. If she chickens out, we'll buy her a pizza from the Greek place around the corner she loves."

That was after they'd been together for a year, when Thomas had become more adventurous, always within the protective shadow of Marcus' sophistication. But Marcus still hadn't expected him to suggest it. It had been one of those remarkable confluence of events. The right mood, the right timing…

They'd shown up with a bottle of expensive wine, pancake fixings and a vibrator, giving her exactly the fantasy she'd requested, something even now she said she couldn't believe she'd been seduced into doing. Even though she simultaneously claimed it was one of the most intensely sexual experiences of her life.

While Marcus teased her ever after, claiming that was just a sad commentary on her love life, he had to admit it had been quite a charge for him and Thomas as well.

As she'd said, they *were* guys, and even though women were not their preferred bed partners, watching Thomas sit behind her on the bed shirtless, holding her arms, had made Marcus hard in no time. He'd let loose his full Master nature upon her, commanding her to spread her legs, taking the vibrator in deep as she undulated. Thomas' arm muscles tightened to hold her as she pulled against him in response, his eyes fastened on Marcus' hand, his attention coursing down Julie's naked body to Marcus' equally bare one…

When she fell asleep at last, curled between two male bodies, another fantasy, they gazed at each other in the dim light, wanting each other fiercely, but not moving. At least until she mumbled, "Guys, guys—you're going to impale me". She'd clambered over Marcus like a cranky sister, but then placed her hand on his back in quiet wonder as he turned Thomas, took him from behind. Marcus had felt the pressure of her palm, her caressing fingers as his back flexed under her touch. Felt her stillness as Thomas groaned, as they both found their climax.

They'd had a fleeting worry that the night would somehow make things awkward, but the next day, Julie was Julie. She gave them both hugs, her eyes wet, told them it was the best present she'd ever been given, and asked, "Where are my damn pancakes?"

* * * * *

Thomas glanced over his shoulder as Marcus came onto the porch, phone still in hand. "You remember Julie Ramirez?"

Thomas slanted him a grin. "Uh, yeah… Let me see. Isn't that the woman who runs the theater across the street from your gallery?"

"The same." Marcus gave him an equally droll look and spoke into the phone. "He thinks he remembers you. Vaguely." He glanced back at Thomas. "She happens to be in the area visiting a friend and wants to know if we'd be willing to take them to a place where the men aren't interested in women. They want to dance."

"Only if groping is allowed."

"You got that?" Marcus paused, chuckled. "She says only if you're willing to follow through and make it worth her while."

"Spoilsport." Thomas grinned more broadly. When he did, the agonizing fist around Marcus' chest loosened, just like that, and things felt better. "Sure."

It told Marcus he wouldn't send Thomas away one moment sooner than he had to. Every agonizing moment was worth it, just for that smile. He was lost. Fucking gone. That was it. Just lost, taken over by the soulful brown eyes of a North Carolina farm boy who somehow knew how to reach inside people and read their hearts, while being as unworldly as a duck living in a pond. It was the genius of his art. He explored the universe of people's desires inside and out, while he'd never hardly been anywhere but home and New York City.

It made Marcus remember what Julie had said, when she'd found out Thomas was gone for good. She'd sat next to Marcus on the edge of her stage that was set up for the evening's presentation by some as yet unknown playwright.

Marcus didn't know why he expected something normal, the usual empty platitudes. He'd even steeled himself for them, but then she looked steadily at him a moment and said, "You fucking dumbass. Why aren't you going after him, hauling his butt back here? He's the one for you, Marcus. He was *it*. You've got to get him back, okay? Because you're only going to be half of you without him."

*****

When they got to the nightclub in Connecticut, Julie was waiting. She went right for Thomas and pulled him down to her for a hug while Marcus went to park the car. "Hi, Thomas," she said softly, holding him. "It's so good to see you."

It twisted Thomas' heart in his chest, the unqualified acceptance. She pressed her face into his neck. "I've missed you. He's missed you, dammit. So much. Where did you go? Have you told him you missed him?"

"Yeah." *In a way.*

As if she heard his thought, she held him tighter. "Have you told him *you* missed him? With your mouth? Not just your penis?"

Thomas grinned despite the squeezing pain the words caused. "Aren't you ever going to learn tact?"

"Tried that once when I was eight. It didn't work for me."

Marcus was coming across the parking lot. Thomas saw a man completely in control, the Maserati in the background, his mouth firm and sensual, hair loose on his shoulders, body moving with a grace that fairly screamed how good he was at sex.

Julie sighed. "You know, I see him every day, and I still can't keep from drooling. He could just walk up and down the street and people would throw money at him all day long just to look at him. Do you think you'd doubt his love if he looked like me?"

"What?" Thomas pulled his attention away to give her a startled look.

"When you love someone, you tell them. Unless you're afraid they don't feel the same way. You and Marcus were together, how long, and neither of you ever said it?"

"He did. Recently." Thomas stopped, pressed his lips together.

"So the problem is you." Julie's eyes twinkled, but her mouth remained serious. "What I'm saying is, what if he looked like me, an ordinary, average-looking person who has bills and a toilet that needs fixing? Who, like most of us, starts each morning thinking, 'can I get out of bed and do all this without totally fucking up?'

"Who fights with vanity pounds, looks at the gray sneaking into her hair and thinks, 'God, I'm only thirty-four.'" She nodded toward Marcus. "He may look like someone who stepped out of the pages of some romance novel, but he's real, Thomas. So real that when you put the fantasy and the reality together, you have this fascinating, complex person with a lot of layers, which makes him good at burying the things you don't want to see."

"You've thought a lot about this." It made him uncomfortable, to hear an echo of Walter's observation in her own.

"The two of you matter. A lot of us don't get the chance at what you have."

Thomas looked away. "Your toilet needs fixing?"

Making a face at him, she pinched his arm hard enough to make him wince and shoot her a narrow glance. "Yeah, Mr. Avoid-the-Issue. That one crossing the parking lot is useless when it comes to plumbing. But I let him tinker with it awhile just to watch him bend over and wear a T-shirt." She pushed away from him as Marcus made it to the curb.

"I can't believe you wasted one of your hugs on this riffraff. Are you trying to convince him to feel sorry for you and come fix your toilet?"

"Well, since your firm ass isn't getting him to stay, I figured maybe the offer of being up to his elbows in sewage would."

Thomas noticed she softened the words by putting her arms around Marcus and giving him an equally generous hug. It tugged at his heart painfully again, the reminder of the life he'd left when he left Marcus. He'd spent over a year in North Carolina convincing himself he'd never fit in New York, that there'd been a lot of moments he'd been homesick. Yet with one hug, Julie had reminded him he'd also found a place there.

Pushing those thoughts away, Thomas followed Julie's gesture toward a woman approaching from a separate part of the parking lot. She wore a simple black cocktail dress, more suited for a country club than the nightclub scene, and her brown hair was pulled back from a too-thin face. She hesitated as she was passed by two fairly demonstrative couples. The men were joking and making passes at each other. At her nervous glance, one of them called out, "You lost your way to your bridge club, sweetie?"

"Ellen." Julie waved her over and linked their arms. "Ellen, Marcus and Thomas. M&T, Ellen. Let's go dance our asses off. And since I've got a lot of ass," she wiggled it for emphasis, "that's going to be a lot of dancing."

"Julie, are you sure? That man who just passed me, he wasn't being very nice…"

"He was just being catty," Marcus assured her. "If he bothers you again, Thomas will bitch-slap him and send him home crying."

Ellen managed a small smile. Julie hugged her shoulders, giving both men a significant glance. "C'mon, sweetie. Let's go have some fun."

* * * * *

The club was noisy and festive. It didn't have the glitzy polish of a New York City

club, but the men there were in high spirits, intending to dance, drink, have a good time and find some action. Julie led the way through the crowd, hauling Ellen by the hand.

Anticipating the open-mouthed stares that usually attended Marcus' entrance into such a place, Thomas nevertheless didn't realize he'd tensed up until he felt a hand settle around his waist, a firm palm over the curve of one buttock. Marcus' other hand latched into Thomas' shirtfront to haul him in for a firm, open-mouthed kiss that was hot, possessive. His fingers caressed Thomas' nipple, his thigh pressing firmly against his groin.

"Mine," he murmured in his ear. "Got it?"

As he started to ease back, giving Thomas an even look, the fist of tension was replaced by something just as fierce, but a lot more welcome. Before he could think too much about it, Thomas clamped his hands on Marcus' hips and brought him back against his body to return the favor, plundering Marcus' lips, lashing him with his tongue.

"Same goes," he muttered against Marcus' mouth, even as he slid his hand between them, boldly cupping his lover's stiffening erection in the discreet press of their thighs, covered by the crush of people around them and the darkness of the club, the flashing lights.

When he drew back, Marcus' eyes were blazing green. "Christ," Marcus swore softly as Thomas' fingers slid away. "You're going to pay for that."

"I hope so, Master." Thomas gave him a quick grin, slipping away as Julie bounced back between them. She seized Marcus' hand as the DJ ripped open a fast tune.

"My God, a trip back to the eighties. Paula Abdul. I was so afraid it would be that hip-hop mess."

"You can hip-hop. I've seen you." Marcus forced himself to tear his eyes away from Thomas' broad shoulders flanking Ellen as he guided her toward the dance floor.

"Yeah, but I've never been able to do it with a straight face." Julie shouted in his ear to be heard as they got closer to the speakers blasting the music. "Not since I realized hip-hop in fast forward can look like someone who needs to go to the bathroom hopping up and down, grabbing their crotch."

Laughing, Marcus grabbed her by the waist and swung her onto the floor. "We'll see if we can't get him to do some Ricky Martin after this. Something sultry."

"Oh God." She rolled her eyes. "If you go all Antonio Banderas on me, I will wet my panties."

Thomas found Ellen a good dancer. The trick was getting her to relax, so he kept it easy, stayed attentive, worked through a few steps with her. It was hard not to get distracted watching Marcus laugh, twirl Julie out and back into him again. He held her up against his body in a couple *Dirty Dancing* moves to tease and flirt, but of course Thomas didn't do the same to Ellen. Not only was she too uptight for that yet, his body's reaction to watching Marcus would make it downright embarrassing.

That kiss was still making his lips tingle. Paula Abdul was denying that it was her man's wealth or looks that got her going, that it was just something indefinable about the way he loved her. Though he'd never be such a geek as to own up to the idea that an eighties dance song was speaking straight to his soul, it didn't change the fact that Thomas felt as if she was delivering the gospel down from the mountain, packaged in a sultry rocking beat.

Marcus *was* beautiful, he *was* rich. Hell, he was the prince of anyone's fairy tale. But it was deeper than that. Julie had caught it as well. *Good at burying the things he doesn't want you to see…*

Somewhere behind the impossible green of Marcus' eyes, the truth lay. It was closer to the surface in these three days than it had been during their almost two years together. Possessiveness. Violence. Flashes of sorrow and an almost desperate hunger.

I love you.

Did he? Was that what Thomas' own burning ache was, like his soul was being scalded every time he thought of being without Marcus? He'd stopped painting at home, like an addict going cold turkey, because it was that feeling that made him paint himself into a near fatal frenzy. As if by losing himself in his art, Thomas could be pulled into the canvas and become it, never again to emerge into the desolation of a life that couldn't include Marcus.

Emerging into that reality after an intense art session was as stark and cold as being born, leaving his soul naked, shivering, defenseless. So sensitive to light and sound, his mother's innocuous call to come to dinner made him want to pummel something organic with his fists until it was a mass of blood and bone.

Julie called out to Ellen, got her to laugh at their antics. Thomas pulled her up close and spoke into her ear so she could hear him over the noise. "Let's show them how it's done. All you have to do is trust me." He winked at her, making her flush, and spun her into a fast turn, a modified ballroom step that he turned into a dip and then pulled her up before she could get worried and stiffen up.

Dancing was the first thing he'd ever done that shocked the hell out of Marcus, who assumed that no Southern boy with his background would dare to be a good dancer. But his mother and sister loved to dance, and his father wouldn't. His mother had taught him all her favorites before he was ten, and he and Rory would take turns impressing her with moves they incorporated into it, acrobatic feats, using Celeste as their test victim.

Rory gave it up when he joined sports and the other boys called him a fag, the ones Thomas pointed out sat on the sidelines at school dances while he and Rory got to turn, twist and gyrate with any girl they wanted to ask.

Back then, he'd covered any doubts about his behavior with comments like that. His intimidating physique that could lay out anyone who got into his face about it didn't hurt, either. However, the basic plain fact was he loved to dance. Dancing with or near Marcus…it didn't get better than that. Marcus' grace at dancing was unpracticed, powerful and unselfconscious.

But Thomas had a few moves of his own. He gave Marcus a challenging wink now and went straight into a full pull-through, making Ellen shriek as he took them into the bebop era to the cranked up Stray Cats tune. Bless the eighties for its unapologetic ebullience, tinged with the naïvety of a teenage virgin trying to appear worldly. By the nineties all that was over, of course.

"Want to try something even better?" he shouted at Ellen. She nodded, smiling, flushed with the exertion. He realized now she was a very pretty forty-something. She had a few appealing lines, more gray in her long brunette hair than he would have expected. But she had lively green eyes that, when sparkling with nervous laughter, made the shadows and sadness markedly evident in her face less so.

He transitioned into a two-step with the switch to a song from the *Urban Cowboy* soundtrack, catching his hand gently on the back of her neck as he turned them, holding her hand at his waist and adding some fancy heel-toeing that had Julie hooting and other dancers calling out encouragement.

"Oh, it's on now," Marcus called back. When the next song started, a sultry Latin number, he launched into the tango.

Thomas couldn't hold a candle to him on Latin moves, and Marcus knew it well enough that it could be called cheating. But watching Marcus dance Latin, who the hell could possibly care? Marcus was just so easily sensual…

When he pulled off those decidedly macho sequences, his expression going all serious and stern, moving around Julie, to all appearances holding her bound to his will, Thomas couldn't even think about dancing. Marcus finished with a quick throw that brought her up against him and slid her down to a resting place on his thigh, his hand low on the small of her back.

Ellen was chuckling. She rose onto her toes and spoke into his ear breathlessly. "I think we're going to have to surrender on that one."

She didn't know the half of it. Trying to take his mind off the desire to get Marcus alone somewhere and rape him, Thomas gave her a mischievous grin. "How about a nice, slow shag then?"

A giggle escaped her at the double entendre. She put her hand to her mouth, embarrassed, but he caught her fingers and whirled her into another dance.

* * * * *

A half hour later, Julie collapsed in a booth and accepted the rum and Coke Marcus brought her. He sat down next to her, knee bumping hers companionably. "Wow," she said. "I haven't danced like that in forever. And look at them—still going. Oh Lord, the *Macarena*. If they burst into *YMCA*, I'll have to go back out there."

"It's a provincial gay dance club, dearest. Count on it." Marcus gave her a smile, tapped his Shiraz against her glass.

"So." She cocked her head. "You're even deeper gone over him than you were before he left. That must suck."

Marcus lifted a shoulder. "Relationships move on. I'm glad he at least wanted to visit. Ah...*Christ*. You little bitch." He stopped, squirmed, stuck his hand down his shirt to grapple with the ice cube she'd dropped down the front of it.

"God only knows what's been done in the shadows of this booth, probably ten times already tonight," she said dryly. "I don't want to be up to my knees in bullshit as well."

Marcus lunged at her, ice cube in hand. Shrieking, she knocked it out of his grasp and sent it skittering over to the next table, earning a startled look from the group of men there.

"Straight girl." Marcus waved apologetically. "Loss of motor control due to all the unavailable testosterone in the room."

Satisfied, they went back to their conversation. He narrowed his gaze at her. "Revenge is best served cold, anyway. No pun intended."

She smacked him in the arm. "Asshole."

"Busybody."

"So why not just chain him in your secret dungeon room this time? Surround him with canvases, take away his clothes?"

"Are you trying to turn me on?"

"When it comes to Thomas, it doesn't take much. It never has. Being around you two is like being around an erotic film fest, all that barely suppressed sexual heat. I've burned out vibrators in one night after hanging out with you two for an hour."

"There's a visual I'm not sure I needed."

"Oh, shut up." Julie settled back, laying her head on Marcus' shoulder and subsided, sipping her drink.

"You really need to get yourself a man and stop being such a fag hag." He made his tone light, teasing, but she rolled her head around and looked up at him, brushing his chin briefly with her fingers.

"You know that night, why I never tried to get you to make it an annual event, like any sane woman would have? Hell, weekly. It's the way the two of you did it. So in concert, as if reading each other's thoughts. Then the way you looked at one another. If you don't have that, and you really want it, then it's too hard to be around bare naked displays of it too often—no pun intended."

She smiled. "That vibrator's the best lover for me right now. I haven't even gotten close enough to the real thing to have my heart broken, not really. The guys who hurt me, they hurt me because they didn't love me. When your heart's broken by someone who loves you back, that's the only heartbreak that's worth the risk. There's always a chance it will come back to you even after the heartbreak. If I can't have even a chance at that, I'll settle for something I know up front is fake."

Marcus wasn't sure what to say to that. He watched Thomas try a new step with Ellen. She was the instructor this time. She laughed as he took the step, made it his own and gave it a little more panache.

"Sometimes I think when he walks out, that'll be it. I'll just…break. Never pull it back together again. It's like somehow he crawled in and replaced all the shit I'd been using as glue, and now…" Marcus stopped, realizing he'd never spoken such thoughts before. He'd barely acknowledged them in his own head. He shook his head. "Never mind."

"Marcus." Julie put her hand over his, her face reflecting her surprise. He pulled away from her touch, ostensibly to pick up his wine. "You aren't giving up, are you?"

Wistful piano notes and a sax accompaniment introduced Aretha Franklin's *Ain't No Way*. Her poignant opening line, about loving someone who wouldn't let her give him everything that she was, filled the club. The song was so powerful a stillness spread into every corner, pushing the fast dancers to the shadows and bringing lovers to the floor.

Marcus shook his head. "Hell, no." He downed the rest of a whiskey he'd bought to chase the Shiraz. Rising, he offered her a hand. "Help me go do a partner switch. I don't want to cut in on Ellen and leave her hanging."

Ellen had looked uncertain when the slow song started, but Thomas drew her into his arms and was doing a slow mix of waltz and two-step movements with her, holding her as she relaxed in his arms. The music was far too loud for talking, so she'd just put her head on his shoulder and swayed with him. To make her smile he'd been making short comments in her ear about the other dancers.

He'd noticed her wedding ring. Though it was on her left hand, the way she touched it so often, as if for reassurance, he was willing to bet she hadn't lost her husband to divorce.

"Mind if I cut in?"

He'd tried to take his mind off Marcus for about two minutes, but here he was, larger than life, the pulsing heat of the club as intimate a cocoon as being wrapped together in a much smaller space.

Ellen looked between the two of them. "Why no," she said, smiling uncertainly.

Julie stepped neatly in front of Marcus and took the hand Thomas had released, pulling Ellen over to her. She winked. "Sweetie, in a place like this, when someone asks to cut in, you need to realize he could be cutting in for either partner."

"Oh. Oh." Ellen flushed. Thomas reassured her with an easy grin and a quick stroke of her hair as Julie tugged her into female arms. "This song's too good to waste. Let's you and me dance. You can close your eyes and I'll whisper to you in Gaelic. You can pretend I'm a really short Liam Neeson."

As Julie maneuvered her away, Thomas shifted his gaze to meet Marcus'. His smile faltered at the edges. They'd danced in clubs before, but usually to something fast. He'd actually never slow danced with a male lover before and wasn't exactly certain how to go about it.

Marcus moved closer, his arm sliding around Thomas' waist, fingers hooking into the belt loop of his jeans as he took Thomas' other hand and brought it to a reverse position on himself. Thomas felt the shift of Marcus' hip and the muscles above it as Marcus moved them into a slow, easy rocking step, allowing a gentle bump and shift on the downbeat. He rested his other hand on the side of Thomas' neck, his palm curving around so his fingers played beneath the collar of Thomas' T-shirt, caressing the skin damp from the heat of the dancing.

It left Thomas with his other hand resting naturally on Marcus' biceps, moving with him. Since he'd mainly done this type of intertwined dancing with women, adjusting or working out leads should have been difficult. However, Marcus simply took the lead and Thomas just as easily followed it. As they made the slow turn, Marcus' thigh shifted so it pressed between them. His hand drifted lower, sliding into the back pocket of Thomas' jeans, pressing him more firmly against him. Thomas' left leg brushed Marcus' hardening groin.

"If you try a dip, I'm punching you out." Thomas attempted to dilute the intensity of the moment.

Marcus didn't respond. Not in words. He held Thomas closer, until they were moving as one creation, managing it so easily Thomas noted some admiring glances, but it was a vague awareness. Marcus stretched his other arm high around Thomas' back, holding him with a grip on his opposite shoulder so his head found a natural resting place alongside Marcus' jaw and temple, his lips close to that tempting throat.

Eventually Marcus brought his other hand out of the jeans' pocket to cover Thomas' on his hip, while Thomas slid his free arm around his lower back, holding him, moving in the same rhythm, feeling him against him, heart to heart as they turned, stopped, turned again. Marcus' body guided him, arms holding him, making Thomas achingly aware of his touch.

Here in front of everyone, where sex wasn't an option, Marcus had gone for the more devastating tactic of intimacy, the slow possession of Thomas' senses. He turned his face, mouth brushing Thomas' cheek, and Thomas' fingers reflexively convulsed on his hip.

It *was* sexual, but it wasn't about sex. Not with Aretha pleading for her lover to just let her love him, so she could give him all he needed. She begged for him not to tie her hands. When Marcus' hand tightened on his shoulder, Thomas knew he was listening to the words as well.

"Everything you hold in your arms is yours, pet," Marcus murmured. "Everything."

Thomas pulled his head back, intending to kiss Marcus senseless, anything to shut him up, but Marcus wasn't letting him get away with that. And Aretha wasn't going to shut up, either, building to a wailing crescendo capable of wrenching his guts out.

Marcus caught Thomas' head, cradling the side of his throat with one hand, holding him with a thumb placed on his lips, a light but unshakable collar. It put them eye to eye, turning and moving to the soulful song, unable to hide from what was in each other's gaze.

One more day. They had one more day together like this.

In four days, Thomas had gotten inspired enough to sketch out a solid dozen ideas. He could say it was caused by the removal of the dam he'd built inside himself, but he knew that was bullshit.

He'd been a talented artist. But Marcus had opened the well inside Thomas to connect to a muse whose inspiration was pure magic, drawn from what the heart of love and life was all about. What Marcus was to him. Whenever Thomas was immersed in a creating session, it was as if he was somehow guarded by the explosive yearning that being part of Marcus' existence kept switched onto high volume.

Even before Marcus, his muse had been inspired by the belief that there was something like what he felt for Marcus out there. So while his art hadn't needed Marcus before he met him, Marcus had taken him to higher levels, capable because of the way Marcus made Thomas feel. Not just about Marcus, but about himself. About anything, everything. There was no settling or going back from that.

If he left Marcus, his muse would die again. Thomas finally realized it. The muse was a two-way street. She drew from his heart as much as he drew from hers. Instead of an expression of his life, his art would again become the self-destructive drug he would inject into himself to get through the rest.

With an oath, Thomas broke free. Aretha blessedly faded away and was trounced by a vacuous techno-pop dance beat that would allow him to go through the empty, mindless motions of turning and dancing.

Much the way his life would be after this week was over.

Chapter Thirteen

ꟾ

Chaining him up in his "secret dungeon" naked was sounding pretty damn appealing. Marcus took Ellen to a table for a drink while Thomas cut up the floor with Julie. Good luck doing some of those moves with a hard-on, he thought with dark satisfaction, even as Marcus pushed down the bleak truth that he could keep Thomas in a permanent state of arousal and he'd still choose to leave again.

"I've never watched men together."

He arched a brow in Ellen's direction, expecting to see her gazing with avid fascination around her. Instead, she tossed back the whiskey sour like water, her fifth of the night, and studied him, blinking, a little glassy-eyed. "Watching the two of you…it doesn't really matter. When you know the real thing, you recognize it."

Desperation gripped her features. "You're so pretty. You're the prettiest man I've ever seen." Ellen reached out, touched Marcus' face. "Why don't I want to sleep with you? Why does it hurt to look at your face and feel nothing?"

Marcus' brow drew down in puzzlement as he caught her clumsy fingers, but she pulled away and laid her cheek down on the table, narrowly missing the drink.

Julie had apparently registered what was happening, for she and Thomas came back from the dance floor.

"I'm sorry, Marcus." She gathered Ellen to her as she started to cry, soft, muffled sobs punctuated with hiccups. "I thought…I'm such an idiot. Ellen's husband," her voice lowered as if Ellen couldn't hear her, and maybe she couldn't, lost in her grief and the alcohol. "He died a couple years ago and it's been really hard on her. I thought if I took her out with guys who aren't really guys—"

Marcus and Thomas exchanged a look. Julie's face suffused with color. "Oh, Jesus, how awful did that sound? Of course you're guys. That's not what I meant. Guys who don't…no pressure, you know? Oh, geez, just tell me I'm a total asshole."

Ellen lurched up from the table and Thomas caught her arm to steady her. "I'll take her out for some air," he said quietly, squeezing Julie's shoulder and shepherding her friend away.

Marcus rose as Julie clenched her hands together. When she reached for her purse, he waved her money away. "The tab's mine, remember? I make the money around here, after all."

"Marcus…"

"Hey." He tipped up her chin, ran his knuckles alongside her face. "I know what you meant, Julie."

"If I hurt your feelings… God, Marcus. I think I'd rather cut off a limb than make you think I don't love everything about you. Okay, yes, I've often, fervently wished you went for short brunette females instead of gorgeous guys like Thomas, but that's not what I mean. And it's not because you were one of my first major benefactors."

"Julie." Marcus let his expression relax into a slight smile and leaned in, nose to nose. "Shut up."

"Okay, shutting up."

When they emerged from the Club, they found Thomas and Ellen sitting on the curb of a landscaped natural area outside the front of the club. Ellen was cradled in Thomas' lap while she sobbed. Thomas held her close as her hands clutched his back.

Julie squatted behind her, rubbing her shoulder. "Oh, sweetie, it's okay. I'm sorry. I thought this would help."

"It does. It did." Thomas said. "Don't worry, Julie. She just drank too much. We got rid of most of it." He inclined his head toward the shrubbery. "Now we're having a cry, then we'll be better. Sshhh, baby, it's okay..." He rocked Ellen as her sobs increased, the clutch of her hands. "Give us just a few minutes, okay?"

Julie wavered, uncertain, but Marcus put pressure under her elbow and took her off a few paces, turning them so with the help of the landscaping and their bodies they were partially screening Thomas and Ellen from the invasive, curious glances of those exiting the club.

"I thought this would help. She's been in such a funk, and it's been two years."

"Thomas doesn't say anything he doesn't mean," Marcus reassured her. "If he says it's helping, it is."

Julie watched Thomas with him. "You know, it's so obvious what a pure heart he has. He's the type you can take home to Mom."

"That should stand him well with the girl his mother wants him to marry," Marcus remarked acidly.

Julie glanced at him, startled, but Thomas was rising. He pulled out a pocket handkerchief, dabbed at Ellen's eyes and made her smile blearily when he had her blow her nose. Pulling her back in for another hug and kiss, he rubbed her back reassuringly. When they began to move, she was wobbly on her dress heels. Thomas simply bent and picked her up, sending Julie a meaningful glance and head jerk to tell her to lead them to her vehicle.

"Tell Thomas I'll meet him at our car," Marcus said, turning on his heel. "I'll see you next week."

Julie stared after him, but he was already striding away.

Thomas registered Marcus moving away from them and the shift in mood it signaled, but he followed Julie to her roomy SUV. When she opened the door, Thomas put Ellen in the passenger seat, pulling the seat belt over her and buckling it. Ellen looked at him, her eyes still wet. "Thanks," she said.

He shook his head, kept hold of her hand. "You owe me another couple dances. I think we can wipe the floor with them next time, when you're not in the mood to be such a pathetic lush." When he gave her a wink, she managed a watery smile.

Closing the door, he turned, coming around to the driver's side. Before he could open it for her, Julie gave him another one of her hard, reassuring hugs. "Thanks," she murmured. "You just reminded me why I'm tempted to come kidnap you from North Carolina myself."

Drawing back, she looked at him. "Tell him, Thomas. Even if you're going to leave again, he needs to hear it. People think it makes it harder if you say it when you know you're going to go, but it doesn't. It makes it worse thinking someone's ripped your heart out of your chest and just didn't really give a crap."

Thomas gave a half smile. "I hear you, Julie." His gaze shifted. Ellen had leaned over and pressed her palm to the driver's window. He reached out, placed his on the other side. She nodded, her eyes wet. Then her head disappeared as she curled up on the seat like an exhausted toddler, oblivious to her surroundings. "You're staying with her tonight, right?"

"Lord, yes. She'll be in good hands." Julie gave him a searching glance. "Fuck you, I'm not saying good-bye. I can't do it again."

Getting in, she got Ellen propped up and closed the door. When Thomas tapped on the window, Julie gazed at him, her eyes sheened with tears.

"Lock the doors," he mouthed.

She managed a smile, put one fingertip to the glass where Ellen had put her whole hand. He did the same, nodded. He could no more make promises to her than he could to Marcus, but as he watched her pull out of the parking lot, the sense of belonging he'd had at the beginning of the night deserted him.

He walked in silence to the Maserati. Marcus leaned against the passenger side, bringing Thomas up short.

"You going to get my door for me?" Thomas raised a brow. "I think you've been hanging around too many women tonight."

"How did you know what she needed?" Marcus' green eyes studied him, sharp and filled with something unreadable.

Thomas shrugged. "Women get weepy. She wanted a hug. I have a sister, Marcus."

"No. Julie was ready with the hugs. You took her away, took her outside." Marcus put his hand on the car latch when Thomas would have reached for it. "It's locked anyway. Tell me."

Thomas sighed, gave him an irritated look. "Type A's don't break. They might shed a few tears at a funeral, but they immerse themselves in the arrangements, changing names on the bills, all that shit. Then something will trigger it. Feeling a man holding them, the way they used to be held, but not… Being held by a man's different than being held by a woman. Right?" He gave Marcus an ironic look. "That's what she needed. That was the trigger."

"Like your mom."

When a muscle flexed in Thomas' jaw, his expression going impassive, Marcus knew he was treading in that area that was always the red zone for them. So he was surprised when Thomas responded.

"Yeah. It happened to her. She was trying to get something down from the second shelf. I'd come into the kitchen and she said, 'Robert, will you get that?' And that was it. It scared the shit out of Rory and Celeste, but I just picked her up off the floor, sat down with her in my lap and rocked her, let her cry it out. She held onto me tight, buried herself…" His voice wavered slightly, then he cleared his throat, looked away. "It wasn't… she wasn't confused, you know. She knew I was her son."

"Don't be stupid," Marcus said. "I know."

Thomas nodded, a very controlled movement, his gaze holding Marcus' with forced steadiness. "That's how I knew. For Ellen."

It made more sense to Marcus then. The meshing of the son with the memory of his father. It had added to the burden and yet deepened the bond, given Thomas the insight and strength to reinforce his stubborn resolve. Marcus might have observed it gave his mother another weapon to hold against her son, her vulnerability more powerful than the sharpest words, but he didn't.

Instead, he made a noncommittal noise, unlocked the door. "You okay?" Marcus asked, when Thomas didn't move.

"Yeah. I was actually thinking I should be asking you that."

But Marcus could see the picture that Thomas' words had painted, that was playing behind his eyes now. It had been the pivotal moment. The moment when Thomas hadn't been just the surrogate. He'd *become* the head of the family. There was nothing, no matter how much he wanted or needed for himself, that would make him abandon that. If he did, Thomas would abandon an essential part of who he was, a part that made him the man Marcus loved so much.

He couldn't make Thomas choose between him and his family any more than he would have a year ago. He'd known it subconsciously, watching him with Ellen.

So that was that.

"I'm fine, pet. C'mon." Marcus cleared his throat. "Let's hit one of those little hole-in-the-wall diners on the drive back and get a late dinner."

When he passed his knuckles alongside Thomas' jaw and squeezed the back of his nape, it was almost the gesture of a brother. But as he backed off, Thomas was sure Marcus had been about to do something more. His body had drawn taut, anticipating it.

He knew enough about Marcus' moods to know not to reach after him. He stood there, though, undecided until Marcus got to the other side. He needed to say it to someone. Maybe Marcus would turn away from it, but then again, maybe he was the only one who could understand. Because just maybe it was true, that Marcus did love him the way love was supposed to be. Even though that didn't change anything.

"Marcus?"

"Hmm?"

Thomas met his gaze across the top of the low sports car. "I really miss my dad. He didn't…you know, understand me, but he did… Love me."

His throat closed up tight and suddenly there was something huge welling up in him, something he tried to stomp down, but it sprang leaks, made it hard to breathe. Like one of his attacks, but not. Almost worse.

"Never mind," he managed.

When Marcus came around the car, Thomas shook his head, backed up. He was disoriented enough by what he was trying to control in himself to bump into the door. He fought it back as Marcus put his arms around him without a word. Thomas gripped him, held onto the broad back, smelled the combination of smells that were Marcus, felt the soft stuff of his shirt he was crumpling, his fingers opening and closing.

"You held out a lot longer than your mother," Marcus said. "Let it out."

The words were a quiet push over the edge of a cliff. But Marcus put his hands to the back of Thomas' head, leaning to sandwich him between the grounding points of his body and the car. When Thomas would have pulled back, tried to fight it down, fight it away, thinking that's what he had to do, Marcus held on, telling Thomas he wasn't getting away. Didn't need to.

Because Thomas' mother, Celeste and Rory had needed him, Marcus was sure Thomas had avoided any opportunity to be overwhelmed by the painful emotions, thinking if he kept them at bay long enough, they would simply go away.

Thomas' shoulders heaved as he choked on a sob. It came forth in a sudden, strangled burst, the rough tearing sound of a man's grief, so much more hard-won than a woman's easy tears.

"I was here, pet. I was always here. Even if you told me you needed me just for an hour, for this, I would have been there." Marcus spoke gruffly into his hair, holding him tighter. "Why is it so fucking hard for you to believe I love you?"

Thomas didn't reply, but Marcus didn't expect him to do so. He held him, the parking lot, the lights, even the breeze against their bodies just vague impressions as the storm of emotion passed. He wasn't surprised that, like the violence of a summer squall, it didn't long.

As Thomas pulled back, he ducked his head away to swipe at his eyes, embarrassed. Marcus offered him a Starbuck's napkin from the car with a half smile. "Take it, you stubborn ass," he ordered, caressing his cheek. "Do you want me to hold it to your nose and tell you to blow, like Ellen?"

"Bite me."

Marcus obliged, leaning in, his nose brushing Thomas' cheek, breath barely brushing the hair over his ear. He cupped the opposite side of Thomas' head in his palm and set his teeth to his jugular, staying that way, motionless, letting Thomas feel the restraint of it, the certain possession and reassurance he intended to convey in the one gesture.

At length, he felt Thomas' hand lift, grip his waist. Otherwise, Thomas was just as still, submitting to the hold with a mere quiver running through his muscles, as powerful a reaction in this moment as a climax. Marcus spoke, his voice rough.

"You think I wouldn't want to wipe your nose, your ass or any other part for you when you need it, Thomas? Now, or fifty years from now?"

Thomas had closed his eyes, for his lashes brushed Marcus' cheek. "Don't," he said, low. "Just don't."

Marcus stepped back, but he could tell he flustered Thomas when he opened the door and guided him in, hand lingering over his elbow, his hip. "Come on. I want to get you back home and into my bed as soon as possible."

"You promised me food. Real cooking, where they use grease."

""Whine, whine, whine. God, worse than a two-year-old."

When he got into his side of the car, he met Thomas' eyes, flashed teeth. Ran a hand along the side of his head, ruffled his hair and was rewarded with a tired but genuine smile. As much as he'd like to take his lover over and over again, he was pleased Thomas was hungry.

For the short time they had, Marcus realized he didn't care where he was or what they were doing, as long as Thomas was part of it. The sands of time would run out whether or not they watched the clock. For now, he'd just enjoy watching Thomas eat a cheeseburger.

* * * * *

They found one of the diners that met Thomas' specifications about halfway back to the cottage. A local hangout just off the highway where people tended to look up when you entered but then went back to their business. They were certainly used to Connecticut tourists on the way to the hills. The waitress told them to pick any table and before long she slid a cheeseburger, fries and tall Coke in front of Thomas. Marcus ordered a Chef's salad and a bottle of import.

"I'll probably pay for this later." Thomas fished the roll of antacids out of his pocket and flicked out two, added them in with his next bite. "Maybe that will help."

Marcus suppressed a comment with effort, tried to eye Thomas with light amusement as he wolfed down the cheeseburger. "Keep that up and your ass will get as wide as that cow of yours."

"First I'm too skinny, now I'm getting too fat. Shallow bastard."

"You know it." Marcus grinned, took the beer to his lips. "Seems like fucking your brains out at least once every twelve hours does good things for you. This is the first time since you've been here I've seen you eat with an appetite."

"Jesus, Marcus." Thomas glanced around. "Keep it down."

Marcus' lips tightened. "What, you think any one with sense would look at us and not realize we're together? We're in New England, not on the moon."

Thomas shook his head. "Not that. Language. There are mothers here. Older people."

When Marcus' gaze shifted, he saw that in addition to a cadre of men their age at the counter there were several groups of senior citizens and one family with a little girl, the latter obviously travelers who'd stopped for pie and a rest break. He turned his regard back to Thomas. "You're a piece of work, you know it? You live in New York City for what, over two years? And absolutely none of it rubs off on you."

"You say that like it's a bad thing," Thomas teased. "Besides, that's not true. You did."

Marcus eyed the senior citizens. "Why is it older people deserve respect just because they're old? Pedophiles and sleazy politicians have been known to live to ripe old ages, right along with Mahatma Gandhi."

Thomas glanced at him, sat back. "Want a French fry?"

"What does that mean?"

Thomas crossed his arms on the table, rolled out two more antacids and took them down with a swig of Coke. "Are you ever going to tell me about you? Who you were before you became what you are now?"

"So I make a remark about old people, and automatically it's got to be some chip on my shoulder about my parents?"

"No. Not automatically. But it does connect, doesn't it?" Thomas cocked his head. "There's like this hellmouth inside of you. Every once in awhile, I knock on the door and get a blast of heat from it, but you won't let me inside."

"If I wanted to be psychoanalyzed every time I made a nasty comment, I'd go straight and find myself a girl."

"Then stop acting like a shrewish bitch and don't curse in front of the old people, who we'll assume deserve manners until they prove otherwise. Society does have to have some basic standards of moral behavior to have a civilized structure."

Marcus shut his mouth with a snap. Thomas' eyes danced and Marcus could tell he was waiting to see if he'd act pissed or try to steal his fries. He went for the latter. Thomas intercepted with a block.

"Am I going to have to separate you boys?" The waitress, an older woman with dangling rhinestone earrings that were a sparkling contrast to her clean jeans and embellished diner shirt, came to pour Thomas some more Coke.

"He started it," Marcus pointed out, making her chuckle.

Even as he watched Thomas banter with the waitress, Marcus knew his lover probably deserved an answer.

I told him I loved him. What the hell more is there?

Proving it. Being willing to be vulnerable. To let go of some control.

Fuck off.

"Marcus?" Thomas had spoken, apparently a couple times. "You okay?"

Other than arguing with voices in my head? Just fine. "Fine."

"You know," those dark eyes were studying him intently, "you don't have to be perfect, Marcus. Sometimes it would be a hell of a lot less intimidating for the rest of us if you showed you weren't invincible."

"Get over it."

Thomas wasn't asking questions that Julie or Josh or even Lauren hadn't tried to get at in the past, questions he'd deflected without a passing thought. But when those eyes were on him as they were now, it was like Thomas had the ability to forcibly get him to say things better left buried and unsaid.

Why was it a man who'd grown up in the middle of a nowhere Southern town, who had not an ounce of sophistication, no polish, had the ability to twist his insides like this? Make things raise their heads that Marcus had long ago exorcised with extreme prejudice? It was a surge of toxic waste he had no intention of dumping on anyone, let alone Thomas.

"Marcus." Thomas spoke more sharply this time, concern edging his tone. Marcus snapped out of it, shoving the memories away and slamming the door. Jesus, his hand was shaking under Thomas' grip. "Your phone's ringing."

Thank God. He jerked away harder than necessary, fumbling for it.

Thomas had no polish because there was no veneer on Thomas, nothing but a hundred percent who he was. With Thomas, it wasn't that his whole family didn't know who or what the fuck he was. It was that they wouldn't accept it, and he was trying to live up to their expectations. He didn't want to disappoint them because he loved them. And they loved him.

Whereas Marcus had six inches of lacquer he'd worked his ass off to refine until it went bone deep. It *was* him, through and through, damn it. Just like the alchemists who'd sought to turn non-precious metals to gold, he'd turned veneer and polish into solid oak. That was the end of it.

He glanced at the phone display. Blinked. "Hell, it's Lawrence, probably trying to get another week on the show displays. He thinks if he calls me at night, he'll get my voicemail, the spineless prick."

At Thomas' pointed look, Marcus grimaced. "The spineless *very bad man*."

Thomas' smile should have loosened the tight band around Marcus' chest, but it didn't. Because the call wasn't Lawrence. "I'm going to have to yell. I'll go outside to take this." Marcus said it casually and rose, avoiding Thomas' gaze and moving around the table to stride for the door.

Just fucking ironic, perfect timing.

Thomas watched him go, speculating. He took another swig of his Coke. Suppressing a sigh, he turned his attention to finishing his dinner rather than why he always hit a brick wall when he tried to push into any part of Marcus where Marcus didn't want him to go. Had he ever surrendered, let someone just walk into a room of his soul, trusting them to treat what they found there gently? What could be there that was so awful?

* * * * *

As Marcus listened to his brother, he stared into the dark mural of silhouettes formed by the scrub trees and underbrush behind the restaurant. There was a pretty retention pond area complete with cattails. It was lit dimly by the bug-encrusted light mounted by the back kitchen entrance. Lily pads moved like ghosts across the water's surface. He'd walked away from the bright front lights where Thomas could still see him. He needed to pace, to feel like he wasn't trapped.

"Yeah, I heard you. A couple months. Does she—" He closed his eyes. "What do you need? Okay, I'll send it. In fact, I'll just set up a separate account. You can pull from it as you need it. You're going to have a lot of unexpected expenses. No. Okay. Bye."

He clicked off. Too late, the scuff of a boot on gravel alerted him and he turned.

There were three of them. He'd noticed them in the diner at the counter, knew enough about their kind that he should have kept his guard up, shouldn't have been so stupid as to wander away from the front of the restaurant.

"What's this we got in the dark, all alone? A pretty, pretty girl, all by herself. Wearing fancy shoes and an expensive watch."

Only one of them believed in chitchat. The other two were moving in. They could have tried to get him to hand over his watch and wallet, but they weren't thieves. That wasn't what had made them get up and come out here, and they all knew it, including him.

"You need to stay in your city and keep your queer ass out of our hangouts. Don't even like to eat near you."

"I suppose it *is* uncomfortable, being around someone who actually knows how to chew with his mouth closed."

That gave them pause. Marcus could have tried to bolt, call out. Someone in the kitchen probably would have heard. But he didn't. When they charged forward, Marcus snarled and flung himself at them, outnumbered and taken by surprise, but in the perfect mood for a fight.

* * * * *

Thomas pushed aside his plate and looked up in time to see the manager glance at the second waitress, a younger, worried-looking woman. At his meaningful look, she rolled her eyes and made a "boys will be boys" expression toward the three empty spots at the lunch counter. Three men gone, their plates not empty, beers left unfinished.

He met the manager's eyes and knew. Son of a bitch. Thomas exploded up from the table and headed for the door, even as he heard the man call out, "We don't want any trouble. Son, you need to—"

He shoved out the door, so violently it hit the wall. The choice was obvious when he didn't see them out front. Pivoting on his foot, he ran around the corner toward the back and saw two figures on the ground. One was off to the side not moving. The other was being kicked by two men still on their feet.

"Get up on your knees," one of the men snarled. "That's something a cocksucker should know all about. I'm going to piss on your faggoty ass like I did your fancy car, and then I might let you live."

Thomas' fist took him in the kidney. The man stumbled, trying to turn, but Thomas followed it with an uppercut that knocked his head back and took him clean off his feet, slamming him down on his back. Roaring his fury, Thomas yanked him back to his feet and drove him into the restaurant wall, knocking the metal trashcans out of his path.

They crashed into the outdoor light mounted by the kitchen door, breaking the bulb and casing, eliminating all but the cloud-covered moonlight. The other man stumbled after them. Thomas drove his knee hard into his opponent's groin to ensure he'd be out of commission a moment longer and spun. Grabbing up a trash can lid, he met the other man with it, thrusting upward to knock his teeth together onto his tongue, resulting in a spurt of blood. Another punch pushed the man back.

Thomas whirled, ducked under the strike of the man who'd scrambled back to his feet behind him. Grabbing him by the shirtfront, he slung him to the ground, bowling him into the legs of the other man trying to charge forward again. The man stumbled over his fallen comrade, but managed to lunge over him.

Thomas landed a kick in the prone man's midsection to keep him on the ground and hammered at the other one's face with a fast series of jabs, hearing the satisfying break of cartilage from his nose and a cry of pain. He fell back, holding his face.

When the man on the ground grabbed his jeans' cuff, Thomas stomped on his chest, put his foot to his throat.

"Stop it. Stop. Please, stop." It was the young waitress, who'd come at a run. "Stop, that's my brother."

Fists clenched, Thomas glanced over at her. Even in the semidarkness, the fury in his snapping dark eyes apparently warned her to stay back. He kept his attention on his opponents, but they were done. The third man seemed mostly unconscious still, though groaning a bit. Marcus' work.

The other man was on his knees, cupping his gushing nose. The brother she was defending was curled up like a shrimp and staring up at him through a swollen eye. His lip was bloody, his breath labored from Thomas' pressure on his throat.

"No. It's a piece of shit that calls itself your brother." Removing his foot, Thomas gave the man a disgusted shove with it that rolled him over on his back, his arms flopping out.

The broken shards of brown glass gleaming dully in the fitful moonlight and the jagged-edged bottle lying near them told Thomas why Marcus had likely focused on disarming the unconscious man first. Which in turn had put him at the mercy of the two men fighting with just their fists.

Thomas gave them one last glance and turned his attention to Marcus. He'd made it to one knee, but wavered there, his long fingers tented on the ground on one side to balance him, the other hand holding his ribs, his head down.

"Here, hold on…" Thomas got to him, knelt to take the bracing hand and guide Marcus' arm up over his shoulders, reaching out to touch Marcus' jaw. "C'mon, look at me. Let's see. Oh, holy Christ."

They'd cut him with a bottle. Marcus' beautiful face. His perfect, beautiful face, laid open from the high point of his cheekbone and across his nose to his jaw. The lower half of his face was wet with blood. Bits of gravel were in the gash. His clothes were torn and dirty.

Then Thomas noticed the blood soaking his shirt and waistband. "Jesus." He had his hands there and was pulling it away to see before Marcus could stop him. The bottle jab had cut him just below the hip bone and made it to the pubic area, cutting through the slacks and underwear beneath. Fortunately, it appeared to be a shallow strike.

"He was trying to cut my dick off," Marcus coughed. "Said I didn't need it. Lucky for you I'm quick."

The murderous rage that had settled into an uneasy simmer flared, a fuel for hellfire. Thomas was up and ready to go another round, but Marcus caught his shirtfront, held on. "No," he said, spitting a mouthful of blood. "Enough."

He wouldn't accept Thomas' help to rise, making it to his feet on his own, but Thomas could feel the pain vibrating off his stubborn, prideful silhouette.

"Where the hell did you come from, man? You don't fight like no queer."

The brother spoke. He was sitting up now, helped to an upright position by his sister who was crouched by him, her mouth tight. The man with the broken nose was staying far back, almost lost in the darkness, but Thomas kept a watchful eye on him.

"North Carolina." As Thomas stepped forward, he was satisfied to see them all shrink back as if he were much closer. "Where I learned exactly how to field dress a deer, so cutting you into chunks and feeding them into the pond back here is sounding pretty good. What the hell is wrong with you? What makes you so fucking special? You could have killed him."

"Pet." Marcus spoke, stiffly lurching up next to him. "Come on. He's not worth it, and I need stitches."

"Should I…can I call an ambulance?" The manager had come out and obviously was wavering between support of his regulars and the possibility of involvement in a lawsuit. He had a flashlight, and swept the ground with it, briefly hitting their faces. He lingered on Marcus' with a gasp and muttered curse before Marcus turned away. Thomas shifted in front of him, compelling the manager to lower the beam.

"No," Marcus said emphatically before Thomas could respond. "We'll stop somewhere and get them to stitch this up." He started to move forward at a careful hobble.

The waitress' brother was getting up. She, like Thomas, tried to help her sibling and was shaken off.

Marcus stopped when he was even with the man and looked in his direction, six feet between them. It seemed to Thomas he was detachedly studying his battered features. "It's the shy, quiet ones you have to watch," Marcus advised, briefly looking toward Thomas, then back at his opponent. "Was it worth it to you?"

The man spat blood on the ground.

"Look at me." Marcus snarled.

The man's gaze shot to him in reaction. In that moment, Marcus lunged forward.

The manager's light flashed up at the waitress' startled scream. Thomas saw in an instant that Marcus had refused help and his movements had been so careful and stiff because he'd been holding the broken bottle close against his side.

He struck the man across the face, splitting open his skin as precisely as a surgeon, and then followed up with the other hand which was holding—Jesus Christ—a brick.

The man's jaw broke with a crunch that Thomas could hear, though it was lost in another shriek from the waitress. She tried to launch herself at him, but the manager had already grabbed her as Thomas hauled Marcus back.

The man was back on the ground, holding his face, moaning.

Marcus managed to land a kick in his ribs before Thomas caught him about the chest, trying not to hurt him further, but Marcus was as oblivious as a pit bull who'd strangle himself if necessary to finish the job.

"Marcus," Thomas hissed. "Come on. We're going. Stop. Please stop."

Marcus throttled back his forward motion, but apparently he wasn't done yet. Even when angry or sarcastic, Marcus' voice was velvet and rich. But the voice that came out as dark and deadly as the night itself was almost guttural, someone Thomas didn't know. "The bottle is so we're even, you son of a bitch. The jaw is because I know what you did to me, you would have done to him." He jerked his head, indicating Thomas. "And that's how a New York street kid fights. Even a queer one."

With that, Marcus gave in to Thomas' urging and moved away from the rear of the restaurant, allowing Thomas to keep an arm around his back to support his steps. As Marcus gave him more of his weight after they turned the corner, Thomas hoped he hadn't made a mistake in refusing the manager's offer of an ambulance.

When they got to the car, Thomas saw they'd smeared something on the windshield. It looked like leavings from the garbage. From the smell, one of them had in fact urinated against the tire. Thomas was thankful they hadn't left the windows open or had the headlights smashed out, but he assumed with the car being in the front, that would have attracted too much attention.

Leaning Marcus against the car, he fished his keys out of the torn slacks without asking, his fingers brushing the bloody gash. Thomas felt tears sting his eyes. "Ah, Jesus."

"Forget that. It's the ribs that feel like shit. Goddamn. I haven't had anyone sneak up on me in a fight in twenty years, and I get laid out by some redneck piece of shit in the middle of nowhere." Marcus' arm wrapped around his midsection. "Can't draw a breath without it hurting."

"We're getting you to a hospital."

"No, you're taking me back to the house. I'll be fine."

"Horseshit." Thomas shook his head. "There was a hospital about five miles from here. We passed it on the way down and you know it. We're going."

"No, we're not. I don't want to go there. They have a terrible reputation. They kill people who come in with nosebleeds."

"You're lying."

There was a stubborn set to Marcus' face, but Thomas didn't give a rat's ass. He stepped forward, bumped Marcus' toes.

"You're going. And you're not in a position to say no." At the flash of fire in Marcus' eyes, Thomas changed tack. "You could have broken bones, a punctured organ. If not for you, do it for me."

Marcus blew out a breath, winced as if even that caused him pain. Thomas suspected it did. "That was a low shot."

"Whatever it takes," Thomas responded.

Marcus nodded, a resigned look coming to his eyes, shadows of things that Thomas didn't understand. "Fine. Let's go."

Thomas helped him in the car, seeking something to change the suddenly tense atmosphere. "New York street kid? Was that the truth?"

Marcus grunted. "Pretty, wasn't it? Just drive, Thomas. You do know how to drive something other than farm equipment and junk cars? It works about the same way."

"The Maserati is like a small combine," Thomas retorted, but before he closed Marcus' door, he fished out some wet towelettes from the glove compartment. He pressed one to Marcus' jaw, his own flexing. "I'm sorry I didn't get there sooner."

"There are no sorrys to be said on this one, pet. They're the only sorry ones. The world sucks sometimes. But a lot of times it doesn't." Marcus managed a grin that looked gruesome and feral with the blood on his teeth. "Jesus, you kicked their asses sideways. I'm so impressed I'd be hard as a rock if I didn't feel like shit. Let's get the hell out of here."

Chapter Fourteen

ꙮ

The small hospital only had two on call doctors. Those capable of walking in had to wait for the doctors to finish with the victims of a more serious car wreck that had come in before them. Fortunately, there was only one other walk-in, a four-year-old with a bad tummy ache. She was being held by her mother, who kept eyeing them suspiciously.

"Because we look like we've been in a gang fight," Thomas muttered.

When they first came in, the nurse had regarded them in the same manner. "You been in a fight?"

"No, a really competitive golf tournament," Marcus had said dryly. Thomas winced at the "fuck off and mind your own business" New York undertone. She'd thinned her lips and thrust the clipboard at Thomas. "Fill this out."

It had felt odd to help Marcus do that. His name, medical history. History of illness. Though Marcus had claimed not applicable and "none" to most of it.

"I shouldn't have let you go out there by yourself." Thomas stretched an arm over the back of the bolted plastic seats, grazing Marcus' shoulder. He didn't want to be rebuffed for hovering, but he needed the contact.

"Let me?" Marcus eyed him from his one non-swollen eye, then closed it. "You my keeper now?"

"Sometimes I get the feeling you need one. Weird, huh?" Thomas shifted so he was sitting sideways on his hip. Propping his head on his fist, he reached out and pushed Marcus' hair back from his temple, rubbing his thumb against the unmarked slope of his left cheekbone.

"I'll say." But the fact Marcus submitted without further comment to the stroking told Thomas how bad Marcus was probably feeling. He snagged a pillow from a gurney and put it between Marcus' head and the wall to give him something to support his head and neck.

"It's not your fault, pet," Marcus murmured. "None of it."

"I should have been there sooner," Thomas repeated.

"It's just a face. Just flesh and bone. When you die, it all rots away." A corner of Marcus' mouth twitched. "Should I be worried? You're going to dump me if I stop being pretty?"

"You're pretty?" Thomas was glad Marcus' eyes were closed so he wouldn't see the war between anger and concern in his expression. "I mean, you're old, almost forty. Your pecs are starting to sag like my grandmother's breasts..."

When Marcus swung a hand out to deliver a weak-knuckled slap to his abdomen, Thomas caught it. Instead of thrusting it back, he held on, a light grip of Marcus' wrist, his fingers tracing Marcus' palm. Marcus stayed still for a moment or two, then his fingers moved, a caress to Thomas' sternum with his knuckles before he pulled away to switch hands on the ice pack they'd provided for his face.

"What happened to that whole thing at the farm, your argument about not solving anything by being confrontational?"

"This was a little different. They hurt you."

Marcus made a noncommittal noise, laid his other hand on his knee, carefully stretching out one leg. "I think we're going to be here for a while."

"Let me check on things."

"Let *you*. That's more like it. Need to remember your place."

"Shut up and wait here." Thomas approached the front desk, the nurse who narrowed her gaze at him as he came. He knew he had blood on the front of his shirt. Probably splattered on his face.

Maybe he should visit the restroom. But he didn't want Marcus out of his sight.

"I told you the doctor—"

"I know," Thomas said. He glanced back, saw Marcus had his eyes still closed, jaw held taut, breathing shallow. "Can he have something for the pain until then? He doesn't have any allergies."

"I can't administer drugs without the doctor's permission."

"Do they…do they do good stitching here? He—" Thomas abruptly pulled out his wallet, fished out something he knew he shouldn't be showing, and slid it across the counter to her. "I know he's surly and unlivable at the moment, and even on a good day he can be like that, but that's what he normally looks like, inside and out."

The wallet picture was one of many that had been done at one of Julie's post production parties by a professional photographer. Despite her budget trepidations, she'd known the promo brochure was important. Marcus had been listening to someone, his head turned at a slight profile, dipped a bit. The photographer had reproduced it in black and white and come up with a finished product that was reminiscent of a still of a legendary great, such as Gary Cooper, Jimmy Stewart, Rock Hudson.

Julie had given this one to Thomas. He kept it behind a couple of other things in his wallet that didn't get disturbed much. An old video club card, his county library card. Even so, the corners of the photo had gotten dog-eared from the nights he'd taken it out to look at it in the quiet darkness of his room at home. He laid it on the nurse's clipboard.

"It's not who he is," he said in a low voice. "Not what's special about him, but it's still important. It's…his armor. His way of coping." As the words came out of his mouth, compelled by some instinct, Thomas knew it was true. It protected whatever it was Marcus so steadfastly refused to tell him, to tell anyone.

The nurse gave him a quiet look, reached out and patted his hand. "Dr. Tillman does very fine stitch work. My boy split open his forehead on a rock last year and you can barely see the scar anymore. You go sit down with your friend and we'll get to you as soon as possible, I promise."

Thomas nodded, tucked the picture away and returned to Marcus, whose eyes were still closed.

"Did you offer her sex to get me in faster?"

"Should I have?"

At the squeak of wheels and a lingering shadow, Thomas glanced up, surprised to see an orderly pushing a hamper full of dirty linens stop to peer at Marcus. Leaning over further, he took a step forward, his light brown eyes studying the gash, or so Thomas thought.

"Dodger? Is that you?"

"This day just gets better and better," Marcus mumbled under his breath, so low Thomas was sure only he'd heard him.

When Marcus lifted the ice pack and raised his head, the orderly's face creased into a smile. He looked as pleased as if Marcus didn't have blood all over his jaw and shirtfront, his eye swollen shut, arm gripping his ribs as if he were holding his insides in.

"It is you!"

The nurse gave the orderly a sharp, admonishing look at the enthusiastic shout. Immediately, he quieted with an apologetic look, clasping both hands over his mouth before he leaned over again, spoke in an exaggerated whisper through his fingers. Perhaps in his late thirties, the man had lanky dark hair to his shoulders, combed back and held with a rubber band, eyes that were a trifle wide, and a mass of scar tissue around his left eye, which was hidden beneath a permanent patch.

Under his hospital smock, the man wore pressed jeans and a clean striped shirt. For some reason, his appearance gave Thomas the impression of a first grader setting out to school, carefully prepared by his mother.

"Your shoe's untied, Toby."

This from an older black man who approached and immediately flanked Toby with the protective demeanor of a parent. Putting a hand on Toby's shoulder, he compelled the younger man to kneel and begin the apparent thoughtful challenge of tying his shoe. "It's Dodger," Toby repeated.

"I see that. How you doing? Never thought I'd see anyone nail that face of yours." His face creasing into a well-used terrain of lines, the man reached out and shook Marcus' unoccupied hand. Since they were having to shake with the same side hand, Thomas noted it was more like they squeezed grips as long-time friends.

"They got lucky," Marcus said. "How're you doing, Owen?"

"He's head custodian," Toby said proudly. "Employee of the month. That looks like it hurts." He straightened and reached out to touch. Thomas watched, intrigued as Marcus sat still, let Tobias place his fingers with an odd gentleness on his jaw below the laceration.

"I didn't know you two were out here. Last time we'd talked you were still in Boston."

From the briefest flicker in Marcus' eyes, Thomas knew he was lying. And he understood why Marcus hadn't wanted to come to this hospital. From Owen's steady look, he apparently knew it was a lie as well.

"Yeah, well, this was better for Toby. Small town, everyone knows him. He does a good job here."

"Mr. Stanton." The nurse spoke. "The doctor will see you now, Exam One. Sorry, you have to stay." She gestured to Thomas. "You can come in after awhile, but…"

"The doctor has to make sure you aren't the one who beat me up," Marcus finished, giving her an arch look. "Does this pussy look capable of beating anyone up?"

The nurse, unfazed, arched a brow. "Well, seeing as all the blood on him appears to be yours, I'd say yes." Her brows lowered. "But I'm here to tell you that *I* can whip your ass if you don't clean up your language and get yourself in Exam One before Dr. Tillman decides to make you wait until tomorrow and goes to get herself a nice, well-deserved latte."

Toby giggled. "She's nice, Marcus. Mean, but nice. Like you. Don't be messing with her. She'll tear you *up*." As he rose, he patted Marcus' shoulder, then abruptly put both his arms around him, holding him. Thomas stiffened at the same time as Owen moved forward, but Toby held Marcus as if holding an egg. "I'm sorry," he said, and Thomas was amazed to hear the man muffle a sob. "Marcus. My friend. He's my friend."

"Come on now, boy. Marcus has to get his face fixed up." Owen's face was full of pain and regret.

Toby shook his head, grip tightening. "Better if he's ugly. Safer."

Though he could see Marcus was being gentle about extricating himself, Thomas could almost hear the vibration of his distress. He rose, intending to help, and suddenly Toby turned on him. "Did you hurt him, like Nurse thinks?" He shouted it, lunging at Thomas.

Thomas fell back, startled. Despite his injuries, Marcus was surprisingly quick, vaulting forward and catching Toby by the collar, hauling him back, though he let out a painful grunt.

"No, Toby. No." He snapped it out through gritted teeth. "Thomas is like you. He takes care of me. He brought me to the hospital. He beat up the guys who hurt me. Though he did take them by surprise," he added with grim humor. His face was white, strained lines around his mouth.

Thomas shot him a narrow look, but the teasing had fallen short. Owen was having a quick word with the nurse on duty, who was obviously getting a little concerned about Toby's agitated state.

"All of them? He beat up all of them? They're all gone?"

"Yes," Marcus said after a moment. Suddenly he looked tired and in desperate pain, for reasons that Thomas could tell had nothing to do with being beaten up tonight. "Now, go on back to work. There are people waiting for you to help them, okay?"

Toby nodded, his brow creased. He gripped the handle of the cart with both hands and pushed it on down the hall, stopping to look back once, his expression puzzled. Then he turned the corner, disappearing.

"Bed pan," Marcus said abruptly. Thomas lunged up but Owen was already there. Marcus grabbed it, turned to face the wall and got violently sick. Thomas stood by, close, wanting to touch, help, but oddly restrained by Owen's light hand and a quick, silent shake of his head. When Marcus was done, he was sweating. He lowered himself into the chair, his arm shaking. The nurse fortunately appeared with a wheelchair.

"You may have yourself a bit of a concussion, Mr. Stanton. I think we better take you in this."

The fact he let himself be helped into the chair like an old man, rather than telling the nurse what she could do with the wheelchair, frightened Thomas worse than anything.

"I'm going with him."

"I'll come get you just as soon as Dr. Tillman says it's okay," she promised, but in a firm tone that brooked no argument.

"Marcus." Thomas closed his hand on his wrist.

"I want to get the hell out of here," Marcus said abruptly. He lifted his head and pinned Thomas with a hard green stare that was almost glassy. "No matter what. They're not admitting me here. I want to go home after they stitch me up, even if I pass out. You got it? You nod and don't mean it, I won't forgive you."

Thomas tightened his grip. "I'll take care of you, of everything. Don't worry about it."

"Promise me."

"Not if your life's in danger. If they say you have a punctured organ or a concussion, then tough shit. Get over it. You stay here. Anything else, I'll get you home."

Marcus sat back in the chair. "Asshole."

"Stubborn bastard. Let them take care of you." Thomas had to close his hands into hard fists to keep from reaching out again as they wheeled him down the hall and out of his sight. "Goddamn it," he muttered.

He whirled on Owen. "What the hell was that about?"

Owen ran a hand over his balding head. "Of all the places Dodger could show up, this would've been the last I'd guess. Like Fate, isn't it?" He shook his head at Thomas' searing look of impatience and moved back to his own cart. "Not my story to tell, son. If you're the right person to tell, he'll tell you. But I don't know you."

"He doesn't tell anybody anything."

Owen stopped, his hands clasping the handle. "Sometimes when you lose everything, the last thing you want to do is remember. And telling is remembering. You do what you said you'd do." His dark gaze fixed on Thomas. "If it isn't too serious, get him out of here. Best for him and Toby."

Watching Owen retreat down the hall, Thomas wanted to put his already swollen knuckles through the sheetrock of the hospital's sea green wall. Fortunately, it wasn't long before the nurse let him go back to Exam One. Marcus was stripped out of his shirt, his slacks open in the front. The doctor, a small-boned woman in her forties who barely came up to his chin, was checking out his ribs. A nurse had prepared a tray of sutures.

"Looks like they're going to give me a wrap, stitch me up and then we can head on," Marcus said.

"If the X-rays say so," Dr. Tillman corrected. "You his family?"

"Yes," Thomas said without hesitation. "Is he okay?"

"Other than being arrogant as hell, which I don't think can be surgically removed, I think he's going to be fine. He was lucky." She glanced sharply at Thomas, taking in his appearance. "Do you need medical attention?"

"No. Not my blood."

"He's obviously a better fighter than you," the doctor observed to Marcus.

Marcus curled his lip. "I'm getting tired of hearing that. I was taken by surprise. They jumped me. He had the advantage of jumping them."

"Mmm. I'm going to go check those X-rays."

When the doctor and her nurse left them alone, Thomas approached the table, ran his hand up the curve of Marcus' bare back. There were bruises rising there from where they'd kicked him. He wanted to go hurt them some more. "You hanging in there?"

"Hanging. I just want out of here. Christ, what a stupid thing to do, wandering behind that place."

"Guess talking to Lawrence really stirred you up."

"Huh?" Marcus gave him a blank expression, then he shrugged, looking away. "Yeah."

Thomas dropped his hand, swallowed the hurt. "Who *was* on the phone? And who the hell are Toby and Owen, and why does Toby call you Dodger?"

Marcus' eyes shuttered. It was a look Thomas knew. In the past it had frustrated him, annoyed him, made him angry. Now, fury just erupted. Somehow, if he'd known more about who was on the phone, Marcus wouldn't have gone outside to a place he never should have been, to hide the conversation from him.

"Not going to tell me, are you? It's okay to slap me down for leaving to take care of my family, but maybe that's because whatever happened with yours is so awful you don't want me to have anything to do with mine."

"Get out." Marcus' eyes went freezing cold, his face a hard mask, the cleaned but unstitched slash making him look far more dangerous. "I don't want to deal with this crap right now."

"I've never gotten in, so how the hell can I get out?" Thomas snarled. "You want me to be your family? You let family in. Knowing they'll hurt you, you do it anyway, because that's what love is. You let them in to hurt you, love you—"

"Leave you?"

Marcus surged up now, coming nose to nose with Thomas despite having to hold his side to do so. "Why should I pour out my guts to someone who considers me family only when it's convenient, which means he's never considered me family at all? You've got a permanent hard-on for me, but hey, join the rest of the world. You're right. Go home. Go home to North Carolina and be everything your family wants you to be."

His expression hardened further. "But you better be ready for the fact it will *never* be enough. Years from now, when you've done what you think they wanted you to do and you're coming home every night to sit in your recliner with your beer gut and your passive aggression drowning in cable, you'll be hating that girl you married. The family you thought you loved. And you *still* won't be enough, because what they want is for you to be truly happy being someone you were fucking never meant to be!"

Venom was pouring off Marcus. Thomas didn't know if it was aimed at him or if it was a poison Marcus was coating his whole world with, but it was all bullshit. All defenses against what he didn't want Thomas to know.

Thomas took one step back, looked steadily at him. Took a deep breath. "Is it that bad?"

Marcus stared at him. Myriad emotions chased each other through his expression. "Worse," he said flatly.

"Does anyone know all of it? Have you ever trusted someone more than me?"

Marcus wanted Thomas to keep fighting, keep it on the level of irrational anger, but Thomas wasn't obliging. And if he couldn't ride out all of tonight's shit in fury, Marcus wasn't sure how he was going to survive it.

"No," he said, sinking back down on the table, feeling the pain in every bone and muscle.

"Okay, then." Thomas spoke after a moment, as if that was an answer he could accept.

"See if you can get that nurse in here and get this done," Marcus said, looking down at the tile floor, a depressing checkered pattern of white and green illuminated far too much by the fluorescent lighting. "Then we'll go back to the house and get you packed. You're supposed to go home tomorrow."

"But I could stay…"

"No." Marcus shook his head. "We said the week. You needed to go back by the weekend. Tomorrow's Saturday. You need to go."

"You want me to go."

The hurt was there. Marcus thought the agony of it, joining the pain in his ribs, was going to squeeze the life from him. He needed Thomas to go now. Not tomorrow, this minute.

"You've got a great start on some excellent pieces," he managed. "Take them home, finish them, let me know when you think you can estimate a completion date. I'll get them picked up and brought to New York—"

Thomas planted his feet between Marcus' braced ones and startled him by catching his face in both hands, tilting it up so Marcus was forced to look him in the eye.

The position crowded him. With his ribs throbbing, there wasn't much he could do to shake Thomas off. God, those artist's hands touching his face, Thomas' expression unsmiling, the dark eyes searching Marcus'. His thumb traced the cut, then moved down over Marcus' bottom lip. When his hip brushed the inside of Marcus' thigh, it was too tempting not to put his hands on Thomas' waist, his hips, draw him forward.

He couldn't fuck a Cabbage Patch doll right now, let alone Thomas, but that wasn't what he wanted anyway. His hands were holding onto Thomas' waist much too tightly, almost violently digging in to his shirt. Almost like Thomas had clutched him, that day Marcus had come to see him at the hardware store.

His arms were rigid bands of muscle as Thomas ran his hands down them, moved just an inch or two closer. It freed Marcus' head to go where it would and he was tired, tired enough to let it fall forward, just barely brushing Thomas. He wanted...but he wouldn't move forward any further. He felt as if he moved at all, he'd break. Thomas closed the gap, that one last step forward, then Marcus' forehead rested solidly in the middle of Thomas' chest. Marcus could feel Thomas' heartbeat through the throbbing of his own skull.

He drew in a breath, looking down at the slope of Thomas' abdomen, the thighs that looked so damn good in jeans, the curve of his cock beneath the zipper. Shoes with socks. Size twelve, wide. Thomas' hands stroked his hair, curled over his head. Bending, he brushed his lips on the crown of Marcus' head.

"I don't want you to go," Marcus muttered. His hands tightened as if he could hold Thomas with just his touch.

This was the root of it. The fight, the anger, the memories of family. It was all about Thomas leaving.

Thomas propped his chin on Marcus' skull, overlapped his arms around his back, holding him loosely. "We knew it would suck, didn't we?"

"Yeah."

"If I could stay, if it was only about what I wanted, I'd stay until you got tired of me and kicked me out. I swear it."

Marcus closed his eyes, breathed him in. For Thomas' wellbeing, he should let him go. Just let go.

"Okay?" When Marcus didn't answer, just sat there, breathing in everything that was Thomas, Thomas sighed, held his tense body closer. He rubbed Marcus' back, easy, caring strokes.

His steadying touch and presence were like a carefully timed release valve, allowing some of the pressure to dissipate so Marcus could breathe. Even when the doctor came back to report the X-rays were clean, he found he couldn't bring himself to draw back, let go.

Not until he had no other choice.

Chapter Fifteen

Three months later

ℰ𝒪

They were done. Thomas stood back, surveying the twelve paintings critically, but he knew they were what he wanted them to be, every one of them. He pivoted on his heel to look at the thirteenth, which was placed in the opposite corner of the work shed.

He'd converted the building into his studio when he'd returned from the Berkshires three months ago. The shed was in the middle of the pasture, previously a feeding area and rain shelter for the herd they'd had years ago. He'd worked on it after store hours, getting it renovated the way he needed it. Kate sometimes came and grazed just outside while he ripped and hammered through the long hours of the night, stripped down to jeans and sweating.

Every drop of moisture rolling over his skin reminded him of the touch of Marcus' hands, the slide of his body over his. Full circle, back to longing and yearning, with too many hours to fill in the dead of night.

He hadn't spoken of his time with Marcus, pushing away his hurt that his family studiously avoided the topic as well. He told them he'd agreed to prepare about a dozen paintings for the gallery. The commissions would be enough to replace the roof on his mother's house, make sure the store had a comfortable winter with a heating upgrade. They couldn't argue with it, though his mother pressed her lips together, saying nothing to support or reject it as she finished making a new pot of breakfast coffee during the Monday morning discussion.

His dad had always joked and called them "Monday staff meetings", but over time they'd essentially become the day that the more significant store issues and strategies were discussed. Other mornings were just for being a family. On those mornings, Thomas found himself quiet, concentrating on eating as much as he could without drawing his mother's nagging to eat more. Half following Rory's latest gripes, their mother's comments about neighborhood goings-on, the volunteer work she'd do this week. When Celeste's next break was.

Thomas brought himself back to the present as he gazed at the one canvas off to itself. It was painful to look at, but he made himself do it. It was leaving in the next couple days, so the statute of limitations for the self-imposed torture was within reach. It was taller than he, and twice as wide. When he looked at it he got pulled into it, as if the painting had the ability to stick a fist in his stomach and reel him in by his intestines.

He'd done most of it this week, working with singular determination through the day at the store, grabbing a sandwich and candy bar from his mother's kitchen and heading to the shed once night fell, the painting calling to him. The craving need to give the deepest part of himself form and substance, at least on canvas, had taken everything else away as he slashed and stroked.

At times, his arm had been wrapped around his middle like a restraint, hand plastered hard against the lower part of his abdomen to compress the burning there, his eyes watering.

Like now, for he'd finished this last painting just tonight. Before him was the finished result. Heaven, and the torments of Hell.

Sinking down on his stool, he studied it. What would Marcus think of it? Thomas wished he could be there to see his reaction when he did. He'd left a message earlier in the week with Marcus' staff assistant that the paintings would be ready by Friday and requested shipping instructions. Marcus was just completing a local exclusive on a much bigger name than Thomas. Remembering how Marcus was during the week of a show, Thomas hadn't expected to hear from him until it was over, but he knew he *would* hear from him eventually.

Since Thomas had returned, Marcus had called him every few days. His mother and brother didn't resort to hanging up on Marcus, but neither one, as well as the demands of the store, gave Thomas much privacy. What wanted to be said filled up the phone like static white noise that got unbearable as he rattled off inanities. It didn't matter what he said, anyway. He just wanted to hear Marcus' voice, even as it left him heavy and aching.

Marcus then mailed him a cell phone, the smartass. Even signed him up and paid for a year's service, noting that he would take it out of his commissions. Thomas left the cell phone in the studio and at night he would check the messages, listening to Marcus' voice. He wouldn't call him back—he used email to respond.

Thomas knew he was taking them back to where they were before the Berkshires, but he'd known that it had to be this way. Time and distance made it possible to do it, at least on the surface. Beneath the surface he feared he was disintegrating, being consumed by the black hole inside his gut a little more every day.

He'd taken Rory for an X-ray today, loaded up four grain trucks, helped Mrs. Smith find a socket set. Marcus had likely had coffee at Starbucks, done an interview for an art magazine, rubbed elbows with God knew who.

Over time, Marcus had begun responding on email. The first email Marcus sent had one word in the subject line. *Chickenshit.* But after that potshot, they started exchanging information. Not just the progress on Thomas' art, but also details about his family. Marcus hadn't been sarcastic; if anything Thomas had been encouraged by his questions and interest. And pouring his thoughts into Marcus' ear and getting his reaction had helped. It had reminded Thomas that as well as a lover, Marcus always had been a pretty damn good friend.

Rory's doc says if he'd push himself more he could probably do more…

Marcus' response… *So when are you going to kick him in the ass?*

Celeste's dating some guy at college we think will ask her to get married at Christmas…trying to convince her to finish college first… Geez, don't I sound like her frigging dad?

Marcus' response… *You are. You're taking good care of them, giving her the right advice. Don't worry. She seems to have a good head on her shoulders… Thought you'd want to know that Julie's friend Ellen is doing better since our night together…actually started to help Julie out at the theater…*

And so it went. Sometimes no more than a few lines, but Marcus always sent him one a day at least, some longer, some shorter. Like a damn lovesick schoolgirl, Thomas kept them all stored, rereading them, imagining Marcus talking, sitting across from him, feet stretched out and braced on the opposite sofa while Thomas did the same on the facing sectional in Marcus' apartment.

Marcus' arm lying loosely over Thomas' shins as he sipped his wine and they talked. Thomas lacing his hands behind his head in a casual pose, teasing Marcus about his fancy lifestyle.

Marcus had even sent him a box whose contents Thomas was glad he checked out only when he was alone. He'd socked it away in the shed, not daring to look at it again.

Jesus, would it ever stop hurting? He bent over, shifted, trying to relieve the pressure.

Why do you keep answering me at two and three in the morning? What was the last thing I said to you? You make yourself sick, I will come kick your ass personally…

Farm people get up early…

Don't feed me shit…

Some of it made him grin. Other times Thomas' throat clogged up as he ran his fingers over the words on the screen. Even when the cell phone got filled up and he had to delete a lot of the messages, he was weak enough to keep one in particular.

You know I'm not going to let you get away with this forever. You're just pissing me off. The threat in Marcus' voice had a seductive touch that reached through the electronic waves and gripped Thomas in all the right places every time he listened to it. *Do you want me pissed off, Thomas? You want me to come bust your ass, take all your choices away?*

The prince coming to rescue the princess in the tower. Marcus was a prince all right, but Thomas knew this wasn't about rescue. Each time he heard that menacing Master's tone, his cock hardened and his heart jumped into his throat, butterflies exploding in his stomach. He made himself erase it at last and cursed himself for an idiot for the next several days when he wanted to listen to it again, like some addict needing his heroin fix.

He glanced at his watch. Two-thirty a.m. Maybe he could send an email to Marcus now before he made himself go off to bed. At six a.m. the deer corn trailer would arrive and he'd have about two hundred bags to unload.

When he logged on, the cell phone rang on the counter, startling him in the quiet of the early morning hour. Wiping the sweat off his face with one arm, he hobbled to the phone.

He shouldn't answer it. But it was the first time Marcus had called at this time. During the day, there was the pretense that Thomas was doing something else. Working, with family, whatever. To ignore it now would be like ignoring him if he stood right in front of him, and the bastard probably knew it.

Plus he wanted to hear his voice. Why'd he delete that message? Marcus wasn't calling as much anymore, and Thomas didn't think it was because of the email option. It was as if he realized the power of sensory deprivation. *Duh.* Who better than a Master knew the power of turning Thomas' own defense mechanism against him?

Opening the cell, he noticed it had a full battery. Crap. No excuse there. If he mimicked low battery beeping noises, Marcus would see through that pathetic attempt and laugh at him. "Hey."

"Hey yourself." The first notes of his voice, God, the first syllables, made need coil hard in Thomas' stomach, twisting the pain. Thomas leaned over again, tried to breathe. Sought something to say. "I just finished the last one."

"Just now."

"Yeah. How'd you know?"

"You've got that dazed sound to your voice like you're coming out of a month of solitary. How's it look?"

Thomas turned, his gaze sweeping over them, resting on that largest canvas specifically. "I don't know. It's different from the others." Son of a bitch. He slid down the side of the counter, pressed his hand to his abdomen. *Quit.* He didn't want to talk. He wanted to hear Marcus talk, let that voice pull him out of the place the painting had taken him, into a place somewhere in between it and here. "Don't know if you'll like it. If it'll sell like the others. Don't know..." *Don't know anything. But talk. For the love of God, talk.*

"Unfortunately, selling and liking are two different things, because most of the buying public wouldn't know talent if it bit them in the ass. It's my job to educate them, Thomas."

Thomas leaned his head against the cabinet, closed his eyes. "You know, it's funny you've never called me anything but that. Most people assume I'm a Tommy, Tom." Thomas covered the mouthpiece, coughed into a used rag and noticed without much interest he was coughing up flecks of blood again.

"When did you have a full night's sleep last?"

"You nursemaiding me? Girl."

"Yeah, fuck off. When, Thomas?"

Thomas rubbed his forehead, scanned the counter for his antacids, realized he'd taken the last of them an hour ago. "Last night."

There was a pause on the other end, significant enough that Thomas had to squelch the urge to fill in the pause with some type of verbal squirming.

"You want to really piss me off, you lie to me one more time."

Thomas licked the residual powder off the antacid paper. "Then don't ask questions you already know the answer to. Jesus." His eyes watering, he gripped the phone harder. "I don't want to fight about this, okay? I've been staying up late to get the paintings done. It's what I wanted to do. I can't…talk…"

"Thomas." Marcus' voice came through sharp and hard. "You're having one of those attacks again, aren't you?"

"It's okay, they happen. Marcus, I've got to go…"

"Lie down on your side, right now. If you're not going to let a doctor help you, you listen to me. Or I get off the phone and call 911 to send an ambulance to your house."

Alarm shot through him, increasing the fiery sensation. Thomas went to the floor, cursing and muttering, but doing it.

"Now take your hand, lay it over where it hurts. Don't press. Just lay it there."

Thomas complied, holding onto Marcus' voice, fairly sure this wasn't going to work, the pain too intense, but he knew Marcus would do what he said. Also, just holding onto his voice, fulfilling his instruction, was what he wanted above everything else. *Just talk... It would pass.* It always did. He'd had to have that extra strip of bacon this morning, like an idiot. He was hungry and he'd needed the coffee to wake up.

"Have you done it?"

"Yeah. Yes. I'm not a child."

"You're acting like one. Shut up and listen. It's my hand there. Just move it, easy, slow circles. I'm sitting right behind you, leaning over you. I've got one hand on your head, stroking your hair. You feel my fingers there?"

Thomas closed his eyes. Remembered them, felt them. "The way you do when I sleep, but I'm not all the way under."

'That's right." Another pause. "I'm going to talk to you, and while I do, I'm going to keep stroking your head and rubbing your stomach in slow circles."

He could feel it. Honest to God. And it was making it easier to breathe. Maybe it felt so real because he wanted it so much. Marcus' fingers. Strong, long fingers, no scars or blemishes.

"How's your face looking?"

"Sshh... Obey your Master. Be still and let me touch you. I just want to take care of you, pet. Just want you to let me take care of you."

"But...who takes care of you?" There was a silence on the other end, but it was full of so many things it almost felt like Marcus was there, right behind him, his body close, curled up spooning with Thomas like that very first night, and many nights thereafter. "I mean, other than the million guys who'd be willing to hold your hair out of your face when you throw up for the chance to sleep with you?"

"One more comment about my hair and I will get a crew cut." A pause. "*You* take care of me, pet. Just by breathing and existing, you take care of me in ways you can't imagine."

"You say things like that just to mess me up," Thomas said. "Mess with my head. I love your hair. Don't cut it."

"Making demands?"

"Why not? You going to come punish me?"

"I might. Do you miss having your ass strapped by your Master? Serving me with your mouth?"

Something stirred other than the pain. *You know I do.* Thomas couldn't say it aloud, but knew he didn't need to do so. It was a part of the whole empty need in his burning gut that wanted Marcus.

"What are you wearing?"

It brought Thomas up short, it was so cliché. It should have called for a quip or a chuckle, but not when Marcus' voice was sending frissons of energy down Thomas' spine with that note of don't-refuse-me-or-I'll-fuck-you-up command. "I'm kidding," Marcus said before he could respond. "I don't give a shit. Take it all off. Now."

Thomas struggled out of the sweats and set down the phone to remove the T-shirt. Rising, he went to the open top door to latch it. Kate raised her head to look at him. She was dozing beneath a cloud of moths surrounding the light just outside. "Sorry, Kate. Private guy stuff." He imagined Marcus laughing at them, but did it anyway.

He was already barefoot. Laying back down on the throw rug, Thomas felt the rough threads against his tense ass, the bracket of his shoulder blades.

"Keep touching your stomach, slow circles. My hand there. Just above your cock. You're getting stiff, aren't you? Harder and longer, your dick trying to touch the side of my hand, begging for attention."

"Yes."

"Yes, what?" His tone was sharp. Thomas closed his eyes, his heart tripping as his cock jumped.

"Yes, Master."

"Good. I'm going to keep massaging your stomach. I like the way it feels, the ridges of muscle under my palm, the way they tighten up further, every time I rub lower, get closer. I can see your cum leaking out of the slit, your balls drawn up, wanting me to cup them, squeeze them. You want your Master to touch your cock, don't you?"

Thomas groaned, his hand convulsing on his stomach. He wanted more than that. He wanted Marcus' touch, rough and brutal, gentle and teasing. He wanted his ass filled. He wanted to be pummeled, hear Marcus growl, his hand gripping Thomas' hair, yanking it back to grip his throat with his teeth as he thrust and thrust, knocking Thomas' knees out wider, reaching down and collaring his balls as he slapped against his ass, again and again.

"Are you…touching yourself, Master?"

"Would you like that?"

"Yes." God, yes.

"Tell me what you'd like. And I'm not touching your cock until I decide it's time."

"I want to take off your shirt. Rip it off. One button at a time. Put my mouth on your skin." *Bite you, suck on it as if I could eat you one bite at a time and finally not be empty, empty…* "God, I love your body." But more than that. "I love the way you breathe faster when I touch you, when you're getting hard and I know you're going to fuck me, I can see it in your eyes. Not asking me or coaxing me. You're just going to fuck me, and that's the end of it.

"I want to get on my knees, watch you open your pants, take down your underwear and force your cock into my mouth. Hold my head so you can thrust in hard, smell your come, wanting you to jet into my throat almost as much as I want it in my ass. I want you everywhere, Master. In every way."

"I'm touching you now." Marcus' voice was rough, thick. "I'm moving my hand down and fisting your cock. Pumping it in my grip, making your ass come up off the ground. Spread your knees out wide so I can see your balls, finger your ass if I want."

Thomas obeyed, his hand working himself, Marcus' hand in his mind, those green eyes close, his lips, his long, lean body.

"I sent you something. I know you have it there, in your studio where you can lock it up. Have you used it?"

"No. You didn't—"

"Say that you could. Good slave."

Though part of it was Thomas not wanting to use it alone. He'd thought often of that box since it had come.

"Get it," Marcus said.

Reluctantly, Thomas rose again and went to the locked cabinet. His shaking fingers had some trouble with the combination padlock, but then he opened it, removed the box. He'd only taken a brief glance at it, but now he swallowed. It was a vibrating plug of daunting diameter and length with a bottle of warming lubricant. "Pet?"

"I'm here."

"It's my size exactly. You can take it."

"It looks different…detached."

"Grease it up. I want you back on that carpet with it up your ass in five minutes."

"You aren't moonlighting as one of those porn stars, are you? The ones who make molds of their cocks and sell them in catalogs?" Even as he made the joke, Thomas' hands were moving over the texture, putting on the viscous liquid. It was about the right size. If he closed his eyes, he could just imagine…

"You imagining it's my cock you're lubing up?"

"Yeah."

"I thought so. Your voice started to get all low and sexy at the end. You practically purr like a tiger when you're about to get off. Makes me harder. Rub me, Thomas. Let me feel your hands. Am I good and slick? Hard enough for you?"

Thomas nodded. "Yes, Master."

"Good. Get down on the floor again. Keep that phone near. I want to hear your groan as you take it. God, you have a fine, tight ass. Best I've ever had."

Thomas didn't want to touch that, the mixture of jealous and possessive heat the comment evoked in him. He went back to the rug and lowered himself. Putting his feet on the side of the cabinet so his knees were raised, he began to take the greased dildo.

"Rub it against your cock and balls first. I want to feel your cock against my cock."

Thomas grunted huskily as the friction made his cock jump, convulse.

"Yeah, that's it." From the cadence of Marcus' breathing, he knew Marcus' hand was working himself. He was probably sprawled on his couch with his paperwork and an open bottle of wine, the lights of New York spread in a panorama before him while Thomas was in a shed in a quiet field in North Carolina, surrounded by the smell of paint, canvas and old lumber, a silver star and black sky domed over it all. It didn't matter. Thomas' eyes landed on the last painting.

"It's…of us."

"What? The one you just finished?"

"Yeah." Thomas groaned as he rocked. "It's always tougher this way, even if it's the same size."

"Music to my ears, pet. I want you stretched. Take me deep. Don't you clench up. You can take all of me. You did that first night when your hole was practically virgin, when I used my mouth to loosen you up, until you were wiggling and humping up against my face like an animal."

When Thomas arched up, the dildo slid home, filling him, stretching him hard, for though a sex toy could be made like flesh, nothing had the miraculous give and yet firmness of a man's flesh-and-blood cock. Of Marcus' cock.

"You make me sound…like some schoolkid…on his first fuck…"

"You were, in a lot of ways. And I fucking loved it. Someone taught you where the parts were. I taught you how to fuck. You remember the night I fisted you, at the club? You trusted me like you never trusted me before. Am I all the way in, pet?"

In ways he couldn't express. Thomas breathed out the word on a rasp of air. "Yeah. God, that's tight."

"Ah, Jesus, you had to tell me that, make me imagine the way it feels, as if I don't already know. You want a little pain with it. It finally blows your mind past that bullshit worrying you. Stomach hurt?"

It didn't. The power of endorphins. Of Marcus. Thomas closed his eyes. Marcus knew how to make it stop hurting, and yet was the source of all pain, good and bad. Thomas didn't care. He wanted it all.

"Does it have our faces? You don't usually do faces…"

"No… It's all the things…" He couldn't talk. He couldn't. His entire focus was on his cock.

"Start rocking yourself against the floor. Use your ass muscles to work it, use the floor to put it in deep. And my hands are on your cock again, Thomas. Holding you rough, squeezing you, fisting you…"

"Jesus…"

"The picture," Marcus commanded. "Tell me more."

"It's everything…you've ever done to me… Everything I wanted you to do, but was afraid to ask."

When Marcus swore softly in his ear, Thomas felt the power flood him, knowing he'd pushed his Master closer to the edge. He wanted Marcus to come, wanted to hear it, wanted it to take him over. "Your mouth…in my ass…but me too. I'm tonguing you, licking your balls while you're holding my thighs, spreading me, fucking me with your fingers, and you've put me in a cock harness so I can't come, but I'm going to explode. I want to put teeth marks in your ass…

The picture actually didn't show any sexual aids, just all those positions intertwined in a tree of life, hints in the tapestry of its branches as it stood rooted, the lone focus in a field drenched in a setting sun. Arms and legs were entwined to do one thing but interlocking with the next position, so other couplings could be envisioned. The sky was full of powerful rich reds, casting that faint crimson and violet hue over the two men twined at the base of the tree, sleeping on a blanket. It was as if the shadowy images in the tree above were dreams. There was a goat nearby…

It had been so easy, so flowing, it was no wonder it had pulled him in, immersed him. He'd painted red and brown streaks on his face, bare arms and his stomach, finishing the painting looking like some mad Celtic warrior involved in a sacred ritual, carried by the vision of it.

All the ways he wanted Marcus to touch him, fuck him…all the ways he wanted to service Marcus, make him come, make him not want anyone else, ever.

Best ass I've ever had…

The power of the physical made it all about that, even as Thomas knew it was goaded to such high limits by what wasn't the physical. But this was male need, the emotional inextricably linked with the physical so it was the dominant form of experience. It said it all. Meant it all.

"You ready to come, pet?" Marcus' breath was ragged. Thomas could imagine his long frame, fingers working up and down his cock. *His* cock as well, an overpowering dual image that had his lower body seizing, his bowels cramping, ass muscles tight on the plug, on Marcus' cock…

"You…first…" He managed through clenched teeth. "I want you to come in my ass…" He focused on those two figures locked together in dreams beneath the tree, two men in an embrace that could be combat. What would it be like to fuck Marcus…hold him in his arms, feel him strain against his hold the way Thomas did, a delicious wrestling that wasn't an attempt to get away but to get more, to allow the thrusts to be more powerful?

Hold him so he wouldn't get away… Was that what it was for him, restraining Thomas, doing everything to him, knowing he couldn't run away from the power of the feeling? Was Dominating Thomas one of the keys to Marcus' inner gates? The most powerful one of all? Was that the key to the rest?

And should Thomas be looking for a way in, knowing he couldn't offer him anything if he got there? It wasn't fair. It wasn't even kind or equitable, no matter what the poems said. It just was.

He loved Marcus.

For the first time in his life, Thomas said it in his mind consciously. He *loved* him, and the bitch of it was, being sure of it at last, when they were so far apart, sure of it down to the bottom of his worthless soul, meant he shouldn't say it… But love wasn't fair.

Julie's voice. *Tell him… You think it's kinder not to, but it isn't.*

"I love you, Master. Love you… Come for me. Please."

There was a groan, a more vicious curse, the sound of the phone hitting something, and he heard Marcus begin to release, that quick rush of breath mixed with animal grunts that spurred his own. Hearing it, he could hold out no longer…

"Come—"

That was all Marcus could manage or Thomas needed. He grabbed another paint cloth he'd been using, held it over himself as he jerked off with his hand, his ass stretched and burning, as full of Marcus as every other part of him was in his mind.

Love you… God, finally accepting it was as bad as dying.

As they slowed and the radio came back into his consciousness, Thomas became aware of Lonestar's heartwrenching, *I'm Already There,* a song which had entirely too much meaning for this moment. He focused blearily on the Coleman lantern, the dim light it threw on his finished paintings. He held the phone tight in his hand, gasping. If he could, he'd imagine Marcus turning him, still inside him, curved against the back of his body as he slept, his breath and touch on Thomas' throat.

"You bastard," Marcus said at last. And hung up, leaving Thomas aching anew.

Chapter Sixteen

ॐ

"Whenever we drive this route, we love to stop here," Mrs. Preston was saying. "I worry every year you won't be here. John says there are just no hardware stores like this anymore. Not like when he was growing up. I tell him you're even more than that. You're like the general store on those old Michael Landon shows."

Celeste gave Mrs. Preston the change for the bag of taffy she'd selected from the oak barrels of various candies in front of the register. "We're always glad to have you back, Mrs. Preston. Careful, now. I think Mr. Preston's wandered into the power tool section. If he and Rory get together to debate those, you'll never make lunch at Rosa's Deli before the crowd gets there."

"Oh, goodness." Mrs. Preston chuckled and headed in that direction.

Celeste turned her attention to her oldest brother, who was checking an inventory list against the wrench section on aisle one. She'd gotten in last night for her semester break. This morning she'd had to mask her shock at the sight of him. He'd lost the few pounds he'd put on in New York and she was afraid he'd dropped even more.

She had no clue how much sleep he was getting, but she suspected it wasn't much. He'd been working on those paintings every night, according to Rory. As she watched, her brow furrowing, he did that nervous habit he was doing more and more often, pressing two fingers to his side, as if he was holding something in. As if he was in pain.

When she'd mentioned her concerns to her mother, Elaine had kept her back to her, slicing scallops at the counter.

"Christ had to suffer to find faith, Les," she said. "Fasting, depriving himself of creature comforts. Your brother is in a crisis of faith. We have to help him."

But her voice had broken a little, and Celeste wondered who her mother was trying to convince. She was the youngest child and a girl, and therefore her opinion counted the least. It was something a younger sibling accepted for what it was, but Celeste was starting to get angry at all of them, Thomas included. But especially her mother and Rory.

She didn't know how to make them listen, but she wished she did. She'd head back to college in two weeks, and already the relief she felt about it made her most angry with herself. She knew Thomas needed them in some desperate way, and they were all failing him.

"I'm thinking of taking a semester off," she blurted out abruptly.

Thomas' head lifted. He pinned her with that oldest brother no-bullshit stare that always reminded her uncomfortably of Dad. She squared her shoulders. "You need the help around here."

"No, we don't. Not as much as you need to stay on track with your classes."

"Why does everybody get to have what they want, Thomas? Everybody but you? Has Mom been spouting the whole Jesus thing so much you think you're supposed to be a martyr?"

Oh geez. Maybe she was more upset about this than she'd known, because she certainly hadn't meant to blurt that out too. Things had gotten quiet over in the power tool aisle.

Thomas looked startled. He closed his mouth, various expressions crossing his face. "Rory isn't getting what he wants."

"If rolling around feeling sorry for himself and peeing in everyone's cornflakes is what he wants, I beg to differ. In spades."

"Les." He shook his head, ran a hand over his face that was so tired looking. Her brother was beautiful. There was no other way to say it. Growing up, her girlfriends had tried to see him naked in the shower on every sleepover. One or two had told her if he was their brother they'd think about committing a mortal sin. But now he looked so weary, and she was sick of it. "I want to paint. I'm painting now. That's what I want."

"I'm not talking about your painting and you know it."

She knew she'd hit the nail on the head by the way his face shuttered closed, like a trap. She almost heard the bones being crushed by the metal jaws.

"We're not doing this, Les. That's none of your business."

"As much as it is for you to tell me I can or can't go back to school when the family needs me. I'm over eighteen. I can make my own choices. And maybe I think the family needs *me* to make some sacrifices. Maybe that will take away some of the things you're using to keep from doing what you really want to do. Because you're scared. We won't fall apart, Thomas."

"What are you talking about, Les?" Rory came rolling up, his eyes darting between both siblings. "You're scaring customers."

"I'm talking about how it's time for us both to get off our asses and do more. Thomas shouldn't have to bear it all."

"Well I can't exactly get off my ass, sis," Rory snapped. "And I was trying to let Thomas have a life when this happened, and you were at school."

"Stop it." Thomas slammed the clipboard against his thigh, brought both their heads around. "Enough. Les, you're going back to school. Rory, maybe you should think about whether feeling sorry for yourself your entire life is a good career plan. I'm doing what I'm supposed to be doing. That's the end of it." He pivoted on his heel and strode back into the stockroom, leaving them both staring after him.

"You're not the boss of us." Rory attempted to regain the upper hand.

Thomas put his head back out, glared at him. "Yeah, I am, as a matter of fact. Deal with it. I have to make a grain delivery to the Worthington farm. I'll be back in an hour."

"Or two. The Widow Worthington," Les said.

The tension dissipated as Rory and she exchanged a conspiratorial look, siblings in perfect accord.

Thomas rolled his eyes as he took off the work apron and shrugged into a coat. "Cut it out."

"Hasn't had a cow or horse on her place in ten years, but wants you to deliver five bags of grain every month. Just so she can see your cute butt in a pair of jeans. She loves the summer… He might just strip off the shirt if she buys a few extra bags."

Rory made a suggestive gesture that had Les clapping her hand over her mouth, stifling a giggle.

"Sounds like the widow has good taste."

Thomas had heard the bells and assumed it was a customer. He was so jolted to see Marcus leaning against the display of concrete paver samples he almost felt lightheaded, wondering if he was dreaming. Oh hell, he wasn't going to faint. Neither Rory nor Marcus would let him live that one down.

Rory turned his chair, a scowl crossing his face. But Thomas had laid down the law. Marcus was managing a good chunk of their potential income during the off months. If he called, he was to be treated with courtesy and respect. Thomas just hadn't expected him to show up.

"Decided I didn't trust a courier service. Wanted to look at them before they were wrapped for transport and take some snapshots for Hans, even though he's already sent me a check, sight unseen."

He could have asked Thomas to email the pictures. Marcus goddamned well knew that.

"Oh, that's marvelous." Les grinned hugely and spun on her heel, looking between Marcus and Thomas. "Someone buying them without even seeing them. Imagine that. That's so amazing. Thomas, you've just got to be thrilled to your toes."

He was, but for reasons that had nothing to do with his work, watching Marcus' attention caught by his sister's exuberance, a slight smile curving his mouth. The bottle wound was barely more than a faint line. He really *didn't* scar.

"There are people who have seen your brother's work and are willing to pay to stand in line for the next piece."

"As they should." Les sniffed, turning her pert nose in the air. "Just think, before long he'll be so important that he'll do just one piece every year and Donald Trump will bid a million dollars to hang it on the wall of his mansion. You'll become one of those…prima donnas?"

"Diva was what I was thinking," Rory sneered.

"Why don't you get it out of your system?" Marcus eyed him.

"What?" Rory demanded.

"The part where you call me some derogatory name, I call you a bitter cripple and we each feel vindicated."

Rory backed the chair and altered direction. "I would," he flung over his shoulder, "but if Thomas is willing to be your bitch for a meal ticket, I can keep my mouth shut. As long as you don't decide we all have to whore for you."

Thomas stepped forward. He was going to knock him out of that chair, seize his brother in a headlock and pound him. The way he should have done a long time ago…

"Rory."

Rory wheeled his chair around just as Marcus hefted the fifty pound sack of grain at him. Celeste gasped, but the boy reflexively caught it in the air, even as it knocked his chair back a yard, into Thomas' quick hands to bring him to a halt.

Before anyone could say anything, Marcus nodded. "If you can lift that, catch it the way you just did, you can run this place as well as anyone. And the difference between you and your brother is you *want* to do it."

"I can't walk. I have to be able to load a truck."

"You have to be able to run a business. A high-school kid earning money for college can load a truck. If you were my brother and you'd just spouted out that bullshit, I would have wrestled you to the floor and sat on you until you screamed like a little girl." He lifted his gaze back to Thomas' troubled expression. "Of course, all you'd have to do is elbow him in the gut and you could break the lock. He's weak there."

"Son of a bitch." Rory thrust the sack off his lap. "You think I wouldn't do it if I could?"

"Yeah. That's exactly what I think." Marcus stepped forward until he was toe-to-toe with the boy. The green in his eyes was ice. "I knew this kid once. We called him Lassiter. He was in a wheelchair. Great scam artist, but not as a panhandler. He was a pickpocket. Got into a fight one night with two guys in an alley. They killed him in the end, but he beat the hell out of both of them first with nothing but guts and the slugger baseball bat he carried."

There were only a few feet and Rory between them, but he didn't look at Thomas. Marcus wasn't being polite, he wasn't being sarcastic. He was holding all three of them riveted, the alpha male who'd had enough and was more than capable of snapping the pack back into line.

"The only thing that ever scared him was finding out there was something he couldn't do, so he damn well made sure there wasn't anything he couldn't. You've got it all here. He had nothing. So stop being such a little prick and prove to us you shouldn't have died under that tractor's wheels. Because if this is all you want to be, then that's what should have happened."

Marcus shifted his attention to Thomas, nodding to a speechless Les. "I'd like to see those paintings now."

* * * * *

They walked across the paddock, Kate plodding patiently behind them.

"You think I was too hard on him?" Marcus broke the silence first.

"No." Thomas shook his head. "I should be doing exactly what you just did."

"You know how to handle him, pet." Marcus gave him a glance. "It's all tied up with everything."

Thomas curled his hands loosely at his sides, feeling the sudden hard need to reach out and touch. The shed would be empty, could be locked from the inside. Despite himself, his step quickened. Marcus' heavy-lidded expression told him he knew exactly where his thoughts were going.

"Think scratching your itch is what I came down here to do?"

The anger was immediate, given a shove by aching lust and loneliness that was underscored by Marcus' presence. "You didn't come to look at my paintings," Thomas retorted. "You could have done that in New York. So maybe you came down to scratch yours."

"Now why would I do that when I have all that fine ass available to me within walking distance of a Starbuck's?"

Thomas stiffened and Marcus raised a brow. "You're the one who thinks all I need is an excuse to move on to fairer game. I'm just reminding you of that."

"Stop it." Thomas came to a halt, his hands now clenched. "Whatever stupid, fucking, bored urbanite game you're playing, just stop it. I told you I love you, damn it."

"And what do I get with that, Thomas? What's the prize in that Cracker Jack box other than those three words?"

He couldn't match him on these grounds. Marcus was at his verbal best when he was pissed, whereas Thomas couldn't think of the right retort, could think of nothing but walking away before he smashed his fists into the offender's face.

"You're right," he said at last, quietly. He stared across the field, not at Marcus. "It's everything, but it's nothing. The nothing-everything I've got to give, that I only want to give to you and no one else. You're right."

Turning, he walked away toward the shed. He wanted Marcus to see the paintings. He wanted to stand next to the rug where his Master had brought him to climax with just the sound of his voice, the touch of his hand, the imagining of it.

But here they were, in the same old argument. Over and over and over again. God, he was sick of it.

He'd left the shed unlocked so if the courier came when he was on an errand, Les or Rory could let them in to pick up the paintings. He found the door standing open.

His mother was inside, using a Number Three broadstroke brush and a heavy-duty latex to cover the enormous canvas, his tree of life.

It took him a moment to process it, to comprehend that his mother, in her pantsuit and crisp white blouse, her hair sprinkled with paint, was doing what she was doing. Her countenance was rigid, almost manic as she slapped up and down, fast, so thick the paint was running like curdled milk and dripping in glops on the concrete floor. She'd been at her garden club meeting, he remembered vaguely.

"Son of a—"

Adrenaline surged through him at the sound of the fury in that voice. It woke him out of the paralysis of shock. Thomas was quick enough to grab hold of Marcus, but Marcus elbowed him with pinpoint accuracy in the gut and stormed into the shed, slamming the door back so it hit the wall.

His mother spun around at the sound of Marcus' voice. Shock coursed over her expression, as well as apprehension as he advanced on her. Her son she knew would never harm her. What she faced at the moment Thomas knew was entirely different.

Because of that, he managed to straighten, stumble after Marcus. Since he felt like he'd been stabbed, it was no easy feat. Marcus knocked the brush out of her hand and herded her by the sheer energy of his anger away from the painting, putting himself between it and her.

Thomas' attention was darting around the room. Some of the anxiety eased as he saw none of the others had been harmed. Just that one, the masterpiece of them all, the most explicit and raw work he'd ever done. A couple of the canvases close by had been flecked, but he could fix that.

"That wasn't artwork." She clasped her hands in tight balls, and Thomas could see she was trying not to shake, even as she blurted out the words. She'd been crying while she was painting, her mascara blotching the shadows under her eyes that suggested she'd been having some sleepless nights of her own.

She was getting over her initial fright. Whatever great emotion had propelled her to this moment was now ready to engage in battle. Thomas could almost see her on a burro, drawing a stick as her weapon, while Marcus, fully armored, peered distastefully down at her from atop a warhorse. "It was…sodomy. Unnatural. Sinful, unclean. Like you."

Because Thomas loved his mother, he managed to propel himself, despite the sharp pain in his gut, between her and Marcus. Marcus' face briefly flashed with that level of violence he'd seen in the parking lot of the diner. The room was heavy with heat, and more than one demon. He felt them swirling around Marcus, saw them in the way his hands tightened into fists that could easily break his mother's face and limbs. Marcus looked at his mother as if he was looking at someone else, someone he *had* wanted to hurt that way.

"What— What is he doing here?" Her voice was shrill.

"Claiming my property," Marcus snapped. Thomas had a moment to feel the shock of the double meaning before Marcus swept an arm in a gesture around him. "I've contracted for this work that you just deliberately vandalized. Which, if you weren't related to the artist and dependent on him for your wasted, narrow-minded life, I would take out of your bank accounts, your house. Every fucking thing you own."

"Don't you dare curse at—"

He stepped forward, his expression robbing her of the words. Thomas put up his hands to block him. Marcus didn't advance, just pressed against Thomas, his eyes leveled on his mother. Thomas felt the heat of Marcus' body as if he had emerged from hell in truth. "Don't you dare tell me what to do."

"Marcus." Thomas knew words wouldn't diffuse this, so he changed tactics. "Mom, you need to leave."

"I won't—"

"Now," he ordered. He glanced over his shoulder. "Now, Mom. Just… You need to leave."

A muscle twitched in her cheek, a spasm of nerves, her eyes suddenly bright with new tears of frustration. She was still shaking. Something hurt so badly in him he was afraid he was going to rupture. She looked frail, alone. And his paintings were arranged in the backdrop behind her, two choices of his life side by side, and the most important one pressed hard against him. In a way, he wished he could just close his eyes and make it all disappear, stop feeling at all.

She left. The door made a quiet thump, the wood hitting the latch and open padlock hung upon it. Thomas curled his fingers into Marcus' shirt, suddenly aware of how close together they were, Marcus' thigh pressed against him, his chest under Thomas' hands.

Closing his eyes, Thomas inhaled Marcus to try to make the moment into something different, knowing it was likely lost. But his body was aware of how temporary this moment could be, such that it could override almost any distraction to make the most of it.

Behind Marcus, the paint dripped off the canvas. Until now, Thomas had kept the door locked except when he was in here, to make this room about his art and everything inside him that drove it. But he hadn't barricaded it enough.

"Thomas."

"Don't. Just…don't." Thomas opened his eyes, turned his head so the brilliant green eyes were close, close enough to make him dizzy. "All the bullshit aside. Did you miss me?"

In answer, Marcus kissed him. Raw, angry, teeth scraping, his hands shoving Thomas' away to grab the front of his shirt and yank him harder against him. He pushed his thigh between Thomas' legs, backing him up to the counter, unleashing a brutal strength that didn't feel as if there was anything controlling it. Thomas knew he was a strong man, but he'd never gone full out hand to hand with Marcus.

Marcus hooked his hand in the back of Thomas' jeans, hauled him hard up against him, his thigh pressed in tight on his balls, making Thomas feel the steel length of him.

Then Marcus moved his hand to the front, opened Thomas' jeans and reached in, gripped him.

"Les…Rory…" Thomas managed to tear his mouth away and gasp. "They might come check…"

"Then you better let me fuck you with no arguments to slow us down," Marcus growled. He pulled at Thomas' shirt, simply tore it open and shoved him to the floor, making him stumble and fall, roll to his back. Marcus was down on him in an instant, his hand gripping Thomas' throat, holding him flat to the floor in an instant as his mouth and teeth closed over Thomas' nipple.

Thomas bucked, thrust against Marcus, but his knee firmly anchored him and Thomas couldn't dislodge him, even though he gave it his full strength, suddenly fueled by his own delayed reaction to the intensity of what had just almost happened here, what it all meant.

Marcus was terrifyingly invincible when he was furious. And Thomas wanted it so badly he could come from the power of that anger alone.

She'd destroyed it…but she couldn't destroy this, could she? He shoved it from his mind, the idea of Marcus being painted out of his life by slaps of thick white paint. He tried to rear up again and Marcus slammed him back down by that hold on his throat so Thomas could only latch onto his hip with one hand, clinging, pulling, digging in, seeking some sense he was in control.

Marcus worked him in the other hand now, his touch rough, sure, jerking him off with no intent but to prove he could bring it out of him whenever he chose.

"Marcus—" he had to gasp around the hold on his throat, but Marcus was relentless, releasing him only for a moment to pull him over, shove him back down on his stomach, yanking up his hips so Thomas had to scrabble for purchase on the throw rug before Marcus was jerking down his jeans, still fisting his cock, his mouth on his bare spine while Thomas shattered, unable to get a rhythm, unable to do anything but go along on the ride.

He savored every brutal touch, even as he knew this was being taken by force, no choices in truth. Marcus fully intended to fuck him whether he said no or not. His fury and violence had to go somewhere other that breaking his mother's neck, and apparently this was the channel for it.

Thomas welcomed it. Needed it.

Marcus plunged his fingers into his ass, working him with those clever fingertips. Thomas spurted, shouting out hoarsely despite himself.

While he was still jetting milky fluid into the rug, Marcus rammed home deep, hard, ruthless. This wasn't making love, or having sex. Or even fucking. This was ripping Thomas' soul out of his body through his cock. It had all the vicious brutality of rape, every touch intended to punish, to prove Marcus had power over him. Yet, because they couldn't stop being themselves, all Thomas wanted was more. He tightened his ass muscles, moved back against Marcus and earned a snarl, but he kept doing it.

Marcus seized Thomas' hair and yanked his head, holding it at a savage angle, letting Thomas feel his strength, his ability to snap his spine, his life in his hands. Thomas knew he could do anything to him. But that sword, like his life, could have two edges. He worked Marcus' cock inside him, squeezing, stroking as Marcus pumped. Felt triumph when hot seed flooded him, going deep and then overflowing, leaking down his buttocks, his quivering thighs.

Silence brought disquieting thoughts, the smell of fresh paint. Thomas closed his eyes. Marcus sat up on his haunches and abruptly yanked Thomas up by the shoulders, collaring him. He held him back against his body, still embedded in his ass, making him face the painting.

"Is that what you want? Are you going to wait until she whitewashes your whole fucking life?"

Thomas stared at it. A part of the tree still remained, and behind the paint he saw faint traces of limbs, both of the tree and the bodies. As if knowing what the most painful and tempting part of the painting had been, his mother had painted the lovers entwined under the tree first, obliterated them entirely. He put his hand up to Marcus' on his throat, laid his fingers over his long ones.

Stroking the knuckles, Thomas stared at it some more. Moved up to Marcus' hair, the feathering at the forehead, feeling him, working backward in his awkward position down to where Thomas could grip the shoulder of Marcus' shirt and hold on, gripping tightly enough to strain the seams.

Marcus let out a sigh, pressed his lips to Thomas' throat. Bit hard, suckled the skin past the point of pain while Thomas stayed still, trembling. Marcus' hand slid over his pubic area, gently took his semi-erect cock and began to manipulate it, fondle it, making Thomas jerk at the hypersensitivity of its post-climactic state.

"Christ, you drive me crazy. Can you fix it?"

Thomas nodded. "I took photos of all of them," he said thickly, though he shuddered at the idea of another night like the one when he finished it. "Kept the sketches. I can recreate it. I'll just change the lock and make sure she can't get in. You can take the rest and I'll ship it up to you next week."

Marcus nodded. "All right." He took a deep breath, his chest expanding against Thomas' back. "I'm not here just for that, pet. Get dressed. I bought a piece of property. The Hill farm right down the road. I want you to go look at it with me."

Chapter Seventeen

ꝏ

After dropping that major bomb, Marcus withdrew almost politely from Thomas' ass. He asked where he could clean up, which he proceeded to do at the utility sink, using paper towels and soap. As he gestured to Thomas to take his place, he refused to answer any questions, simply told Thomas he'd meet him in the car.

Thomas saw his sister at the door of the store as he crossed to the parking lot. When he opened his mouth, she nodded, waved him on. "We're quiet right now. Just come back for the post-lunch rush."

"I told your sister I would have you back in an hour, assuming you get a lunch break." Marcus was standing beside the rental car. "She told me to take as long as we need."

When Thomas got in, Marcus pulled out of the gravel parking lot, gunned the engine to pull ahead of a slow moving pickup truck. Mr. Gardelli, coming to get more fertilizer, Thomas assumed. Who'd probably be eyeing the fast car and muttering about Yankee invasion. "I like your sister," Marcus commented.

"She wants to ditch the next semester to stay home and help. Says I shouldn't be carrying it all."

"She's right, but not about the college part. You set her straight."

"I did, but she's got a stubborn streak."

"Thank God she's the only one in the family. It can be a pain when they're all infested with it."

Thomas sent him a narrow glance, but Marcus said nothing further, just gave him a bland smile.

The Hill farm was five miles down from the hardware store, set back a half mile from the road. It was a rambling old farmhouse, built in the 1940s, in need of work, sitting on ten acres. Mr. Hill had died last year and Mrs. Hill was comfortably ensconced in an assisted living facility. It hadn't been an actual farm for ten years, but the Hills had had some small plots for a roadside produce stand to supplement their social security.

There was a barn with a loft, a storage building, as well as a well-laid-out yard that Mrs. Hill had once kept cultivated with flower gardens. A swing hung from the old live oak in the front yard, which also had the remains of a tree house from when the kids were younger.

"Have you been inside before?" Marcus asked as they got out of the car.

"Yeah. We grew up with a couple of the kids. Mrs. Hill baked a lot. We stole a pie from her window once and she chased us all about five miles up the road with a spoon." Laughing all the way, Thomas remembered. He remembered he'd hung back to get the brunt of it because Rory hadn't hit his growth spurt and was too young to outrun her, shorter legs and arms pumping. He'd been shouting joyously, still too young to know what the word bitter meant.

Marcus was on the porch, had unlocked the door and was letting it stand open. He turned. Gestured to the barn. "Lot of space there. It has a loft. The whole thing would make a great studio."

Yeah. It would. Thomas was gripped between anticipation and apprehension. He didn't want to think it, hope it, because he knew it wouldn't work.

"Marcus, what are you doing?"

Marcus studied him in that intent way again. "Just what I said I was doing. Reclaiming my property."

He tilted his head toward the door, then stepped in, disappearing. Thomas swore softly, went up the stairs and followed him. He'd always liked the big wraparound porch. Sitting on the bottom step, spitting watermelon seeds at Johnny and May Hill, keeping an eye on Les as his Mom and Mrs. Hill shared cake and talked.

There was no furniture in the big kitchen except for a dusty oak table that had been left there. The paper on the walls was harvest gold seventies floral and stripes, but the smell of old wood preserved by quality care and brought out at this particular time of day by the sun was soothing. There was a quiet to the house, as it waited to become a home again. Perhaps to the two men regarding each other across the room.

"We could restore this together." Marcus put it out there. "Mix of old and new, traditional with our own tastes."

"Marcus, you live in a penthouse."

Marcus shrugged, settled back against the counter, crossing his arms, watching Thomas with those brilliant green eyes. A dragon's eyes. "I live anywhere I want to live. I can maintain a residence here and in New York. There's a small airstrip nearby that can handle private planes. I can fly back and forth as needed to the gallery. Both of us could go there whenever we want to. I have an excellent general manager. She'd be delighted to take on more responsibility."

"You don't belong here. You don't fit. You'd hate it after a week. Local theater consists of the high school's biannual production of Gershwin, or Rodgers and Hammerstein. No gourmet shops."

"There's only one question relevant for you to answer. Do I belong with you?"

Thomas swallowed, looked away. "That's not the issue."

"I just made it the issue. Do you belong to me, Thomas?"

A pause, a quick jerk of his head. He couldn't deny it, had said it before. Marcus' eyes flared, quick and hot, but still he didn't move. The room seemed to be getting smaller.

"Then, next question, same question. Do I belong with you?"

"That's not for me to say. I can't—"

"If it's not for you to say, then it's for me to say. Why the hell are you so afraid to take this for yourself? I say I do belong with you. To you."

Marcus' eyes traveled around the kitchen. "There's a good fresh market right up the road," he mentioned, changing the direction of the conversation, putting Thomas off balance. "The sign caught my eye. Strawberries, flowers and boiled peanuts. Ordinary things, put on a sign like the most amazing treasures. Reassuring, basic. I picked up some excellent tomatoes and green peppers from a woman wearing a purple and red hat that any pimp on the strip would envy."

Thomas choked on a snort. "That's Mrs. Dorsey."

"She gave me a recipe for a seven layer salad that calls for enough mayonnaise to give me arterial blockage. When I told her I'd bought this place, she said if I needed help making the salad for entertaining my friends, her divorced daughters—one or both of them—would be happy to help." His eyes managed to glint with amusement without losing a watt of that immobilizing intensity. Something in Thomas was responding despite himself, like a bird waiting at the door of a cage that was inching open.

"At which point," Marcus continued, "her mother—who, by the way, looks like she sailed over on the Mayflower—elbowed her and said in a stage whisper, 'Betsy, he's far too good-looking. You know he's got to be one of those homos'. Elongated o's, by the way."

Thomas' lips twitched. "I bet Betsy Dorsey just about passed out."

"She was quite mortified. I took Mrs. Mayflower's hand, kissed it and said she had senses as sharp as a vampire's teeth. And I'd appreciate that help if the offer was still open, because I figured she was the one who taught her daughter how to make the salad to begin with."

Thomas pushed off the door, ran a finger through the thick dust on the table. "We're not backward here, Marcus. As long as you don't shove your differences in people's faces, they're pretty tolerant."

"Did I sound shocked?" Marcus asked mildly, raising a brow. "We had a good chuckle over it and Mrs. Dorsey talked me into some fresh squash. I know the problem isn't the community, Thomas. It's your history in it. Your family. What will Mrs. Dorsey say when Thomas Wilder shows up with that handsome Yankee everyone knows is gay? But it's not even about that, because small town people are usually a lot sharper than us big city folk believe. Most of them probably guessed it about you long ago."

He shifted, tilted his head. "Your mother, your family, is a serious obstacle. But what I've realized is that you're the true problem. What you feel you deserve, the faith you have in us. The question isn't *do* I belong in this world of yours, but do you *want* me to belong in it? I'm willing to try, because your mother is right about one thing. You need this part of your life. It's as much a part of who you are as your painting. And…maybe I need it too, because it's the core of you."

Thomas' gaze snapped up. Marcus turned then, as if he suddenly had a need to move, had gone somewhere he'd not necessarily intended to go. Looking out the window, his expression became more thoughtful, his gaze drifting.

"At the hospital," he said at last, quietly, "you said that if it wasn't for your responsibility to your family, you'd stay with me until I kicked you out. Are they your safety net, your mother, Rory and Les?"

"What?" Thomas' brow furrowed.

"If you believed I would never tire of you, never kick you out, would the answer be the same?"

Thomas shuffled, drew a circle in the dust. "As hard as it is to be without you now, I don't think I could handle watching you get bored with me."

"And you think I would?"

Thomas couldn't answer. Though he thought he saw a flash of pain in Marcus' expression, his voice was still even when he spoke next. "How would you feel if you knew I had every intention of making what we had a forever deal? That I consider you mine, not just now or a year from now, but every year after that?"

"Scared shitless." Thomas managed a smile he didn't feel.

Marcus nodded. "I can see a lot of things here, Thomas. I can see us in this kitchen, making dinner for your family. Your mother might be tight-lipped at first, but then we'd all loosen her up. She'd be giving ideas on curtains before she left. I imagine you on that front swing, your feet bare, toes brushing the ground as you sketch that way you do, like everything else has disappeared. I see a tester bed, a firm mattress, able to take punishment. Like you."

Marcus turned now, his lips curving, voice settling into a lower, enchanting cadence. "I see you leaning against the doorway over there. I can imagine moving past you, stopping just a breath away from your mouth, pressing you back into the frame with the weight of my body. I'd be on the phone, brokering deals hundreds of miles away, and yet my hand would be on your cock, sliding around to your hip to cup your ass, watching your eyes go opaque and dangerous like they are now.

"Bending you over the kitchen table, or pushing you to your knees to suck my cock while watching the sun set over the fields, anticipating taking you up to my bed, fucking you and holding you while you sleep… I can imagine you and us a million ways here, Thomas. I will make my home where you are, because you are my home. I don't know any way to say it any more clearly. So now the ball's in your court."

Marcus straightened, faced him squarely. "I want you to move into this house. Make a home with me."

As Thomas stared at him, speechless, Marcus came across the room. "And another thing. I've had enough of this shit." He laid a hand on Thomas' shoulder, then another on his abdomen, curving over the ache, making Thomas wince. "It ends here. You need someone at your back, making sure you're taking care of yourself, someone who's able to truly kick your ass back into line when you don't. And in the words of the country song, slightly altered, I'm wearing the outrageously expensive Italian loafers that can do it."

* * * * *

It was unreal. Like a Twilight Zone episode, only in vibrant color and without the eerie echoing hopeless ending suggesting that human nature *would* always disappoint.

Thomas didn't know what to answer, couldn't think what to say. Then Marcus' cell rang. Marcus glanced at it. His eyes darkened, his lips thinning. "I'll be outside. Look around."

As Thomas watched Marcus leave out the kitchen door, step onto the porch, he felt that brief sense of hope drain away.

He looked around the kitchen. Marcus wanted him to make the ultimate step, and yet in this fateful moment, he was demonstrating he wasn't willing to make Thomas fully a part of his life. Perhaps the Twilight Zone episodes were on target, just like Thomas' original feelings. Even if Marcus did think his feelings for Thomas were love, they wouldn't last. A passing phase, having to do with not being willing to hear the word no. Marcus' subconscious apparently knew it even if he didn't, because he continued to feel the need to keep his secrets.

As he had the thought, Thomas realized that wasn't fair, exactly. Once again they were at the point of "I'll show you my hand if you show me yours." Whatever was in Marcus' past was apparently his most closely guarded secret. Until Thomas was willing to surrender to him completely, he wasn't going to trust. Was that how it worked? A slave's full surrender could win a Master's trust?

Or was it like gradually loosening a tight box lid, taking it up a little on either side, not able to get too far ahead of the other side until it all came up at once? Maybe it was different for every two people.

He stepped out as Marcus snapped the phone closed, exchanged a look with him. Marcus opened his mouth.

"Don't," Thomas said quietly. "Don't lie to me about who that was. If you don't want to tell me, just don't tell me. You've..." He turned and looked at the house. "This is a dream, Marcus. I think it's a dream I want, maybe *the* dream I've always wanted, but I'm not sure of what you want, or even who you are. You always keep it to just you and me, and a person is about a lot more than that. They are what they come from, who their family is, where their deepest secrets and fears lie.

"You know all those things about me," Thomas said. "I've never hidden them from you—when I tried, you just ferreted them out. But in order to live in a house like this, you've got to appreciate the light. An artist needs light like air. To flourish and create. To believe in the art."

When Marcus didn't respond, Thomas turned to face him again. Marcus looked at a loss for words. Not being reticent, not muddling through something insightful to take the wind out of Thomas' sails later. It was like he didn't know how the hell to respond. Marcus was ageless in his looks, but in that second Thomas almost saw evidence of his mortality in the rigidity of his facial muscles.

He stepped forward, the weighty topic thrust aside. "Marcus, you okay? What's wrong?"

Marcus started as if caught doing something wrong, shook his head. Turned away quickly before Thomas could touch him. "I told your sister I'd have you back. Let's go."

"Marcus—"

"Don't." The word snapped out like a whip, and Thomas froze in the act of reaching toward him. Marcus had never rebuffed him. He'd intended to take Marcus' arm, stop him, and the way Marcus recoiled from him, his eyes green and hard, clearly did not invite contact. "Get in the car or walk."

Thomas set his teeth and inclined his head. "Fine." He should feel anger and a sense of justification in his mistrust of Marcus' offer to play house. But as Marcus turned away, Thomas watched him closely, the stiff body posture, and all that didn't seem to matter. Marcus, the epitome of dangerous grace, narrowly avoided running into the side mirror before he found the door handle and got back in.

When they got back to the store parking lot, he parked and got out of the car before Thomas could say anything. Alarmed by the way Marcus shoved open the door of the store, Thomas lunged out of the car and quickly followed him in.

Les and his mother were at the cash register. Rory was on the nail aisle, restocking.

His mother paled at the sight of Marcus, but curled her fingers into resolute balls on the counter, even as Les put a reassuring hand on her arm and cast a worried glance at Thomas. Thomas increased his step and managed to almost catch up before Marcus reached them. He'd taken his organizer from the car and now unzipped it on the counter, inches away from his mother's knuckles. "Pen," he said to Les, in a voice so calm and precise Thomas thought it could chisel rock.

Les mutely handed him the pen and he began to write.

"Celeste says you're buying the Hill farm." Elaine raised her chin. Marcus didn't even glance at her.

"It's already bought. In cash, closing statement signed and deed recorded. I know enough about small towns to know that family connections can muck with a building inspector's report."

"You can't buy us," Elaine said, her voice quivering. "You can't buy my son."

"An intriguing thought, and a pity. I think he'd be far happier as my slave than he is as yours." Marcus kept writing. "Thomas, this is your part on the dozen pieces you've done. The courier will arrive later today to pick them up. It's a good agency so you don't need to worry about them getting to me safely." While he shifted his attention to Thomas, Thomas had the strange feeling Marcus was somehow seeing them all, including him, through some type of distorted filter.

He'd done that once as an experiment, painted an image through a wavering piece of glass. For a little while it had seemed as if he was somehow seeing an alternative but perhaps more true reality of what he was painting. In the same way now, Marcus seemed conscious of all of them, but in a way that felt skewed, raw.

"You'll redo the last one as we discussed or I'll take the extra advance out of your hide." His green eyes focused somewhat, a seductive promise briefly in his voice. Thomas didn't dare look at his mother or sister, alarmed at the tone even as he couldn't help but respond to it. "I want that painting."

Abruptly, Marcus turned and slammed his hand down on the counter, making both women jump. He leaned in, his eyes snapping, face inches from Elaine's frozen features.

"I haven't bought him. I have the goddamned privilege of handling his work. Have you looked beyond your own nose at what those paintings are? They're art. Art is that which touches us down to the soul, tells us this is what life's about. People come into my fucking gallery and stand in front of his fucking work for twenty minutes, because even if they can't put their finger on it, they know they're standing before something so priceless this measly amount," he waved the check, "doesn't touch its value.

"Accepting what people are, what they can't change and loving them with every part of yourself anyway. *That's* what love is about." He glared at Elaine. "You take that away from him, you make him believe that kind of love doesn't exist… It would be better for you to shoot him rather than destroy him inch by inch, year after year. If you do that, you're not saving his soul, you're killing it. If you'd look into his eyes for once, you'll see it. How we love *is* our soul."

Out of his pocket he yanked the rag that Thomas had left on the sink in the shed and foolishly not thrown away. Marcus tossed it on the counter in front of her. "That brown stain covering about half of that cloth isn't paint. It's coming from your son's stomach lining. I want him to see a doctor this week. If he won't go, you hogtie him and make him do it." He looked toward Thomas. "Or I'll come back and do it for you."

"Marcus, cut it out. Mom, that's not—"

Marcus made a slicing gesture with his hand, relocked gazes with Elaine. "If you still actually know what being a mother instead of a missionary is about, you'll get him there and figure out why he's doing it before he kills himself. He'll do anything to take care of you. Of all of you." He sent a hard glance toward Rory. "Get a clue."

As Elaine lowered her gaze to stare at the rag, her fingers reaching out to touch it, Marcus tore off the check, left it on the counter and turned toward Thomas. "I'm headed back to New York. But I'll be back, and we'll pick up our conversation then."

Folding the organizer up, he pivoted and headed toward the door as brusquely as he'd come in.

Various questions were churning inside of Thomas, but seeing Marcus about to walk away brought one of them up immediately. "When?"

The word was out before Thomas could think to stop it, or completely mask the urgent need for an answer.

Marcus turned at the door. There was such a powerful emotion in his eyes that Thomas almost moved forward, his lover's fuck-off routine be damned. He saw something in Marcus' eyes that told him he'd needed to hear that tone of want in Thomas' voice, in front of his family. Marcus had needed it so desperately that it looked in danger of shattering something within him completely. The last word Thomas had ever thought to describe Marcus was lonely, but it was in his face now.

"Whenever you ask me to come, pet," he said softly. "Just not today. No matter what happens, I can tell you this. I will always love you. No matter what you feel you need to be, where you need to go, I'll always know you're mine. I understand that now. So you can at least be easy on that, all right? It's okay. I love you."

His attention shifted back to Elaine and something altered in his expression, became much colder. She raised her gaze under the compelling power of his stare.

"If you ever touch anything he creates again, you won't have this place, your house. You'll be lucky to get a bed in a state nursing home when I'm done with you."

"Marcus—"

"No, Thomas." His mother surprised him by speaking. "Let him say what he's going to say.

"This is your dream, your husband's. Even Rory's. Not his. He loves you. That's why he's here and part of what makes me love him, frustrating though it is to love a fucking noble idiot. But don't give me the slightest opportunity to take it away from you, the way you're trying to take it away from him, because I will. His art is his soul. You attack his soul again like that and I don't care who the fuck you are to him. Clear?"

She stared back at him, making no acknowledgement, though her shoulders quivered with the effort of holding the pose under that intimidating glare. It was the most cowed Thomas had ever seen her.

Marcus nodded as if he'd gotten the answer he expected, turned on his heel and left the store.

Thomas ignored his brother's demand for an explanation, his sister's murmured reassurance to their mother and went after him, spell broken. When Thomas caught up with Marcus at the car, he grabbed his arm, bringing him to a halt.

"What the hell was that? What is wrong with you?"

Thomas was angry at him, but he was more furious with his inability to figure out what the tumultuous current of murky waters under the surface of the whole scene was about. He wanted answers.

Marcus ran a hand over his face, the back of his neck. When he raised his head to meet Thomas' gaze, it was as if the act took great effort.

"I thought…if you couldn't leave, I could bring it here, give you a way…" He shook his head, moved away from Thomas' touch and got into the car. The window was down, but what was swirling around Marcus, the fact he'd removed himself from Thomas' touch twice now, didn't encourage Thomas to take immediate advantage of the opportunity the open window provided.

Fitting the key into the ignition, Marcus held it there. Thomas felt a spear of apprehension as a shudder seemed to run through his arm. Marcus stiffened, his expression shutting down again as he turned over the ignition.

"You may be right. An artist needs light. And I bring my own darkness. Maybe we don't belong together, Thomas. I don't know. I really don't know anything right now." Reaching out the window, he put a key that was sitting on the dashboard in Thomas' hand. "The house is in both of our names. Move in if you'd like. Maybe I was just…maybe I'm just fucking crazy."

"Marcus." Changing his mind, Thomas put his hand on the window ledge and leaned in, not caring who might be watching. Touching Marcus' face, he ran his knuckles along the slope of his rigid jaw. "Stop," he said softly. "Just stop, and slow down. Trust me. Will you ever trust me?"

Marcus closed his eyes, his lips pressing together, so Thomas moved his touch there, fingers tracing them.

Something was terribly wrong, and none of the rest of it mattered.

"No," Marcus said at last, opening his eyes and looking directly at Thomas. "I can't trust anyone. It's just not in me. Not now. Not ever. I've got to go."

He hit the window control then and Thomas had to pull back his hand or have it trapped. "Marcus, dammit..."

But Marcus had already put the car in reverse in almost the same movement and backed it. Normally, he was a smooth, confident driver, but now he pushed down on the gas like a teenager learning how to work a clutch. Thomas had to move back fast to spare the toes of his fortunately chosen steel-toed work shoes.

He didn't want to go back into the store. Everything in him was saying he needed to jump in the store's truck, run Marcus' ass down and figure out what the hell was going on. Marcus had never been like this. So dead, so final. An hour ago, he'd been threatening to set up house just down the road. Despite Thomas' doubts, he'd gotten him hoping, considering. Wondering if it was as impossible as it sounded.

Now Marcus acted like...he didn't know where they were now. Thomas tried to ignore the feeling that Marcus had just started the beginning of the end between them. Over a fricking phone call.

He went back into the store, steeling himself. Something in his face must have warned them, for even Rory said nothing, back to making a quiet clinking sound on the nail aisle. Or perhaps they were both waiting for their mother to detonate. To break down. Instead, she was looking at Thomas' face. "Are you okay, son?" she asked softly.

He swallowed. "Yeah. But I don't think he's okay at all. And he won't tell me why."

She pressed her lips together then jumped as the ledger book she'd opened on the counter began to twitch and make a buzzing sound. "What on earth—"

Les flipped up the ledger book to find a cell phone there. On the third vibration, the ring tone kicked in and Rory's brow creased. "Is that…"

"*Highway to Hell*. Marcus is a closet AC/DC fan." Thomas said absently, then shook his head at Rory as he snickered. "No cracks about closets." Moving to the counter, he picked up the cell. It was an extension of Marcus' arm. For him to be upset enough to forget it made Thomas question the wisdom of allowing him to get behind the wheel of a car.

"Mom, what's the area code for Uncle Ren in Des Moines?"

"515."

Thomas stared at the phone. Iowa. Marcus was getting a phone call from Iowa, and a quick press on the call listing button told him it was the same number his last call had come from.

"Thomas," his mother said. "What are you doing?"

"Getting some answers." He flipped it open. "Hello?"

The line was crackling with static, so he had to repeat it.

"Marcus…is John. Have a crappy connection out here. You there?"

"Yeah."

Thomas waited, straining his ears to hear through the crackling. When Les started to speak to their mother, he shook his head, made a sharp hand gesture for quiet and hoped no customers came in.

"This…" there was a pause on the other end. "This isn't Marcus, is it?"

"No. This is his partner." Thomas managed not to hitch over it, though in his mind there was a significant pause in thought, trying to decide the best word to use. It left it open to meaning business, or more than that. Apparently, either one seemed to ease John's concerns enough, though he added the question. "So you know what's going on?"

"Yes. Marcus left for a few minutes. Is there something else you need?"

"Is he…okay?"

On that, Thomas was on solid ground, and was able to give the key sense of intimate knowledge that apparently would win John's trust and assumption that he *did* in fact know what the hell was going on.

"No. He's definitely not okay."

"Jesus." John blew out a sigh. "Then maybe you can think of a way to say this to him. I talked to Mom. She says she's going to respect Dad's last wishes. She doesn't…hell, no good way to say it. She doesn't want him at the funeral. I mean, she does, but Dad didn't and she's just…

"We're going to need another transfer on the burial expenses. His last days were pretty rough, so I tapped out the account for the hospital. He's got to understand, it tore her apart these last days. All she can think about is how much she loved him and misses him, so of course she's going to support his wishes right now.

"Marcus will want to transfer another six thousand in there Friday. That's when I'll need to pay the funeral home. She's worried to death about the farm, but I told her Sue and I can cover everything. Didn't think it was time to lay on her that Marcus has been paying their way out of every tight corner for the past ten years.

"Maybe…after this all dies down, he could come home for a visit. I think she really wants to see him. Hell, we all do. He's probably told you how she is, all the Bible stuff about Dad being the head of the household and obeying him. Hell, if I tried to get Suzie to go that way, she'd hit me in the head with a two-by-four. It's just the way they are.

"He was a mean old bastard. Stubborn, but Marcus is like that too. Stubborn, mean when crossed. They never saw how alike they were, even as different as we know Marcus is. I…I didn't mean that in an offensive way, okay? I mean…I don't know if you're his partner…or his *partner*. Or both. Ah, hell. Don't know why I'm telling you all this. It just…it's been a hell of a day. Will you just tell Marcus we love him and when this crap is past, he should come home? He really should. I know he won't, but…will you tell him?"

"I will."

When Thomas heard John hang up, he closed the phone and started to slide it in the front pocket of his jeans.

Iowa. Marcus had a family in Iowa. A farm. A father who'd just died.

But he was also Dodger, somehow connected to Toby. On a hunch, he scrolled through the call history, the phone list, and found Owen's name.

One part of him knew this was wrong, but the larger part didn't care. Pieces were missing, but the pieces that were coming together were goading him into the territory Marcus had always declared off limits. Well, to hell with that.

As Thomas cued up the number, finger poised to start the call, he glanced at Les. "I'm going to New York for a few days. I need you to make sure the courier gets those pieces. Okay?"

She nodded, her eyes full of questions even as she glanced toward Elaine.

"Marcus' father died," Thomas added.

"Oh." Les made a little sound as her mother crossed herself, then folded her hands on the counter.

"Maybe he left the phone here deliberately, Thomas, knowing…"

"Mom, enough." Thomas said coldly, stopping his mother mid-sentence. "This isn't a debate. While I'm gone, ask the Brewster kid to come in. He could use the money anyhow."

He turned to Rory, who'd rolled up close to the side of the counter near his mother, attempting to make a wall of their disapproval. Thomas cocked his brow at him. "While I'm gone, you're in charge of the store."

A surprised expression fluttered across his mother's face. "Thomas, Rory can't—"

"I can't—"

"Yes, you can. More than that, you *will*." Thomas stabbed a finger at him, his brows drawing down. "You chickenshit out and let Mom take over, as she'll try to do to baby you and your wallowing self-pity, I will yank you out of that chair and put a foot up your ass. Your legs don't work, but your brain does, your arms and upper body does, and you can use Les and Brewster's kid when you need a pair of legs. I need a good manager to handle things this week. You're that guy."

He gave his brother an even, take-no-shit look. "You can hold more figures in your head than a rocket scientist. So stop focusing on what you don't have and use what you got. Or I'll tell Amanda Brewster you're really a paraplegic and your dick doesn't work."

"She already knows it does," Rory snapped and then colored to his roots. His mother and sister turned, a look of consternation on one face, barely suppressed laughter on the other.

"Well, if you've got the brains to use it, you can do other things." Despite the circumstances, Thomas felt a gut-loosening grin cross his face.

Then his mother's expression shifted back to him. As he met her gaze head-on, he felt a calmness that was new to him. "When I get back, we'll talk. I may be gone several days. You know how to get hold of me."

For once, without further comment, she nodded. He wasn't unaware of how she had her hands folded together, her short nails biting into her skin, but he would deal with that.

He'd been dealing with things for eighteen months, but hadn't felt in control of anything. For the first time since his father died, that feeling was gone. He was going to New York. To Marcus.

Chapter Eighteen

ઇ

He'd kept the entry key to Marcus' place. It had been in his wallet all this time, working its way toward the back, behind the more frequently used assortment of other cards. Credit cards, his driver's license, hell, the video store card that protected Marcus' picture.

It was shortly after two a.m. and he'd seen a light on in Marcus' place from the glass elevator. Top floor. A spectacular view of Manhattan and the water. Because Thomas had to pass through three checkpoints using that access card, as well as a security guard, who recognized him with a friendly smile, he wasn't too concerned about letting himself into a New Yorker's apartment in the middle of the night. He could have called ahead, but chose not to, not wanting to give Marcus the ability to shut him out.

When he let himself in, Thomas dropped his bag in the foyer and then moved through the kitchen. The light had been on in Marcus' office area, but he found Marcus sitting in the dark living room, just inside the open balcony doors. He was in the shadows, next to the fluttering curtains. Thomas might have missed him, except he was smoking and the faint glow of the cigarette tip drew his attention.

Now Thomas leaned against the kitchen doorframe, considering the man he loved.

His fastidious lover was wearing just a pair of jeans, the top button open. The pack of cigarettes was half empty, ashtray full. A bottle of Jack Daniel's Gentleman Jack sour mash and Chopin brand vodka sat companionably together.

He was staring. It didn't seem to be at anything in front of him, so Thomas assumed it was at something inside him, something worth making himself shitfaced drunk. As Thomas watched, he lifted the bourbon to his mouth and chased it with the vodka in an impressive swallow. Straight from the bottle, both of them, and Thomas was willing to bet it didn't even make his eyes water. Wiping the back of his mouth with a hand, Marcus picked up the cigarette again.

"Marcus."

Marcus froze in the act, turned his glance toward the interior of the apartment. The eyes glittered in the darkness and Thomas had the sudden impression he'd walked into the den of a wounded tiger.

"What are you doing here?"

"You forgot your cell phone." Thomas lifted it, moved across the room. Taking a position in the open door to the balcony, he made sure he was square with Marcus, where he wouldn't be ignored. Deliberately, he hooked his thumbs in his pockets, curling his fingers loosely on the front of denim. Watched Marcus' eyes center where he'd intended, then run up his body with a greedy look gripping his features, causing prickles of heat to move across Thomas' skin.

Yeah, Marcus was drunk. But not too drunk, which meant he could hear, and maybe listen some.

Thomas didn't know what he was going to do or say, though. He was here. That was what mattered. The rest would come. "Your brother needs you to transfer six thousand to the account to cover the burial expenses."

Marcus' gaze shifted back up to Thomas' face. Deliberately, he crossed his legs, leaned back further in his chair. Took a deep drag on that cigarette with a style only Cary Grant could have emulated. Thomas could almost see the internal machinations clicking into gear to put the usual shields in place. "You couldn't call and tell me that?"

"I would have been here a couple hours sooner, but there was someone else I wanted to talk to. A story I wanted to hear.

I didn't get all of it. I want it from you. But I got enough to get my foot in the door."

"You think so?"

"I know so."

"Are you fucking with me, Thomas? You think I'm in the mood for that?"

"Do you really think you can love someone without making yourself vulnerable? I told you. That's not how family works."

"I'm not your family, Thomas. I wouldn't even know how to be. Go home. Go away. Go to hell. I don't care."

"Nice try," Thomas said mildly, though Marcus' words spiked against the ball of nerves in his stomach. He knew he was playing against a master poker player. A Master, period. But he wasn't going to back down.

"Owen told me about a street kid they called Dodger. With slick hands and the kind of looks that made sure he could stay ahead of hunger. Just. Over time, two other kids got attached to him. Toby and Emile. He ran with them, protected them. Kept them clean while he did whatever he needed to do. Fifteen years old. A runaway from Iowa. From a father who couldn't accept what he was and a mother who wouldn't stand for him."

Marcus flicked ashes in the ash tray. "You're telling me a story I already know. Go tell it on a street corner. If you set it to music, someone might flip you a quarter."

But Thomas' sharp eyes caught the slight tremor in the fingers. Drink, but also nerves.

"Every Dodger has to have a Fagan," he pressed on, though the images the story had created in his head had made him sick, made him hurt for Marcus. "Yours was Mike Winshire. He'd grown up a street kid as well, become a small operator. Graft, gambling, prostitution, but according to Owen, a strangely gentle man who loved you in his odd way."

Marcus rose out of the chair, swift, but without his usual animal-like grace. Paced out onto the balcony. "I chose every step of my life, Thomas. Mike taught me to survive, taught me to play the right games. If he needed sex, he got it from me and counted himself lucky to be tapping the ass of a pretty kid, because he was an ugly son of a bitch, hung like a damn moose.

"We only had one rule. I'd make him money and be his fuck toy, but my kids were off limits. They ran scams, worked some honest gigs." A muscle flexed in Marcus' jaw and he shook his head. "I made it, they didn't. I stayed in control of my life from the beginning to where I am now." He gestured to the view in front of him, the apartment behind him.

"You can handle anything," Thomas agreed. "So can I. So can my mother. So can Rory. But we all have a breaking point. When we get there, there's got to be someone or something that helps you hold it together. You can handle anything," he repeated. "Except being out of control. What I've been wondering is…are you strong enough *not* to be in control?"

When Marcus turned, his eyes narrowing, Thomas kept going. "You could throw me out of your place, but how do you get me out of your heart? Your head?" His voice quieted. "Your soul. I know I haven't figured out a way to get you out of mine. I guess as long as I figured I wasn't in yours, I could handle that.

"Hell, I could always go home, hide behind my commitment to my family and never acknowledge that the reason I didn't come back is because I didn't truly believe you wanted me so much that it would make standing up to my family worth it. That you'd really be there forever."

He had Marcus' attention now. His Master had gone very still. "But here's the kick in the ass," Thomas continued. "Somehow it finally got through. You do need me as much as I need you. Maybe even more. And in the past twenty-four hours you've needed me more than you ever realized was possible. It's scaring the shit out of you, to the point you're standing there wanting nothing more than for me to get out before it spills out all over both of us."

Thomas pushed up off the frame. Marcus was motionless, though his jaw was held so tight Thomas was afraid it might fracture. His eyes had gone from angry to cornered rage, a rage tinged with desperation. The shadows of his past had him in such an obvious stranglehold that Thomas acted on instinct. Just as he had the first time he'd decide to creep into Marcus' bedroom and lay his hand on his foot.

Reaching out, he put his hand on the side of Marcus' neck, threading his fingers under his hair, finding his nape, massaging him with light fingertips. "Sshh…"

Marcus moved forward a reluctant step, every muscle rigid. Thomas took the cigarette from his tense fingers, put it in the ashtray. Brought him in another step. Inside the doorway, away from the balcony. Tugging the sliding door closed, Thomas enclosed them in hushed silence, shutting out the sounds of the street. It brought him near enough to press his chest against his lover's, the cotton cloth of his T-shirt against Marcus' bare skin.

Thomas dipped his head, pressed his lips to Marcus' shoulder, the fine line of bone. When Marcus' fingers brushed his hips, hooked onto his jeans to grip him tighter, Thomas felt a surge of triumph, and relief. There was a way in. Moving on to Marcus' throat, he nuzzled him there, smelled the abrasive combination of liquor and cigarettes, but Marcus was under it. Thomas set his teeth to him, tasted.

Marcus' breath expelled on his temple as he moved into Thomas now, his hardening groin touching his hip. Thomas reached down, found him and opened the jeans. When Marcus caught his wrist, Thomas stopped in the act of pulling down the zipper. Raising his head, he met the brilliant green of his Master's gaze. The only man he'd ever let own him, body, heart and soul.

"I want to take you, Master," he said. Marcus' attention settled on Thomas' lips in a way that had his own cock rising.

He knew how much Marcus liked to make him go down on him. Almost as much as he liked doing it. But something else was driving Thomas now. "Take you deep and hard in the ass, be where you've never trusted me to be before. I want to tie you down when I do it. I want you to surrender to me the way I've surrendered to you, so you'll know I'm yours and you can trust me. Now and always."

"I…can't." It took a moment to register, but then Thomas realized he wasn't mistaken. Marcus, over six feet tall and almost two hundred pounds of hard, solid muscle, was starting to shake. As Thomas had done the first time Marcus had ever told him he was going to do exactly this to him. When Thomas had started shaking, Marcus' eyes had flared hot…much as his were doing now, he was sure, because the shaking told Thomas that Marcus was going to let him do it.

Marcus moved back, away, dropped into the chair. Thomas followed. Dropping to one knee, he covered Marcus' hand, resting tensely on his knee. The curved knuckles, the veins marking out the finger bones beneath.

Marcus turned his head and watched him, saying nothing, just staring at him with that haunted, fierce expression.

"It's hard for you…the idea of it." Deliberately, Thomas circled one of Marcus' wrists, keeping his attention on his face. As he held the restraint, a quiver ran through Marcus' shoulders, something shifting in his eyes. Fear.

Abruptly Marcus jerked away, throwing the other fist. Thomas blocked it with his forearm. They froze there, their wrists crossed, Marcus' fist juxtaposed in the air with Thomas' open palm.

"Owen said there was one time, a group of men. That was when you went to the hospital, the first time he met you…"

"No. *No.*" Marcus' jaw clenched. "It wasn't like that. No one forced me, no one held me down except when I went willingly. I'm not some rape victim, a molested kid. I worked the streets, I protected what was mine." Something darkened in his eyes as if somewhere his soul was falling into a deep pit. "It was just sex, Thomas. It doesn't mean anything, bending over and taking someone's dick.

"Like us? Just sex?"

"Yes," Marcus snapped.

Thomas smiled. "Don't be a bastard," he murmured. "It's not going to work on me. Not ever again. I love you."

At Marcus' closed expression, he cocked his head. "It never occurred to you the day might come when you'd win me over and I'd surrender to you, did it? I'm yours, Master. All yours. What are you going to do about it? Are you going to be a prick or are you going to surrender and let me love you, the way you want me to?"

Thomas turned his hand then. Slowly, he closed his fingers over Marcus' wrist again. Under his grip he thought he felt the manacles of Marcus' memories, the things Marcus called choices.

He'd never thought of Marcus as one of the damaged. His polish was so bright and brilliant. But it was there in his eyes now, so raw and violent. It confirmed what Thomas now accepted, what finally made him and Marcus make sense. The key had been the unfinished thought Marcus had spoken at the farmhouse. *I need that core of you…* The core Marcus had lost.

Thomas rose to his feet, tugged. Brought Marcus to his feet, coaxed him one step, then another. They were moving down the hallway, Thomas moving backward, his footing sure, keeping his eyes on Marcus', like a dance. If the eye contact was broken, the rhythm could be lost. Marcus' chest expanded with a deep breath as Thomas stopped at the threshold to the bedroom.

"You can do this. You will. Your slave is begging you for the privilege. Please, Master." Thomas grazed his thumb over Marcus' wrist pulse. "I know everything about your body. I know the way your cock likes to be touched, how to suck you into my mouth and make you come. How your fingers clench in my hair when my mouth and teeth mark your skin. I know how your ass tightens when I squeeze it, and I've wanted to get between those cheeks with my fingers, my mouth, my cock."

He was a bottom with Marcus. Always had been, even when he'd topped or taken turns with other men. But he'd wondered and wanted, at least once, to feel this.

They'd moved into the bedroom now. Thomas reversed their positions so Marcus was turned to face the bed while Thomas stood behind him. Another step and Thomas was pressed against Marcus, his cock a tight bulge under his jeans against Marcus' denim-covered, luscious tight-as-a-drum ass.

Reaching under Marcus' arm around to his flat abdomen, Thomas stroked the ridges of muscle before descending to the half-opened pants. Unzipping them fully, he pushed them down far enough to be out of his way. When he ran his hand over Marcus' buttock under the stretched cotton of the briefs, he felt the reflexive tightening. But Thomas sensed some of the tightening was tension.

"It's just me." As he reached over to the night table, he noted the slight tilt of Marcus' chin, his attention following him. There were restraints still in the drawer, as he'd hoped and suspected. Thomas set the bottle of lubricant on top of the nightstand.

"Kneel down, Master." He put a firm, inexorable hand to Marcus' shoulder and began to press.

"Thomas, I…" Marcus shuddered. Thomas slid his hand into Marcus' underwear, his thumb playing in the crease between his buttocks, just a teasing caress before he moved to palm one cheek. To squeeze. With the other hand, he reached around from the other side and gripped the thick root of Marcus' cock. Marcus' head fell back, hair brushing Thomas' temple. Thomas pressed his face into it, inhaling.

He worked his strong fingers over the ridged head, the steel shaft. When he pushed his leg against the back of Marcus', he made his knee bend. Slowly, Marcus went down onto one, then the other. Emotion flooded Thomas' chest, made it hard for him to speak. He didn't think there were words for this kind of moment, anyway.

Guiding Marcus' hand up, he held the arm straight in the air and fit the cuff around the wrist. Then the other. "Lace your fingers behind your head now," he said quietly.

Marcus had a preference for restraints that made his submissives feel that extra step of vulnerability. So now Thomas ran the stiff strap threaded through a loop of the wrist cuff around Marcus' throat, a three-inch thick collar which nudged up his chin. With his thumb, Thomas nudged it up further so he could fit the collar, run it through the other cuff ring and adjust it.

As he slid the tongue of the strap through the buckle, he ran his fingers beneath, made sure it wasn't too snug against Marcus' throat. Then he snapped the joining pieces of the wrist cuffs, the final reinforcement. It effectively kept Marcus' hands laced against the back of his head, unable to lower arms or move his hands at all. It allowed Thomas access to any part of him.

Guiding Marcus back to his feet, he turned him. Gripping his bound forearms, Thomas leaned in and simply seized his mouth. He could do whatever he wanted to that mouth, and he did, playing deep into him, moving to hold Marcus' face to take himself deeper, push his tongue so far in it was probably at the back of his throat.

When Marcus' legs hit the bed, Thomas took him down flat on his back on it, pressing between his legs, still half standing, hard groin to hard groin, the pressure of his body on every available inch of Marcus' as he kissed him, kissed him, and kept kissing him.

He used his hands, running them over the biceps, hard as rock. Along the laced fingers, tugging on the wrist restraints and the collar to tease, underscore his bondage. Marcus strained for him. Arms, upper body. When he tried to raise his legs, buck against him, Thomas shoved them down. Held the powerful thighs to the bed and ground denim against soft cotton, let him feel the full press of his length and need against his testicles, against Marcus' own aroused cock.

Oddly, Marcus said nothing. It was as if his voice was paralyzed and all he could do was move against Thomas, conveying his desire with his body, the expression in his eyes, his now wet mouth. He was trembling still, all over, so hard his teeth were practically chattering. Thomas reached under him, gripped his ass, his fingers opening him, teasing the rim.

"Ah…fuck…"

That got a response. Thomas felt Marcus' cock convulse against him like a separate beast. He moved his hand forward, inside Marcus' snug briefs and gripped the base. He was hot. Jesus, was he hot. When he was sure the near miss had passed, he caressed the tip, then withdrew his touch and licked Marcus' salty taste off his hand while those green eyes watched him.

"Fuck me. Do it."

Instead, Thomas put his hand to Marcus' throat, his fingers sliding under the restraint of the collar to hold him still as he bent to the left nipple and began to nibble. Marcus had the sexiest nipples, the flat brown circle of pigment around them like burnished pennies. He laved them, nipped and then nipped more sharply.

Marcus almost came off the bed. Thomas fought him and won, ending up straddling his waist, his ass pressed down on his cock. Marcus' gaze traveled down his own body to Thomas' tightly restrained crotch area. His chest was heaving from the exertion.

"Show it to me. I want to see all of you."

"Stay where you are." Thomas eased back, stood between the spread of Marcus' thighs and caught his thumbs in the band of Marcus' boxer briefs, ran them down his legs and took them off with the jeans. He wanted Marcus completely naked first.

God, he'd never felt anything like this. He wanted to devour Marcus, drown in that green fire in his eyes. He wanted to be fucked by him forever, taken down on his knees and savaged as punishment for doing this to his Master. But first he wanted to earn that punishment. Earn it well.

For a moment, when Marcus' gaze traveled down his body, Thomas could tell it occurred to them both, that Thomas could make Marcus open his mouth, thrust himself in. But he wouldn't. That was a true act of submission, one he would never force upon his Master.

Despite the rush of this moment, Thomas had no illusions he was a sexual Dominant. The desire he saw in Marcus' eyes when he Mastered Thomas goaded a response from Thomas that was explosive, all consuming, so raw he knew it came from a core identity of who he was. The slave of one particular Master, who was as much a Master as Thomas was his slave.

Therefore, this might be the most difficult thing Marcus had ever done. Thomas didn't want to do anything to destroy the highly fragile, perfect moment. Everything he was doing now was following his intuition of what his Master needed in order to let go, to love. To do that, his slave had restrained him. It was a delicate, completely instinctive give and take, so close to the deepest, darkest areas of Marcus' psyche that it seemed to require the deepest level of Thomas' submission in an unprecedented way.

As he took off his shirt, he felt Marcus' eyes cover his chest. Thomas lay back down on him, putting his knee in between Marcus' legs and stretching out so he brought his chest to Marcus' face, giving him the heat of his body. He closed his eyes, shuddering as Marcus' lips clamped on his skin, mouthing him greedily, sucking on his flesh, tasting him, licking the tender crease of the pectoral, the bump of his nipple, the curve of skin over the last line of ribs before his flat stomach.

He rubbed his hard need against Marcus' abdomen even as he pressed his upper thigh against Marcus' arousal. Marcus strained upward, grinding. Locking his legs over Thomas' ass, he increased the friction in a way that had Thomas fighting his own response, creating a light dew on both of their skins.

He moved back down hip bone to hip bone, chest to chest. Thomas loved the feel of his bare, cleanly shaven skin rubbing over the light covering of silken hair over Marcus' pecs that made a dark arrow down his belly. Marcus kept his pubic area clean though, except for a trimmed mat of hair. Thomas reached between them to stroke it now, to run his knuckle along his cock.

"Jesus…clothes…off." Marcus reared up, bit his throat with a growl.

Thomas pulled back from him, stood and pulled the button free, took the zipper down and shucked off the jeans, kicking off his shoes to make it happen. He suddenly found his hands perspiring, heart high in his chest. The first time he'd done this it had been with someone he'd picked up at an artist's hangout in New York. They'd been two kids groping each other, laughing.

Philip. After Philip fucked him, they switched places and Thomas did him. It had been fun, simple sex, though it had been a wonder for Thomas, having always had to guard his desires so closely, never exercise them. It had been Philip in that first painting, when he'd met Marcus.

This was anything but simple. This was Marcus. Marcus whom he wanted so badly he had to remember to breathe.

One step, two steps. He put his knee on the bed, by the outside of Marcus' hip, and leaned over him. Reaching behind his head, he unsnapped the cuffs, slid the strap free from his neck and laid it to the side. Pulled one cuff free, then the other, running his fingers over the red marks on his wrists where Marcus had pulled so viciously against the restraints.

It was dark in the room, but there were lights from the city outside the bedroom window, enough light he could see the gray tones create a sculpture of Marcus' face, the way his cheeks sloped, the line of his jaw, his lips still moist from Thomas' mouth and his own ministrations on Thomas' skin. Those eyes.

"I've tried to paint your face. Did you know that?"

Marcus shook his head, one slight movement. "No, pet. I didn't."

Thomas remembered it as he ran his fingers over Marcus' upper body slowly, thoughtfully, semi-aware of Marcus' breath catching in his throat, his charged stillness.

Marcus wasn't restrained, but he lay there as if he was, his knuckles on the bed above his head. It only emphasized the mouthwatering line of elbow to armpit, deltoids, abdomen, pectorals. Down to elegant straight hips and a cock that begged for Thomas' touch, his mouth. He looked at him and he hurt. Because it was all his. His. The same way he belonged to Marcus.

Thomas had never really understood it, had been incredulous of such an enormous gift. Yet here it was, the proof in how Marcus just lay here against all his dominant instincts. Needing him, waiting on him, though Thomas knew it was taking everything in him, tearing things inside, for him not to take control.

"You're a masterpiece, Marcus. You never imagine going to the Louvre and getting to take something home like that. Not a kid from a small rural town that doesn't even register on cosmic radar."

"How do you think a kid from Iowa feels every time he looks at you?" Marcus said, his voice barely a sound emitting from the shadows.

Thomas' touch stilled on him, his eyes burning through the darkness, summoning an answering fire from Marcus'.

Marcus closed those green eyes then, turned his face to the mattress. "Thomas…I can't. Do this. God, just do it, or I'm going to break. Hold me together, pet."

Thomas pressed his lips together, nodded and moved to put the heat of his palm against Marcus' thigh. As he exerted pressure, Marcus began to turn. The one leg crossing over, taking him to one knee on the bed, his shoulders flexing as he pushed himself up. Thomas brought Marcus' feet back to the floor, pressed on him so his knees bent, supported by the slight shelf of the bed rail holding the box spring mattress.

Picking up lubricant from the nightstand, he applied it liberally to his own cock, then worked a stream between Marcus' buttocks. They tightened, the display drawing a growl of desire from Thomas as he rubbed more lubricant on himself. Marcus' head swung to look back at him, his eyes coursing over Thomas' slick knuckles, the way he was fisting himself. "I could have done that."

"If you had, this would have been all over."

A flash of teeth, despite the intensity of the moment. It made Thomas want Marcus all the more.

Thomas set it aside and put his hands on Marcus' hips, the oil making his hands slick over the upper part of his buttocks. When Marcus began to look down, Thomas' hands clutched, dug in.

"Look at me, Master. I want you to look at me."

Marcus swallowed, turned his head and met his gaze. Thomas held it as he guided himself in. Slow, easy. Marcus was tight, tight as a virgin. He hadn't been taken this way in a long, long time. Probably not since he'd been a street kid when his ass had been up for whoever had the money or power to take it.

It made Thomas' heart ache, even as his cock nearly spurted at the way it felt to be entering Marcus. He lifted his hips to Thomas, helping, his eyes going opaque, his teeth sinking into his bottom lip as Thomas got past the sphincters and slid home. Slid deep.

"Jesus Christ." Marcus was shaking again and now Thomas leaned over him, wrapping his arm around his wide chest and putting his other fist to the mattress alongside his, biceps to biceps, the line of their shoulders together. Thomas pressed his face into his neck, letting Marcus drop his head now.

"Hold on." He lifted his hips, thrust, and Marcus groaned. Thomas could barely restrain himself at the excruciating feel of it, Marcus' ass muscles holding him, working him, his body rippling with power beneath the hold of his. The smell of his hair, the neck, his skin. *His.*

Reaching up, Marcus grabbed the hand Thomas had against his upper body. The connection became one knotted fist, their fingers holding together so tightly against Marcus' chest Thomas could feel the pulse of blood fighting through their fingers like the hammering of Marcus' heart and his own.

Their curved bodies were two parts of the same heart, and though he couldn't put this on canvas any more than he'd been able to capture Marcus' face there, he knew moments like this were imprinted on the universe, already rendered by a Master Artist far greater than he would ever be.

He thrust, thrust deeper, looking for the place that would send Marcus over, and then he could go. He knew it had to be that way. To be done right, all the way, Marcus had to surrender, to let go. Jesus, it wouldn't take more than a thought for Thomas to lose control. Marcus' back was slick with sweat, his breath coming harsh. Almost too fast, as if he were a winded horse. Thomas tightened his grip on Marcus' fingers, pressing his face hard into his neck.

"I'm here, Master. Let go. Come. God, you feel so fucking good."

Marcus' short nails bit into his hand, into the scars from working around the store. His head dropped even lower, his back curved up high. He'd gone to one elbow, and Thomas leaned down with him, pressing the back of his thigh against his, half up on the bed with him. So slick and hot. God, Marcus had an ass worth dying for. He snaked his other hand under Marcus' waist and Marcus cried out when Thomas gripped his turgid cock, squeezed, began to work the broad head.

"Thomas…no…"

"Give me everything," Thomas demanded urgently. "Don't you hold back on me. Past…time for that." Lord, he was going to just erupt any second, but he couldn't go alone. Wouldn't. "Mine. You're mine. Forever…" His lips stretched back, almost a snarl. "Family. You're part of…my family. My blood. My heart. Forever. Always. Come now, dammit. Come…for me."

Marcus bucked, a roar tearing out of his throat. With relief and a surge of hot lust so strong it made him violent, Thomas slammed into his ass and worked Marcus' thick cock at once, pulling on it, rubbing furiously with sure knowledge as he kept pumping him.

Marcus seized the bed covers, using them as a counter pull as he pushed when Thomas shoved, drawing back and coming together as Marcus' climax rocketed through them both. For a few remarkable moments Thomas held both their weights on one arm, keeping Marcus hard against his chest as he stroked him to the last drop. Then his balls convulsed, beyond the point of no return.

He shouted out his own climax, too powerful to stop the reaction, and a deep guttural cry from Marcus joined his, his hips rocking up to take all of Thomas' seed, heart thundering against their locked fists. Thomas rammed him without thought now, just all physical need and animal feeling, everything right, everything as it should be, no need for a mind when the heart and soul were so large and overwhelming, filling the room with heat.

When at length he slowed, a lifetime later, his hand was slippery with the cum that had jetted out of Marcus. With his warm and wet knuckles Thomas rubbed his Master's cock, up and down as Marcus twitched at the increased sensitivity, all his muscles shuddering.

While at first Thomas was filled with deep male satisfaction at the trembling post-coital reaction of his lover, as his own post-climactic haze cleared off, he realized Marcus was still breathing too fast, too deep. He was rocking back against Thomas as if they were still fucking. Pushing, drawing away, pushing, pushing…

Marcus' hands were clutching the blanket spasmodically. Lowering his head to the covers, he pressed his face there, his back curved in a painful bend as if something far greater than Thomas' weight still rested on him.

"Hey…" Thomas withdrew, pulling him back in his arms, but he had to follow Marcus down the side of the bed to the floor. When Marcus put his arms over his head, covering his expression, his body still rocking, Thomas' heart broke. He wrapped both arms around him as the first sobs crashed over his Master.

He was overwhelmed by Marcus' grief. The way he leaned into Thomas, almost toppling over so he was half curled into Thomas' lap. The weight of what he was carrying seemed to be hurting him too much to allow anything but a fetal position to brace himself against it. Thomas curved protectively over him.

Now knowing what he knew, Thomas suspected the grief wasn't solely for Marcus' father. Eventually, an unloved child realized there was no obligation to love back. But the man Marcus had become could mourn being born into a family where he wasn't wanted, didn't fit. Feel the hurt of standing on the outside of what so many others had. Of knowing there was no way for it to be different, caught between hate and longing, not hate and love.

After talking to Owen, Thomas realized there was another reason he'd fallen in love with Marcus. While he loved Marcus certainly for the individual, sexy, complicated man he was, Thomas also had found a spark of his own father, who had carried so much responsibility and never thought to question or resent it.

When the family farm had failed, Thomas' father had turned to the hardware store *his* father had started, which wasn't more than a side interest at that time. He worked contract jobs in between building it into a thriving concern. At times the money had gotten so tight Thomas' mother had turned to neighbors to provide a meal for them, tucking away her pride.

She'd hidden the knowledge from Thomas' father, and Thomas knew she'd done it so he'd never falter, never think she had a moment's doubt in him. He suspected there must have been times his father had wanted to crack, so afraid he wasn't going to make it all come together, take care of his family, live up to that love in his wife's eyes.

Marcus went out and forged his dreams out of less than nothing, formed his own family, protected them, even tried to protect Mike. And had lost them all. From the violence of his reaction now, Thomas thought it likely he'd never let himself break over any of it, because he couldn't. He couldn't handle the pain of it until…he had someone he trusted enough to see it.

A different version of the same words Marcus had said to him, during that first bad fight in the Berkshires.

Different situations, different men, but the glue always the same. The thing that made it all work. His father had had his mother's unwavering love, his children's respect. Marcus had him.

Hold me together…

"Always, Master," he murmured, holding him tighter. "It's going to be okay. We're together now. Always."

The polish had come at a high, high price.

Thomas kept stroking his hair, murmuring and rocking, until at last Marcus started to rein it back in, pushing himself up, swiping his hand at his nose and eyes.

"Okay?" Thomas kept a hand on his bare shoulder, moving his fingers slow and easy over the firm flesh.

"Yeah. Oh, Jesus. No." Marcus bolted from the floor, disappearing into the bathroom. He managed to kick the door shut before Thomas heard him start to get rid of probably a gallon of Jack Daniels and vodka.

Wincing sympathetically, Thomas rose and went to the adjacent bathing area to run water in the Jacuzzi tub. He selected the temperature Marcus liked and increased it a few degrees up from that. Moving to the sink, he began to clean himself with a cloth and soap, keeping an ear tuned to the bathroom. Three pauses, followed each time by more vomiting. Marcus must have been drinking since he'd last seen Thomas.

The evidence was in the penthouse as well, in the unmade bed, dishes in the sink, paperwork tossed on the floor. Thomas pulled on his jeans, shrugged into his shirt and made the bed while he waited. As the minutes passed, he suspected Marcus was probably in there hoping he'd disappear. He heard the sink running, the sounds of teeth being brushed, a mouth being rinsed that would probably never be able to taste Jack Daniel's again.

"Got a bath out here when you're ready."

"Go away."

Thomas stifled a smile. "Come out here and stop being such a girl."

That did it. The door opened and Marcus stood gloriously naked in the doorway. He'd washed his face, but as Thomas well knew, everything else to use for cleaning up was in the Jacuzzi part of the bathroom. Marcus glared, but otherwise seemed at a loss for words. And he looked tired.

Thomas rose from the bed. "Tomorrow you can go back to being invincible. But for tonight, why don't you let the guy who loves you enough to kiss you with stale liquor and cigarettes on your breath take care of you? Get you into the tub and scrub every part of you that needs scrubbing."

The teasing light died out of his tone, replaced by something else as Thomas stopped in front of him. "Maybe after that, you can try sleeping while I hold onto you and thank God that you kept on loving me until I figured out what a gift you are?"

As Marcus' expression changed, Thomas moved forward another step, put a hand to his face. "Please, Master. Give me the gift of taking care of you."

"I already did."

"C'mon, then. I've got a bath run. It'll do you good."

Marcus gave him a searching look but complied, moving into the bathing area. Thomas tried not to hover, but was nevertheless glad he did. When Marcus lifted his leg to get into the tub, he lost his balance.

"Whoa…got you. Here." Thomas eased him down into the warm water. "Don't think Jack's completely out of your system yet."

"Good thing he isn't. Else, probably wouldn't have let you…" Marcus' face was turned away, his jaw pressed to the cool porcelain. When Thomas laid a hand on his hair, tangled there, he didn't move, but he felt the focus of Marcus' awareness as if he'd fixed that potent gaze on him.

"I'm glad you did. It was about time you let me all the way in. Course, maybe it was the first time I'd earned the right to do it."

Marcus turned and looked at him then, a hundred thoughts passing between them, none of them needing saying.

"I don't know why I care," Marcus said abruptly. "He didn't ask for me. Why should it matter to me what his expectations were?"

"I think he was just the straw," Thomas suggested gently. "Do you have a good memory of him? Even one?"

Marcus looked down into the water. "He took me to the barber once, when I was six. We had ice cream afterward, sat in a park. He put his arm along the back of the bench and talked to me about going to school. How to get along with other kids, not to let them push me around, but not to jump into a fight, either."

"That's your favorite memory of him. That's how you were able to call it up so easily."

Marcus lifted a shoulder.

"Hold onto that one. That's the only one that matters anymore. Why don't you get your hair wet? I'll wash it."

Marcus complied, sliding down and beneath the water's surface, and then emerging, slicking the ebony silk of his hair to his skull. As he settled back, scraping water from his face with his hands, he turned a considering eye to Thomas. It had some of its usual arrogance to it, cheering Thomas considerably. "Remember, shampoo followed by conditioner. Use the ones in the black bottles."

Thomas eyed the array of hair products on the corner of the tub and snorted. "God, I forget sometimes how gay you are."

When he reached across to grab the shampoo, Marcus seized his waistband and hauled him into the tub. Even wrestling him, Thomas managed to be overpowered and held under for at least five seconds, water sloshing over the sides.

He surfaced, spluttering and laughing, and splashed Marcus in the face. "You asshole. You know this flannel shirt is a Tractor Wholesale original? It was a whole twelve ninety-five off the rack. You've simply ruined it."

And found himself dunked again. When he came up this time, he was hauled forward to meet Marcus' mouth in a wet, rough kiss, Marcus' hands holding his head.

Hair treatments could apparently wait.

Chapter Nineteen

ꟸ

Despite the relaxation a bath provided, Thomas could tell Marcus was still dealing with a lot of emotional debris. After their bath, he wrapped a towel around his hips and went back onto the balcony, seeming to need the open air, deep breaths of the freedom he apparently found high above the world below.

There was another chair, but instead of using it Thomas slid down the side of the balcony wall, lacing his hands over his knees. He stayed in Marcus' peripheral vision, his bare sole close enough to overlap the smallest toe of Marcus' nearer foot. An expanse of leg was revealed by the split of the towel, a provocative pose that was entirely unconscious, totally Marcus.

Thomas noticed when Marcus smoked, as he was doing now, he displayed a different set of gestures and mannerisms. As Thomas studied him, he realized when Marcus smoked, he saw the street kid, the boy.

"You've got questions in your eyes, pet. What's on your mind?"

That was the all-seeing, all-knowing Master he knew. But pieces of the puzzle were still missing, holes Owen wouldn't or couldn't fill in. He wouldn't push, but if Marcus was in the mood, Thomas wanted all of it.

"Tell me more, about your life before." *Let me all the way in.*

Marcus glanced at him. "I made it out, Thomas. I make a lot of money. I have friends, culture." An unpleasant, almost cruel smile touched his lips. "I get everything I want."

"Even me?"

"Especially you."

"Arrogant jerk." But Thomas leaned forward, brushed his knuckles over Marcus' ankle, stroked the calf. "Tell me," he repeated.

Marcus took a drag so deep on the cigarette Thomas expected to see the paper burn down to his fingers. Abruptly, he leaned down, snagged the front of Thomas' clean T-shirt. He pulled Thomas to him and kissed him with that hard, forceful and demanding Marcus taste. "That's not who I am anymore. You understand that?"

Thomas nodded, but he couldn't help the desire he had to touch and heal all those scars inside that he could finally see. Why had he been fooled like all the rest, when it had been there, plain before him? "Tell me," he insisted, once again.

Marcus stared at him, straightened. Took another drag and spoke flatly. "I ran away at fourteen, turned fifteen on the streets here. Dad…" the word came out thick. "I knew what I was then, and Dad couldn't accept it. Wouldn't. Tried a lot of the usual things. Beating, tossed me in the cellar for a few days at a time, no food. Prayer… God, endless prayer. I still get nauseous if I get near a church. Whenever I have a hangover, I try to make a point of puking on the steps of one. I figure it's the tithe I owe. Sounds bitter as hell, doesn't it? My mother…"

His tone faltered, then Marcus flicked away the ashes angrily. "Wouldn't say no to him. Figured he was God in the house, so he had to be right, even if he was wrong. We were just a simple, fundamentalist family, Thomas. Not that well educated for all that. A lot simpler than yours. Hardworking, though. Dad's idea of Friday night culture was picking up his beer and cigarettes at the local store and hanging out in the yard talking about how the fags, niggers and wetbacks had ruined America.

"We were the stereotype, what everyone thinks a dumb, white trash family is. I ran. I doubt they even looked for me. I probably could have walked. Maybe even asked for a ride to the bus station." His lips stretched in a humorless smile.

"I eventually got back in touch with my brother. He did okay. Clawed his way into college, runs a laundry business in the area. Watches over them."

"You both do." Thomas tapped Marcus' cell phone, sitting on the ledge with the planter.

"Yeah. Don't know why the fuck I do. Maybe some of that honor thy mother and father shit got so beat into me I can't shake it. I didn't care so much about him. Least I didn't want to. Don't want to. But it happens anyway, as if there's some stupid part of you that says you have to do it, even if your old man's a piece of shit. But Mom…"

Marcus drew in a breath, his nostrils flaring as his chest expanded. He shifted his gaze to stare out at the night. Thomas suspected Marcus didn't realize that the city lights reflected a great deal of the emotions passing through the eyes. "She liked bluebells," Marcus said. "There was this china doll in the gift section of our local department store. She was holding a bunch of bluebells. She'd always stop and look at it.

"Sometimes, when I think of her like that, I think about when she was fourteen, or Dad was fourteen. Maybe they were something different then, wanted to be something different…I should hate her." Marcus shook his head. "If you stop loving someone, it's easier to forgive them. So I guess I never stopped."

He visibly pushed it away, turning the story from that path. "I worked the streets here, hooked up with Toby and Emile. And Mike. Yeah, he was a pimp when you got down to it. He'd smack me around to convince himself he was boss, but we both knew I took care of him as much as he took care of me. It isn't as dramatic as you see on television. Angst is the indulgence of the middle class."

He shrugged. "When you're on the streets running, that's it. You're animals. You survive it, you move on to the next thing. If you dwell on it, you miss the next opportunity. Anyone who hurt me back then, this is my revenge. I'm here in a penthouse apartment with everything I could want. They're not." Marcus put the cigarette out.

"Is that why you didn't come after me sooner?"

"What?" Marcus turned, a startled expression on his face.

Thomas lifted a shoulder. "When I walked out. You…you were my Master. Hell, you didn't ever let me get away with anything. I've never had the upper hand with you. But that one time, you could have come after me, tried to haul my ass back, but you didn't. Was I like them? I hurt you, so that was the end of it? What made you come so much later, when you hadn't come before?"

Marcus stared at him a long moment. "Maybe it was pride, maybe something else," he admitted at last. "The sub has the upper hand in a true Master and sub relationship, Thomas. Always. I can possess you only as long as you want to belong to me."

Thomas swallowed, looked away. "I never stopped belonging to you."

"Maybe it was just hard for me to see that." Marcus cleared his throat. "What are you, some kind of romantic girl who walks out on her lover just to see if he'll give chase? Look…" He ran a hand over the back of his neck. "When you left, it was because you got a call your dad had a massive heart attack. Things spiraled from there. Then there was Rory. I wanted you back. Jesus, those first days without you in my bed, knowing you were somewhere grieving…hell yes, it hurt."

He surged up from the chair, paced. "I wanted to come after you, but I didn't because I knew you were dealing with your family, and I'd be a selfish bastard, entirely."

"You thought you would be an intruder, in a place you didn't belong." Thomas corrected him, made himself say the shameful words. "Because I made you feel that way. Marcus, I'm sorry."

Marcus turned his head, looked at him. In the dim light, Thomas thought the two of them probably appeared terribly fragile, like figures from a dream where something could be lost if even a loud noise snapped them out of it.

"Okay," Marcus said. Nodded once. "Forgiven, pet." He cleared his throat again, looked back over the city. "Thank you."

"So how did you get all the way from working the streets to up here?" Thomas gestured, knowing they needed a different track, for now.

Marcus gave another one of those tight smiles. "Focus. It's working hard every day, giving up sleep, food, friends, everything else you might want for yourself, doing everything half-assed except that one goal. Those simple pleasures of relaxation we all take for granted, the half hour in front of the television, playing with the dog…hell, doing nothing. Every single moment has to be dedicated to that purpose, so everything else is scheduled around it.

"Surgeons know it, pilots, anyone who wants to be the frigging best at what they do. And then when they finally make it, knowing it was the most miraculous combination of luck, timing and working their asses off, when they have the time to take that moment of relaxation, for those nine holes of golf on a Friday afternoon, someone assumes it really wasn't that hard. The privileged wealthy, my ass."

Thomas half smiled. "I know better than to get into politics with you." Or to let Marcus get him off track with the distraction of a spirited debate. "Owen said Mike died for you."

The glint of humor in his green eyes died. Marcus went to the opposite railing, bracing his arms out to either side of him. He'd lit another cigarette and now it was trapped under his fore and middle fingers. The air filtering up between the buildings fluttered the hair across his forehead, but was unable to soften the harsh profile.

"It was that group of guys. Seven of them. Hardcore, into boys and pain. They were each willing to pay a grand, as much as you'd pay for high-priced tail in Vegas. Mike told them no. I caught up with them down the block, told them yes. Got the money, ran it back up to Mike and shoved it inside the door where he'd see it when he got out of the can. All I could think was forty percent of that was mine.

"Toby was my first discovery, I guess you could say. Graffiti artist capable of being way more. All of us were setting aside money to get him into the first year of an art school. The school said if we could get a certain percentage together, they'd take him. That money would have cinched it, with a little left over for Emile. He'd had a rotting tooth and needed to get to the dentist...

"Wasn't Emile...a girl?"

"No." Marcus said it emphatically. "What he was born didn't matter. In Emile's mind, in everything he was, he was male. I respected him that way."

Thomas was watching his face closely. "You were lovers."

"As much as two street kids at that age can be." The cigarette was burning down, the ashes untapped. Thomas rose and moved to his side. Sliding his fingers over Marcus', he removed the butt and stubbed it out. He wanted to grip the tense hand on the rail, but he didn't. He stayed close, though.

"It was a tough night," Marcus said briefly, another humorless smile crossing his mouth. "But they got what they paid for."

"Jesus," Thomas murmured. Marcus slanted a glance at him, and his green eyes were hard, brittle.

"Don't think about it, pet. I don't. No one who lives it dwells on this fucking stuff. You just thank God or your own balls for getting yourself through it, pulling yourself up into something better. The day I see pity in your face, I want your fucking ass out of my life."

"That's not what I'm thinking. And that's bullshit, by the way." Thomas kept his voice mild as he leaned over the rail and laced his fingers, bracing his forearms. It brushed his side against Marcus', clad only in the terry cloth. Marcus flinched, but he didn't move away. "You know, the very first time I looked at you, I thought, what the hell could he possibly want from me except maybe the thrill of a one night fuck with some halfway decent-looking piece of ass from down south?"

Marcus' eyes narrowed. "What kind of horseshit—"

"It's actually not easy to love you," Thomas interrupted. "You're arrogant as hell, moody, and a lot of times just a mean son of a bitch. Even when I didn't know about your past, I knew you had some pretty dark places. It *is* killing me, thinking about what you went through, how I couldn't be there to help or protect you. But when you've reached for me in the night, demanded I submit, I was helping heal those wounds, wasn't I?"

He met Marcus' gaze. "I understood it somewhere deep down. You don't feel lonely when you're with me. All those things about me you make fun of, just like me with your cologne and fancy ways—that's everything and way more of what we need from each other, isn't it? Everything down to the soul of what we are. That's why we fit."

When Marcus didn't immediately respond, Thomas shifted his gaze down to the street, to where a doorman was walking an elegant Great Dane. "You're what my art's all about, Marcus. We see something and think we know it, understand it, but really we're lucky if we ever understand any more than a small piece about anything. The infinite of the universe is in each one of us. You're grace, faith. Hopelessness, despair. Violence and anger. Beauty."

His attention flicked briefly up, lingered on Marcus' mouth, the column of throat, sweep of shoulders, expanse of chest, down to the snug hold of the towel. "Pain. You overwhelm me," he said quietly. "And every time I see you or think of you, I can't grab a brush fast enough. I thought I couldn't paint you, but it turns out I've been painting you all along, from the beginning, before I even knew you."

Thomas reached out then, no longer worried about the reaction. From the stillness between them, like the stillness he felt when immersed in his work, he knew he stood inside Marcus and Marcus stood inside him in this moment. Laying his hand on Marcus' face, Thomas cupped the jaw, fingers over the ear, touching the still damp strands of his hair. He increased the pressure on the side of Marcus' neck, moving forward himself until their mouths met, tasted. Savored.

Marcus' lips parted and their tongues caressed, wet, straining heat. It was easy then to bring him closer, take his hand to his waist, the small of Marcus' back. Thomas' thumb caressed just inside the hold of the towel, his other fingers resting on the fine curve of his buttock. Marcus remained nearly motionless. Not resisting, not passive, but like he held an explosive energy too compressed to dare movement.

It was as if he knew Thomas was experiencing this so deeply that reaction wasn't needed. This utter stillness *was* the reaction.

Thomas drew back, studied his face. "All that time on the street. There's not a scar on you, Marcus."

Marcus lifted a shoulder. "I don't scar. I never have. Mike..." He gave a half-derisive chuckle that was too full of pain for Thomas to summon a smile. "Mike used to say I must be an angel, though he didn't know if I was from Heaven or Hell. I can get sick, my bones can break, but my skin always heals. Never shows anything."

"No. That's your eyes. They show everything. It's all there." The scars, the wounds that didn't heal, the story of who he was. It was all there. And even more. Something bigger than the experiences. Something more than mortal. It made Thomas wonder if Mike had been right.

The artist in him could imagine a woman with Marcus' jaw and fair forehead being lovers with an angel who had those amazing green eyes and to-die-for body. A one night fantasy the woman would think was a dream, as if visited by a succubus.

Nephilim. Child of an angel. That's what he'd call the painting.

Marcus was looking at him, a half smile on his lips, an unexpected expression after the dark memories he'd been visiting. But Thomas understood it now. When immersed in his feeling for Thomas, none of the past existed for Marcus. It was all just swept away.

"You're painting, aren't you? I can tell. You have that dazed look. Go." Marcus gave his shoulder a light shove. "Go up to the roof and do your thing."

"You're just trying to stop talking about this."

"Yeah. It's enough for one night." Marcus brushed his shoulder more casually with his knuckles. "I promise to tell you more. But not tonight, okay?"

Thomas captured the long fingers, took a step forward. Then another, moving Marcus back in counterpoint into the shadowed dark corner of the balcony.

"What are you up to, pet?" But Marcus' voice had gotten throaty. That look was still in his eyes, heat and vulnerability, a raw, primal openness that Thomas wanted to guard jealously forever, the gift he now believed only he'd been given.

When he got Marcus to the corner, he put his hand down, took the edge of the towel and tugged it free, leaving his Master standing full and strong, naked and pale, touched by the gold and red lights of the city, limning the hair resting on his shoulders and the light thatch across his chest.

Kneeling slowly, Thomas slid his hand down Marcus' taut abs, the slope of his thighs, nuzzled his Master's cock with his lips, teasing as his breath drew in harshly.

"Jesus…"

Thomas opened and took him in deep, feeling with fierce joy as he grew harder, thicker. Marcus' testicles shifted convulsively under the caress of Thomas' thumb, the taste of his come already leaking from him. Putting his hands on his thighs, Thomas dug in, holding onto Marcus to take him deeper, sliding down every marvelous inch.

Marcus put one hand high on the stucco wall, the other going to Thomas' shoulder, gripping hard in the collar of his shirt, hard enough to tear except Thomas was moving with the rhythm of the flexing hand, anticipating Marcus' rock forward on the balls of his feet, the press of his ass back against the wall and forward again.

When Thomas glanced up, the look in Marcus' eyes almost overwhelmed him. A desire so strong it was indescribable, as if something had been unleashed in him that was unquenchable. His expression said he could fuck Thomas to death and still need more, because what he wanted was so much more than his ass.

Thomas had never seen this naked expression that revealed the unshielded heat of Marcus' need to control, his need for Thomas' utter surrender to give himself some type of peace. A level soft meadow in which Marcus' soul could fully rest and know what he most wanted belonged to him in every way.

"Thomas..." A breath, a guttural groan and Thomas sucked hard, hollowing his cheeks, flicking the sensitive underside with his tongue, finding the perineum with his finger and pressing just enough, teasing.

"Jesus, fuck..." Music to his ears. Thomas held the vision in his mind. Marcus as a fallen angel, head dropped back against the wall, six feet of wings stretched out on either side of him, feathers glimmering in the sparkle of a city that moved on, the mundane world and magic intertwined together, one so unaware of the other. When Marcus' thighs flexed under his grip, convulsing, he braced himself, prepared as Marcus came with sudden violence, clutching Thomas' shoulder with bruising fingers, thrusting against his face.

"Love your fucking mouth..."

Poetry, the rough male response to fucking, being fucked. Invaded, penetrated, filled, taken beyond satiation to exhaustion, all the answers there in post climactic aftermath, at least for that powerful, still moment of repleteness.

When it was over, Marcus was leaning fully against the wall, chest expanding and contracting like a bellows. His knees were…quivering. Filled with satisfaction and emotions too strong to form words, Thomas stayed on his knees and put his cheek on Marcus' thigh, lips nuzzling the now drained cock, rubbing his knuckles slowly up and down the opposite column of thigh, brushing Marcus' testicles with the movement, teasing his hip bone.

As Marcus' touch moved from Thomas' shoulder to cup his head, a deep breath left Thomas. He was aroused, of course, but he wanted to stay this way awhile. Just be this.

"When do you go back?" Marcus' voice. Hard to read if Thomas didn't know him, heart, blood and bone.

Thomas raised his head, looked up that incredible terrain of curved muscle. As he rose, he stayed close, his body pressed against his lover's. Marcus shifted, his thigh pressing knowingly against Thomas' hard cock. His hand slid to Thomas' nape, that possessive kneading touch. But his mouth was taut.

Thomas' lips curved. "Don't worry about that right now," he murmured.

Marcus nodded. Looked out into the night and worried.

* * * * *

Marcus found a pair of loose cotton lounging pants and they went to his roof garden. While Thomas sketched, Marcus fell asleep on the grass, too exhausted by drink, sex and emotion to do anything different.

When he was snoring in an amusingly offensive way, Thomas squatted at his side, removed Marcus' cell phone from beside his elbow and moved to the far end of the roof. He found the number he was looking for, took a deep breath, and hit the preprogrammed button to dial it.

"Hello?"

A man. Shit. Thomas had hoped to talk to the woman first, not the man that Thomas knew Marcus had once fucked. He forced himself to rally. Marcus was his now, and this man was married. "Josh?"

He didn't know his last name, knew nothing except they were the closest friends Marcus had, if Julie and Marcus' own references to them were true.

"This is Thomas. Marcus' Thomas." He didn't know how else to go about saying it.

A pause, then a surge of alarm that came through clearly, even over a cell phone connection. "Is he okay?"

"Yeah…yeah. Well, no. Actually, not really. His dad just died, and I was thinking he could use some friends right about now. Do you…do you live nearby?"

"Jesus, he hasn't told you anything about us, has he?"

Thomas hesitated, not sure what to say to that. Apparently the significance of that pause came through clearly as well.

"*Oh.*" A self-conscious chuckle. "Figures that's the only thing the asshole would tell you. He hasn't told us much about you either. It's from what he *doesn't* say that we figured out who you were to him. No wonder his stomach's been bothering him, if his dad was sick. I knew that son of a bitch was lying about it not being him. Here, I'm putting Lauren on. Tell her what's happening with him. She's a doctor."

"No, it's not—" Thomas heard an exchange of words and then he was relieved, despite the misunderstanding, to find himself talking to the woman.

"What are his symptoms? Are you at a hospital?"

"No, and in about five hours, his symptoms are going to be a massive hangover." Thomas chuckled wearily despite himself, ran a hand over the back of his neck. "Look, I probably shouldn't be calling you, but I think you two are his closest friends, and he got some bad news today. I'm thinking if you're nearby or planning to come this way soon, you could—"

"You're not bugging out on him."

"No," Thomas said automatically, in response to the sharp tone of her voice. "That's the thing. I'm going to have to go home in three or four days, and I'm hoping—"

"Thomas, you do realize you're the love of his life, don't you? So are you sticking this time or not?"

"I'm sticking," he said, the simplest answer.

A pause. "Oh. Well, good then. We'll be up tomorrow night. Josh will cook. We'll have a quiet night in. I'm going to let you talk to Josh some more."

"No, I—" But she was gone. Thomas shook his head.

"Sorry, didn't realize she was going to go after you like that. Women, Jesus. So tell me how he's doing? And tell me when the hell did he get a dad? First we've heard of it."

"I only heard about it a couple days ago…"

A few minutes later, when Thomas finished, Josh stayed silent for a long pause. "Christ. Marcus and I have been friends a while, and I didn't know anything about his family."

Thomas felt a tightening in his gut. "I know. Me either, until this week."

Another pause, as if Josh was having some trouble getting out the words. "Listen, Thomas, Lauren is my Mistress. She and Marcus shared me one night. Long story short. One time, special circumstances. She's everything to me. Marcus and I were never lovers. Got it?"

"Okay." Thomas got his mind around it, took a more secure grip on the phone. "Okay."

"She's a girl, so she's going to say it the girly way—*ow*. But..." Josh's voice got serious again. "She's right. You're everything to him. Don't fuck him up. Okay?"

"I..." Thomas looked over at the sleeping man, his arm thrown over his eyes. "He's everything to me too. I've got it straight now. He won't shake me. But there's one more thing I've got to do. That's why I need you here. After I take care of it, he's never getting rid of me."

"Good. Because he's a royal pain in the ass and you have our sympathy."

Thomas grinned. After a few more moments of confirming plans, a guilty shock as he realized the two of them were at the tip end of Florida and would have to arrange a flight in, he hung up. Only to find Marcus awake and watching him.

"Josh and Lauren will be here for dinner tomorrow night," Thomas informed him.

"Meddlesome prick. You think you have the right to handle me?"

"When you need handling. Why don't we invite Julie over tomorrow morning if she's back from Massachusetts? We'll fix her breakfast."

Marcus considered him. "Okay," he said at last. A sudden exhaustion crossed his face, the simmering belligerence just evaporating, making Thomas' heart hurt for his lover. "I don't have much in the kitchen. And the place is a fucking mess."

"I'll take care of it. Why don't you just keep on napping? I'm going to finish this idea up, then I'll wake you and we can head to bed."

Marcus lay back on the grass. "Fine. But be sure you wake me. You're feeling so nurturing right now, I don't want you scooping me up in your manly arms and carrying me back downstairs."

Thomas sent him an arch look. "Will you beat on my broad chest with your feeble fists if I do?"

"And ruin my manicure? Not likely. I would have Julie sock you in the eye though. In the morning."

"Then shut up and go to sleep. I'm working. Trying to make you money to keep you in the manner to which Donald Trump wishes he could become accustomed."

"Music to my ears. Tomorrow night I'll have my biggest commission source and the one artist I know who can give him a run for his money in my house." Marcus raised a brow. "Come to think of it, maybe I should keep you two separated, like the President and the Vice President, never in the same building."

Thomas snorted. "J. Martin is your biggest commission check, another guy you've never let me meet."

"You and the rest of the world. He's very private. Likes living on some ass-end remote island off the coast of Florida."

Thomas stopped dead. His charcoal made an uncontrolled smudge as he forgot to remove it from the paper during his swift turn.

"*J* can actually stand for a name beginning with *J*," Marcus pointed out. "Like Joshua. Josh."

"I was talking to *J. Martin*? That's Josh? Holy—why didn't you tell me? Holy Christ. I… You *fucked* J. Martin. Holy Christ."

Thomas broke off, scowled when he saw Marcus with his hands laced behind his head, eyes dancing with laughter at his reaction.

"So *now* it's okay that I fucked him?"

"You *dick*. I'm going to throw you off this roof."

"Security will not let you stay for dinner tomorrow night if you kill me," Marcus said, rolling to his feet more quickly than expected as Thomas came after him. He dodged around a tree anchored in a massive clay planter.

"I'll make it look like a suicide," Thomas promised.

Marcus feinted left, but he was too tired and still too full of alcohol. Thomas tackled him and they rolled over the grass, throwing elbows. Somewhere along the way, Marcus was laughing and Thomas forgot to be annoyed, suddenly just pleased to see his Master laughing, roughhousing as if they were teenagers. Thomas rocked back on his heels, shoving him away. Marcus sat up on his elbows, giving him an indulgent expression. "You're pretty good to have around, pet. I could get used to it."

"Don't expect me to clean up your apartment ever again. This is a one-shot deal."

"That's why I have a maid service. Call them on my Rolodex. They'll put it all back together and we'll stay in bed, until dinner. They're used to working around me."

Thomas shook his head. "J. Martin. Marcus, he's like—"

"You'll be as good as him. You're on your way now." Marcus said it bluntly, watched the deep flush of pleasure rise in Thomas' cheeks. "And he is a complete slob, a bohemian of the worst sort. Lauren has to make him wear shoes most days. You two will get along just fine."

"And he's…like me."

Marcus easily picked up the direction of his thoughts. "Josh is a sexual submissive, like you, only he prefers women. One woman. Lauren. She's extraordinary, and if I ever tried to lay a finger on him without permission, she'd break all ten of them." Reaching out abruptly, he caught Thomas' arm and pulled him to him, tumbling them over in the grass and suddenly having enough strength to pin Thomas under him. "The same thing I'd do to anyone who touches you."

He traced Thomas' bottom lip with his thumb, his eyes getting smoky and intent. "We're going to let the maid service do the apartment. I've got better things for you to do with your energy."

"Insatiable monster."

"You bet your fine ass."

"*Your* fine ass," Thomas corrected, a moment before his mouth was seized, his breath taken so he couldn't tease his Master further.

Chapter Twenty

ഇ

Marcus made fun of him when Thomas struggled over what shirt to wear, and eventually borrowed one of Marcus'. But then, as if Thomas weren't nervous enough, Marcus had to be on the phone when the doorbell rang.

As he moved to the door, he admonished himself firmly. "I will *not* act like a starstruck idiot."

How Josh Martin's photograph stayed out of the papers was a testament to just how good Marcus was at simultaneously protecting and marketing artists. Even so, the fact that he was such a good friend and yet Thomas had never known much about him, like the most horrendous parts of Marcus' life, bothered him.

But that kind of secrecy was over. Marcus and he had talked a lot in the past twenty-four hours, enough that Thomas was able to push the feeling aside as he came face-to-face with one of the men who had inspired his own work. Thomas had pictured J. Martin a lot of ways, but he found Marcus' description accurate.

In his early thirties, with brown and black hair streaked with blond, Josh was tall, about Thomas' height. His gray eyes shifted restlessly. He was dressed casually in jeans and a snug dark T-shirt, revealing Celtic design tattoos around his wrists. Wire-rimmed glasses increased the stunning intensity of his gaze, but it also made him more boyish and sensually appealing at once.

The woman who had her hand threaded through the crook of his elbow had blue eyes like crystals and straight blonde hair that moved like rippling lake water over her shoulders. A pediatric specialist and surgeon, Thomas remembered Marcus saying, and he could see her resilient character in the firmness of her delicate chin, the decisive slope of cheekbone, giving a hint of the type of Mistress she was as well as the type of physician.

Thomas realized with some amusement they were studying him as thoroughly as he was studying them.

"I told you he was beautiful. Just as I remembered." Lauren spoke first.

When Thomas raised a puzzled brow, she prodded his memory. "At the club *May I Have This Dance?* a few years back. I was the Mistress in the balcony."

"She's got a way of breaking the ice, doesn't she? 'Yes, last time I saw you, you were being stripped naked in front of a bunch of strangers, myself included.' Kind of makes it hard to be formal, not that we were going to pretend to do that." Josh extended his hand. "Let me guess. He's on an important overseas call to underscore how terribly important he is, and remind us that, as the artists, we are completely replaceable and expendable."

Thomas grinned despite himself. "You must be the expendable and replaceable J. Martin."

"Josh. You must be my replacement, if everything Marcus has told me about you is true."

He'd pulled off the casual first comment well, Thomas thought, but that one completely flummoxed him. Fortunately, Lauren came to his rescue.

"You're exactly as I remember you, except a little thinner and more serious-looking. Is Marcus making you look after that ulcer?" She brushed Thomas' cheek in a kiss, laying her hand on his forearm as she did so, a light but confident grip. "We'd have been here sooner," she continued, "but the whole year has been about the European tour. Keep in mind there are advantages to being a starving unknown. If Marcus makes you a success you might as well manacle yourself to your studio."

"I'm in favor of anything that involves Thomas and chains."

Thomas turned to find Marcus had joined them. He gave a wicked grin, then stepped forward to embrace Josh and Lauren at the same time, one in each arm, his face brightening.

While he didn't put it past Marcus to pull such a calculated stunt as Josh had just described, in this instance Thomas knew he'd actually been on another call with his brother, finalizing the burial arrangements. For that reason he was glad for the timing of Josh and Lauren's arrival, their presence obviously having the ability to chase some of the stress lines from around Marcus' mouth.

"Thomas, take Josh to the room you're using as your studio and show him what you did on the roof last night."

"Oh, I don't think—"

"I know that, you're an artist." Marcus waved a hand. "Go take a look, Josh. You'll like what you see."

As Thomas reluctantly complied, he threw a narrow look at Marcus before disappearing down the hallway with Josh. Marcus slid an arm around Lauren's waist and shot her a smile.

"He wants to kill me right now, but it's the easiest way to get him over his jitters. We'll have to go dig the two out of there in a half hour because they'll be so busy impressing the shit out of each other and planning their next show together. That should take some pressure off Josh. He can scale back a bit, take some time to relax. I know he's been working his ass off."

"So have you. I've seen all the faxes and emails." Lauren studied him, then stepped up without preamble and put her arms around him. Drawing Marcus against her in a close, emotion-absorbing hug, she rubbed his back with her palms. "I'm so sorry. No, don't pull away. Just hold on a moment. Don't you know how important you are to us?" she scolded gently. "Josh absolutely wants to pummel you. It should have been you calling us instead of Thomas, but I'm glad he did. You look like shit."

Marcus lifted his head, startled. "I do not."

Lauren grinned. "The invincible pretty boy ego. Eternally sensitive but as enduring as the Rock of Gibraltar." She ran her thumb beneath one of his eyes. "You're always a god, Marcus. But for you, you look like shit. Which means anyone else would be set to go out on a model runway."

"Ego restored." Catching her wrist, he squeezed lightly and lowered their now linked hands to swing between them. "I'll be all right. I have Thomas."

"I noticed. When you came into the room, he was the first thing you looked for, like a captain seeking a port in a storm. *Do* you have him, Marcus?" She looked as if she regretted the question, but Marcus could understand why she asked it. Thomas had left before…

"We'll see. He hasn't resolved things with his family, or even told me how he plans to do so." This morning Marcus had woken up with the apprehension Thomas would be packing his bags. Thomas had been silent on the subject, and for once Marcus hadn't had the strength to demand an answer, seize what his Fate would be.

He was in limbo and he knew it, but he just…couldn't face it yet. He'd heard everything Thomas had said last night during their intense encounter, the implied promise, but that was… Well, he knew Thomas loved him, would tear out his heart for him when Marcus was in pain. He also knew Thomas felt the same way about his family in North Carolina.

He saw in Lauren's face she knew it wasn't like him not to force the issue, but instead of saying anything, she gave him a considering look. "Well, since we expect the boys to be occupied for the next half hour, why don't I offer you my limited culinary skills to help with dinner?"

"Or you could keep me company in the kitchen and take a glass of wine."

She made a face. "Am I that bad?"

"No, of course not. You toss a good salad. Particularly if it comes in one of those premixed bags."

She smacked his arm, but agreeably accompanied him to the kitchen, pouring herself a glass of wine as he checked on the status of the dinner he'd had brought in by caterers. Normally he would have enjoyed the preparations of cooking for friends, but Marcus had preferred to spend his time wrapped around Thomas. Talking, fucking…sleeping, starting all over again. He had muscles that hadn't been sore in years.

"Why haven't you ever told Thomas about us, for heaven's sake? Are you ashamed of us? And Josh said he didn't even know you had lived with Thomas. Why hide us from one another?"

Marcus lifted his shoulder. "I haven't had many relationships, Lauren. In fact, with the exception of Thomas, the last one I had of this intensity was when I was fifteen years old. Everything else has been club relationships. I never wanted someone that close to me."

I didn't want to be hurt when they were killed, or worse, decided they didn't want to love me back.

He hadn't realized that about himself until this morning, when he'd held Thomas close, watched the sun rise and told his pet things he'd never even told himself.

Her irritation appeared to die away at the harsh honesty in his voice.

"Marcus, if you want him…I know it's tough. God, do I know. But you have to make yourself as vulnerable to him as you're demanding of him. Show him who you are."

"I did," he said quietly. "So now…I guess we see what we'll see."

But as he turned away to check the stove temperature, Lauren could feel his fear of it like a tangible thing. She caught a flash of heartbreaking sadness in his eyes she'd never seen there before. Along with his obvious fatigue, it made her afraid for him.

Marcus, who never appeared vulnerable, seemed as breakable as a ceramic sculpture. She hoped like hell Thomas was telling the truth about his plans to stay this time.

* * * * *

After only a few minutes, any self-consciousness Thomas felt about Josh's status as an art giant vanished. They talked brush techniques, use of color and light. Josh gave him some sculpting tips, his specific milieu. Though it wasn't Thomas' best medium, there were a few pieces in his head he wanted to do.

Josh moved a lot as he spoke, the gray eyes brilliant. He used a scratch sheet on Thomas' easel to demonstrate his points. One part of Thomas' mind just cartwheeled like a giddy toddler with the thought, "I'm standing here getting tips from J. Martin", but the artist in him couldn't be suppressed for long. Before he knew it, he was beside Josh, pointing out other options, taking what Josh was suggesting to a different level, using it as a springboard for other possibilities.

The chance to stand with a peer and immerse himself in their shared world and language… Sometimes being an artist, obsessed with his art, was like being an alien. There was no one to really talk to about it, who *wanted* to talk about the minutiae involved in creation that was so amazing and miraculous—to the artist alone.

Aside from the acclaim, the layers of experimentation and skill Josh had honed were as obvious as a perfectly cut diamond. Thomas stood shoulder-to-shoulder with a true creator, what he'd always called his favorite artists in his mind. There were things in Josh's work that no one but an artist could understand how miraculous they were to render.

Standing here talking about it was the most fantastic fucking charge, and Thomas knew no matter where he went with his art, to whatever showings or fame, this was what it was about for him. This moment with another creator who understood the singular intensity to bring to life that which burned inside of him, from whatever source it came.

Though Marcus wasn't an artist, he knew Marcus felt it in a different yet similar way. One of the many things Thomas knew that drew them together.

Lauren leaned against Marcus' shoulder as he propped himself in the doorframe, the two of them watching. "They don't even know what a miracle they are, do they?" she said softly.

"No." Marcus found he had to clear his throat to say the words, watching the focus of Thomas' dark eyes, the quick smiles and frowns, lines between his eyes. Even the way his body was aligned with Josh's at the easel. "It wouldn't matter if they did. It would just puzzle them. That's why Josh is where he's at and Thomas is going to be right there with him, if he'll let himself. I suspect there were people who stood like this watching Michelangelo or Matisse. It's like…"

He shook his head at himself, a light smile crossing his face. "Like watching God at work in His studio."

It was a sacred, spiritual gift to watch him work, to be part of the inspiration that made Thomas the creator he was. Marcus realized he wanted to come home every day to this, wanted to know Thomas would be part of his life. The part of his life that would keep everything else in balance.

Shadows gripped him at the thought. If Thomas changed his mind once Marcus got his grief and emotional shit under control, if he tried to withdraw again… Marcus knew he didn't have the energy left to fight him. After all the harrowing years when he never let himself entertain the notion, even in his darkest moments, Marcus now knew he would have a compelling reason to take his own life.

He should hate Thomas for doing that to him. For dredging up all the loneliness and rage of his past with the comparison of all it could be now. The hope or promise of an unconditional love from someone who accepted and wanted Marcus for all he was. But of course that wasn't the way it worked. Marcus just wanted and loved him all the more.

Feeling Lauren's shrewd eyes on him, he dropped his hand and gave her ass a hard squeeze in the short skirt she was wearing.

"Marcus Stanton." She hissed, elbowed him in the ribs hard enough to make him wince, as he wasn't fully healed from the diner incident. Her exclamation drew the artists out of their absorption. They turned with matching looks, twin deer caught in headlights.

"Just checking out your wife's ass," Marcus explained. "It's as firm as ever."

"It's actually a bit softer," Josh responded. "I like it that way."

"I hate you both," Lauren announced. Thomas smothered a smile when she sent him a searing look. "Way too much testosterone in this house. Don't any of you doubt for a moment I can take all of you down. Even you." She shot a narrow glance up at Marcus.

"Sounds like something I'd like to see. After dinner." Josh grinned. "Is dinner ready?"

* * * * *

Ice not only broken but completely dissolved in the warmth of newly discovered friendship, dinner was an animated discussion of food, art, politics, television and even some about D/s clubs the three had visited in Europe or that Thomas and Marcus had visited together.

Thomas found Lauren and Josh were more like him, keeping their play intimate and preferring one another, using the clubs primarily as stimulating viewing entertainment.

They didn't linger long on the topic, and he couldn't deny that he was glad, because when Marcus had been at clubs, that meant he'd picked up one or more partners, even if it was just for a night.

After dinner, he and Lauren cleared the dishes while Josh and Marcus went to the living area to discuss the show, prepare drinks. After a few minutes, however, Thomas noted Marcus wandered out to the balcony, excusing himself and encouraging Josh to check out his music selection while he lit a cigarette.

"Is he okay, Thomas?" Lauren asked softly, helping him rinse the bowls. "Really?"

"Yeah," Thomas nodded. Josh was following his own gaze, studying Marcus, his brow creased in similar concern. "He will be. A lot of stuff's broken loose in the past few days. Old wounds. He's messed up now, but he's trusting us enough to let it show. That's good. It's good you came. I think he trusts you two more than anyone."

"Not more than you. You sound sure he's going to be okay because *you're* going to make sure of it." She met his surprised look with a smile. "You really have come home to stay. Does he realize that?"

Thomas lifted a shoulder, embarrassed by the praise but also disturbed by the question. "I hope so. I'm going to have to prove it to him. It's probably not going to be in a way he'll like."

"And that's why you want us here. You think he's pretty fragile right now."

She moved closer, standing shoulder-to-shoulder with him at the sink. She smelled good, a light powder, feminine aroma that made him miss Les, his mother.

Thomas glanced back at the balcony. Last night, Marcus had had a nightmare. A bad one where he woke soaked in sweat, trembling. To soothe him, Thomas had eased him back to the mattress, held him tightly. Laid a light kiss on his face, his neck, then shifted and spread them over his whole body until Marcus was trembling for other reasons.

It was a different, more erotic version of what his mother had done for him as a boy. If he had a nightmare, and they'd been few, she'd sit on his bed and kiss his face, his belly, blowing on it to tickle him, the soles of his feet, his hands. His chest, over his heart, sometimes laying her head on it to listen to it thump. She'd said that everywhere she'd placed a kiss, the fear would run away. Until it would give up and run away entirely.

"Yeah," he said, going back to her implied question. "I think he's pretty damn fragile right now."

* * * * *

Owen had told Thomas that Marcus was fearless. *Never saw a kid so not afraid of anything. If he had fear, he hid it places no one could see. The night that gang of monsters dumped him off and ran, he looked so bad that Mike brought him to the back door of the hospital. He talked an intern into coming out and treating Marcus in an alley, because he refused to bring him in where he might get caught as a runaway. I came out to help the intern.*

Dodger was bleeding everywhere, beat all to hell. He regained consciousness while the doctor was looking him over. The first thing he asked was if Mike had found the money. The second was could somebody bring him a fucking towel so he could wipe the blood off his face?

Marcus had explained it. *My father tried to use fear to make me what he wanted me to be. That's when I decided not to be afraid of anything. Then you came and I remembered that true fear is knowing you have something you can't bear losing.*

In the desolate comfort of the three a.m. hour, Marcus had given Thomas the rest of the story in terse sentences, a few syllables to explain what had built his own foundation.

When Mike went after the men who had effectively gang-raped Marcus, they'd stabbed him. Mike made it back to his place and refused to let Marcus call for help, so he'd died while Marcus held the edges of his gut together.

Tobias had been in a gang before he got together with Marcus and Emile, and he could never completely shake the old loyalties. Six months into his first semester of art school, Toby let one of his old gang buddies pressure him into covering his back for a robbery, and his head was bashed in with a tire iron.

On the wall of Marcus' living room, a canvas with the bold, angry colors of Tobias' work shone like jewels. The other three walls had been painted a relaxing blue-green, but Marcus painted his walls specifically for the art hung upon them, so Toby's wall was bare white, giving the art the full focus. When Thomas looked at it now, the significance of it being there was obvious.

Now he can't paint inside the lines of a coloring book... Marcus' words haunted the dark corners of Thomas' mind like a ghost.

Behind Marcus' back, determined to pull his weight, Emile took a blowjob gig meant for Marcus. While they didn't know for sure, Marcus suspected the john found out Emile was not anatomically male. Pissed off by what he would perceive as deceit, the john had taken his revenge. Emile was strangled, his body dumped like garbage in one of the landfills. It had taken Marcus and Toby a week to find him.

At the age Thomas had been playing in a baseball league and dreaming about the possibility of going to art school, Marcus had been in the sewers of New York, scoring a warm corner for him and his street rats against bigger, meaner vagrants.

Toby taught me that talent needed to be represented, nurtured, protected. So I ferreted it out, conned and hustled buyers and investors, got where I am today. I don't even have a high-school diploma, let alone a college degree, but do you think anybody ever assumes otherwise? You learn the right language, the right way to present yourself, no one even questions it.

Despite that offhand comment, since Thomas knew how difficult and highbrow the art world truly was, he also knew Marcus' acceptance in that world was right up there with biblical miracles. But what was hustling and charming his way into the intimidating art society of the Upper East Side when he knew what it was to fight packs of wild dogs for food found in the garbage? To hold your surrogate father while he died, holding his guts in, blood up to your elbows? The man who just happened to smack you around and tap your ass when he had the desire for it, but you loved anyway for reasons too complicated to explain?

You have a purity I've lost, pet. But in some ways, the important ones, you're not naïve. You understand the darkness without ever having been in it. You see the world as it is, all its misery and pain, all the beauty that somehow rises above it, and you accept all of it. You accept me.

When Marcus touched him Thomas saw it in his face now, how he drank in Thomas' balance, his quiet stable nature. Yeah, they fit. Yin had to have a yang. The art was the dot of darkness in Thomas' life and the dot of light in Marcus' that made them a part of each other, connected them. He'd always been thankful and awed by his gift, but now Thomas saw it had a higher purpose. Even if he became world renowned or crashed as an art nobody, the greatest treasure it had brought him was that connection with Marcus.

* * * * *

Lauren was watching Thomas shrewdly. "Marcus treats everything as a work of art," she said abruptly. "Something endlessly fascinating in both its perfection and imperfection. So it makes sense that he would wait for that feeling with the man he'd love forever. Josh told me that on the way here. Have faith, Thomas."

Thomas' mind gingerly touched her words, as if they were an animal that might bite. But they also made him remember something else Owen had told him.

"You ever notice how he doesn't look at himself in a mirror?"

Why would he need to? Thomas had asked it, half humorously.

"No." Owen shook his head. "I don't mean look at his hair when he's brushing it, or his jaw for a shave. He never looks at himself. It's his face that got him out. But it's his face that lost him his soul. The way he looks at you, son…he thinks you're holding it for him."

Nodding to her, he skirted the living area with a gesture to Josh, and stepped with only a brief hesitation out on the balcony.

Marcus was standing with his back to him, wineglass in hand, considering the city below. The shirt lightly blowing against his body, stretching across the broad shoulders. The pressed slacks defining his thighs and perfect ass. Studying the tilt of that sculpted face, the light fall of hair feathering his shoulders with the breeze, Thomas couldn't imagine anything further from the roots of a farmer's son.

And he wasn't seeing the surface. Beneath the New York City art dealer, even beneath the farmer's son. Down to the raw, open soul. Would Marcus have faith in *Thomas* at this most vulnerable juncture? Because Thomas didn't want there to be any more questions between them. Time to stop putting it off. Tomorrow he'd leave. Later tonight he'd talk to Marcus and make him understand.

Taking another step forward, he slid his arm under Marcus', flattened his palm on his chest and pressed his body up against his, feeling the flex of the firm ass as Marcus tilted his head.

"Let me pleasure you, Master," he murmured. "Lean back on me." Knowing they were turned so his act was disguised, Thomas slid his palm down the flat abdomen and found Marcus' cock, cupped him. That organ capable of giving so much pleasure hardened under his hand. Putting his lips to Marcus' ear, he nuzzled, despite the fact Josh and Lauren were in the penthouse.

"What are you doing?"

"Arousing you the way you always arouse me, when I can't do anything about it. I want to know how much you want me." Thomas found the side of Marcus' throat, nipped. "Knowing you'll have to wait and suffer the way you make me suffer sometimes."

"You might get punished for that later."

"I don't think you'll be able to hold out that long."

Marcus curved his hand over Thomas'. "Look in the living room."

Lauren had gotten her wine and was standing next to Josh, her hand on his nape as he sat on his heels, looking at the music choices. When he turned his head and kissed her just above the knee in her short skirt, her hand tightened on his neck. She murmured, "Behave", earning an unrepentant heated smile from Josh as he curved his fingers around the back of her knee, his thumb coursing along the upper part of her thigh.

The pose, him on his knees, the way it changed the look in her eyes, the intent look in Josh's that said he knew exactly what it did to her, was so familiar that Thomas couldn't help but get more aroused himself at the sight.

As Josh's hand climbed higher, he and Lauren still not cognizant of Marcus and Thomas' regard, she watched him, a soft look in her eyes. But her mouth firmed and she reached down, grasped his wrist to stop him. He kissed the back of her knuckles, caressed her with his cheek, brushing his hair against her bare skin and the soft gleam of the wedding band on her finger.

Devotion. Utter. Permanent. It was like much of the subject matter of Thomas' paintings. The shape of it could change, yes, but not the fundamental things that were the foundation. It was in the way they looked at each other.

"Perfect timing," Marcus said quietly. He caressed Thomas' back, that lingering touch just over his buttocks, easing him back into the room.

Lauren's head lifted. Josh merely rested his temple against her knee, his hand still firmly wrapped around her leg while her hand teased the strands of unruly brown and blond hair beneath her touch.

"I'd like the two of you to hear something." Marcus gestured Thomas to a chair but remained standing. Josh rose and took the sofa, reclaiming his drink as Lauren settled in under his arm with her wine.

"It means a lot to me, the three of you being here tonight." Marcus took a position at the fireplace, before the mantle. He cleared his throat, lifted a shoulder. "I haven't had many people in my life I've truly loved, that stuck. I'd forgotten what it means to have people who care enough about you to give up things for you. Be there when you need them."

He'd captured their attention fully, for certain. Thomas glanced over to see Lauren and Josh both intently watching him. Thomas turned his attention back to find Marcus' gaze specifically on him, and when his voice lowered, became somewhat more unsteady on the next words, Thomas leaned forward, his brows drawing down.

"Once, a long time ago, I gave you a chain, and I told you if you broke it, we'd go our separate ways and I'd wish you well. You remember? You mailed it back to me after you left, for Rory."

Thomas nodded. "I remember."

"That wasn't about being magnanimous. I was being a cowardly asshole who wanted to make sure I didn't let you get too close, even as I was doing everything I could to pull you inside me. So it's no wonder when you left, I felt ripped apart. You asked why I didn't come after you for so long. I was angry that I'd allowed myself to get that vulnerable again. That I'd set all the rules in place and it didn't make a damn bit of difference.

"Every day you were gone, I just missed you more, and I went ten rounds every one of those days, making sure I didn't call, didn't do all those desperate bullshit moves people stupid enough to open their hearts do."

Thomas swallowed. He heard Lauren say softly, "Oh Marcus," but Marcus pressed on, his eyes locked on Thomas'.

"I'm saying this in front of them, because it was Josh and Lauren who made me go after you. It's hard, especially for a Dom, to realize that to get what you really want you have to give up control completely, just hoping to hell that Fate doesn't kick your balls into the back of your throat. I've been there, one too many times, and I wasn't ever going to do it again."

A grim smile touched his mouth. "But I figured out that it's worse to do without you than to take that risk. So I hatched my strategy to sell your paintings and come back to get you, to deal with what we had.

"I don't want to be magnanimous anymore." His expression changed, that stern Master look, so unexpected that Thomas almost rose out of the chair, but something in Marcus' look kept him pinned to it just as effectively. "You're mine, Thomas. With your family, without your family, wherever we need to be, whatever we need to do, we need to be together.

"I will take a lifetime of you, good, bad, terrible, to anything without you. I love you. And as much as you're mine, I'm just as much yours. Maybe more, though until the other night I was afraid to admit that to you, or to myself."

He was not going to get teary-eyed like Les over some Hallmark commercial, but damn, if Marcus wasn't making it tough. He wasn't done yet, though. *Jesus.*

Marcus turned, slid a box out from behind the framed print propped on the mantle and extended it to Thomas.

Thomas rose now, feeling at a loss for words. He had no idea where this was going, or what it meant, but he knew from the stunned look on the faces of the couple on the couch, he wasn't the only one who was nonplused.

Thomas opened the box and blinked despite himself. "You changed it."

Marcus nodded. "I took the originally broken gold chain, had silver welded in as a decorative inlay. This chain, as small as the links are, is an unbreakable alloy. Once you put it around your waist and lock it with the fastener," his green eyes gleamed with that light that could spin Thomas' brain to his groin in a blink, "only I can get it off you." He reached into the box, touched the loop that was pinned to the velvet base. "And instead of a tail of chain, this goes around your cock. You'll wear my collar at all times, pet."

Thomas touched the slim chain, the same metal disk lock. *Mine.* Looking far more like something that would be put on a prisoner. A willing one.

He pressed his lips together. "When did you do this?"

"Before I came down to buy the farm. I'd brought these with me as well."

Thomas raised his gaze to find Marcus holding a second box. When he slid the top back, Thomas could only stare at the matching pair of men's rings. One gold, one silver, a single etching on each, a bold line like a lightning strike.

Thomas blinked. Blinked again. He thought either his senses had all been incapacitated or Josh and Lauren had become statues. Because everything was suddenly so still Thomas was as unaware of their presence as any other inanimate objects in the room. He wasn't including those rings as inanimate objects, though, not with their ability to inject this hot flood of feeling through him.

"I want you to marry me, Thomas." Marcus' attention had weight and heat on every exposed, raw part of him. "We can get a license in a state where it's legal, have a ceremony wherever you want, however you want. And I don't care if there's no law for it on the books, it will be the law between you and me and whatever God there is. I want it to be impossible for us to leave each other without a hell of a lot of paperwork, ugly custody battles over furniture, whatever.

"I want to marry you," he repeated. "I want you to know that every morning when you wake up and see me that I want to be there, that I made an oath to be there. To stand by you. And that there's no one else for me. Not ever."

Thomas swallowed. "I've never thought of it. Never even considered it possible." He gave a husky chuckle. "Marcus, Jesus…"

"Yes or no, pet. That's the only thing that matters."

It was the urgent note in Marcus' voice that pulled Thomas away from his own reaction. He raised his gaze to Marcus' face. When he saw the look in his eyes, the tautness around his unsmiling mouth and the tension in his face, Thomas was reminded of what had transpired over the past few days, his own thoughts when he was with Lauren in the kitchen.

Though Marcus wouldn't see it this way, he'd given Thomas the best possible opening for the conversation he'd intended to have with his Master later tonight. What Thomas was going to do to prove himself to Marcus, to win the trust Thomas knew would be required to love each other for a lifetime of ups and downs, good times and bad.

Thomas' world righted itself, giving him a calm peace. He stepped forward until they were eye to eye.

"No," he said.

As Marcus' expression changed, he pressed on. "Tomorrow, I'm going to go home and tell my mother how I feel about you, the life I intend to have with you. I'm going to deal with Rory. I'm going to make it clear who I am and what I want, and how it's going to be. Then, I'll come back and say yes."

He put his hand over Marcus' on the box, tried to ignore how the fingers had gotten rigid. "The words you just said to me mean everything. So I owe you the same. I won't ever have you wonder if you just overwhelmed me, coaxed me into this. I'm standing up to you, Master. To Marcus Aurelius Stanton, turning you down flat until I can go get my life in shape and deserve you. Then, I'm going to ask *you* to marry *me*."

Chapter Twenty-One

It had been hard to say. The right thing to say, but so hard. From the worry in Lauren's face, Thomas knew she had the same concern he did. That although Marcus heard the words, nothing in his past or present gave him the ability to believe them. When Thomas left for his family in the past, whether for a short trip or to break it off, he *left*. Which is why Thomas had to prove to Marcus that wasn't going to happen again.

He couldn't think about it too much, because it tore him apart to leave Marcus suffering, to only be able to convince him through the deed, which required the passage of time.

Marcus thwarted in his intent was not a pleasant person. Sex had been savage, stilted, and Thomas had woken alone, aching and bruised, to find Marcus already gone to his gallery. He'd left a Thermos of terrible coffee for Thomas' cab ride to the airport. The rings and the chain were still on the mantle where Marcus had put them. Thomas deliberated, then took them with him. He wanted to look at them, think about them, remind himself. He wanted Marcus to see he'd taken them.

The connecting flight had been delayed, so he'd gotten home late, after midnight. He'd found out from a sleepy Les where his mother was.

Somehow, the tranquility of the one a.m. hour seemed appropriate for the conversation. That, and his urgency to get back to Marcus. Following the gravel road, Thomas walked the mile to the church under a silent starry sky. He was accompanied by the Murphy's coon dog, who saw him pass their house and fell into step with him, always up for a stroll.

Even a Catholic church as small as theirs was had a tabernacle, where vigil prayer went on twenty-four hours a day over the extra communion wafers that had been blessed by the priest as the actual flesh of Christ. The Catholics in the area, including his mother, took turns. Apparently, she'd chosen the 12:30-1:30 a.m. time slot, probably because she wasn't sleeping well.

She hadn't slept well since their father died, really. Still learning to sleep in a bed by herself, he assumed. A couple times when he'd woken earlier than her, he'd seen her curled up in Les' single bed.

When she took a late hour like this, Thomas' practice of faith had been to meet her on the steps to walk her home. He'd taken over that responsibility as a teenager, when his father had to work long hours. He wouldn't let the boys help with things that interfered with their homework. So this was one thing Thomas could do.

It was a ritual he remembered now with deep affection, how his mother would loop her arm through his as they walked so he could keep her from tripping over loose rock. He'd talk about problems, skirting around the one that was uppermost in his mind. She'd walk silently next to him, pauses he now knew reflected her understanding of what his real worry was. She'd tell him to pray, to ask God to help him to find his true self.

Tonight, he looked up at the stars, the vastness of the sky and the world in which he lived, and knew who he was. All he wanted was for her to accept that, the way she accepted God's wisdom for the many things she couldn't understand.

As he thought about it, it was all about family. Les, Rory, Mom. Marcus. It wasn't a spigot that turned on and off, no matter how his Mom or even Marcus wanted to believe it was, to uphold their view of the world, or to protect a heart that had already been invaded. He was in Marcus' heart, in his soul, and he couldn't be shut out. Same with his mother. Just as Walter Briggs had said.

When there was full surrender, a lot of things became clearer. To be head of a family meant something far different than just being there—it meant making the hard choices he knew would be best for all of them, as Marcus had demonstrated to him that day in the way he'd handled Rory.

Tonight he would tell his mother he loved Marcus. Tomorrow, he would make sure Les knew she shouldn't get married until she finished school, and he'd invite her boyfriend down and make sure he understood the same. Rory would get off his butt, figuratively speaking, and start pulling his weight. Then he would go to Marcus.

The asshole had left him one message. A business card next to the coffee, one of his gallery associates, with a scrawled note saying "If you don't come back, deal through John on your paintings. It will be easier for both of us."

Thomas had torn up the card and left it on the table. Idiot.

When he got there, Elaine was just coming out, pulling her light jacket over her shoulders. She saw him, a momentary start, then recognition. Smiling, she came down the steps. He hugged her when she was still a couple steps up, so they were eye to eye.

"Hi, Mom."

"Hello, son. I'm glad you're home. You didn't have to come out here. I'm sure you're tired from your flight."

"I wanted to come. I wanted to talk to you. Here."

Elaine's eyes stilled, studied his face. "All right. Why don't we sit here, on the stairs?" As if she felt better with all the symbolic strength of God at her back. He didn't fault her for that, but he hoped she'd use it as a comfort, not a reinforcing army to turn this into a combat.

He sat next to her, pressing close as he usually did when they walked, to give her warmth. She seemed to have shrunk some since Dad died, and seemed more fragile and often cold.

Though he knew he was risking the hurt of having her pull away, he took one of her hands, enclosed it in both of his.

"I do pray, a lot, Mom. I always have, because I believe you. And I believe in Him. You know that?"

She pursed her lips, looked down at their joined hands. "I know that, Thomas. I know you love God. You've always had a very loving heart."

He nodded. "I try. I'm worried about what I'm about to say to you, but I really need you to hear it. I consider Marcus my family, the way I consider you, Les and Rory my family. The way Les' boyfriend will become our family if they get married. Marcus has no family, nothing but me. I want to give him all of mine, because I can't imagine a better family for him to be a part of. If I can only give him myself, so be it. But he doesn't just need me, Mom. I think he needs all of us."

He took a deep breath. "If you can't accept that, then I'll integrate you both into my life, but I won't turn my back on Marcus anymore. You understand?"

She did free her hand as he expected, but to cup the rosary in her hands, stroke the base of the wooden cross with her fingers. Thomas had made it for her in shop in seventh grade, learning how to make the round beads, sanding and smoothing the small cross piece, carving it out of one piece of wood. He'd chosen a pretty piece of oak for it.

"I need you to say something, Mom." Closing his hand into a tense fist at his side, where she couldn't see it, he tried to keep his tone mild. "Or, if you don't want to, I can walk you on home."

"You were always so articulate, so well spoken. Quiet, but when you spoke, you had your thoughts in such good order it was like poetry at times. Whereas Rory still trips over his tongue around girls or even my friends." She smiled, though there was a wistful sadness to it that made him want to put his arm around her. "He was right," she murmured. "I did always know. It wasn't even in those things, because Martha Wingfield's child is…like you, and he's as rough as a fence post. But it was a clue for me, I guess."

"Mom, what…who's 'he'?"

"Your friend Marcus told me something once," she said abruptly. "That time he came down here to talk you into going to the Berkshires." At Thomas' expression, she shook her head. "He didn't tell you about it. Neither did I. I guess the both of us said more than we should. I didn't pay attention to it, but sometimes…"

She glanced back up the steps at the face of her church, her eyes lingering on the stonework on the front. "There are those who hate Catholics. For no reason other than we're different. It's that way for a lot of people, I know. But I've been thinking that it's not the differences that frighten people. That's not the root of it. It's that we can be different and yet be so much the same.

"It didn't sink in then, what he said to me that day. And I don't think what I said sank in, either. But the odd thing is I think it did later for both of us, on almost the same day. That day he got the call about his father. Like so many things that God tries to tell us, we have to do it the way we think is best before we try doing it His Way. And sometimes he sends us reminders if we stray too far. That's how much He loves us."

"Mom." Thomas put a hand over hers again and found it colder, so he caught both of them and sandwiched them in his, warming them along with the rosary beads that dangled off the side of his palm. "You're confusing me."

She smiled. "So much of what goes on in your head when you paint, that's a universe beyond my understanding. But when it's like this, the day to day, you've always been a person who likes plain speaking. That day, when he was so angry about what I did to your painting…" She took a deep breath. "The look on his face. There was nothing more important to him than protecting you, protecting your happiness.

"Sometimes, when you're desperately, foolishly in love with someone, you find out what they keep in the shadows of their soul has nothing to do with you or how they feel about you. Sometimes they're afraid if they let that out, let go of what they've been trying too hard to handle a certain way for so long, things will change. They don't realize that's what love is about. Being willing to open up and change the way they do things, do it together. Be different, in the new way."

"Marcus isn't desperate or foolish."

"Oh, Thomas. When it comes to you, he's quite both." She freed a hand and ran it down the side of his face, stroked through his hair. "This is getting curly again. You should visit the barber. Rory's is getting long too. Maybe you could go together." She sighed.

"I didn't want to see it, because it confused me. How could I see the same things I felt for your father, and he for me, in the way the two of you are together? Not the kissing and touching, or the things you say. It's deeper than that. The way you look at each other, even in the most casual moments. The way the air around you just seems right when your loved one's in the room, in the house."

Her eyes were distant, soft. Sad. "The way you finish each other's sentences, think of thoughts the other one has a moment earlier. The way you laugh and smile easily with each other, at jokes that if other people said them, it wouldn't be the same. And still, none of that comes close to describing it, you know? It's this feeling so much a part of you that you don't have to feel it."

Thomas nodded, struck speechless, held still by that gentle, maternal touch on his hair.

"I thought...it was easy when I thought it was sinful, something to do with the flesh. But what I'm seeing is more than that. It's love, and love isn't a sin. So how can God be so cruel as to give that feeling to two men or two women if it's a sin? I've always believed God to be compassionate. Loving."

A tremulous smile touched her face. "This is very hard for me, Thomas. Can you help me understand?"

It was the first time he'd been invited to talk to her like this. Thomas wasn't certain how much would be too much, but grasping the resolve that brought him here, he knew he wouldn't take the risk of it being too little.

"You're right, it's not just about..." She colored some, looked away and Thomas had to bite back a grin despite himself. He squeezed her arm, drawing her attention back to him.

"I mean, he's hard not to think about that way because he's overwhelming. And I guess at first I thought I was just like anybody else. Hormones, etcetera. But I think about other things, want other things with him as well. Like being with him every day. Figuring out dinner, what to watch on TV. He has this thing when he's on the phone, I can tell if he's pleased or getting pissed just by the way he twists a pen in his fingers. To hold onto his temper, or to focus, he doodles, does weird Celtic stuff like a tattoo artist on paper.

"When he took me to the Hill farm, Mom…it was there. Like he'd stepped into my mind and figured out what I wanted the most, even before I knew it. It's like he's the one who holds the book of my life, and I'm waiting with all this breathless excitement to see him turn the page. I can see us being there, close to you, going back and forth to New York when we're needed, but renovating it, building a home there."

"You didn't fall in love with New York?"

"I fell in love with Marcus," he said simply. The first time he'd ever said it so easily to his mother. The first time he ever thought he *could* say it. "New York was home because he was there, the way this is home because you, Rory and Les are here. If that's where he wants to be, and as long as I know you're okay, I'll be happy there. But there's something about here, North Carolina…there's a peace, a steady constancy to it."

"Out of all my children, you've gone the furthest away in distance, as well as in your hopes and dreams." Elaine nodded, her eyes as steady and thoughtful. "But your heart, the core of you, has always been about home, family. And I think that's where the puzzle falls into place for me."

He raised a brow. "How so?"

"We may not always act like it as we should, or deserve it, but there's something instinctual that makes us want to love our family unconditionally. That's why we're called a family. And you said that Marcus doesn't have that. He would have found it in various places, with friends, but that's not the same. It was you who called to him. He knew you epitomized everything that family is about. Loyalty, sacrifice, no matter the personal cost."

She laid her hand on his stomach then. He shifted, but she made a noise, holding him still. "Love and joy. Laughter. He couldn't have made a better choice. And because he was smart enough to seek it in you, he may be a finer man than I gave him credit for being."

"Mom." Thomas' throat was tight as she curled her fingers into the front of his sweatshirt.

"And you may not listen to Marcus, but you'll listen to your mother. You're having an appointment with Dr. Lassiter next week or I'm making it for you. You're going to get a complete physical. If he says you've got something like an ulcer going on, you're going to do whatever he says to make it better, even if that means you cut back on your hours at the store."

"But we've got the planting rush about to—"

"My eldest son happens to be a very important artist who makes boatloads of money. We'll be hiring some help. And Rory…what you did before you left, it was good for him. You're right. We were wrong to treat him as if he were helpless, as if he deserved our pity. He's still a man, and he deserves to be treated like one. He'll be the general manager of the store. Your father left me in charge of operations until I say otherwise, and I'm demoting you. You're holiday help and part-time grunt only."

He looked away, this time at the church. "Mom, are you okay with…this?"

She turned to look as well. As she did, she leaned back against him, putting a hand up along the side of his face. It encouraged him to put his arms around her, squeeze her tight, until she made an "oof" noise that made him grin, even as tears stung the back of his eyes.

"I don't know, Thomas," she said at last. "I know what the Bible says. I know what I've been raised to believe. But I've always turned to the church in comfort during the hardest times of my life because I believe He's about Love at the root of everything.

"Though I don't understand it, I can't deny it anymore, that what you feel for one another is as real as what I was given with your father. If you don't take and make a life out of that, you'd be a fool. And I didn't raise a fool. So I think it's time for it to be between the two of you and God, and I'll pray for you both."

He squeezed her again, holding her tightly so his heart wouldn't break. "I love you so much, Mom. I never stopped. I never would have, no matter what."

Her shoulders hitched in a little sob. She put her face into his shoulder and he felt her swallow, then she drew back, squared her shoulders and gave his hands a pat. When she gave him a quick smile, her eyes glinted and she swiped at an escaped tear.

"Let's get home now. Tomorrow you'll go back to New York and get that smart-mouthed Yankee's butt on a plane back here. If you aren't back in time for your doctor's appointment, I'm coming to get you both. And I can promise you, New York is not ready for me."

* * * * *

"I thought you'd left."

Lauren paused at the open door of the gallery, arching a brow. "And a good morning to you too. We thought we might stay one more day."

"Statue of Liberty's open for viewing. Then there's the Guggenheim. I'm busy." He glanced at her. "Where's Josh?"

"Getting us coffee down the street. He'll be here in a minute." She glanced over at the woman going through a box of receipts. "You must be Linda, his general manager. We heard good things about you the other night."

Linda nodded with a smile, a wary glance at Marcus.

When she and Josh had been unable to get Marcus to answer his cell after lunch, Lauren had suggested they try the gallery, since it was not far from their hotel. Since they both knew Thomas had headed back that morning, they'd agreed they weren't going to return to Florida until they were sure Marcus was going to be okay. She was glad they'd gone with that intuition.

Lauren put her hands on her hips. "Linda, I think you want to take a personal day. Your boss is acting like a jerk, and I'm more equipped than you are to slap him around until he pulls the stick out of his ass."

Marcus raised his head, met her cold blue stare with one of his own. "You come here to fight?"

"No. But if you're rude to me one more time, that's what it's going to be."

Marcus slapped the ledger closed, extended it to Linda. "File that in the back."

"Please," Lauren added. "He meant to say please."

After Linda disappeared, Lauren made her way to the counter, one casual step at a time, surveying the layout and artwork in this front area. Marcus stood behind a high walnut counter. His restless energy made him prefer to work on his feet. He'd told her it made a better impression on clients if the proprietor was standing when they arrived anyway, as if waiting just for them. With his forbidding expression today, she thought they might scream and run the other way.

When she got to the counter, she pivoted on her heel, presenting her back to him to see what art he'd chosen to place in his direct line of sight.

There were a couple of Josh's sculptures on pedestals of course, the first thing people saw when they came in. But on the wall, with a distinct but discreet block letter sign, "Not for Sale—Other Work by This Artist Available" was a farm scene. A man leaning shirtless against a fence, watching the sun set, the image so vibrant and strong, so real, that anyone would feel they were standing just a few feet behind that man. Watching. Absorbing everything he was.

She turned back to face him. "You put him here, where you could see him every day."

"Get out, Lauren. I mean it. You don't want to be around me today, and I'm not in the mood for games."

Lauren put her palms flat on the carved and polished wooden surface and looked up into his face. Marcus was truly intimidating when he was pissed and broody, and there was an even deeper level to it, something volatile and dark, layers of past poison injecting itself into the present. Everything pulsing off him said he wasn't in control, and what's more, he didn't really give a fuck that he wasn't.

She'd once stood toe-to-toe with Josh, called forth his demons and unleashed them upon herself. She'd taken him down with nothing but nerve and the expert use of a whip that, in the face of a powerful man's rage, hadn't lasted five seconds. The nerve had. The love had.

Marcus was a different entity, with even more violent spaces. She could sense that, but just like with Josh, she believed she knew the core of the man. So when she reached up with both hands to frame his face, she wasn't surprised when his hands caught her wrists. But he didn't push her away. He held her there, his grip squeezing her as if she were a lifeline.

"You're a great Mistress, Lauren," he said quietly. "But you're a woman. I'm stronger, bigger and a hell of a lot meaner than you'd ever dream of being. You value our friendship, you don't fuck with me today."

Thomas had said something about the polish being all seared away when they were in the kitchen. She understood it now, seeing the coldness in his eyes.

"Marcus, if you value our friendship, you'll take your hands off my wife. Now. I mean it. Because I *am* bigger and stronger."

Josh set down the coffee cups on the entrance table and moved forward, his gray eyes hard. He took Lauren's elbow, drew her away. When he did, Marcus let go.

Josh took her wrist in one hand, looked at the red marks and looked at Marcus.

"Josh—"

He'd leaned over and snagged the front of Marcus' shirt before Lauren finished the thought. "What the hell is the matter with you?"

Marcus yanked loose, shoved Josh back and came around the counter.

"Stop it, both of you."

But Marcus wasn't after Josh. Lauren realized it a blink after Josh did. They both lunged after him, but it was too late.

Marcus ripped the framed picture off the wall hard enough to tear a gash in the sheet rock and broke it over his knee. The frame snapped like kindling in his frustrated hands. He tore the canvas loose as Lauren cried out and Linda emerged from the back, her eyes round. Taking the coffee, he dumped it over the now ruined canvas.

"Marcus—" Lauren leaped forward.

Josh picked up the nearest statue, a hefty bronze of a Minotaur, and yanked Lauren back as Marcus turned on her, rage gripping his features. Josh struck him across the jaw with it, knocking Marcus back into the wall.

"Josh!" Lauren tried to move forward again, but Josh held her firmly.

Marcus was breathing hard, leaning against the wall. Blood slipped through his lips, proving the blow had made an impact, not just in the evidence of the blood but in his sudden stillness, hunched against the wall as if he couldn't move, as if frozen by the horror of a Medusa's gaze. A look into his Fate, his life without Thomas.

Josh handed the statue to Lauren. Despite the fact he needed her to be his Mistress on a lot of levels, he didn't assume the mantle of submissive in any way when her wellbeing and protection was at risk. "You stay right here," he ordered her. "Not a step."

He moved to Marcus. When he got there, he reached out, laid a careful hand on Marcus' shoulder.

Marcus raised his gaze, and it was as if Josh was looking into a hell-filled abyss, all the conflict and turmoil roiling in the green of his eyes. "He's coming back, Marcus," Josh said.

Marcus shook his head. "He'll get down there, and it will all be about his mother and…what he has to be. He can't walk away from his responsibility to them."

"He's not walking away from anything," Josh said firmly. "That's why he is going back, Marcus. Have faith in him."

"I do. I know who he is, everything about him." Marcus abruptly straightened, shrugged past Josh and squatted by the mess on the floor. Running his fingertips over it, the layers of now wet paint mixed with coffee staining his hand. "I know him inside like it's my own inside, my breath and bone. This painting…it captured his soul."

Is it bad to just stop? Maybe it hurts less. Maybe Emile, Toby and Mike were the lucky ones.

Marcus shook his head again. Stood. "I'm sorry," he said with forced politeness to Lauren, and included Linda and Josh in his gesture. "I can't be here today. Linda, please close up. Don't clean this. I'll do it later."

Lauren did step forward now. "Where are you going?"

Instead of answering, he looked at the statue in her hand and shifted his gaze to Josh. "You hit me with a Royce sculpture? Do you know how frigging expensive that piece is?"

"It's bronze. Something even harder than your head would be needed to dent it. And I'm not the one who just shredded the painting you paid thousands of dollars for at an auction."

"Your hand." Lauren caught it, and Marcus noticed the gash caused by the wood frame, the nails. "When was your last tetanus?"

Marcus pulled away. "Leave it." He stared down at the wreckage. "It will heal over. It always does. Doesn't even leave a scar."

When he was a boy, they'd had a cat on the Iowa farm whose eyes were always messed up, as if the poor beast suffered allergies. Upon eventual inspection, they discovered his eyelids grew inward and his lashes were abrading the surface of his eyes. Of course, by the time they figured it out, the corneas were scarred such that the cat lost part of his sight, but he lived a fully functional life anyway.

It occurred to him then that he might have a peculiar phenomenon like that cat. Perhaps the scars from all of his wounds were on the inside, a protection method that allowed him to maintain his looks, his most potent survival weapon. But somehow, along the way, the wounds had begun to fester. Because of Thomas, his torment and savior both.

He had to make peace with it. He had to go back to the beginning. Where he could turn the wounds into calluses, before he bled to death internally.

Chapter Twenty-Two

ꟹ

As Thomas chuckled and rose, offering his mother a hand up, the cell phone Marcus had given him began to buzz in his coat pocket. He withdrew it as they made their way down the stairs. When he glanced at the display, he started. "Mom, I'm sorry, I need to take this one."

"Is it Marcus?"

"No." He flipped it open. "Josh? What is it?"

The minute he'd seen the hotel number on his screen, a cold spear of anxiety had thrust through Thomas' chest, tightened in his stomach. Why would Josh call him at this time of night, unless it was about Marcus?

He listened, his brow drawing down, his mouth settling in a straight line. "How long? Since after lunch? Is she okay? Good. He wouldn't have forgiven himself if he'd really hurt her. Yeah. I'm worried too. I'll call him. Maybe he'll answer for me."

He cut the call, responded to his mother's worried look. "It's Marcus. He..." He shook his head, ran a hand over the back of his neck. "I think I stirred stuff up from his past, Mom. Bad stuff. I don't think he really believes I'm coming back to him."

"And you're here, where you can't help him."

"No." On that point, Thomas held firm, despite the fear in his gut. "This is the way to prove to him I'm serious, that he doesn't have to manipulate or use force to keep me. That I'm choosing to be with him. I think this has more to do with him, with the demons of his past."

His mother digested that, an odd look on her face. "Call him, honey. Right now."

Thomas was already dialing. Six rings and he knew it would go to voice mail on seven. Four…five…

C'mon, you stubborn bastard. Pick up.

"Yeah."

"Where the hell are you?"

Marcus blinked at the explosive tone. "In New York, last time I checked."

"I know that. Where? Exactly. And if you say it's none of my business, I will point out that the person you ask to marry you does have a right to know where you are. Basically forever. All the time."

"You haven't agreed, but I can assure you I'm not off somewhere sticking my dick into an inappropriate orifice."

"Marcus, cut it out. Where are you?"

"Where I grew up."

"You're on foot?"

"If I drove the Maserati down here, I'd have to be selling a crate of crack out of the trunk or drive it to a chop shop myself and collect the take for the parts. I took the subway."

"Okay, why are you in the part of New York City most likely to get you killed, at nearly three in the morning?"

Marcus studied the dark alley in front of him. He could hear the subtle sounds of the street people burrowing down, trying to make themselves invisible to the nocturnal predators.

He'd passed a few of those early on, and given them as threatening a look as they could hope to deliver. The streets never left a man, and it showed. They'd been keeping their distance, but he was an oddity and eventually one would be stupid. Some dark part of him had been looking forward to it.

"Josh really should have been a woman. You too, maybe. Even though I wouldn't have paid the slightest attention to either one of you."

"Marcus, I swear to God, you are really pissing me off."

"Why? Because I'm taking a stroll down memory lane?"

"Because—" There was a murmur of conversation, some type of low level argument, then another voice came on the line. One he didn't expect.

"Marcus, this is Elaine. I don't know what you're doing, or why. But I told you something that day, a long time ago. You remember it?"

"I might. You said a lot of things that day I ignored."

"Stop being a wiseass. I told you not to sacrifice my son on the altar of your past demons. He's here tonight, telling me he loves you with all that he is. He's one of the best men I know, so if he tells me that, it must mean there's more to you than the arrogant smartass that has darkened our door before."

Marcus stopped in place, his hand clutching the phone. "I doubt that's true," he said, grasping for something to say, his mind scrambling.

"You promised to love him, and be with him forever. Is that true?"

"Yes."

"Then you don't do that by deliberately putting yourself in harm's way for no good reason. That's spitting on the love he's offering, that you offered to him. You have to take care of each other if you're going to spend a lifetime together.

"He's coming back to New York, I hope to bring you down in time for Thanksgiving and start working on this second home of yours. The front porch is going to need work. The baseboards are rotting, which you'd know if you'd had more sense than money and waited for the inspection report. So get your ass out of that slum and home where it bel—"

The line crackled and disconnected, cell service interrupted, leaving Marcus blinking in shock. "Yes, ma'am," he murmured and turned to face two street kids. One of them already had a knife out.

They thought they'd got him cornered. He bared his teeth in a feral grin and pocketed the phone. He'd take that fight now, just because it would feel so damn good.

* * * * *

He knew Thomas was arriving on the seven p.m. flight, so Marcus was surprised when the doorman told him that he'd gotten here a couple hours earlier. He'd hoped to change clothes, do something to prepare himself mentally. Despite the unexpected conversation with Elaine, until he saw Thomas' face, Marcus wouldn't believe it. He was torn between wanting to leave the building, avoid what he was most afraid of facing, and needing to see Thomas, even if it was for the last time.

Jesus, stop being such a pussy and get it over with. Marcus stabbed the entry card into the slot and turned the door handle.

He found Thomas in the living room. He was sitting on a chair, his back to Marcus, studying a painting he'd set up on an easel in the middle of the room.

"I don't want your pity," Marcus said gruffly, first thing. He realized he sounded defensive, just as Thomas had when he first got out of the car in the Berkshires. *One week.*

Thomas snorted, not turning. "Why would I pity you? I couldn't survive on the streets of New York *now*. You did it at fourteen. I bet you don't remember this painting."

Marcus' gaze shifted, registered a swirling tapestry of greens, intriguingly formless and yet substantial at once. Another time he would have allowed himself to be immersed in the subject, but he wasn't interested in a painting right now, just the artist.

When he stepped closer, he saw the corner of Thomas' mouth tug up in a wry smile. "Yeah, you didn't pay any attention to it the day I did it, either. You remember that time you came to my place in the summer? No air. All the windows open, and it was still an oven. I'd gotten back from that job stocking for the freight company. I was tired and so hot, but this was in my head, taking over everything. I finished it in three hours. A really intense three hours."

Now Marcus remembered. When he'd let himself in, Thomas had been lying there in nothing but the gold waist chain, Marcus' statement of ownership. His hand had been idly stroking himself into a semi-erect state as he studied his newest painting. Any interest Marcus had had in Thomas' work that day had evaporated before the need to possess that sweat-slick, muscled flesh.

"When you came in that night, I was thinking about you and that picture. My Master and my art, the two things I can't survive without."

Still not looking toward Marcus, Thomas rose and moved to the painting, drawing Marcus' attention back to it.

"It's just shades and shades of green." Thomas' fingers passed over one of the formless places that somehow became a contour, the hint of…something, as if there was something living in that canvas that responded to his touch.

"I never got past your eyes. Couldn't even sketch you. I look at you in my mind, in person, it doesn't matter… Your body's a fucking feast, your face…it's like an angel escaped from heaven and gave you his face. But that day I stretched the canvas, the way I felt about you had gotten so huge inside of me that I knew I was going to do something. *Had* to do something."

"I started touching the canvas, a lot like this. Just ran my fingers over it. Back and forth…back and forth…" Marcus watched, mesmerized by the motion of those fingers. "Then something in my mind focused on the way it felt. The canvas. Rough, just waiting.

"That's when I got it. The rough canvas. God paints our bodies over that, over our heart and soul. It's the eyes that tell us what we're really seeing, what's underneath. So all I painted in the picture were greens. Patterns, random slashes, shapes over shapes, shadows, emotions, it's all there." Thomas gave an absent chuckle, slid his other hand into his back jeans' pocket and cocked a hip. He was still caught up in that painting, while Marcus was caught up in him, every motion and word.

"Up until that point, I'd gotten so frustrated, trying to paint something that was everything about what my heart was, what it wanted. I thought if I couldn't paint that…Jesus, it was like being Superman and knowing what the kryptonite was. But it wasn't the rock, it was Lois Lane. The same thing that could bring him to his knees was the thing that made him most want to be Superman. The very thing that made me want to be an artist. You. The beginning and the end, and everything in between."

When Thomas turned at last, Marcus couldn't speak. He just couldn't. Thomas looked at Marcus with brown eyes that were serious, more intent than Marcus had ever seen them. He was looking at Thomas the man, certain of who he was and what he wanted. And he wanted Marcus.

It was there, in the quiet peace, the love and acceptance. His. Really his. Promised. Committed. Forever.

Thomas blanched. "Jesus Christ."

"They look much worse," Marcus assured him, glad Thomas seemed too distracted to notice the break in his voice. Thomas crossed the floor to examine the lacerations on Marcus' face, across the bridge of his nose, his swollen lip and eye. "And hell, I gave them money anyway."

"I'm going to wait until you get better, and then I'm going to smash your face in all over again." Thomas shook his head, then stepped forward one more step and crushed Marcus' mouth with his own, a week's worth of need and worry in it.

Marcus was set back by the ferocity of it, but it didn't take him long to rally. He got his arms over Thomas' so he could grab his head, hold him steady and plunder. Oh God, so good. So sweet, the taste of Thomas' mouth.

Violent, cleansing adrenaline had him tearing at the front of Thomas' shirt. Buttons clattered as he just ripped it open, hooked his foot and took them both tumbling to the floor. Thomas shoved against him, but Marcus wasn't going to be denied this. He tasted Thomas' heated skin, bit the sensitive nipple and Thomas' grip on his neck flexed, back arching.

Yeah, that was it. He got him with the nipples every time. Marcus sucked on the small nub, scoring it with his teeth while his hand went down, squeezed Thomas hard through his jeans. Hard as a rock and enormous. His slave hadn't even jerked himself off, he'd bet.

He wrestled him out of the jeans and Thomas' hands got between them, tore open his slacks just as Marcus caught the glitter of the slim gold and silver chain. Thomas was wearing it. Low on the lean hard waist, riding against the hip bones, the lock securely fastened. The loop adjusted around the cock. *Mine.*

"Wait, wait." Thomas was gasping. He grasped the edge of Marcus' open shirt. "I want… I know you're supposed to wait. But fuck it. I want to do it now."

Marcus' mind, in a whirl from lust and emotion, didn't follow him until Thomas retrieved the pair of rings from his discarded jeans. He sat back on his heels, suddenly speechless as Thomas reached out.

"Please, Master," he murmured. "Your hand."

Marcus put it out there and watched a million expressions cross Thomas' face as he fitted the silver ring on Marcus' finger and slid it home.

Reaching for the other ring, Marcus took Thomas' hand to do the same with the gold. He gave a half chuckle at everything welling in him. So ridiculous, so perfect. "I'm fucking nervous, can you believe that?"

Thomas' eyes were suspiciously bright. Just the two of them in the dim living room, their clothes half on, half off.

"Thank you, Thomas," Marcus said at last. "For saying yes."

"It was the easiest and the hardest thing I've ever done." Thomas' gaze fastened on Marcus' hand, the silver ring, the way it shone. What it said.

"Can I get back to fucking your brains out now?"

Thomas grinned. "You forget how to be a Master? Why are you asking?"

He dodged the tackle, but Marcus caught him. As his Master took him to his knees, pushed him to an elbow, he brought Thomas' left arm back, holding it against the small of his back. It was a restraint that made Thomas even harder, particularly when Marcus linked hands with him and Thomas felt the metal of the two bands brush each other, clink.

Marcus' free hand cupped his ass, took a firm hold of Thomas' right buttock. Bent and teased him with his tongue, licking up his rim in the way that drove Thomas insane. The chain loop dug into his cock as he thickened and grew. He writhed, struggled, cursed and then groaned when Marcus drove in deep, still holding him fast with that arm pulled behind his back.

"You wait until I give you the command, pet. You can't let go until I say you can."

I'm never going to, Master," Thomas managed. "Never again."

Epilogue

ꟃ

As Lauren helped Thomas with the cravat, she decided she'd been overly blessed with the number of beautiful men in her life.

"Marcus looks gorgeous, doesn't he? God, I'm going to pass out when I see him and make a total ass of myself."

She tugged on the silk, thought about decking him as he shifted and ruined her second attempt at it. To quell the urge, she reminded herself of the cardinal rule. The bride could do no wrong on her special day. Wisely, she tucked her tongue into her cheek and kept that thought to herself.

"*You* look gorgeous, Thomas. Now hold still or I'm going to choke you into a faint so I can do this without you moving around so much. I'm a professional doctor, I can do it."

"Is Josh helping Marcus do this?"

Lauren snorted and cursed, chuckling as she ruined it herself this time. Seeing Thomas grin, she narrowed her gaze at him. "You did that on purpose. I had to tell Josh not to wear gym socks with his dress shoes. The only way Marcus would let Josh touch his cravat is if *he* was passed out. Ah, hell. Julie, go get Tyler. He knows how to do this stuff. Third row from the back. He'll be sitting with a stunning woman with white hair."

Julie slid off her perch on a nearby chair, gave them a brilliant smile and disappeared.

"He's here with his mother?"

"Hardly. I said white, not gray. She's his wife." She gave him an arch look. "I should have really fixed your ass and told you Josh was giving Marcus one last quickie before he's off the market." She reached out and ran a hand down his lapel, straightening the white rose in the buttonhole. "But the truth of it is, he's even more nervous than you are."

She raised soft eyes to him, registering his astonishment. "You and I know about this stuff, Thomas. Love, commitment. It's really new territory for him. He's been so afraid to give his whole heart to anyone, and he's given it to you." After a brief pause, her lips tightened. "How did things go in Iowa? I still can't believe you insisted on a visit there before you did this."

Thomas sobered. "I wanted him to know that he didn't have to hide anything about who he is, or who he was, from me. It went about as he told me it would." He shook his head. "His mother said she couldn't see him right now. We left after about an hour."

But Thomas had gone back in for just a minute, while Marcus spoke to his brother outside about his mother's financial arrangements. His mother stood isolated, alone at the kitchen counter, slicing a tomato into the tiniest pieces Thomas had ever seen in his life.

He came within three steps of her, studying her housedress, so like the ones his mother wore in the morning, the smooth gray of her hair pulled into a barrette at her neck. Her husband had probably liked her hair long. He knew he liked Marcus' that way and suspected the thick, healthy strands had been inherited from her. She didn't turn around when he spoke, but she stopped cutting. That was the only acknowledgement he needed.

"Your son asked me to spend my life with him. To marry him." He made himself say it, though he knew many people thought wanting to commit their whole lives to someone spiritually was only a heterosexual person's need. "I know it would mean a lot to him if you attended, but even if you don't, I wanted you to know. He's always going to have someone looking after him. I'll be there to hear his good news when he's excited about something. If something makes him mad, I'll help him work through it, because he has a hell of a temper."

"His father had that," she said, then pressed her lips together.

Thomas nodded. "So he comes by it honestly. If he's sad, I'll be there too. I'll do whatever needs to be done to help him be happy. He's not going to be lonely. I'll spend the rest of my life wondering how I got so lucky, even though he tells me he's the lucky one. So…I just want you to know that. Being his mother, I'm sure knowing someone's going to be looking after him is important to you."

Then he turned and left.

"Doesn't he remind you of Marcus?"

Lauren's whispered question brought him back to the present, and the reality of finding himself face-to-face with Tyler Winterman.

He also found he had to agree with her. A hundred percent sexual Dominant in a six-four frame, Tyler had an easy confidence and authority. While he wasn't as pretty as Marcus, he certainly held him toe-to-toe in charisma, enough that Thomas found himself a little fumble-handed and tongue-tied around him, despite the fact Tyler was obviously, solidly straight.

But feeling his hands on his throat, tying the cravat, his face so close, Thomas couldn't help but flush. He guessed he would always be a shy Southern farm boy, but that was okay. That's what Marcus wanted.

"So are you going to give Marcus that auction piece you bought out from under him?" Lauren teased. Tyler stepped back, eyed the cravat critically, nodded. Then shot Lauren a look. "I made a photo of it," he said in a rich Southern drawl. "It has a very nice frame."

Tyler's wife stood at the door. She reminded Thomas of the other side of the entrance to an Egyptian pyramid. A pharaoh and his queen. The way her gaze moved over Thomas told him she was a Mistress. Josh had told him that, but it still boggled the mind, two Dominants married.

When Lauren saw his gaze shifting between the two of them, she tugged his sleeve. "Don't try to figure it out," she murmured. "It fits, is all. It works for them."

Apparently it did, for as Tyler came to her side, the woman with moonlight-colored hair and pale blue eyes yielded to his arm sliding around her waist. He pressed her against the door with his body for a simple brush of her lips that, though brief, was full of heat.

"Newlyweds," Lauren rolled her eyes.

"Yeah, thank God we're past all that," Josh said. He'd arrived in the opposite doorway and now stood watching them. "I see you have enough company to keep you from bolting. But I'll be happy to distract them if you're having second thoughts. Not many artists are brave enough to marry their pain-in-the-ass manager."

"I thought you were in the other room to keep Marcus from bolting," Thomas said dryly. Julie chuckled, moving under his arm to wrap her arms around his waist and give him a hard hug. Thomas smiled down at her, squeezed her shoulders.

"I was." Josh shifted. "His mother and brother are here. That's why I came to get you. Tradition and all, but—"

Thomas was already past him and out the door, moving down the hallway.

The door to the other dressing area was ajar. Thomas stopped in the opening and surveyed the three people facing each other in an awkward triangle. Marcus' mother had worn a pretty pink dress that managed with some artful tucks and gathers not to hang too obviously on her too-sparse frame. It helped soften the harsh lines of her worn face. Her other son had a reassuring hand at her elbow even as he kept his gaze fixed on Marcus.

Thomas rapped his knuckles lightly on the frame, all uncertainty melting away in the face of Marcus' speechless, pale expression.

"Connie, thank you for coming. You look beautiful." Thomas took her free hand briefly. Coming to Marcus' side, he touched his back, an obvious protective and reassuring gesture. "John. We're so glad both of you could come."

He looked up to see Tyler and Josh at the door, Lauren and Julie just behind. Reinforcements. Friends who cared.

"We're going to start in a few minutes. I'm going to ask Tyler and Lauren here," Thomas nodded, turning Connie and putting his hand out to direct John, "to take you out and get you settled. I think we'll break tradition, such as it is," a ghost of a smile touched his features, seeming to surprise them both, "and have you seated with my mother and sister. Mom's about as overwhelmed by all this as I'm sure you are, and you'll be an anchor for her."

Tyler stepped forward on cue and offered his free arm as Lauren guided Marcus' brother. Thomas turned back to Marcus when they ushered them away. Josh, Marcus' best man, did his part and quietly closed the door.

"Marcus?"

There was a muscle twitching in his jaw, one hand clenching. Thomas reached out, closed his hand over a rigid biceps. "Hey. You okay? I invited them. I didn't tell you because…well, I didn't want them not coming to ruin it. I hoped, but hell, it shocked me to see them, just about as much as it did when Mom told me she and Les were coming."

"Goddamn it." Marcus turned away, drew a deep, shuddering breath. "You know you're every fucking miracle in my life, right? Everything that's told me I ever did anything right?"

Thomas' throat closed up and he simply put his arm around his lover, the man who was his Master and would soon be his spouse, always. "And you've always been my best friend, from the beginning. Helping me to be everything I could possibly become. So let's go get married so we can screw legitimately."

Marcus coughed on a snort. "I think there'll be some disagreement with that."

"Fuck them. I love you. Want to see what Les made us as a gift?"

"You're opening gifts without me?"

Thomas laughed and went to the table. "Shut up and look."

This changing room had become a temporary storeroom for the earlier gifts. Thomas took Les' out now. It was needlepoint, a framed print. At one time, he would have worried that Marcus would laugh at something so provincial, but now Marcus took it and a smile spread across his face, dispelling the shadows. It made him such a sexy picture in that tux it almost took Thomas' breath. He had to look down at the picture as well so he wouldn't make a fool of himself.

It was a rendering of the country mouse and city mouse folk tale. She'd stitched a city skyline behind the country mouse, a rolling field and black-and-white cow behind the city mouse. Each mouse had features of Thomas and Marcus. At the bottom she'd carefully stitched the wedding date and the modified quote:

What therefore God hath joined together, let no one put asunder.

"She wasn't sure if we'd like it, but…"

"It's perfect, like her." Marcus said, obviously moved by the work she put into it, the sentiment it conveyed. "And what's this—"

Thomas tried to get it back, but Marcus snatched the note Rory had included.

You know, they say sons marry their mothers. I'm thinking Marcus seems about as bullheaded as Mom. So good luck. You'll need it. Oh, and if you and the New York fruit could arrange to be home the week before Christmas to help with the tree deliveries, we could use the extra hands.

Thomas burst out laughing at Marcus' look of affront. "He's comparing me to your mother?"

"Well you do have that kind of disapproving purse to your lips right now… There are definite resemblances. I mean, her hair isn't as well conditioned as yours, but maybe you can give her tips on that."

"Horse's ass. Remind me to bring a crate of New York apples and oranges for the obnoxious little cripple."

When Marcus shoved at him, Thomas ducked away and put the picture down with the other gifts.

It made him think of something else, though. While he tried to push the thought away, of course Marcus saw the shadow of it cross through his eyes.

"What is it, pet?"

"I guess that holds true for me too. I'm like your mother. Just because someone tells you that you have to act a certain way to prove you love them, doesn't make that the honorable thing to do, or the right thing. Sometimes, making them realize you need to do the right thing *and* can still love them is what's right. I'm so sorry, Marcus."

He faced him, met him eye to eye. "Thank you for fighting for us both until I figured it out."

"Well," Marcus shrugged, finding himself at a loss.

Thomas touched his face. "You aren't getting all weepy on me, are you? You Yankee boys, you cry a lot. Now Tyler Winterman, he seems a big strong Southern guy, no tears… And he can tie a cravat too, which you know is very important for my day-to-day fashion requirements."

Marcus caught his wrist. "Don't test me, farm boy." He shot him a smile. While he knew Thomas was teasing him, he nevertheless felt the need to add, "You're mine, pet. Mine to protect and love."

"Same goes. I'm yours. Master." Thomas moved closer, his dark brown eyes getting that intent focused look that made Marcus' thoughts immediately shift to what they might be doing to celebrate their first night married. "And I'm going to take care of you too. Whatever way you demand, and a lot of ways you won't."

"I can think of a few demands now." As Marcus closed the gap to taste Thomas' lips, Thomas' fingers dug in at his waist in that strong, urgent way Marcus knew so well.

Strength and gentleness. His farm boy. Strong, sexy exterior and a steel core, with a generous, shy heart that was all his. Forever.

His family.

Also by Joey W. Hill

Behind the Mask *anthology*
Chance of a Lifetime
Enchained *anthology*
Holding the Cards
Ice Queen
If Wishes Were Horses
Make Her Dreams Come True
Mirror of My Soul
Mistress of Redemption
Natural Law
Snow Angel
Threads of Faith
Virtual Reality

About the Author

ꟗ

I've always had an aversion to reading, watching or hearing interviews of favorite actors, authors, musicians, etc. because so often the real person doesn't measure up to the beauty of the art they produce. Their politics or religion are distasteful, or they're shallow and self-absorbed, a vacuous mophead without a lick of sense. From then on, though I may appreciate their craft or art, it has somehow been tarnished. Therefore, whenever I'm asked to provide personal information about myself for readers, a ball of anxiety forms in my stomach as I think: "Okay, the next couple of paragraphs can change forever the way someone views my stories." Why on earth does a reader want to know about me? It's the story that's important.

So here it is. I've been given more blessings in my life than any one person has a right to have. Despite that, I'm a Type A, borderline obsessive-compulsive paranoiac who worries I will never live up to expectations. I've got more phobias than anyone (including myself) has patience to read about. I can't stand talking on the phone, I dread social commitments, and the idea of living in monastic solitude with my husband and animals, books and writing is as close an idea to paradise as I can imagine. I love chocolate, but with that deeply ingrained, irrational female belief that weight equals worth, I manage to keep it down to a minor addiction. I adore good movies. I'm told I work too much. Every day is spent trying to get through the never ending "to do" list to snatch a few minutes to write.

This is because, despite all these mediocre and typical qualities, for some miraculous reason, these wonderful characters well up out of my soul with stories to tell. When I manage to find enough time to write, sufficient enough that the precious "stillness" required rises up and calms all the competing voices in my head, I can step into their lives, hear what they are saying, what they're feeling, and put it down on paper. It's a magic beyond description, akin to truly believing my husband loves me, winning the trust of an animal who has known only fear or apathy, making a true connection with someone, or knowing for certain I've given a reader a moment of magic through those written words. It's a magic that reassures me there is Someone, far wiser than myself, who knows the permanent path to that garden of stillness, where there is only love, acceptance and a pen waiting for hours and hours of uninterrupted, blissful use.

If only I could finish that darned "to do" list.

I welcome feedback from readers - actually, I thrive on it like a vampire, whether it's good or bad. So feel free to visit me through my website www.storywitch.com anytime.

Joey welcomes comments from readers. You can find her website and email address on her author bio page at www.ellorascave.com.

Tell Us What You Think

We appreciate hearing reader opinions about our books. You can email us at Comments@EllorasCave.com.

Why an electronic book?

We live in the Information Age—an exciting time in the history of human civilization, in which technology rules supreme and continues to progress in leaps and bounds every minute of every day. For a multitude of reasons, more and more avid literary fans are opting to purchase e-books instead of paper books. The question from those not yet initiated into the world of electronic reading is simply: *Why?*

1. ***Price.*** An electronic title at Ellora's Cave Publishing and Cerridwen Press runs anywhere from 40% to 75% less than the cover price of the exact same title in paperback format. Why? Basic mathematics and cost. It is less expensive to publish an e-book (no paper and printing, no warehousing and shipping) than it is to publish a paperback, so the savings are passed along to the consumer.
2. ***Space.*** Running out of room in your house for your books? That is one worry you will never have with electronic books. For a low one-time cost, you can purchase a handheld device specifically designed for e-reading. Many e-readers have large, convenient screens for viewing. Better yet, hundreds of titles can be stored within your new library—on a single microchip. There are a variety of e-readers from different manufacturers. You can also read e-books on your PC or laptop computer. (Please note that Ellora's Cave does not endorse any specific brands.

You can check our websites at www.ellorascave.com or www.cerridwenpress.com for information we make available to new consumers.)

3. *Mobility.* Because your new e-library consists of only a microchip within a small, easily transportable e-reader, your entire cache of books can be taken with you wherever you go.
4. *Personal Viewing Preferences.* Are the words you are currently reading too small? Too large? Too... ANNOYING? Paperback books cannot be modified according to personal preferences, but e-books can.
5. *Instant Gratification.* Is it the middle of the night and all the bookstores near you are closed? Are you tired of waiting days, sometimes weeks, for bookstores to ship the novels you bought? Ellora's Cave Publishing sells instantaneous downloads twenty-four hours a day, seven days a week, every day of the year. Our webstore is never closed. Our e-book delivery system is 100% automated, meaning your order is filled as soon as you pay for it.

Those are a few of the top reasons why electronic books are replacing paperbacks for many avid readers.

As always, Ellora's Cave and Cerridwen Press welcome your questions and comments. We invite you to email us at Comments@ellorascave.com or write to us directly at Ellora's Cave Publishing Inc., 1056 Home Avenue, Akron, OH 44310-3502.

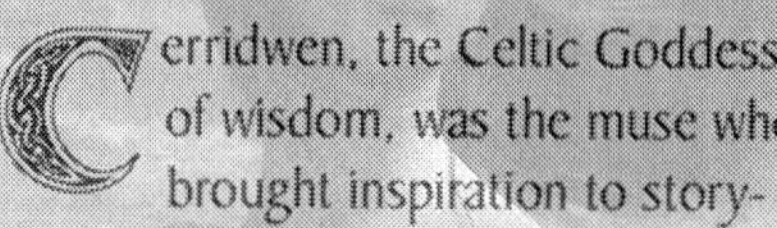

Cerridwen, the Celtic Goddess of wisdom, was the muse who brought inspiration to storytellers and those in the creative arts. Cerridwen Press encompasses the best and most innovative stories in all genres of today's fiction. Visit our site and discover the newest titles by talented authors who still get inspired - much like the ancient storytellers did, once upon a time.

ELLORA'S CAVE
ROMANTICA PUBLISHING

Made in the USA
Lexington, KY
25 May 2010